D1365352

The Book of Love

Egan made no move to push her away or still her hands. She loved the hard, full feel of him through the plaid.

"The Nvengarian *Book of Seductions*," Zarabeth said softly, "instructs a lady to measure her lover with a piece of ribbon and to keep it by her bedside as a reminder when he is absent."

"I've heard much about this *Book of Seductions*," he gasped. "Required reading, is it?"

"When a lady comes of age, she studies it most carefully."

"So she can drive a man mad?"

"I believe that is the intention."

His groan turned into a growl. He swung around and seized Zarabeth by the shoulders, backing her into the nearest standing stone. The magic from it seared her body, and she gasped at the heady sensation.

Even better was Egan leaning into her, his knee sliding between her legs. "Which seduction is this?"

JENNIFER ASHLEY

Highlander Ever After

DORCHESTER
PUBLISHING

DORCHESTER PUBLISHING

January 2011

Published by

Dorchester Publishing Co., Inc.
200 Madison Avenue
New York, NY 10016

ISBN 13: 978-1-4285-1085-2
E-ISBN: 978-1-4285-0266-6

The "DP" logo is the property of Dorchester Publishing Co., Inc.

Printed in the United States of America.

Visit us online at www.dorchesterpub.com.

Acknowledgments

Thanks go to my editor, Leah, for holding my hand through this book so I could make it the best it could be. Also to Erin and others on the Dorchester staff for their hard work behind the scenes. And as always, thanks go to Forrest, for being there through thick and thin.

Highlander Ever After

Prologue
Letter from a Prince

To Egan MacDonald
Castle MacDonald
Ullapool, Scotland

Egan, my friend, I am sending you precious cargo. Nvengaria is once again rife with plots, and I have re-called Grand Duke Alexander to help me fight them. I am not entirely worried—Alexander has the most de-vious mind I have ever known, and between the two of us we will deal with the insurgency. An imperial prince of Nvengaria has to expect a rebellion every year and a serious one every decade—it is the way of Nvengarians to be restless.

But trouble has come to my cousin Zarabeth. As I told you, she married one in the Council of Dukes— Sebastian is his name—and he is thick with the ring-leaders of this current plot against me. He is intelligent and commands loyalty, and I cannot take his threat lightly. Zarabeth braved certain death to escape from his stronghold and make her way to inform me of his treachery.

Of course, his faction immediately denounced her and offered a reward for her death or capture. This need not worry you, because I will find and punish the perpetra-tors, and once I mop up Sebastian's resistance, she will be safe. But I cannot send her to her father; nor can she continue here because the palace, as usual, is filled with treachery.

I remember visiting you at Castle MacDonald before my father's death, and what I remember most is not the spectacular views or the excellent fishing, but the fact that it is extremely hard to reach. I think it an excellent place to tuck my little cousin, and she could have no better protectors than you and your Highlanders.

I am sending a guardian with her—Baron Valentin, a good man and loyal to me and to Princess Penelope.

Keep Zarabeth safe for me, my friend, and when Alexander and I have suppressed things here, I will have you return her to Nvengaria. Penelope would be happy to see you, and you've also made a friend of Meagan, the grand duchess of Nvengaria, who has melted the ice floe that was Alexander.

Keep her safe.

By my hand
The twentieth of September, 1820

Damien

Imperial Prince, Nvengaria

Postscript: Penelope sends her love.

Chapter One
The Devil's Teeth

October 1820
Ullapool, the Western Highlands, Scotland

Egan barreled out of the tavern onto the dock. The news had to be a mistake.

A curtain of rain soaked the wooden pier and the stone buildings, heightening the fishy, briny smell of the harbor. Rowboats were just breaking through the rain and mist, a blue-coated captain standing in one's bow. To the west the harbor was closed in by a series of rolling hills, leaving a gap that led to the open sea and wind-whipped waves.

Egan frantically tried to make out the other passengers, desperate to find Zarabeth. He'd been told her ship had broken up offshore, but he refused to believe he'd failed her already. She would be on one of these boats pulling in, laughing that she had got wet, none the worse for wear.

He hadn't seen Zarabeth for five years but hadn't forgotten one strand of her black hair, her deep blue eyes, and her sweet face with its slightly pointed chin. She'd been a beautiful young woman when last he'd seen her, poised to take her world by storm.

So beautiful he'd forced himself to walk away.

Sailors leaped onto the docks from the rowboats,

then reached back to haul out the drenched passengers. The boat with the captain contained three men in the garb of faraway Nvengaria, but no sign of Zarabeth.

Egan's blood ran cold as the captain approached him, his eyes weary in the rain. "Are ye himself?"

"I am Egan MacDonald. What happened, man? Tell me and be quick about it."

"We lost a mast, and the hull cracked open. I thought we could limp into harbor, but the ship broke up just outside. My first officer, he put the young lady into the first boat, but . . ." He cleared his throat. "We lost sight of it in the mist. We searched. . . ."

Pounding rain soaked Egan's bare head, but he scarcely felt it. "Where?" he shouted at the captain. "Where did ye go down?"

"By the Devil's Teeth."

Egan's heart lurched. The Devil's Teeth were razor-sharp rocks below the mountain called Ben Duncraig. Ships or fishing boats that ran up on them were shredded into useless bits of lumber.

Egan turned away, calling for a horse. The captain tried to stop him. "There's no point, man. The boat will have been washed out to sea."

"If she were dead I'd know." Egan grabbed the bridle of the horse the hostler brought him and scrambled into the saddle.

A hand on his ankle stopped him. He looked down into the grim eyes of one of the Nvengarians, a man with a craggy face, black hair, and a hard mouth. "I will go with you," he said in heavily accented English. "I was sent to guard her."

"I can move faster on my own," Egan told him, squarely facing the man's intense gaze. "She saved my life once. I'll not leave her t' die."

Before the man could say more, Egan spurred the

horse and charged from the docks for the road that ran along the shore.

I am here; please help me.

Zarabeth silently screamed the words as she clung to the black rocks, the pounding sea threatening to drag her back into its depths. Her rowboat had cracked in two, icy waves tossing the pieces far north of the harbor mouth.

She'd clung to what broken boards she could find until rocks had swirled out of the fog. Then she'd reached for them and grabbed on. The first officer had gone down and not come up, or at least Zarabeth had not been able to see him through the mist and rain. Either way, she could no longer sense his anguished thoughts and knew he was dead.

She was terrified at the same time she was furious. She'd traveled from her tiny country in the Balkans across the length of Europe, through the German states to the North Sea, and endured a hazardous ocean journey to land here on the west coast of Scotland. She'd come so close to safety, so close to seeing Egan Mac-Donald again. But now she would die.

What use was magic now? One of her charms, a piece of gold wire twisted over a stone, still hung between her breasts. It was supposed to ward off an enemy's physical attack—well, that had worked in the literal sense. The first officer had slipped when he'd tried to put his hands around her neck, and an instant later the ship had crumbled beneath them.

Too bad the charm did not also ward off sharp rocks or death by drowning.

I'll have to add that in next time.

Zarabeth was freezing—she'd die of cold and exposure even if she didn't drown—but she didn't regret what she'd done to bring herself here. Sebastian was a monster, and he'd made her life unbearable for the last five years. When she'd learned a few months ago that he was a traitor, she could no longer even pretend to be a loyal wife.

She'd crept away in the middle of the night and gone to her cousin Damien, imperial prince of Nvengaria. He'd helped her, had started divorce proceedings for her, and, when things got too dangerous, shipped her off to Scotland for safety.

Only she would not reach safety. Or Egan. She'd planned to apologize to him for being such a fool that night five years ago. The world had taught her that dreams and reality were vastly different, and she planned to tell him so.

Now her only regret was that she'd never again see his face or watch his hardest expression suddenly dissolve with his warm grin. She'd never again hear his rumbling voice that comforted her like nothing else could.

Egan MacDonald, the only person she'd ever met whose thoughts she could not read. She'd saved his life once, and he'd stayed with her family while recovering. When he came back years later for a visit, she thought he'd be her knight in shining armor like the legends of old; except he wore a kilt and rough leather boots. But he'd made it clear he still saw her as the little girl who'd helped pull him from a ditch. Even so, she'd waited for his rescue all these years.

It was likely he wouldn't come now, and she'd be dead and unable to scold him for it.

Help me, Egan.

Over the pounding of the surf against rock, she thought she heard hoofbeats on the hard road. She raised her head but could see nothing through the spray and rain and mist.

Then out of the dark loomed a knight gleaming from head to foot in armor, his mighty warhorse pawing the ground, sparks flying from his hooves.

The knight flung himself off the horse and descended the treacherous rocks toward her. His figure resolved itself into a Scotsman in a dark blue and green; then suddenly he blurred and vanished.

A dream, she thought dimly, and everything went black.

Egan hauled Zarabeth's limp body up from the rocks, cradling her against his chest. Her skin was clammy and cold, and so wet. The damned rain wouldn't stop.

Her black hair hung in tangles, her hands cut and bloody from clinging to the rocks. Her dress was torn, revealing the white of her breasts, a strange piece of jewelry glinting gold on her pale skin.

Get her warm. The thought pounded through his brain. He wrapped her well in his cloak, but she was too cold, too lifeless. He'd never get her back to Castle MacDonald before she froze—it was too far, and night was falling.

He laid her across his saddle and mounted behind her, cradling her against his chest. He turned the horse back up the road to Ullapool, knowing an inn lay at a crossroads not far from there. It was not much of an inn, but there he could get Zarabeth warm and dry.

When he reached the inn, the proprietor and his wife quickly acquiesced to his demands—they'd never refuse anything to a MacDonald. Soon he had Zarabeth in a private bedroom with a roaring fire in the hearth.

Egan helped the innkeeper's wife peel off Zarabeth's clothes, feeling sick as he saw the bruises on her pale body. She was so cold, shivering, and she would not wake up.

The innkeeper's wife rubbed Zarabeth vigorously

with towels and blankets. Then Egan laid her in the bed, piling on the quilts. The woman hung Zarabeth's sodden dress and underclothes in front of the fire, shaking her head at the gashes in the fine cotton.

After the woman had finished and was gone, Egan sat down on the bed beside Zarabeth. Damn, she was still too cold. The room had already filled with warmth, but none of it seemed to touch her.

Egan stripped out of his coat and kilt and peeled off his wet shirt, his own body warm despite the wet. He spread his clothes in front of the fire to dry, then slid under the covers. He spooned himself against Zarabeth's cold, limp body, worried that she lay so lifeless.

"Take my warmth, love," he whispered. "Take all ye need."

If she heard him she made no response. Egan pressed a kiss to her hair, remembering the Zarabeth who had kissed him so sweetly in her father's house five years ago. Her lips had warmed him, her smile welcoming.

He'd been drunk and enchanted and ready to take her on the floor. That night he'd realized that the twelve-year-old hellion Zarabeth who used to take him fishing and endlessly taunt him had become a woman— a beautiful, charming woman he wanted with every breath.

Her lips had tasted of warmth and spice, and his hands had sought the curve of her hips. She'd been wearing a dress that bared most of her bosom, a pendant similar to what she wore now hanging in the shadow between her breasts. He'd wanted to catch the pendant in his teeth, lick the salt of her skin. Itched to pull the dress down to bare the sweet darkness of her nipples.

Leaving her had been the hardest thing he'd done in his life. He hadn't spoken to her or seen her or even had a letter from her from that day to this. And now here he was in bed with her.

I'll stay until she's warm, then go.

His mind said that. His body knew that he'd ridden hard in the cold rain and dragged Zarabeth to safety and was exhausted from chill and worry.

He fell asleep.

Zarabeth woke to incredible warmth. She cracked open her eyes, then shut them again because even her eyelids hurt.

She lay under heavy quilts in a prickly bed with a thin pillow. Breathing hurt, but she lay in splendid comfort and felt no signs of fever.

The thought trickled through her brain that she was no longer clinging to sharp rocks in a stormy sea. She nearly wept with relief, forgiving the mattress its prickles and the pillow for being flat. For a time she lay still, eyes closed, and enjoyed life and safety.

After a while, she realized several more things—first, she had no idea where she was, and second, she was not alone in the bed. A warm bulk lay next to her, long and strong and protecting her like a wall. It was also snoring.

She pried open her eyes. It did not hurt as much this time, and she was able to see Egan MacDonald lying on his side next to her, his head pillowed on his bent arm.

She nearly stopped breathing. The man she'd dreamed about for five years—in intense, deeply erotic dreams—lay under the covers with her. When she'd last seen him he'd been devastating—hair rumpled, brown eyes half-closed, lazy smile as he'd murmured, "What is it ye wanted to tell me, lass?"

If anything he looked stronger and more solid, his skin darkened by sun and wind. The lazy smile had been replaced by a little frown in his sleep, and his eyes were closed, dark lashes resting against his cheek.

His large hand had spread out on the coverlet, as

though he'd been reaching for something but fallen asleep midway there. Misty sunlight picked out gold strands in his hair, light brown weaving through darker brown.

She'd always loved his wild hair and how the colors were variegated, had always longed to touch it. She indulged herself now, sliding a finger through the twisting curl that rested against his cheek.

The hand on the quilt moved, and his lips curved in a half smile. He still slept, but he turned his head to nestle his cheek into her palm.

Zarabeth moved the pad of her thumb across his cheekbone, back and forth, feeling the burn of unshaved whiskers. His smile faded as he drew a long breath, and his hand on her hip grew heavy as he drifted into deeper sleep.

Zarabeth continued to rub the roughness of his whiskers until her own eyelids drooped and she fell into dreamless, contented slumber.

She awoke facing the edge of the bed. Her body was spooned to Egan's, his chest to her back, his strong arm flung around her waist. She realized this time that they were both unclothed.

A fold of blanket had wedged between them, but she felt every line of his body burrowed into hers, including the thick arousal that nudged her through the fabric. A silver armband encircled his bicep, the metal cool against her skin.

She still had no idea where she was. The room was tiny and whitewashed, filled mostly with the large bed. A fire flickered in the small hearth, and early sunlight leaked through the half-shuttered window.

She tried to slide out from under Egan's arm, but he murmured in his sleep and tightened his clasp. One hand came up to rest on her breast, his palm cupping it through the blanket.

"Egan," she whispered.

"Mmm." He nuzzled her ear; then his lips touched her hair, so warm. "Hush, love."

Love? For a moment she pretended he meant her. She liked the thought of him kissing her and calling her *love.*

"Egan, it is Zarabeth."

He went still a moment, then jerked awake. He wrenched himself up with unflattering speed and landed on his feet, snatching a length of tartan to wrap around his lower body.

Zarabeth sat up, pulling the blankets to her shoulders. Egan made a delectable picture, his hips hugged by the plaid, the cloth dipping to reveal a hint of dark hair below his navel. His skin was tanned by the sun—he'd been dark since his army days—and his tight arms were marked with narrow white scars, the intricately patterned armband glinting on it.

Dark hair hung in tangles to his shoulders, unruly as ever, and unshaved whiskers stubbled his face and jaw. His chest was sculpted with muscle like the rest of him, and dusted with dark hair. Flat, copper-colored nipples drew to tight points as he regarded her almost fiercely.

Her blood heated at the sight—her Highlander, tall and very male.

" 'Twas only to get you warm, lass," he said gruffly. "Nothing more."

Zarabeth couldn't stop gazing at him. "I'd say that I was warm."

"I meant to leave ye, but I fell asleep."

If only he didn't look so repulsed to have awakened pressed against her.

Out of habit, she slid into her brisk society-hostess voice. No one out-eleganced no-nonsense Zarabeth of Nvengaria. "Very well, we can pretend you left when I slept."

His eyes narrowed. She could never fool him, and he knew it. Egan could always see through her, no matter that she never had any idea what was going on behind his hard gaze.

He made himself lean over the bed and rest his hand on her forehead. "No fever. Good. I got ye out in time."

Flashes came back to her: the storm, the breaking ship, the wild and terrified thoughts of the sailors and crew, the despair of the first officer as he flailed away from her, and his last fading thought—*I'm sorry.* The freezing, greedy sea that tried to pull her from the rocks to her death.

Egan touched her cheek. "Are ye all right?"

She gasped and looked up to find his face an inch from hers. She'd always loved his eyes, deep brown flecked with gold.

She remembered the first time he'd opened those eyes and looked at her. That had been after she'd found him in a ditch by the side of the road, half-dead. Her father had taken him home to be nursed back to health. When Egan had finally awakened, Zarabeth had been sitting by his bedside reading fairy tales to him in Nvengarian. He'd stared at her in confusion before demanding to know in his luscious Scots accent where he was.

She tried to keep her voice from shaking now as she answered. "I am well."

He stood up again, holding the tartan closed with one tight fist. "Good. I'll tell the landlord to get ye breakfast."

"Where are we?"

"An inn up the coast from Ullapool. Closest thing I could find—couldn't risk dragging ye all the way back to Castle MacDonald with you that wet and cold."

She shivered again, but only from the bewildering

memories of the wreck. "We are even then, you and I. I rescued you from a ditch, and you pulled me from the sea."

Egan's brows raised the slightest bit. "No, lass, you and I will never be even."

What did that mean? She peered into his eyes but could see nothing behind them, as usual. The only man she'd ever loved, and she couldn't read him.

Egan turned to stir up the fire, lifting another log onto it one-handed. She enjoyed watching his hips move against his plaid.

"How did you find me?" she asked him.

"I heard ye calling out. Even over the storm I heard ye calling from the rocks below. Good thing I did. I climbed down, and there ye were, clinging to the Devil's Teeth, fainted dead away."

He snatched a much-wrinkled gown from the rack near the fire and tossed it onto the bed. "Dress yourself, and I'll have them bring a meal to ye."

He took up a large linen shirt and woolen stockings from the bottom of the bed without letting loose his grip on the tartan. "Keep warm," he admonished. Then he banged out the door and was gone.

Zarabeth sank down into the bed, hugging her knees to her chest. A few tears leaked from her eyes, and she quickly wiped them away. She'd grown too accustomed to being constantly watched to let her emotions show. So many people watched her for so many different reasons.

One thought in her jumbled mind stood out from the rest. Egan had said he'd heard her call out, but she hadn't, not in words. She'd been too exhausted to shout for help with her voice, needing all her strength to hold on to the rock.

She'd called out only with her mind, and Egan had heard her.

Chapter Two
Castle MacDonald

I'm going straight to hell.

Egan guided his horse down the narrow trail that skirted the top of the cliffs, directly above the spot where he'd found Zarabeth. Zarabeth sat in front of him, her sweet backside tucked between the spread of his legs, hips swaying with the movement of the horse. Wrapped in a dry cloak the landlord's wife had lent her, she looked like little more than a bundle of wool in his saddle.

He held her securely—for her safety, he told himself. Yet her nearness churned up every secret lustful thought he'd ever had of her, no matter how many times he reminded himself he had no business having such thoughts. Not only was Zarabeth still married, despite her husband's treachery, but she was the daughter of one of his closest friends, a man without whom Egan would have died long ago.

So here he was, with his dear friend's only offspring perched on the saddle before him, thinking of how her backside felt against his thighs. This after waking up pressed against her body, his hand on the curve of her breast, its nipple a hard point against his palm. He remembered the exact size and shape of it, and the easy way she fit into his hand. Even the wind cutting from the mountain couldn't banish the direction of his thoughts.

Straight to hell.

They'd left the village behind, heading toward Loch Argonne and Castle MacDonald. The road at this point hugged the coast but would make its way inland around the corner of Ben Duncraig.

"It's breathtaking," Zarabeth said over the wind, the lilt in her voice as sweet as ever.

"I know, 'tis bloody cold."

"No, I mean beautiful." She swept her hand to the rise of the mountains, the sharp blue sky, the sea dropping away at their feet. "You must love it here."

In the seconds before Egan had awakened fully this morning and realized he was fondling the woman he'd vowed to protect, he'd experienced deep joy. Her warm body tucked against his, her hair tickling his lips, the scent of her so fine. He'd wanted to stay there forever.

His conscience liked to stick it to him with a knife.

"Love is going a bit far," he said to clear his thoughts. "Can be bleak and cold of a winter's night."

"Not with a warm fire and your family around you. Damien said you had a large family who live at the castle."

"Oh, aye, you'll be mobbed. I sent word last night with the innkeeper's boy that I'd found ye and would bring ye back safe."

She looked back at him, worried. "And Baron Valentin and my footmen are truly all right?"

"Unhappy but unhurt. I sent them to the castle. Cousin Angus's wife-to-be will likely fuss around them till they're driven mad."

Zarabeth turned around again. "I still think it is beautiful here," she said a bit defiantly.

"Well, ye go ahead and think that."

"I will. With or without your permission."

She shifted a little in the saddle, rubbing straight against him, and he stifled a groan. She wasn't doing that on purpose, was she? The young Zarabeth had enjoyed tormenting him, but she'd been through so much since he'd last seen her.

What he needed was a lush female he could lay himself on and thrust between her legs until this madness went away. But in his fantasy the woman had Zarabeth's pixielike face, her Nvengarian blue eyes, her long lashes, her smile. She'd stretch out her arms and welcome him to the body that had imprinted itself on him this morning for a few fiery seconds.

Zarabeth watched the scenery in silence, unaware that he was aching under his plaids and thought he might drop dead of it before they reached Castle Mac-Donald.

Nothing so dire happened before he swung the horse up the road that led to his ancestral home. Loch Argonne stretched like a broad sheet of silver between mountains, the lake both treacherous and beautiful. Castle MacDonald perched on a rock cliff overlooking the loch, an impregnable fortress that had stood eight hundred years, reachable only by a road that wound tortuously up the mountain.

The horse perked up as they climbed the hill, knowing he was home. At the top, the old-fashioned gate that had been wedged open for the past thirty years welcomed them, the horse's hooves echoing hollowly through the narrow gatehouse. A coach could just fit through, and the stones bore gouges from carriages that hadn't done it quite right.

Beyond the gatehouse lay the courtyard and the wide-open doors of Castle MacDonald. Highlanders poured out of the castle as they approached, all talking at once as they swarmed around Zarabeth—cousins Angus and Hamish, nephews Jamie and Dougal, neighbors Adam and Piers Ross, and Gemma MacLean, Angus's betrothed, chivvying the lot of them.

The Nvengarian footmen rushed out behind Gemma, no less anxious, quarreling over who would hold the horse and who would help Zarabeth down. The hard-faced Nvengarian who'd stopped Egan on the docks followed more slowly, his gaze resting on Zarabeth, then Egan. This must be the Baron Valentin Damien mentioned in his letter.

"The poor lass, is she all right?" Gemma MacLean demanded, elbowing past the crowd and lifting her capable hands to Zarabeth.

Before Gemma could pull her from the saddle, blond, blue-eyed Adam Ross laced his strong hands around Zarabeth's waist and lifted her to the ground. "There you are," he said, flashing his perfect smile. *Bloody interloper.*

"I am very well," Zarabeth said in English. "Egan found me quickly. I was warm and dry in no time."

Her assurances and her bright smile made the others relax, Angus heaving an audible sigh of relief. "Thank God for it," his big cousin rumbled.

The Nvengarian footmen started an argument over who would build the fire in her room. Egan gave Zarabeth another narrow look as she stood serenely waiting. Exhaustion etched her face, yet she smiled as though hostessing a supper ball.

"She needs a rest," he growled at the Highlanders hemming her in. "Do ye not all have something to do?"

"Gracious, yes." Gemma flapped her skirt at the men. "Get on with ye. 'Tis my wedding day, and I want it perfect."

Angus and Hamish exchanged guilty looks and rushed indoors, followed by Jamie and Dougal at a dead run.

"Your wedding day?" Zarabeth asked, startled.

"Aye, but don't ye worry, love. I'm having Angus

MacDonald make his vows to me today, don't matter what happens. Rain or shine, whether we're in the kirk or on top of a tor, he's pledging himself to me, and that's that."

Zarabeth enjoyed the wedding ceremony inside the small stone kirk, the simplicity of the service soothing her aching head. Back at the castle, Gemma rushed about preparing for her own wedding feast, shouting orders at her new husband, Angus, who in turn bellowed at his brother Hamish. When Zarabeth asked to help, Gemma, a gillie's daughter, seemed horrified that a highborn lady should dirty her hands. But Zarabeth stubbornly insisted. As the wife of a duke, she'd seen to many entertainments designed to impress a thousand highborn guests. Plus she'd do anything to keep from thinking about how she'd woken up nose-to-nose with Egan.

Not that she had to work hard to avoid him. He'd disappeared after the wedding and did not return until late that afternoon, when the additional guests for the feasting and dancing began to arrive.

Supper was a loud, laughing business in the great hall on the first floor of the almost vertical Castle MacDonald. The two-story room had high windows, thick ceiling beams, and whitewashed walls that held an assortment of weapons, from wicked-looking axes to ancient claymores and spears. A boar's head hung over the enormous stone fireplace, whose huge fire heated every corner of the room. The castle majordomo, Williams, gave churlish commands to the sunny-faced maids who served the feast.

It was all was very different from her husband Sebastian's orchestrated affairs. The Highlanders shouted orders at the maids, who shouted right back at them, and every few minutes someone voiced a loud joke that had the whole room roaring with laughter.

After the feasting the tables were cleared out of the way and the dancing began. The wedding couple were dragged immediately to the middle of the room, and circles formed around them.

A fiddler and a drummer struck up a merry tune in the corner, and the swish of plaids and laughter soon accompanied the dancers. Some of the men sported plaid knee breeches and trousers instead of kilts, but most women wore skirts of plaid, though a few dressed in fashionable garb that would be found in London.

Baron Valentin had managed to save some of the luggage, but all of Zarabeth's clothes had been lost, the gown she'd been found in ruined beyond repair. While the baron wore his blue military coat with a green sash from shoulder to hip, Zarabeth had to make do with a hastily altered gown belonging to Egan's absent sister, Mary.

Zarabeth liked the MacDonald plaid of dark blue and green laced with red and black, and the lightweight, warm fabric. She fingered the skirt, knowing she touched a piece of Egan MacDonald's heritage.

With so many people in the room, Zarabeth found it more difficult to shield the thoughts clamoring about her. Gemma was thinking, *Och, when ye marry a Highlander, ye marry the pack of 'em.* Angus's thoughts were less coherent but filled with embarrassed happiness and anticipation of the wedding bed. A general cacophony of joyousness permeated the room, and Egan . . .

Egan reposed alone by the fireplace, one hand resting on the mantelpiece as he sipped his whiskey and watched the dancers. His unruly hair had been pulled into a tail, but curls escaped it—he'd never been able to tame his hair. He looked every inch a Highlander in his full kilt, with a swath of excess fabric slung over his shoulder. Zarabeth tried to shut out the noise of the wedding party and focus on his thoughts, but as usual she found only silence.

Egan had said little to her since they'd arrived at Castle MacDonald, but now he caught her glance and left the fireplace to come to her.

"Are ye well, lass?" he asked as he reached her.

She made herself turn a stunning smile on him. "Since I'm no longer drowning, clinging to rocks for dear life, or freezing, I appear to be perfectly fine."

Except that Egan stood too close, his warmth touching her along with the masculine scents of wool and whiskey. The wedding band on her finger seemed to throb.

"Ye should be resting," he said in a low growl. " 'Tis late, and this lot should find their own homes."

"No, no, I find it most diverting. So different from Nvengaria."

Egan's gaze pinned her. "Ye seem cheerful for a woman who's survived a shipwreck."

"Well, I did survive it, that is the cheerful thing." Zarabeth swallowed, unable to keep up the smile. "The first officer did not. He . . ."

She remembered the man's hands reaching for her neck, then his scream as the boards splintered beneath him and he fell into the sea. The magic charm around her neck had glowed warm.

"Do no' grieve overmuch about the first officer," Egan said grimly. "I returned to Ullapool after Angus and Gemma wed to investigate a bit."

Ah, so that's where he'd vanished to.

"The ship's captain managed to save a locker belonging to the first officer, and he showed me its contents— damning letters and papers. The first officer had taken a bribe to sabotage the ship offshore and to take ye into a boat by yourself. He'd been paid plenty to row ye up the coast, where someone was to have picked ye up and taken ye to another ship. One thing to console us is that his money is at the bottom of the sea with him."

Zarabeth recalled her few glimpses of the first officer's thoughts—very few, since Baron Valentin had made her keep to herself during the voyage. "I thought something was wrong," she said slowly. "And when he pushed me onto the boat I had a feeling . . ." He'd shielded himself well, this man, until the very end.

"I put my men to tracing who he worked for," Egan said. "They were able to track a man to a tavern in Inverness, but he'd fled by the time they arrived."

"A Nvengarian?"

"A Scotsman, but none knew him. His accent put him from Glasgow, likely hired there. I sent men down to Glasgow to investigate, but I'm no' hopeful. But even if we never find him, he'll have to stay in hiding and not bother ye."

"Let us hope," she said with feeling.

"Those who live on my lands are loyal to me. If there are any strangers lurking within twenty miles, I'll know all about it."

"I feel very safe here in this castle, I can assure you."

Egan gave her another of his narrow-eyed looks. "Oh, do ye, now?"

She gave him a narrow-eyed look right back. "I do, now. Quite a fortification."

"It's a sieve. Too many windows, and tunnels that lead out to the hills."

She sensed he was goading her to some retort, but she couldn't imagine what. She ignored his remark and made a flirtatious flip of her fan. "It was very good of you to rescue me."

"I could no' verra well tell your father I left ye to die, could I?"

No, she supposed he couldn't. Egan would do anything for her father, including climb down impossible rocks to drag his daughter from the sea.

If only he hadn't grown still more attractive since she'd last seen him. He was thirty-six now—why did he not have a balding head, a large waist, and a sagging face? Why did she still want to drink him in and love every sip?

To stem her irritation and confusion she returned her attention to the dancers. She'd met all of Castle MacDonald's Highlanders today during the rush of the wedding preparations, and she thought she'd sorted them out. There was Angus MacDonald, Egan's cousin, now married to Gemma. He was a large man about Egan's age, with russet hair and dark brown eyes.

Near him was Hamish, Angus's "wee" brother, who was as large and bulky as Angus. The two younger lads were Dougal Cameron and Jamie MacDonald—Dougal was seventeen and the son of Egan's sister, Mary, who was presently in Edinburgh.

Zarabeth watched Jamie, Egan's fifteen-year-old nephew and heir, bounce across the dance floor, his kilt flying. Zarabeth knew that Jamie's father had been killed in the war, in Portugal. It had been after Charlie's death that Egan roamed Europe, grieving, and ended up half-drowned in a freezing ditch in Nvengaria.

The handsome blond Highlander who'd helped her down from the horse this morning was Adam Ross, Egan's nearest neighbor. He and his brother, Piers, were regular visitors to the castle, though at one time their families had been deadly enemies. Their kilts were bright red and green with blue, in contrast to the Mac-Donald blue, green, red, and black.

Adam Ross, spotting Egan and Zarabeth standing alone, made his way to them, smiling his handsome smile.

"I hope you will be pleased with our Highland hospitality, dear lady," he said.

Zarabeth turned a grateful smile on him. "Indeed, I find Castle MacDonald lovely. So quaint and full of history."

"'Tis drafty," Egan growled. "And cold. The castle is no' but a pile of rock, most of it falling down. We try to keep it in repair, but nothing lasts."

Zarabeth glanced back at the hall. The room looked worn, but the firelight bathed the vast chamber in a warm, friendly glow. It was a room that must have seen much—weddings, deaths, births, quarrels, and happiness.

"'Tis the curse," Jamie said, whirling to a stop in front of them. Jamie had long, coltish legs and arms, a young man still growing into his body. "The curse of the MacDonalds. That's why the place is forever falling down."

"Curse?" Zarabeth asked with interest.

Egan glared at his nephew. "There is no curse, lad."

"Of course there is a curse. Three hundred years ago, a witch pointed her finger at Ian MacDonald and cursed him." Jamie held out his hand, forefinger curled, his voice becoming a high falsetto. "'A curse on the MacDonalds!'—and it's no' been the same since. Ghosties and beasties all over the place."

"Nonsense," Adam said, winking at Zarabeth. "Stories your nanny told you to keep you from running about the house in the middle of the night."

"Nanny Graham was a wise old woman," Jamie said indignantly.

"Nanny Graham was mad as a weasel." Adam laughed. "She thought her hat stand was the Duke of Cumberland and tried to shoot it."

Jamie scowled. "She only tried to shoot it a few times." He turned back to Zarabeth. "See the sword up there?"

He pointed to a sword hanging by itself to one side of the massive fireplace. It had a thick blade and a plain hilt, a weapon made for fighting rather than show.

"That is the claymore of Ian MacDonald. The legend goes that to break the curse, the sword must be used by the laird for a brave deed, and then the laird and his lady—a woman of magic herself—must chant a rhyme and break the blade together. Only then will the curse be lifted." His expression turned glum. "But the times of brave deeds are over, unless ye count me and Dougal putting a sheep in Uncle Egan's bedroom. That took much courage, and he thrashed us something horrible. And we don't know what the rhyme is. I've never been able to find it."

"How interesting," Zarabeth said. It intrigued her even more that the story made Egan look uncomfortable and angry. He was scowling like a bear whose den had just been invaded.

"Enough of the curse nonsense, lad."

"But, Uncle, I think it only fair that Zarabeth knows she's living in a castle with a curse."

Egan's brows lowered still further, making him look like a dangerous man who'd been pushed to the edge. Jamie still looked mutinous, and Zarabeth feared that Egan would drag him off by his ear.

He was saved as Gemma whirled by, gripping a red-faced Angus by the hand. "Jamie MacDonald!" she shouted. "'Tis my wedding day, and ye'll dance wi' me. *Now.*"

She grabbed Jamie with her free hand and pulled him into the sea of plaid. The fiddler burst into a new and louder tune and the drummer joined in, filling the hall with more raucous music.

Egan's gaze remained fixed on Jamie, his expression troubled. "Jamie and his curse. The lad needs to learn the more practical side of running the castle, no' go on about magic and fairy tales. He'll be laird someday."

"He enjoys it," Adam told him. "There's more to being laird than crop rotation and mending roofs. It's knowing about the people and their stories."

"Aye, he knows every tale every farmer's granny tells, but nothing about cattle or collecting rents without beggaring the tenants."

Adam clapped Egan on the shoulder. "Leave off the discipline tonight, my friend. Let the lad celebrate." He looked to where Jamie leaped up and down with enthusiasm, kilt flying. "Not only are Angus and Gemma finally wed, but Zarabeth has arrived safe and sound." He smiled at Zarabeth and held out his hand. "Will you favor me, my lady? Egan, do you mind?"

Egan shrugged, still watching Jamie.

Zarabeth lifted her chin. "I would be pleased, Mr. Ross."

"Excellent. And I am Adam to you."

Zarabeth carefully touched Adam's thoughts, but she found nothing more than a spark of interest in dancing with a young woman he found attractive. He had pride in himself—though she didn't need to read his mind to know that—otherwise, he was simply a handsome man wanting to get to know a woman.

She flashed him her sweetest smile. "Then I thank you, Adam."

"Excellent." He held out his arm to lead her away.

Egan's thoughts, of course, were a blank to her, but the scowl on his face said it all.

Chapter Three
The Curse of the
MacDonalds

Adam Ross wasted no time, Egan thought as he watched Adam and Zarabeth join hands with the other dancers. The circles moved in and out, clasped hands rising and falling, as the fiddler played faster and the clapping pounded through the room. In the middle of it, Zarabeth danced, her dark hair shining and her eyes sparkling with delight.

And didn't she look fine in MacDonald plaid? The narrow skirt outlined her legs and rounding of her hips, and the décolletage hugged her fine bosom. She was wrapped in his colors—all he had to do was claim her.

Egan forced his hands to unclench. It had been a long time since he'd seen her, and she was much different now. Unfortunately, she'd only become more beautiful. Her hair was more lustrous, her lips redder, her eyes more sparkling, and she carried herself with confidence and poise.

But she'd changed in other, troubling ways. He sensed a darkness in her, more than what could be explained by her flight from Nvengaria and the dangers she faced. Her smile was still bright but out of place, considering all she'd been through. Damien's letters describing Zarabeth's husband as the devil incarnate had made Egan's blood boil.

I will find ye, Zarabeth, he thought. *I will strip away*

whatever layers you're hiding behind, and I will no' stop until I have the truth of ye.

"You think deep thoughts."

Baron Valentin had moved to Egan's side.

The baron had typical Nvengarian coloring—black hair, intense blue eyes, dark skin. Nvengarians were descended from Magyars and Gypsies, which came out both in their looks and their temperaments. They were a wild, unpredictable people who believed in magic, and after all Egan had seen, he believed in it too.

The Gypsy ancestry seemed to run true in Valentin. Egan put him at about thirty years old, and he stood ramrod straight, nearly as tall as Egan's six-foot-five inches, his blue eyes large and framed with black lashes. He wore a midnight blue frock coat and breeches and high black boots. Several knives hung from his green-and-gold sash.

As a baron, Valentin was in the third-highest order of aristocrats in Nvengaria, right after dukes and counts. He had the sharp-eyed look of most Nvengarians and something else that hinted of danger.

Egan began in fluent Nvengarian, "Why did Damien choose you to bring Zarabeth here?"

If Valentin was surprised by Egan's language skills, he made no sign. "He trusts me. Why did he choose you to hide her?"

"He trusts me, too."

Valentin gave him an assessing look. "Today I went all over this castle, inside and out. It is defensible at the gate and at the bottom of the cliff, but once inside there are too many holes, too many nooks and crannies. It is not a safe place."

Egan knew the truth of this, but for some reason felt defensive. "It has stood against MacDonald enemies for eight hundred years."

"Wild Scotsmen with swords and axes, not Nvengarian assassins with silent feet and poisoned darts."

Egan understood his point, and it worried him too. "Someone will be with her at all times, plus a guard on her bedchamber door, and she'll no' go out without armed escort."

"And these Rosses? I have looked into everything surrounding the MacDonalds, and the Ross clan were your sworn enemies. Would they not betray Zarabeth in order to thwart you?"

"Adam Ross is a good man," Egan said. "The blood-thirsty days are over. The 'Forty-five ended it, and the Clearances are seeing to it that we can never be strong again."

He could see that Valentin didn't quite believe him, and Egan knew why. Nvengarians nursed grudges for generations, hundreds of years, while Highlanders had recently learned that to survive, they needed to bury the past.

The Highlanders were only just now recovering from the atrocity of Culloden, although Egan knew they'd never truly be the same. Those who might have attempted vengeance on the English were now laboring in the factories of Glasgow, leaving the Highlands silent and empty.

Even the plaid patterns his clan and the Rosses wore were recent acquisitions. The Highlanders had been forbidden to wear the plaid or speak their own language since Culloden. Not until the Highland regiments began in the army and the ban on tartans lifted did interest in plaids rekindle. And now that being Scots had been romanticized in the novels of Walter Scott and others, societies had devoted themselves to the restoration of the clan tartans. All the plaids in Egan's family had been destroyed; not a scrap from before Culloden remained.

"I will watch this Adam Ross," Valentin was saying.

"Ye do that. He'll be watching you, too."

Valentin gave a brief nod. "As it should be."

Egan looked the man up and down again. Valentin hadn't actually explained why Damien trusted him. He was smooth and careful, like all Nvengarians, but Egan now noticed that his eyes were a little different, a very dark blue, the irises slightly larger than normal.

"Oh, God," he groaned. "Ye aren't one of those bloody logosh, are ye?"

Logosh were demon shape-changers that lived in the mountains of Nvengaria and could choose what shape they'd take, animal or human. Egan's friend the Grand Duke Alexander had turned out to be one of them, his chosen animal shape a panther.

Valentin's brows rose. "You are perceptive. Though I am not full-blooded. My mother was half logosh, and I possess some of their powers."

That explained a few things. Logosh were ferocious, but as long as Valentin protected Zarabeth, Egan would welcome him.

The dance wound to a close with much cheering and applause, and Valentin moved away to circle the dance floor like a wolf prowling his territory.

Another dance started, but Egan saw Zarabeth give Adam a polite smile and beg to be excused. Adam led her to a chair like any gentleman in a London ball-room, where she fanned herself and smiled brightly.

Too brightly. She was almost brittle. What had happened to the girl who'd fished with him from the river behind her father's house, the flirt who'd asked with a teasing glint if it was true that a Highlander wore nothing under his kilt?

"No one will take it amiss if ye rest yourself up-stairs," Egan said to her when he reached them. "Ye've been through much today."

Her smile remained in place, but her voice held an edge of coolness. "I am perfectly fine, Egan, thank you."

She had dark smudges under her eyes, and the hand that held the fan was trembling. If Adam noticed, he made no sign of it. He gave Egan a lazy smile, as if to say, *Push off, old friend; you're getting in the way.*

Egan held out his hand to Zarabeth. "Then mebbe you'll dance with me?"

She raised her brows. "A kind offer, but you are indeed right that I had a tiring journey. Perhaps I should simply sit and enjoy the music."

"Leave the poor lady alone, Egan," Adam said. "Run off and be laird or something."

Egan ignored him, exaggerating a polite tone. "Then mayhap Your Grace would like a turn on the terrace to cool down? The view of the moon is fine from there."

Adam snorted. "You haven't got a terrace."

"Mary fixed it up. Zarabeth will like it."

At last he saw a sparkle in her eyes, a glimpse of the old Zarabeth answering his challenge.

She put her gloved hand in Egan's and allowed him to lift her to her feet. She gave him a cool look but turned her warmest smile on Adam. "I shall be fine with my old friend. Thank you, Mr. Ross, for looking after me."

"A pleasure indeed, my lady." Adam made a perfect bow and smirked at Egan.

Egan led Zarabeth away rather abruptly.

The "terrace" was little more than a crenellation that jutted from the main castle, likely used in violent days as a lookout for whatever enemy was expected to pour across the valley. The moon was round and full, glittering white, the breeze sharp but bearable.

Zarabeth stepped away from Egan. She hated it when he wouldn't talk to her, but she had difficulty standing close to him as well. He was too large, too masculine, too real. She'd thought about him for five years, but it was one thing to imagine him, another to have him standing next to her, warm and solid.

In her dreams he belonged to her, but she knew the true Egan belonged to no one. Women the length and breadth of Europe ate their hearts out over him—they'd been eager to tell her so.

The silence stretched too long. If the bloody man wanted to talk to her, why did he not say anything?

"Quite lovely," Zarabeth blurted, sounding to herself like a tongue-tied debutante. "Ingenious."

Egan swung her to face him, his fingers points of heat in the cold. "What is the matter with ye? Ye were shipwrecked and nearly drowned, a man tried to kidnap ye, and ye'd have died had I not heard ye calling. Any other woman would have taken to her bed in hysterics by now. Yet ye smile and dance as though the world is bright. You're smilin' so hard your face might crack."

Her whole body might crack if he kept holding her like this. "Perhaps you'd be happier if I fell to the floor wailing and tearing my hair? A pleasant way to celebrate a wedding."

His voice softened to the little growl that had always made her heart speed. "This is me, Zarabeth. Are we not still friends?"

Her practiced smile faded. "Are we?"

"I always considered us so."

Her face heated with embarrassment as she thought about the night when she was eighteen, the last time she'd seen him. She hoped he'd forgotten what a little idiot she'd been.

He'd spent the evening at the village tavern and returned long after the household had gone to bed, smelling of the strong Nvengarian whiskey that he liked. She'd spent the time he was gone perfecting a love charm to use on him.

She remembered the eagerness with which she'd sat at her table, candles lit, inscribing runes of love and devotion on her crystal. She'd been certain he'd be hers that night.

She'd hung the charm around her neck and waited for him in the deserted drawing room, calling out to him softly when he entered the house. She remembered the warm closeness of the room, the scent of wax from the spent candles, the deep shadows that were familiar rather than frightening.

Egan had come in, smiling his Highlander smile and asking, *What is it ye're wanting, lass?* She'd put her hands on his wide chest and asked him to kiss her.

He'd hesitated at first, then leaned down and rested his lips lightly on hers. When she began to kiss him back, he'd groaned and pressed her against the wall. He'd opened her mouth with hers, giving her a man's kiss, a lover's kiss. His tongue had swept into her mouth, hot friction that made her knees weak.

She still could feel with clarity the wall behind her, the molding against her hips, the coolness of the wallpaper on her back. Egan's mouth was firm on hers, tasting of whiskey and maleness. The cleft between her legs had ached, and she'd nearly slid to the floor in a puddle of warmth.

He'd whispered her name, laced his arm around her back, kissed her again. His mouth had been hot, his tongue a point of pleasure, licking and probing, claiming her. She waited for him to say the words she'd longed to hear—*I love you, Zarabeth.*

Instead he'd backed away suddenly in horror, looking much the same as he had this morning when he'd leapt out of the bed at the inn. He'd held his arm outstretched to keep her away from him and gasped, *You're no' for me, lass.*

She'd tried to argue with him, make him see reason. She'd been a clinging little fool, and he'd rebuffed her and gotten himself out of the house as quickly as possible.

Zarabeth had returned to her room, stifling her tears by being furious with him. She'd smashed the crystal, erasing her silly spell. She should have remembered that her magic never worked on Egan. When next she saw him, she'd be cold and haughty and pretend she did not care.

Except he'd never come back.

She looked up at him now, her gaze going to his mouth. A few lines creased the corners, but his lips were still strong, still satin smooth. . . .

She wanted to kiss him again.

Zarabeth took a quick step back as the need to kiss him flooded her body. What was the matter with her? Hadn't she learned her lesson by now?

"Perhaps we should go back inside," she said hastily.

"Not yet. I want ye to tell me what happened, Zarabeth. What your husband did t' make ye like this."

"Like what?" *Vulnerable? Afraid?*

"Brittle. Simpering."

She glared. "I do *not* simper."

His entrancing mouth curved into a small smile. "That's better."

"I don't wish to speak of it. Not now, Egan. It's too fresh, too awful, too close to me."

She knew that if she did pour out her troubles, she'd fling herself at him, probably weeping and begging him to make it all better. She'd be the clinging fool he'd run away from all those years ago.

"Damien said you are divorcing your husband," Egan was saying.

"Yes, Damien is taking care of it for me. It is quite handy to be a cousin to the ruler of the nation."

His gaze sharpened, and she realized she was doing it again, making light conversation about serious things.

"I know the laws of Nvengaria," Egan said. "A divorce does not ruin ye there, but I suggest we don't mention it to m' sister."

"I can keep a secret."

His shadowed eyes seemed to burn. "That's obvious, lass."

"Meaning what, exactly?"

He leaned into her, his large body bending over hers. She knew she should back away, yet at the same time she wanted to stay in the curve of his body and enjoy the warmth.

"Ye have so much dancing behind your eyes," Egan said softly. "One day I will discover all that is there."

"Will you?"

He cupped her shoulders, his warmth making her want to crumble. "I will, lass. I promise ye."

Was he doing this on purpose? Driving her mad for once being young and stupid? Or did it simply amuse him to torment her?

At least being married to Sebastian had given her fortitude. She'd hardened and did not fear what she used to fear, and she'd certainly not back down from a challenge made by a handsome Highlander.

She lifted her chin. "Very well then, that's settled. Now let's rejoin the party. I'd love you to show me a true Highland dance, and if you think I ought to be frail and tired, I will sit on a soft chair and watch you."

Zarabeth started to turn, but he stopped her. "Oh, this is far from settled, love."

His eyes were dark, his lips parted slightly. She remembered again precisely how satin smooth his lips were, how strong his arms.

She also remembered that for all his laughing charm

and good nature, Egan MacDonald brooked no foolishness from anyone.

"What do you mean?" she asked, suddenly nervous.

"Ye will find out, lass."

That sounded ominous in the extreme. When she didn't answer, he took her hand and pulled it through the crook of his arm. She wore gloves and he wore a coat, but the rock-hard muscle under the cashmere shot fire to her heart. Dear God, it would be difficult living under the same roof with him when she wanted to melt every time he touched her.

He seemed oblivious to the turmoil raging inside her as he more or less dragged her back to the great hall.

Cajoling Egan to dance had been a grave mistake.

Adam sat at her side once again, on hand to look after her. Zarabeth found it hard to catch her breath, and made the excuse to Adam when he asked that the wind had been a bit too brisk.

"He should not have taken you out there," Adam said severely. "You were sent here for your protection, not to catch your death of cold." He abruptly went to fetch her some warm wine.

Cold was not what had her gasping, and she knew it. It was Egan, blast the man.

The crowd on the floor parted as the fiddler struck up a tune, and Egan became the center of attention. She heard cries of, "Make way for the laird," and, "Aye, show them how it's done, cousin." They circled around him, and Zarabeth rose to see.

Two sabers had been laid on the floor, crossed at right angles, and Egan began to dance carefully between them. Hands on hips, he started a slow, almost understated jig, his upper body ramrod straight and still. When the musicians sped up Egan danced faster, his eyes trained on the swords at his feet. He lifted one hand overhead for balance, the other remaining on his waist.

He kept perfect time with the music, his hips swaying against the folds of the kilt, an athletic man moving with grace. More than one woman's eyes roved over him, and Zarabeth heard their thoughts speculating whether a man who danced like that would be as powerful in bed.

Zarabeth wondered the same thing.

The crowd clapped along as Egan danced faster and faster, and Zarabeth found herself clapping too, palms tingling. The music caught her and closed her off to everything but it and the man dancing fast and skillfully in the middle of the circle.

At last Egan threw up both hands, landed on his feet outside the crossed sabers, and roared, "Enough!"

The party burst into wild applause, and the musicians wound up with a flourish.

"All hail our bonny MacDonald," someone shouted, and whiskey glasses shot high. Some of the younger lads clamored for Egan to teach them the sword dance. Egan glanced over and saw Zarabeth watching him.

His smile also held a challenge and a large dose of self-confidence that made her quiver.

She would have to go very, very carefully.

In the morning, one of the castle's smiling red-haired maids helped Zarabeth dress in another plaid gown and told her that breakfast could be found in the great hall. Zarabeth had learned from Gemma that most of the maids came from one family, the Grahams, who had produced seven daughters and three sons, all of whom worked for Egan. She remembered Jamie mentioning a Nanny Graham, and wondered if all these young women had sprung from her.

Zarabeth's footmen waited outside her bedroom door, having stationed themselves on each side like sentries. They were fine specimens of Nvengarian youth, Ivan a little taller than his brother Constanz, both muscular, black-haired and blue-eyed, with innocent but eager faces, both on their first venture away from home.

"Good morning," Zarabeth greeted them.

They thumped fists to chests and bowed, then fell into step behind her as she wound her way down the staircase to the great hall.

The room had been put to rights since last night's feast, and now an immense table flowed down the center, covered with platters of food. Only two people ate there, Jamie MacDonald and Egan himself.

Egan and Jamie sprang to their feet when she entered, Jamie wiping his mouth from the enormous forkful of food he'd just shoved past his lips. Ivan rushed to hold a chair for Zarabeth, but Egan beat him to it, drawing out the high-backed chair next to his own.

Jamie called a greeting as he sat back down. "Ye look bonny this morning, Zarabeth. The night did you well."

"Yes, I was very comfortable, thank you."

She slid into her seat while Egan gazed at her with watchful eyes. Really, was the man going to be suspicious of everything she said?

Egan shoved her chair to the table with a strong hand, then dropped back into his own seat. There seemed to be a great deal of food put out—sausages, boiled eggs, ham, and some flat cakes she didn't recognize. She peered at it all, pleasantly hungry for the first time in months.

"Will there be porridge, too?" she asked eagerly. "Egan talked of it all the time he stayed in Nvengaria, and I have so looked forward to trying it."

Jamie snorted. Egan only stared, still challenging her.

"Williams," Jamie bellowed as the servant entered with another plateful of sausages. "Has your wife fixed no porridge this morning? Tell her to send up a bowl for our guest."

Williams looked surprised. "Porridge? Them's good bannocks and fresh eggs. Surprised the hens are laying, what with the mad crowd we've had here."

He looked so amazed that Zarabeth flushed. "This will be excellent, Williams. Please thank your wife for me. Perhaps I will try porridge later."

Looking puzzled, Williams trudged away.

Jamie was still laughing as he helped himself to the pile of flat oatcakes called bannocks.

Egan said, "Scottish servants like to speak their minds. Mebbe not what you are used to?"

Zarabeth looked at him in frank astonishment while her footmen both tried to fill her plate at once. "Nvengarian servants can be the most forthright in the world, as you well know, Egan MacDonald."

Egan's lips twitched, as though he were pleased with her answer. "Aye, I do know it."

Then why on earth did he ask?

Frustrated, she attacked her breakfast, but slowed as she found the food delicious. She said so, earning an indifferent nod from Jamie, who said it was as usual.

" 'Tis a lovely morning," Egan said abruptly.

Jamie looked up at the high windows in surprise. " 'Tis raining, Uncle."

"All the better. Good fishing to be had in a light rain." Egan bent his gaze on Zarabeth. "Are ye up to it, lass? A little fishing in one of the best streams in Scotland? 'Twill be a bit muddy, of course. Not an activity for the delicate."

Aha. Delicate indeed.

Zarabeth met his gaze steadily. "But of course. I seem to recall times we went out when the weather was much worse. I will brave it to try fishing in this famous stream."

Jamie peered up again at the wet windows. "You're both mad."

"You'll come with us," Egan told him. "Ye need to better learn the lands and the wilds if you're to be laird."

"I've told ye. I don't want to be laird."

Any humor Egan found in the conversation deserted him. "You are my only heir. You'll be laird, and that's that."

"Not if you marry and have sons."

" 'Tis no' likely, lad, even with you scheming to find me a bride. Ye'll be laird, and that's an end to it."

Jamie scowled, but Zarabeth's interest sparked. She turned to Jamie. "Find him a bride?"

"Aye," Jamie said, brightening. "Aunt Mary and me are workin' to get Uncle Egan married off. We have criteria and everything."

"Criteria?"

"Shut it, Jamie," Egan warned.

"No," Zarabeth said. "I want to hear this. It sounds like a fine idea." It didn't, in truth. The picture of Egan standing in the small stone kirk as Angus had yesterday, plighting his troth to a happy, pink-cheeked bride made her sick at heart. But she kept a bright smile trained on Jamie.

Jamie ticked each point off on his fingers. "She must be Scottish, well-bred, pretty, of tolerable personality, and either practice magic herself or be descended from someone magical. Oh, and she must be rich. Bloody filthy rich."

Zarabeth lifted her brows. "Why must she be magical?"

"Because of the curse, of course. The laird must

marry a magical lady without shame, and then they say the spell that breaks the sword."

"Jamie," Egan said again, his look thunderous.

"That's why Aunt Mary went to Edinburgh," Jamie rattled on. "To bring back eligible misses to meet him."

Egan growled. "I'm to be protecting Zarabeth, not letting the place be overrun by debutantes."

"There's nothin' to worry at, Uncle. They'll stay at Ross Hall. No sense in bringin' the lass here until after the weddin', or she might run away when she sees the ruin of this place."

"Ye'll not bring them here at all. Ye can send them straight back to Edinburgh."

Jamie took another mouthful of sausage. "Be reasonable, Uncle. Ye need to marry, and quick, before ye grow too old. A rich lady will give us money to fix the leaking roof, and we'll make sure she's young enough to give ye a dozen children."

"Enough. 'Tis a mad scheme, and I'll have none of it."

"And I'll have none of being laird," Jamie shot back. "Ye only want me to be laird so you'll pass *me* the curse of the MacDonalds."

Egan climbed to his feet and shouted, "For the last time, there is no bloody curse!"

A tearing sound cut through his words. Zarabeth looked up in time to see a piece of the beam over her chair come loose and plummet toward her.

She screamed and dove sideways at the same instant Egan leaped from his seat and yanked her out of the way. The beam crashed to the table in a splinter of wood and porcelain as Jamie scrambled back.

Zarabeth ended up with her back to the wall, Egan hard against her. The wool of his kilt was rough through the thin fabric of her borrowed gown, his hands on her arms bruising.

The pressure of his body and his masculine scent stirred her already maddening feelings for him. If they'd been alone, she'd have slid her hands under his hair and coaxed his mouth to hers.

She almost did it. Her hands rested on his chest, and she rubbed her thumb over the bare, dark skin of his throat. He looked down, his eyes darkening, his pulse throbbing under her touch.

"You all right, lass?" he asked softly.

She nodded, keeping her voice light. "I am used to dodging attempts on my life. I am Nvengarian, after all."

She could not stop her thumb from caressing him again, loving the hot feeling of his skin. She realized with dismaying clarity that she ached for him as much as she ever had.

Jamie had his hands on his hips, surveying the damage. Ivan and Constanz surveyed it with him, but they made signs against the evil eye, sure demons had done it.

"No assassin," Jamie surmised. "Naught but a loosened beam, pegs worn out after several hundred years."

Egan abruptly released Zarabeth, the sudden absence of his warmth making her shiver.

"Aye," he said. "Castle MacDonald is a ruined heap of stone, held together with a wish and a prayer."

"'Tis the curse," Jamie muttered. Then, catching Egan's eye, he looked at the wreckage of the table and said quickly, "Aye, well, I suppose it's porridge for us all now. Williams, tell your wife."

The rain had turned to fine mist by the time Zarabeth tramped along the path toward the river following Egan. Egan looked splendid in a linen shirt, a dark kilt, and boots, his curly hair bound in a queue. Jamie wore a similar costume, but he sulked a bit, keeping up a muttered monologue that only a madman would drag them out to fish in the rain.

Gemma had loaned Zarabeth sturdy boots and a warm mantle, all the while admonishing Egan not to wear her out. Gemma had sent for the village seamstress to replace Zarabeth's lost clothes, and Zarabeth would have to stand for many fittings later that day.

Egan had merely glanced at Zarabeth and said, "She's hardy enough to do both."

Zarabeth ground her teeth and promised herself she'd show him just how hardy she was.

Conscious of the danger, Egan had a contingency of his own men and Baron Valentin fan out into the hills and woods and patrol as they walked. Zarabeth's two footmen accompanied her, as usual. Zarabeth, having been married to a controversial duke in Nvengaria, was used to bodyguards and had learned to quietly accept their presence. Egan ignored them also, but Jamie didn't like it; he continued to mutter that the men would scare away all the fish and he'd have caught a cold for nothing.

They crested a low ridge and trudged down the other side to the flowing river below. Mountains rose around them, some of them with snow already on their peaks, tops lost in the mist. The path ended at the river, which was about four feet deep at this point, rushing through shallows and burbling in pools cut into the banks.

Egan turned and trudged through wet grass and mud at the same speed he'd moved down the path. Zarabeth lifted her skirts and determinedly followed.

He stopped at a rock that jutted out into the river. To one side, the water sent up cold spray. On the other, the eddies slid into a quiet pool, which was thick with fish darting in and out, silver scales catching the light.

Egan rested one booted foot on a rock, his kilt hanging

modestly. The wind pulled at his hair and his shirt, making him look very much the rugged Highlander of old. If he'd had a claymore instead of a fishing pole, he might be saying a prayer to the old gods before he joined his fellows in battle.

He turned his head and regarded her, dark eyes enigmatic. "Just right for it."

"Lovely," Zarabeth returned. "A bit cold, but I daresay the fish find it lively."

Now that he had arrived, Jamie stopped sulking. He took in the abundance of fish, tested the wind with his finger, and began to string and bait his pole. Zarabeth's footman Ivan began to bait her hook for her until she took it away from him.

"I can do this," she told him in Nvengarian. "You go patrol with Constanz; I will be fine."

Ivan's eyes welled with tears. She knew he and Constanz blamed themselves for the shipwreck as well as the fallen beam this morning, as though they could have held the ship and castle together with their bare hands.

Zarabeth patted him on the shoulder. "You are doing well, Ivan. I thank you and Constanz for all you have done for me on the journey."

Ivan looked morose. "But we failed you. You must put us into the dungeon and feed us scraps that the pigs do not want."

"Egan doesn't have a dungeon. Besides, I need you and your brother looking out for me out here in the world."

"We will never fail you again. We will never, ever let you come to harm. I swear this on my mother's bones."

"Your mother is still alive," Zarabeth said with patience. "You must go patrol now."

Ivan bowed deeply. "As Your Grace wishes." He spun smartly on one booted heel and marched off to join the other guards.

"What was that about?" Jamie asked.

Zarabeth impaled the worm on the hook and wiped her glove. "He thinks he should be shut in a dungeon because he did not prevent the shipwreck. I told him Egan did not have a dungeon."

"But he does," Jamie said. "We store the whiskey and ale down there now, but it used to be a dungeon. Still has bits of manacles and things on the walls. Mrs. Williams says there's ghosts in there—she's afraid to go down. She hears the poor souls moaning and wailing, she does, those that were tortured to death."

"That's no' but invention," Egan retorted. "It was used as a holding area for prisoners captured in war, who were let go as soon as they were ransomed. There was no torture at Castle MacDonald."

Jamie winked at Zarabeth and turned away to cast his line.

"Insolent pup," Egan muttered. "Stand just here, Zarabeth; this is always a fine spot."

"I know how to fish." Zarabeth stepped away, knowing she wouldn't be able to concentrate on fish with his warm body next to hers. She wanted to lie down with him on the riverbank, despite the mud, and have him wrap them both in his plaid. Wouldn't that look fine, a highborn lady of Nvengaria rolling in the grass with a Highlander?

She suppressed a shiver. She didn't care how it would look; she could only imagine how glorious it would feel.

Egan turned away. Zarabeth cast the line into the water with gentle flicks of her wrist, earning an admiring look from Jamie.

They fished in silence for a time, the only sound the rushing water and the wind in the tall trees that lined the hills. The wind brought the cool scents of pine and rain and water, soothing to her soul.

Zarabeth hadn't fished in years, but it came back to her: the quiet waiting, the simple plop of the lure going into the water, the mild excitement of a tug on the line, disappointment when the fish flipped away. After a while, Jamie moved a little way down the stream, stopping now and again to test a new spot. Egan and Zarabeth stayed where they were and fished until they'd caught several. Egan dumped them into a net that bobbed in the river, and the fish zoomed about the small space, looking for a way out.

They are like me, Zarabeth thought. *Searching for freedom.*

Egan planted his pole in the bank and stretched himself out on a flat-topped rock. Zarabeth admired his long, strong body in scarred boots and worn kilt, linen shirt stretching across his chest. He was a powerful man, latent strength in his body. Some might mistake his languor for laziness, but they'd be deceived. Egan was like a feral animal, taking his ease in the sun but able to spring up with wild energy when he needed to.

Zarabeth stuck her pole next to his and sat down on the rock. "I see through you, Egan."

"Do ye now?" he asked mildly.

"I know why you brought me out here. You think I have become such a refined lady of society that I've forgotten all about how to get my feet muddy. Well, I've not become so lofty that I cannot tramp about in the rain."

Egan raised himself on his elbows, his ankles crossed. "I never thought ye'd grow too genteel to fish."

"But you teased me until I came out here today—to prove I still would. Why, for heaven's sake?"

He shrugged, muscles moving beneath his open shirt. "I thought ye might enjoy it."

She grew exasperated. "Why must you be so maddening?"

He grinned. "I thought ye might enjoy it."

Egan, the man she could never read. He looked back at her, eyes half-closed but with an alert gleam beneath his lashes.

"What do you want me to say?" she asked, irritated.

"Mmm." He shifted his body, as if looking for a more comfortable spot. "Do ye remember, lass, what ye asked me on a day like this that first time I was in Nvengaria? You gave me a sly look and dared me to tell ye what a Scotsman wore under his kilt."

Zarabeth felt her face heat, wishing he'd forget how childish she'd been. Egan had already been a grown man, five-and-twenty years old and she twelve when she'd found him injured, in a drunken stupor, and nearly frozen to death. He'd been an officer in a Highland regiment that had fought at Talavera, where his brother had died. Feeling responsible, Egan had lost all sense of purpose. After returning Charlie's body to Scotland, he'd wandered Europe, using whiskey and brawling to help him forget the pain of his guilt. Egan had stayed with her family for some time, then returned to his regiment rejuvenated. He'd come back to visit Zarabeth and her father in 1815, fresh from Waterloo and handsomer than ever.

If anything, he'd grown still more appealing. His face showed the lines of life and battle, and she wanted to feather kisses over every one.

"I was a child when I said that," she said hurriedly.

"'Twas a fair question. I never did tell ye, did I?"

"No, you laughed so hard you couldn't speak."

Egan chuckled. "I remember that."

He had roared with laughter, leaning back on the grassy bank under the warm sunshine with his arms over his stomach. Zarabeth the girl had looked at him and realized she loved him.

He stood now, towering over her. She looked right at

the hem of his kilt, which was frayed with wear, his brawny knee just showing beneath it.

"Well, lass," he said, voice rumbling and soft, "I think 'tis time your long patience was rewarded."

Chapter Four
Under a Scotsman's Kilt

"Egan!" Zarabeth sprang to her feet. Her heart beat swiftly, her face burning.

He gave her a look of mock astonishment. "Do ye think I have no modesty, woman? Jamie!" he called.

Jamie looked around from downstream. "Wha'?"

"What are ye wearing under your kilt?"

Jamie stared as though not certain he'd heard right. "*Wha'*?"

Egan cupped his hands around his mouth. "I said, what be ye wearing under your kilt, lad?"

"Leather breeches, what d'ye think? It's mother-loving cold out here."

Egan waved his thanks and Jamie turned away, shaking his head.

Zarabeth hugged her arms to her chest. "What on earth did you do that for?"

"Ye wanted to know."

"You are ridiculous."

Egan looked enlightened. "Ah, now I have measure of ye. Ye wanted to know what *I* wore, not just any Scotsman. Well, I'll tell ye, lass." He took a step closer to her, curving over her as he had in the hall. "I'll tell ye— someday. I promise ye that."

He stepped away and leaned over to grab his fishing

pole. His kilt moved to reveal the strong backs of his thighs, which were not covered by anything at all.

He straightened up, saw her gaze, and roared with laughter. "Are ye trying to look now?"

She stepped back. "Certainly not."

She lost her footing on the rock and plummeted downward. Egan caught her in his strong arms, and for a moment she was in his embrace.

His large hands splayed across the small of her back, warm and powerful. He looked down at her, his eyes dark, the vee of his open shirt letting her see his hard chest dusted with dark curls.

He was going to kiss her. His gaze swiveled to her lips, eyes flicking across her top lip, then the bottom. She waited for it, heart pounding, knowing she wouldn't stop him.

She was shameless. Sebastian had destroyed her trust and hurt her so much. Zarabeth was empty and paralyzed, and here was her Highlander to soothe her heart.

She couldn't stop her tongue from wetting her lower lip. Egan's chest rose and fell with his swift breath, and he leaned a fraction nearer, gaze riveted to her lips.

She wanted him with a savagery she hadn't thought herself capable of. If he chose to lay her in the mud and take her body or throw her over his shoulder and rush to the castle, she wouldn't stop him.

His gaze flicked to her eyes, and the moment broke.

"Egan," she whispered.

"We should go back," he said in a low voice. " 'Tis too cold. I should never have brought you out here."

"Not yet." She tried to smile, pretending she hadn't just been dying to kiss him. "I'm tired of hiding myself, tired of living in a gilded cage."

"A definite lack of gilding at Castle MacDonald," he

said. "Not to mention a bloody great lot of Highlanders." His voice remained low, as though he didn't want to frighten her away.

"I don't mind them."

Boldly she raised her hand and touched his face. He stood still, letting her caress him as he had in the great hall. No tearing away as when he'd realized he'd fallen asleep with her at the inn, no look of horror.

She made herself lower her hand and step away, breaking his embrace. He let her go, his fingers closing on her elbow to steady her to the ground. He was right: the day had grown colder, and they needed to retreat indoors.

Zarabeth walked down to the bank to retrieve her pole, and Egan brushed past her to get the net, which looked strangely empty. She peered at it as Egan lifted it.

"There's a hole in it," she said, dismayed.

Egan studied the net, then lowered it regretfully. "Aye, they've gotten away. Back to freedom."

He walked past her, grabbed his pole from the rock, and started down the path, calling to Jamie on the way.

Jamie had caught a string of fish and dangled them as they climbed the hill to the castle. Zarabeth followed, aware of Egan hulking behind her and her footmen trailing in the distance.

She could still feel the imprint of Egan's hands on her back and her vast disappointment that he'd chosen not to kiss her. She needed him to kiss her, needed the feel of his lips and the bite of his tongue and the heady sensation of being in his arms.

But Egan had a deep sense of honor. She'd always known that, and her father had reminded her of it when Egan left Nvengaria five years before. Though she was twenty-three now, she'd always be little Zarabeth in his eyes, daughter of a man he greatly respected. Egan would keep his honor, and Zarabeth would eat her heart out.

A shiny black carriage with polished wood and spokes picked out in gold stood in the courtyard as the three of them entered through the open gate. A red-coated coachman busily scraped mud from its painted surface.

Egan stopped. "Bloody hell."

"What is it?"

Zarabeth instinctively drew closer to him, and her two footmen flanked them, hands near weapons. She was too canny to believe herself safe even out here in the wilds, though she was certain no one sinister had lurked at the river. She'd sensed no thoughts but those of Jamie and the patrolling men.

"My sister," Egan groaned. "God help us."

A lady in a much-decorated blue traveling gown and a headdress stuck with too many ostrich feathers was already in the front hall. Mary Cameron looked much like Egan, the same brown eyes, the same riot of dark curls. The household servants swarmed around her, scurrying upstairs with boxes and valises.

Zarabeth sensed Mary running over lists in her mind of things she needed to do, her thoughts focused and anxious. But she also sensed something behind Mary's surface: loneliness, defensiveness, and a sense of being left out. It was as though Mary kept the lists going steadily to keep from thinking more troubling thoughts.

Mary stripped off her gloves impatiently. "How could you, Egan?" she said, not noticing Zarabeth behind him. "We at last have a visitor of consequence, but could you be bothered to send word when she was expected? What do I learn when I alight but that she's already here?"

"I could scarce send ye word when her presence is supposed to be secret," Egan said.

"Not secret to me, your own sister. Dougal had to tell me. At least *he* loves his mama." She frowned at Jamie, who still held the string of fish. "Get those to the kitchen, Jamie. They stink to high heaven—what would *she* think?"

Jamie merely said, "Hello, Auntie," and trudged down the stairs toward the kitchens.

Mary swung around again and at last saw Zarabeth. Words died on her lips, and her expression moved swiftly from alarm to anger to dismay.

"Your Highness." She made a deep, overly formal curtsy. "I apologize for not being here to greet you as a hostess should."

Zarabeth slid off her dirty gloves and went to her, holding out her hand. "I am not a princess, Mrs. Cameron. You do not need to address me so."

Mary shot to her feet. "But Egan told me—"

"My title as a young woman was *princess*, but my family is not royal—only distantly related to the ruling family. It is like Russian families, where all the children of dukes are little dukes and duchesses. After a while everyone is a duke or duchess." She smiled to show she was not offended.

Mary looked mollified. "I apologize. My brother is the worst at protocol. How would you like me to address you?"

"If you call me Zarabeth, I believe we shall get along quite well."

Mary blushed again. "Then it is my delight to welcome you to our home—Zarabeth."

Egan looked heavenward behind her back. "This is Castle MacDonald, Mary, not a society salon."

Mary looked at Egan and nearly shrieked. "What a

mess you are. What will our Edinburgh guests think of you? If they see you in that state, smelling of river and fish, they might dash right back to Edinburgh, so do clean up. There's a good brother."

"They can hie back this night, for all I care, and have done. I'll have no part of this scheme."

Mary ignored him and smiled at Zarabeth. "I am so happy to meet you at last. Let me sort myself out from my journey, and I will have Williams give us tea." She held out her arm to Zarabeth, who took it, knowing exactly how to behave in this situation, at least.

As they went up the stairs, Baron Valentin entered the castle, returning from the fishing expedition. Mary's step slowed. Valentin, even in his human form, had a primal and dangerous air, as though no civilized house could hold him.

Mary's eyes widened as she watched him move to Egan, but Valentin did not stop or ask to be introduced. He'd likely either been told by others in the house who she was or concluded it himself. His gaze rippled over her, and Zarabeth sensed his sudden sharp spike of interest. Valentin's eyes met Mary's for a brief, intense moment before he looked away.

Egan met him in the lower hall, and they walked off together.

Mary stilled, staring at the place Egan and Valentin had stood. "Who . . . ?"

"Baron Valentin," Zarabeth said, taking her arm again. "Sent to guard me. You will grow used to him."

She did not add the reassuring platitude that he was quite kind once you got to know him, because Zarabeth did not know whether Valentin was kind. She knew very little about the enigmatic logosh. He had kept to himself during their travels, despite her attempts to draw him out. Nor could she read many of his thoughts—he was adept at keeping his innermost secrets secret. She was surprised she had gotten his jolt of interest when he looked at Mary.

Mary continued up the stairs with Zarabeth, but her gaze returned to the lower hall again and again, her expression troubled.

Mary insisted Zarabeth enjoy a hot bath after her "fishing ordeal."

"My brother had no call to drag you out into the mud and rain," she said indignantly. "It was really too bad of him."

Zarabeth insisted she'd been happy to go, but Mary, seeming nervous after their encounter with Baron Valentin, rattled on. "He never has learned how to behave in polite society—I have heard stories of him wearing hunting kilts to the palaces of Vienna. So embarrassing."

Zarabeth knew Egan played what he called the Mad Highlander on purpose. He'd pretend to be an ignorant, backwoods Scotsman with a heavy accent, and his antics made everyone laugh. He did it both to put people at ease and to hide his shrewd intelligence when necessary.

While Zarabeth bathed, Mary sent in clean dresses—heavily embroidered lawn gowns flounced at the hems. Zarabeth ignored them in favor of one of the plaid gowns Gemma had altered for her yesterday, telling the worried maid that she found it a novelty.

In truth, she did not want to go back to being a highborn lady just yet. In the tartan gown she could make herself believe she'd escaped, that she was safe in this remote and strange land.

After dressing, Zarabeth dismissed the maid and left her room for the gallery that circled the main staircase. The huge clock at the top of the staircase chimed, sonorous and slow.

Zarabeth had not had time to explore the castle, having been busy since the moment of her arrival, and now she looked about with interest. Castle MacDonald was tall and square, rising straight from the rocks in a pile of sharp-cornered stone. A polished wooden staircase wound through its heart, obviously more modern than the building around it, and each floor was encircled by a wooden-railed gallery. This place had been built for battle, little luxuries like the polished railing, paneled doors, and runners in the halls added when battle had ceased being a way of life.

Paintings of MacDonalds hung on the stone walls of each floor, portraits ranging from recent years to those from the dim past. She found Egan's father at the end of her gallery near the clock, a broad-shouldered man with a severe manner and Egan's gold-flecked eyes. Next to him was painting of a woman with a warm smile and dark brown ringlets, the shape of her face so like Egan's and Mary's that Zarabeth knew it was their mother.

A portrait of Mary hung nearby. She stood straight and tall, chin lifted, her hand on the back of a chair in which a very young Dougal sat holding a puppy. Mary stared out of the painting haughtily, as though letting the world know she could live fine on her own, thank you.

The painting on the other side of Egan's father's caught Zarabeth's attention—at first Zarabeth thought it a portrait of Egan, but a closer look revealed that it was not. The young man had Egan's openness of manner, a smile on his face, and a wicked twinkle in his eyes. He wore an army uniform—kilt and red coat, his tall hat under his arm. The youthful face looked excited, eager for battle.

This must be Egan's younger brother, Charlie, she surmised. His portrait held pride of place at the head of the stairs next to Egan's father. Egan had been in the same Highland regiment, but though Zarabeth scanned the walls, she found no portrait of him.

Zarabeth quietly took the stairs upward. She found no portraits of Egan on the floors above hers either, only landscapes of Loch Argonne and faded portraits of MacDonald men and women from centuries past. There were fewer rooms as she went up, the doors faded and worn like the paintings.

A door in the middle of the gallery three floors above hers stood ajar, and she heard Egan's baritone rumble from behind it. She paused to listen and realized to her astonishment that he was singing.

Zarabeth had heard Egan sing before, usually loudly and horribly out of tune, belting out Scottish ballads in elegant drawing rooms to entertain as the Mad Highlander. This time he sang in a low voice that was surprisingly musical.

She could make out lyrics about lying on a plaid in the heather with a bonny lass. Her treacherous imagination put herself on the plaid with Egan, lying beneath his strong body, the purple-flowered heather stretching to the horizon. She imagined his fingers in her hair, his lips on her mouth, his body nestled between her legs.

Zarabeth closed her eyes in the silent hall, swaying in time with the music. It was a sensuous song, but sweet, full of the love of a Highlander for his pretty maid. If only . . .

She heard a soft splash and popped open her eyes. Egan was taking a bath.

A proper young lady, a society hostess like Zarabeth, should turn and quietly make her way back down the stairs. It should not even *occur* to her to tiptoe to the door and peek inside.

Hardly daring to breathe, she pressed her face to the crack and positioned herself so she could see the room.

Egan lay in a tub in the middle of it, his back to the door. His head was tilted backward, his damp hair massively curly, as he sang gently to the ceiling. His arms rested on the sides of the tub, brawny muscle slick with water.

Zarabeth imagined creeping up behind him and running her hands along his arms and shoulders. She would cradle his head against her chest and not care that the damp ruined her gown. He'd open his eyes and smile at her, then pull her down for a bathwater-soaked kiss.

She had no business thinking these things, or peering at him like a love-struck dairymaid. But each time she tried to make herself turn and go back downstairs, her slippers seemed stuck to the floor.

He ceased singing and hummed the tune, his voice wrapping around her like silk. She could listen to him forever.

She'd just convinced herself it would be prudent to retreat when he braced himself on the sides of the tub and stood.

And then an army couldn't have dragged her away. He rose like a god from the sea, water cascading from his body to slosh over the tub's sides. She froze as his beautifully sculpted back, strong thighs, and tight backside came into view.

His skin was tanned from the sun, a bit lighter where his kilt would cover him, as though in summer he wandered about in the kilt and nothing else. The thought made her throat dry.

His hair hung halfway down his back, heavy with bathwater, rivulets trickling to his buttocks. Muscle rippled as he rubbed water from his face.

Good-natured Egan MacDonald was a beautiful man, and Zarabeth had always known it. He'd charmed every lady he'd met in Nvengaria, and the girl Zarabeth had been eaten up with jealousy. The woman Zarabeth could only stare in awe and understand why ladies tried to ensnare him.

Whistling, Egan reached for a robe. The mirror over the fireplace slanted downward, revealing the full front of his body before he pulled on the dressing gown.

Zarabeth nearly slid to the floor. When he'd stood next to the bed in the inn, his plaid had been pulled firmly around him. Now nothing blocked the view of his tight abdomen and the stem that hung full and thick from a thatch of dark hair.

The sensual beauty of him made her veins warm and her pulse speed. She wanted nothing more than to enter the room and slide her hands inside the loose robe. His body would be warm and wet, the gaze he turned on her dark with desire.

She must have made some gasp or noise because he turned his head, not in alarm but nonchalantly, as though not worried about who might be watching. His gaze came to rest on the gap in the door, but he made no sign that he saw her.

Zarabeth took two silent steps backward, then turned and sped noiselessly down the gallery, her heart beating fast and hard.

Zarabeth wore one of Mary's gowns the next afternoon to call with Mary at the home of Adam and Piers Ross. Zarabeth had spent the previous afternoon being fitted for gowns, but of course it would be days before they were ready. She'd welcomed the tedious measuring with Mary and the seamstress to keep her mind off Egan—not that it had worked.

She relived the moment of Egan rising from his bath again and again, her mind showing her maddening pictures of him beckoning her inside, a sinful smile on his face. He'd take her into his arms, soaking her dress with his wet body, and pull her into the bath with him.

She dreamed this all night and awakened damp with sweat, her hand pressed to the joint of her thighs. She'd groan and tried to banish the dreams, but they crept in as soon as she shut her eyes again.

Egan had been convinced to go to Ross Hall, though he remained obdurate about the marriage scheme. He refused to ride in the chaise with Mary and Zarabeth, stating that he'd join them later. He had business to take care of—Mary did remember that Zarabeth's life was under threat?

"I think you'd ride with us, then," Mary said, "if you're so keen to protect her."

"Ye have Baron Valentin and plenty of outriders. Hamish and I need to meet someone."

"Oh, very well," Mary said crossly.

Zarabeth for one was glad Egan would not ride in the carriage with them. Sitting across from him in such a close space would never do. Not with his feet an inch from hers, his hard body taking up too much room. She'd do something foolish, like launch herself at him. Best he follow later and she ride alone with Mary, far from temptation.

Ross Hall lay five miles from Castle MacDonald, across a river and along a winding road. The journey took a little over an hour and ended in a green park with a pair of ornate gates.

They turned into a well-tended drive that led to a broad spread of a modern house with glittering windows and Doric columns. Trees that were red and gold with autumn arched toward them as they rode up the lane, branches scraping the top of the coach. The day was clear and crisp, yesterday's rain gone.

It all seemed so normal, a carriage taking Zarabeth to

pay a call on a neighbor, servants in knee breeches swarming out to meet the coach. But Highlanders with pistols had surrounded them as they rode, and Zarabeth had glimpsed riders back in the trees and scrub. Baron Valentin had gone with the outriders, disappearing altogether when they reached Ross Hall.

Inside the Ross mansion was an arching, echoing hall covered with paintings. Zarabeth recognized work of the Scottish painter Ramsay, along with Gainsborough, Reynolds, and Stubbs.

Adam Ross met them, every inch the lord of the manor. He wore a knee-length kilt of Ross plaid, but his lawn shirt, watered waistcoat, and dark frock coat could have been found in the clubs of London.

Zarabeth smiled. "Your home is most lovely."

"My father had an eye for architecture," Adam said modestly. "He designed much of it."

Servants took their wraps, and Adam led them into a high-ceilinged drawing room filled with delicate-legged furniture, a pianoforte, and more paintings. Every corner screamed with wealth, and there were no drafts or signs of falling beams.

Two men in their fifties scrambled out of chairs to stand next to two matrons of the same age, both of the women plump and dressed in the very latest mode. Except for their hair and eye coloring, the women could have been mirror images of each other.

Two younger ladies leaped from the pianoforte, both dressed in virginal pale muslin. They each had ringlets hanging from their foreheads almost to their eyes, giving them the look of young fillies peering through forelocks. One girl had blond hair; the other's was as dark as Zarabeth's. They had bright eyes and brighter smiles, and curtsied deeply.

"Your Grace," they said at the same time, then glanced at each other, annoyed.

Mary made the introductions. The two girls stood mute while their mothers and fathers were presented. But the girls' thoughts, sharp and fierce, clamored through Zarabeth's shields.

My curtsy was better. Why did the princess not bow more to me if my curtsy was better?

Is that what Nvengarian princesses wear? It looks as dowdy as anything Mary Cameron has.

I shall play first. The princess will want me to.

And both of them thinking frantically, *Where is Mr. MacDonald? Why has he not come?*

With difficulty Zarabeth focused on her conversation with their parents, making the right responses at the right times. One family was the Bartons, the other the Templetons. They were both Scottish-born, but spoke English without a trace of the Scots accent Zarabeth loved. She sensed no danger from them, only rather empty thoughts about how rich Adam was and hope that Egan proved to be just as wealthy. A good match for their daughters would be something to boast of.

The daughters were Faith and Olympia, golden-haired Faith belonging to the Bartons, and dark-haired Olympia to the Templetons.

"Your gown is lovely," Olympia said. She was the one who'd thought Zarabeth's dress dowdy. "It must be *très rigueur.*"

Zarabeth ignored her garbled French and answered politely, "You are too kind."

"I have read all about Nvengaria," Faith said. Her thoughts clanged that she thought the subject too dull for words and she'd quickly left off. "I have never been there. I will go to Paris instead."

"Paris is a fine city," Zarabeth agreed.

They were all seated, Adam still playing host, though with a slightly pained expression. *What was Mary thinking?* His thoughts spun past her.

But from the girls' clamor, neither of them had any intention of leaving until she landed the famous Egan MacDonald, a handsome laird, in marriage.

The ladies had no idea how handsome. From the conversation that followed, Zarabeth concluded that they'd never met him. She hoped no one could read *her* thoughts, because they strayed many times to the vision of him rising from the bath, wet and gleaming, the mirror letting her see every inch of him.

Every inch.

If she did not control herself, she would wear a permanent foolish smile. Egan was shredding every morsel of self-control she had.

Mary engaged the Edinburgh guests in lively conversation. Adam sipped tea and wished the Templetons and Bartons far, far away. His brother, Piers, had escaped to Glasgow. *Coward.*

When called on to perform at the pianoforte, Olympia rather surprisingly offered to let Faith go first. Mrs. Templeton was pleased that the gesture showed Olympia's generous nature. Olympia's thoughts were: *I play so much better than she does. I shall seem even better after they hear her mess.*

Faith began her piece, a rather clanging version of a Mozart air. Mary listened to the tune with sparkling eyes and an excited flush. Adam cringed and hid it by rapidly drinking tea. The Bartons were proud, the Templetons sneering at Faith's effort.

Faith finished and bowed, and they all clapped. Olympia glided to the piano with her nose in the air, opened her music, and began.

She played marginally better than Faith, but ruined the effect by starting to sing. Her off-key treble warbled up and down, trying to grab notes that the most practiced opera soprano had trouble reaching. Adam got abruptly to his feet and strode to the window.

Overcome by emotion, Mrs. Templeton thought happily.

A strange sound reached the drawing room, echoing outside in the hall. Mary jumped and nearly spilled her tea, and Adam remained frozen in place, his thoughts like a chiming bell: *Oh, no, he wouldn't.*

It came again, a roar like a bear. Olympia faltered at the pianoforte, then plunged determinedly on.

The double doors of the drawing room suddenly burst open to admit Hamish MacDonald in a riding kilt and muddy boots. He stopped for effect, then shouted, "All hail Egan, laird of Castle MacDonald."

Chapter Five
The Mad Highlander

Olympia's piece crashed to a halt. Mary rose, her hand at her throat, and the other guests looked around with interest.

Hamish stepped aside, and Egan dashed into the room, brandishing the sword of Ian MacDonald that usually hung in the great hall. Zarabeth took one look at him and collapsed onto the sofa, hand tight against her mouth. But no one noticed her laughter because they were looking at Egan.

He wore his dark hunting kilt and rough linen shirt, his boots caked with mud. His hair hung loose and wild, and he'd painted his face and neck dull blue.

No, Mary groaned in her thoughts. *Oh, no.*

Egan tossed the sword aside, and it landed with a clatter beyond Adam's fine Chinese rug.

"'M I late, Mary?" he asked in a voice that vibrated the windows. "We were chasing brigands across the hills and lost the time."

His accent was thick, almost unintelligible. He pivoted in a swirl of plaid and made for the guests. "Wha' have we here, naow?"

He peered first at Faith, standing wide-eyed against her mother, and then Olympia, who'd frozen at the pianoforte.

"Are ye playin' a song, lass? Donnae stop. I like a tune t' tap me feet tue."

"Egan," Mary said faintly.

"Go on," Egan said to Olympia, putting his wild blue face level with her sheet-white one. "Is it a ballad t' make m' cry, or a reel I can hop tue?"

"It's Handel," Olympia stammered.

Egan straightened up, looking puzzled. "Is it Scots?"

"He was German," Olympia whispered. "I think."

Mary quickly stepped between him and the pianoforte. "My brother does like his little joke." Her laugh was strained. "Go and change, Egan. Your playacting has amused us."

Egan ignored her, spinning to the tea table. "Is that whiskey ye have?" He lifted the teapot, removed the lid, and sniffed it. "Och, it's tea. Adam Ross, why have ye filled yer pots with tea? Have ye run out of the best malt?"

Adam coughed into his handkerchief and didn't answer.

Egan snatched up a plate and a huge hunk of teacake, then swirled to the sofa, giving Zarabeth a broad wink. He climbed onto the sofa and perched on the back of it, his muddy boots planted on the cushions while he ate.

"Look, Mary," he said proudly. "I'm usin' a plate this time."

Mary rushed to the French doors and swung one open. "Perhaps we should go into the garden, Mrs. Templeton, Mrs. Barton? Mr. Ross's gardens are some of the best in Scotland."

"But we've seen them already," Faith began. Her gaze was riveted to Egan, her expression not as horrified as it should have been.

"Yes, of course, Mrs. Cameron." Mrs. Templeton bustled over. "Come along, Olympia."

Olympia said, "Yes, *maman*," in a sweetly compliant voice, but her thoughts were rebellious.

Egan stuffed the last of the cake in his mouth. "Ye're quite right, Mary. 'Tis a fine day. I'll come wi' ye and show ye how t' toss the caber." He flung down the plate and ran out the door, nearly colliding with Mrs. Barton. "Yer pardon, ma'am." He swept her an exaggerated bow, and she shot out into the garden with him close behind.

Hamish followed them all slowly, his hands behind his back. Zarabeth and Adam Ross remained, alone in the room. As soon as they were gone, Adam collapsed onto a chair, threw his head back, and laughed.

Zarabeth stopped trying to hold it in and laughed until her sides ached. "Wherever did he get the blue paint?"

"My gardener's painting the sheds," Adam answered, wiping his eyes. "I never thought he'd do it. Mary will never let him hear the end of it."

"You knew he would dress up like this?"

"He threatened to last night. Said if Mary insisted on parading debutantes in front of him, he'd dress up like a wild Highlander and scare them off."

"I do wish she would have brought young ladies more . . . thoughtful," Zarabeth said. "Perhaps a little older as well."

"Yes, Egan needs a courageous woman. One who can put up with him and his Highlanders and live at Castle MacDonald. The place is a run-down ruin."

Zarabeth sat up and poured Adam and herself more tea. She felt defensive of Castle MacDonald, indignant that Adam in his fine house would scoff at it. "It suits my needs, and Egan will fix things now that he's home. He is a wealthy man, I believe."

"He hasn't always been. The MacDonalds lost much after Culloden and took a long time to recover—most Highland families did, including my own. Egan invested the money he made in the army—prizes and such, plus selling his commission—and he was canny enough to make plenty of blunt. But Castle MacDonald is eight hundred years old. His tenants' roofs are snug and tight—Egan sees to that—but there's buckets all over the castle to catch the rain. There's not enough money for it all, but none of the MacDonalds will stand for leaving the castle and living in an ordinary house." He glanced around his modern, comfortable drawing room.

"Why don't you live in a castle?" Zarabeth asked, lifting her teacup. "Your house is lovely, but built recently, was it not?"

"Ah, the Rosses *had* a castle. Not far from here, up against the mountain." He gestured out the window, where a craggy hill reared its head in the distance. "It was destroyed, brick by brick, and the foundations crushed. No laird will live again at Castle Ross."

"Why?" She sensed pain in his fleeting thoughts. "What happened?"

He set his teacup in his saucer and gazed at her with frank blue eyes. Adam Ross was a handsome man, one who liked his comforts, but she felt from him the same kind of raw courage that lurked in Egan and his family.

"At Culloden my great-grandfather killed the son of a noble English family, and that family retaliated. My great-grandfather had died in the battle, but troops came to Castle Ross and turned his wife and servants out into the winter. My grandfather was only a small boy at the time, and they didn't even give him a blanket to keep warm. The English pulled down the castle, shot cannon at it for fun, and when they finished not one stone was left standing on top of another."

Zarabeth's defensiveness dissolved into shock and sympathy. "I'm sorry. What happened to your grandfather and his mother? Where did they go?"

"Egan's family took them in—the first time Rosses

and MacDonalds helped each other. My great-grandmother lived on with them, and my grandfather grew up in Castle MacDonald. Eventually the family who exacted their vengeance on us died out themselves. My own father studied in Edinburgh and became a brilliant engineer. He invented a new sort of valve and made a bit of capital at it. I've made some contributions to the engineering world as well, papers and such. The Rosses are now scientists instead of fighters."

He glanced around the room again, the place so comfortable and elegant. The beautiful plastered room with its paintings and mirrors was a stark contrast to Castle MacDonald, which was all gray stone or whitewash and beams. This room was warm all the way through, unlike the drafty castle.

And yet Adam wore a wistful look, as though he'd trade all this luxury for his ancestor's home in a heartbeat.

"You are brave," Zarabeth said.

Adam brought his gaze back to her, his handsome smile flashing. His thoughts chimed loud and clear: *Ah, she likes me.* His eyes warmed. "You are kind to say so. Most people tell me how lucky I am to have all this."

"You *are* lucky. But I understand that a gilded palace cannot mend all the hurts in the world. It is only a place, filled with things."

Adam gave her a thoughtful look. "Tell me how it is that you, a foreigner, understand when all my neighbors, good Scots like me, have no idea?"

"Perhaps because I have lived in a gilded palace, and learned that one can be more content with a simple hearth."

He smiled again. "I believe you and I will rub along well, my lady. Shall we join the others? And promise not to laugh?" He came to her and guided her to her feet.

"Poor Egan," Zarabeth said. She slid her hand through Adam's strong arm and let him lead her to the door. "We must save him."

"From a fate worse than death." Adam grinned, and they went out into the gardens.

The water in the bucket was freezing cold as Egan sluiced it over his face and arms in the courtyard of Castle MacDonald. The blue paint stubbornly adhered to his skin, resisting his attempts to scrub it off.

Hamish handed him a brush.

"Stop laughing at me, man," Egan growled.

"But the performance was legendary, cousin. They'll talk of it for years."

"Well, it didn't do what I intended, did it? The bloody girls were still looking at me like a choice morsel in a butcher's shop."

" 'Twas the dancing in the garden. A lass likes a man who can dance."

Egan snarled and busied himself in the bucket again. He scrubbed hard as Mary's carriage screeched and rattled through the gatehouse and came to a halt not three feet away. Egan stubbornly stayed by his bucket.

A blue satin skirt trimmed with green and two elegant slippers stopped just outside the circle of wetness, but they didn't belong to Mary. Egan looked up, water dripping, at the breathtaking beauty of Zarabeth. Her face was pink from the wind, her curls slightly mussed, but she still managed to be neat and clean. He was a mess, with his shirt open to the waist and his arms sunk to the elbows in soapy water.

He wanted to lick his way from the pointed tips of the beaded slippers to the curls at her forehead. He wanted to peel off those tidy clothes and get her all wet and soapy with him.

Good thing his kilt hung loose, or it might tent out

embarrassingly. All she had to do was stand before him and he lost every shred of sanity.

"Where's Mary?" he asked.

Zarabeth's dimples showed. "She stayed behind to soothe her guests."

"I imagine they're hieing back to Edinburgh as fast as they can?" he asked hopefully.

She shook her head. "The young ladies are intrigued by you and have begged to stay. There is no hieing, I am afraid."

"They like men who paint themselves blue and behave like savages, do they now?"

"A handsome savage with wealth and a castle. They find you romantic."

"Och." Egan scrubbed his hands over his face, streaking the blue. "Next time I'll ignore them completely."

"Then they will do anything they can think of to catch your attention. Misses Faith and Olympia have quite set themselves to snare you, if only to see which one can have you first."

"Good God, 'twas easier to fight the French."

Zarabeth's smile deepened, the hint of the mischievous hellion of her girlhood gleaming through. "The marriage mart is a much more frightening battleground than any in the Peninsular War, I wager. I advise you to never let yourself be alone with either of them, day or night, even for a few seconds, lest they claim themselves compromised."

He stifled a groan. "They wouldn't."

"I am afraid they just might."

He peered at her. "Whose side are ye on, lass? Ye seemed all set with Jamie to see me wed."

Her blue gaze flicked from his for a moment. "You need a wife, and Castle MacDonald needs a mistress. But I'd rather see you happy, Egan, as I would any friend."

"Thank God for that. Promise me that ye'll not leave my side when those two little demons are about. I'll protect ye from assassins, and ye protect me from *them*."

Her smile returned. "A bargain. I met a few eligible ladies from genteel Scottish families on my travels, and I believe I know a few who might be a match for you." She looked him up and down. "Even if you're still blue."

He wasn't sure which rankled more—her laughing at him or her blithe offer to find him a wife. He decided to punish her a little.

The courtyard was clearing, the stableman leading the carriage horses to the stalls under the castle, and they were relatively alone. Egan lowered his voice and leaned toward her.

"So, lass, ye were determined to find out, were ye?"

She looked puzzled. "Find out what?"

"What a Scotsman wears under his kilt." His smile widened as a flush crept up her cheeks. "Is that why ye ogled me in the bath yesterday?"

She took a quick step back, her laughter gone. "I was not ogling you."

"No? What would ye call it then?"

"I did not mean to look. I was only—" She broke off as he gave her a wise smile.

"Ye meant to, lass. I saw ye plain as plain." He leaned closer, pleased she was so flustered. "Tell me, did ye like what ye saw?"

He tracked the swallow as it moved down her throat, and then she looked up at him, her eyes dark. "Yes," she said. "Yes, I liked it very much."

Something twisted in his gut. He'd expected her to blush and stammer, or to loftily tell him he was conceited and march away. He hadn't expected a quiet declaration or the need in her eyes when she said it.

He touched her face. Her skin was satin soft, her blush

warm under his fingertips. Her lashes lowered until they curled black against her cheek, but she did not move away.

My Zarabeth. Always mine.

A dribble of blue, painty water trickled from his finger across her cheek. Zarabeth abruptly stepped back, swiping the wetness away with her glove. Without looking at him, she swung around and hurried to the castle, scrubbing away the evidence of his touch.

That night Zarabeth was wrenched out of dreams of Egan trickling blue paint all over her naked body by a commotion on the stairs.

She sat up to listen, but sound was muffled by the thick door. She sensed frenzied thoughts—anger and fear from many people. Something had happened. She threw on a dressing gown, shoved her feet into slippers, and opened her door.

Every Highlander in the house had collected on the stairs: Angus, Hamish, Dougal, Jamie, and Egan. With them was Adam Ross, dressed for riding and looking grim. Mr. Templeton, father of the silly Olympia, stood below him, his face ashen.

Zarabeth's two footmen joined the fray, along with Baron Valentin, awake and dressed. Zarabeth slipped out the door and nearly staggered at the weight of distress in the hall. She stilled herself, drew a breath, and with effort closed her shields between herself and the others.

Gemma hurried around the Highlanders to Zarabeth. "Miss Templeton's gone missing," she said. "Adam and Mr. Templeton have just brought the news. The lads are going to form a search."

Olympia Templeton, a young woman with hair as dark as Zarabeth's own . . .

Zarabeth's blood ran cold, and her gaze sought Egan's. He gave a slight shake of his head.

From Mr. Templeton's garbled explanation and Adam's more lucid one, she learned that Olympia had gone walking in Adam's garden alone this evening after she and Faith had quarreled over whom Egan had liked better. She hadn't come in by dark. Mrs. Templeton had assumed she was in her room sulking, but when she did not appear at supper, the woman had become alarmed. Olympia never missed a meal, sulks or no.

A search of the house and gardens had ensued. Faith had found Olympia's bonnet lying crushed in the grass at the end of the garden and had gone into hysterics, believing Olympia abducted by Gypsies. Adam suggested they come to Castle MacDonald on the off chance Olympia had somehow made her way there.

She had not. Egan had roused his cousins and nephews and Baron Valentin to make a thorough search of the castle. They had all just returned with nothing to report.

"I'll get men from the village," Egan said. His broad Scots accent faded somewhat as he assumed the role of commander. "We'll divide the surrounding area into sections and have a party go over each thoroughly. We will discover what's become of her."

Mr. Templeton looked slightly less panicky, but Zarabeth noted that Egan had not promised they'd find her alive.

Egan directed everyone to the great hall and asked Angus to fetch maps. He made his way up the stairs to Zarabeth as the others began to move.

"Dress yourself," Egan told Zarabeth. "Ye'll come with me."

Zarabeth's eyes widened. "Is that not dangerous?" She was itching to join the search but trying to be prudent.

"Very dangerous. That's why I want ye with me, where I can watch ye with both eyes. I don't want ye out of my sight."

Zarabeth opened her mouth to argue, but Egan's glare

shut it again. "Very well," she said so meekly that the glare turned suspicious. Perhaps she shouldn't overdo it.

"I'm coming too," Gemma said. She held up her hand as both Egan and Angus started to protest. "And ye needn't shout at me—I'm going, and that's final. When ye find that poor girl, she'll need looking after—or a good spanking—and I'm the one as can deliver both."

Chapter Six
Danger in the Heather

You think someone kidnapped her, mistaking her for me," Zarabeth said to Egan.

She was bundled against the cold and huddled against Egan in his saddle, but a sharp wind swept down from the mountains, icy with snow. Winter came early in the Highlands. If someone had abducted foolish Olympia, Zarabeth hoped they were keeping the girl warm.

Egan's rock-solid arms wrapped around Zarabeth, his broad hands holding the reins steady. "I never said so," he rumbled.

"You didn't have to. It is what I think, too. If she wore enough wraps and the abductors saw only the color of her hair, they might have assumed she was me. Men hired here in Scotland might not know me by sight."

"Which is exactly why ye are riding wi' me," Egan said. "I don't want ye straying two steps from me while ye are in my care."

"Then I'll likely see more of you in the bath."

She meant to say it under her breath, but Egan heard. His arms tightened. " 'Tis no' a laughing matter. I'll keep ye safe if I have to shackle myself to ye. I'll not face Prince Damien or your father and tell them I let ye come t' harm because of my modesty."

"I'm certain we can come to some arrangement."

"Aye."

He said nothing more, but Zarabeth wondered if he'd thought about the other side of the problem—if she had to stay glued to him he would likely see her in *her* bath.

Modest Zarabeth of Nvengaria, daughter of Prince Olaf, should be shocked by such a thought. But the vision of Egan leaning against her door frame while she bathed, perhaps entering the room to trickle water down her back, made her hot all over. Her woolen mantle suddenly seemed too warm.

The howl of a beast in the distance slapped her back to reality. The moon soared out of a tear in the clouds, tingeing the land silver-white.

"Ye should tell him not to make noise like that," Egan said in her ear.

Zarabeth started, then realized that of course Egan would have guessed that Baron Valentin was a logosh. Valentin had not joined the riders but had slipped away alone.

"I think he cannot help it," she said.

"If he's found something, he ought to shout, 'Over here.' Not cry out like a beastie. Logosh give me the willies."

"I will tell him—and Grand Duke Alexander."

"You are amusing, lass," Egan said.

"Should we go to him? He might have something to report."

" 'Tis a bit trackless out here. If we wander off in the dark we may miss him."

Zarabeth knew she could find Valentin, and probably Olympia, by casting for their thoughts. She'd never revealed her ability to Egan, worried about distancing him even further, but they had bigger worries now than Egan discovering her secret. She'd just have to make him trust her.

"Of course we won't get lost," she said, trying to sound confident. "Valentin would not call out if he didn't think we had a safe way to reach him."

Egan gazed off into the moonlit distance. " 'Tis too dangerous. We'll go around."

"It might be too late then." Zarabeth felt panic welling in her as she sensed Valentin's worry heighten. "I know Valentin. He wouldn't guide me wrong."

Egan hesitated a long moment, his sharp gaze focused on her. Then he nodded. "I hope you're right, lass." He swung his horse toward the noise, and Hamish followed with Gemma. He instructed the other riders to continue their search pattern.

Zarabeth opened her mind. She felt the mass of riders fanning out northward behind them while Egan and Hamish angled due east. She heard loud and clear the riders' worry for Olympia and thoughts on how cold it was, their nervousness about the strange animal howling among the hills. She even sensed the horses' fear of the beast overlaying annoyance that they'd been dragged out of their warm stables.

Valentin's mind was sharp, like blue-white light. He'd shifted into a wolf, and his thoughts were more animal than human—the joy of stalking prey and the hot, metallic taste of blood.

There was also another thought in his head, stronger than the others: *Protect*.

Near him, almost masked by Valentin's presence, she found the panic of a young girl.

"That way," Zarabeth said, pointing to the left.

Egan gave her a look. "How do ye know?"

"I just do."

He continued to look at her expressionlessly, then called back to Hamish to change course with him.

They found Olympia huddled in a cleft of rock above the river. Egan and Zarabeth had fished farther downstream; here the river rushed over boulders and plunged out of sight into a black gorge. Zarabeth thought she spied a flash of fur and blue eyes in Egan's lantern light, but then it was gone. She wasn't the only one who had secrets to hide.

Hamish thundered up behind them, playing his lantern over the scene. "Have ye got her?"

Egan swung from the saddle and lifted Zarabeth down with him.

"The poor mite, is she there?" Gemma called. She was gentleness itself as she went to the terrified Olympia. The girl looked up, her white face plastered with mud, tears tracking the dirt. She flung her arms around Gemma's neck and sobbed against her.

Olympia's story, when they at last got something coherent from her, was simple. She'd tired herself walking in Adam's garden and must have fallen asleep ("after all, it is quite a *long* walk"), because the next thing she knew, it was dark and a man had seized her. Another man tied her hands and gagged her. Then she was dragged down the hill and thrown across a saddle.

The men rode with her for miles and miles, then met another man with a gruff voice who'd rudely pulled Olympia's head up by her hair to examine her face. The new man had started shouting at the others in such broad Scots she hadn't understood what he said. He'd taken her from the horse and dropped her to the ground, then rode off with the others, still shouting.

She explained all this while tucked up in bed at Ross Hall, with her mother hovering anxiously, a horde of maids attending her, and Faith looking a bit envious. Egan and Adam, the only two men Mrs. Templeton had allowed in the room, listened to her tale.

Olympia could not describe the men who'd abducted

her or the one who'd left her among the rocks. It had been too dark, she'd been hanging upside down on the horse, and she'd been crying.

"By 'broad Scots' she might have meant Glaswegian," Egan said as he and Adam discussed it downstairs with the others.

"Aye," Hamish agreed. "They swallow every consonant known to man. Can never bloody understand wha' they're sayin'."

"Is she all right?" Zarabeth asked.

Her blue eyes held concern. She was beautiful, sitting against the curled end of a Duncan Phyfe sofa, firelight glistening in her hair. Her expression also held guilt.

" 'Twas not your fault," Egan told her quickly.

"She was taken because of me."

"It is *my* fault," Mary cried. "I brought those girls here. We should have done this in Edinburgh, where things are civilized."

"Then it might have been Zarabeth snatched," Egan said. "And I wager she'd not have been turned loose so easy."

"They want only me." Zarabeth met Egan's gaze without dread or terror. She was simply stating a fact. "They're not interested in hurting anyone else, which means they believe they are men of honor, doing an honorable deed."

"Which makes them all the more dangerous," Egan said. "God save us from fanatics."

Because it was nearly sunrise, Adam Ross gave them all breakfast before the MacDonalds rode home again in the light of day. Mary stayed behind again. Egan left her apologizing to the Edinburgh guests, saying that kidnapping was unusual in the Highlands.

"Perhaps in this day and age it is," Egan said as they rode out, Zarabeth once again on the saddle before him.

"But only a hundred or so years ago we were happily stealing women from clan to clan, forcing reconciliation through marriage. Not that it worked for long."

"The ladies, they objected?" Zarabeth asked, a gleam in her eye.

"Oh, most strongly. Sometimes they carved up their new husbands with the man's own claymore and fled back home."

"Is that true? Or one of your Mad Highlander stories?"

Egan chuckled. "It could be true. But to be safe, we won't let Gemma near a claymore."

They returned to the castle to endure a midday feast that Mrs. Williams had cooked up, never mind their already filling breakfast. The fallen beam had been cleared from the great hall and the table moved, but the gaping hole in the plaster remained, reminding Egan of the many repairs the castle needed.

Baron Valentin presented himself at the luncheon, in human form and fully dressed. He good-naturedly took the ribbing from the other Highlanders that he'd missed all the fun of the chase.

Afterward, Egan walked Zarabeth upstairs, continuing his vow not to let her out of his sight.

"I spoke with your baron," he said. "If not for him, we'd never have found the lass out there in the dark. She might have died of exposure before daylight."

Zarabeth scuttled into her chamber when Egan opened the door for her. She was exhausted, her eyes dark, and she was trying to stifle her yawns.

"He must have scared her, poor thing," she said.

Egan snorted. "She can believe herself a brave little heroine for not being eaten by a wolf."

"I suppose that's true."

Egan leaned against the mantelpiece, letting the

warmth of the fire slide under his kilt, while Zarabeth sat heavily on the sofa.

"Ye have an interestin' collection of friends," he observed.

"Good and loyal friends."

"Aye. And many more here."

"I'm grateful for all of them," she said. "Believe me."

He lounged more negligently. She was fighting fatigue, but stubborn Zarabeth would never admit it. She would keep pretending to be the polite hostess until she fell over.

"Your face might shatter, love, if you keep trying to hold it steady," he said.

That earned him a glare. "It's been a tiring night."

Egan shrugged, pretending his heart wasn't beating fast and hard. "Rest then. Ye are safe enough here with me."

"With you? What are you talking about?"

"I told ye last night, remember? I'm no' letting ye out of my sight."

"Yes, but I didn't think you meant it literally."

"I meant *every* minute."

"Egan, you cannot possibly stay in the same room with me. It's not proper."

He folded his arms. "This is my house, and I'll stay in what room I please."

"You have to be mad. Mary and Gemma will never allow—"

"My sister and Gemma are not charged with protecting ye. I am."

"Egan."

"Zarabeth."

She came to her feet, her eyes sparkling as she faced him. Her head was up, her cheeks flushed, and she looked beautiful.

"I see," she said. "You'll save my life but ruin my reputation? What would my father say?"

"He'd likely say, 'Thank you for protecting my mule-stubborn daughter.'"

Her eyes flashed. "Mule-stubborn? Thank you very much."

Egan left the fireplace and met her in the middle of the room. Her shoulders were back, her blue eyes holding a challenge.

"When ye came here, lass, I didn't see the Zarabeth I knew," he said. "I saw a woman in hiding, putting on a mask of the gracious lady to all around her. The hellion is gone, and I wonder what you did with her."

Her color rose. "I grew up."

"At first I thought 'twas simply that ye were scared. That I understood. But there's more, isn't there?"

Her glare intensified. "How could you know? You left my father's house and never returned. Not for my wedding, not to visit my father—even when you came back for the wedding of Penelope and Damien, you never tried to see me."

She flung the words at him, and they stung because he knew she was right. But he couldn't explain why he'd stayed away—because he could not have remained only friends with her. He'd have thrown honor to the wind, not caring she was married, and tried to coerce her into a sordid affair. Some Nvengarians had open marriages, and he'd try to convince her to do the same. He'd wanted Zarabeth then and he wanted her now. The time apart had only heightened his desire.

"I don't recall seeing ye or your charming husband at Damien's weddin'," he said. "I looked for ye." He had, fearing at every moment to see her, fearing his reaction when she arrived on the arm of another man.

Her gaze flickered. "Of course he would not attend. It was political—Sebastian was never a supporter of the imperial prince. He had wanted Grand Duke Alexander to win."

"And when Alexander threw his backing to Damien?"

"Sebastian deserted Alexander. Missing the wedding was a protest."

From what Damien's letters to Egan had indicated, Sebastian belonged to an opposition party that believed that the country would be better off without an imperial prince. Sebastian and his friends had moved from angry mutterings in the Council of Dukes to out-and-out rebellion, complete with weapons and plans to assassinate Damien. How Zarabeth had discovered this, Egan didn't know, but she'd bravely left her husband and crept off in the night to warn Damien. It killed Egan to learn what she'd been through and how much danger she'd faced.

"Why didn't ye send for me, lass?" he couldn't stop himself from asking. "Why didn't ye tell me ye were so unhappy and needed help? Did ye forget I was your friend?"

The anguish in her gaze pierced his heart. "You never came back."

"I had no choice but to leave ye that night."

He'd been about to ravish his best friend's daughter, not hours after Olaf had indicated his high hopes for eighteen-year-old Zarabeth's marriage and future. That future did not include a Scotsman who buried himself in whiskey and indulged himself with barmaids. Olaf wanted Zarabeth to marry a duke or perhaps foreign royalty. She was highborn, and she should fly higher still.

A drunken laird whose ceiling regularly fell down did not count as highborn, at least not to Olaf. Egan MacDonald did not get to live in a spun-sugar palace with the beautiful princess.

Zarabeth stared angrily at him now, her eyes just as blue and seductive as they'd been on that faraway night. "You left because I shamelessly begged you to kiss me?"

she asked. "You should have laughed and told me not to be silly. I would have been hurt, but I'd have come to my senses in time."

His throat tightened as he remembered the long, lonely ride away from her house that night, the knowledge that he'd lost something—that he never could have had it in the first place.

"But I would no' have stopped, no' have laughed," he said softly. He stepped close to her and cupped her cheek with his palm. "Ye think I did no' want what ye offered me? I was drunk, and ye were pretty in the firelight. I would have put ye on that floor and had my way with ye, no matter what ye thought about it. Ye wanted a kiss, but I wanted everything. *Everything.*" He dragged in a breath. "Ye'll never know how hard it was to turn and go."

Her throat moved with her swallow. "I would have given you everything you wanted that night."

Heady thought. Her smile had been so damn sweet, and his body had been aching for her. He should have been given a medal for being able to leave her.

"Aye," he agreed. "Then bitterly regretted it."

"You broke my heart," she said softly.

He'd broken his own heart ten times over. "I'm sorry, lass. Your father meant the world to me. He gave me back my life when no one else believed in me. I loved him for that and couldn't repay him by ruining his only daughter. I had to choose."

She looked down, lashes shielding her eyes. "I came to understand that, of course. Why throw away a friendship for the whims of an eighteen-year-old girl?"

He drew the ball of his thumb along her chin, wanting more than anything to let his fingers trail down her throat, to part the buttons of her bodice and touch the warm roundness of her breasts. "I never meant to hurt ye. But I would have hurt ye worse if I'd stayed."

Her lips parted, red and kissable. He could bend and touch her mouth with his, slide his tongue along her lips and taste her. He wanted to feather kisses down her throat, catch the top button of her modest dress in his teeth.

Perhaps her eyes would soften and she'd make a sound of surrender, pull him to her as she had that night all those years ago. He could slide his hands into her gown and pull it down, smoothing her skin under his touch.

Egan made himself curl his fingers into his palm. She needed protecting, not ravishing, and he was old enough to leave her be.

Never mind that he was throbbing hard, every bone in his body aching for her.

"In retrospect," she said as he stepped away, "I'd rather you *had* ravished me that night. I'd not have married Sebastian, which would have saved me a world of trouble."

He certainly didn't want his imagination going *there*. He'd have taken her down to the floor, pulled her skirts up, and pressed his very stiff cock into her warm, intimate place. He'd have taken her virginity, her trust, and her friendship. He'd have ruined her, and she and her father would never have forgiven him. Better that he had backed off, as he did now.

"Ye're tired, lass," he said carefully. "Ye should sleep."

Her brows went up, and she returned to her bantering tone, unaware of his roiling thoughts. "If you insist on sleeping on the sofa, I may get no rest at all with you snoring away. I'll have a ruined reputation *and* lose a good night's sleep."

"No, ye won't. I planned t' bunk down outside the door."

She stopped. "What? But you said . . ."

He watched her flush as she worked out that he'd

never actually said he'd sleep in the room with her. "You are horrible, Egan MacDonald."

He gave her an exaggerated bow. "I live to tease. I'll go now, so ye can preserve your modesty."

His heart thumped as he imagined her slowly stripping off each item of clothing after he left. She'd stretch like a cat, rubbing her tired limbs before pulling a nightdress over her nakedness.

She rolled her eyes. "Oh, do go away, Egan." She turned, and Egan quickly left before his rising arousal could betray him.

Zarabeth slept very little.

She thought over her argument with Egan and knew she'd been ridiculous to grow angry at him for not coming back to her in Nvengaria. He'd had no idea what Sebastian was like or what she'd gone through— no one had, not even her father, until Zarabeth had left Sebastian and told the whole story to Damien.

She couldn't have sent for Egan during her marriage, because Sebastian or his hateful secretary, Baron Neville, read every letter she wrote and always found the ones she tried to keep secret. And then she would be punished. He never beat her, for that would show. Sebastian wouldn't want to spoil the performance he put on for the world. But his twisted mind could come up with very creative punishments.

He'd made Zarabeth dress and behave to his dictation at all times, speak and write only to certain people, attend only certain events. Disobedience to these instructions resulted in more punishment to Zarabeth, or worse, to her maids. Eventually he'd managed to wear her down and sever every tie to her old friends and even her family.

Sebastian had watched her every move, but he'd never detected her abilities. She'd learned of his plan to assassinate Damien from a stray thought in his head. She remembered the terror of that night, the realization that she could no longer pretend to the world that nothing was wrong—knowing she had to stop hiding and act.

As twilight fell, she heard Egan's snore through the door and allowed herself a few tears—not of anger but of relief. She felt safe here in Egan's stone castle, with him guarding her.

She rose and wandered to the window. The October day had grown dark, ropes of white stars casting their light over the valley. The loch lay in a shimmering silver sheet, a moon path stretching across it.

She loved it here, and she understood why Egan did, too. It was a part of him, this wild, remote land. He might have avoided it for years, but it had called him back.

She heard the door open, then felt warmth behind her. Egan. He hadn't undressed, sleeping in his linen shirt and a kilt. The heat of his tall body encompassed her as he pointed around her through the window.

"See there?"

Zarabeth followed the line of his outstretched finger. She thought she detected faint movement in the darkness, but she couldn't be certain. "What am I looking at?"

"My men. At least a dozen patrol the valley at all times. They go in shifts t' keep rested and alert. Had Olympia been staying at Castle MacDonald, the men who came for her would never have gotten near her. This is a safe place, never worry about that."

She tried very hard not to lean back against him. "I still feel responsible for Olympia."

"Not your fault she wandered off by herself. 'Tis dangerous to do so even in times of peace. Ye'd not have been so foolish."

Zarabeth dropped the subject, but she'd never feel easy about what had happened. Olympia hadn't understood her danger.

"Who are your men?" she asked. "I thought the days of lairds with their own soldiers were over."

"Some are from families who still consider themselves the laird's retainers. Some are soldiers from the peninsula who had nothing to return to, and some have lost land and don't want to turn to the factories for work. They are all loyal and happy to help keep you safe. I would no' call them an army, but 'tis good to have them."

"You have done so much for me, and I haven't said thank-you enough."

"I don't blame ye for it." His voice was low, a whispered rumble.

"It is not because I am not grateful. I am just . . . I am having difficulty being around people who are kind."

"Kind? My family? Mebbe ye're asleep and dreamin', lass."

She hid a smile. "Goodhearted, if you do not like the word *kind*. Your family is goodhearted. So are the Rosses."

"If ye'd like to think so."

"You're teasing me." She turned and found him too close. "You always liked to tease me."

" 'Tis my hobby," he said. "I canno' seem to leave off."

Her heart was hungry and sore, and she was so tired. Up here in the dark, high in the castle under the stars, she could believe they were the only ones in the world.

She touched his face. His whiskers scratched her fingers, and his eyes glinted under his lashes as he looked down at her. Her heartbeat sped up.

Don't.

You will regret . . .

She no longer cared.

She rose onto her tiptoes and kissed the corner of his mouth.

He made a noise like a groan and turned his head to meet her. Their lips rested together, the kiss half-formed, until Egan captured her lower lip between his teeth, a gentle nip that disguised his strength.

His breath was warm on her face. Zarabeth expected him to jerk away, to push her aside and tell her again she was not for him. But the line between his brows only increased as he deepened the kiss.

Maybe time and the outside world didn't matter here. Maybe this was a magic castle and she could have her heart's desire as long as she didn't leave this room.

She nearly laughed at her own foolish thoughts, but instead of breaking the kiss, she slid her arms around his waist and welcomed him in.

Chapter Seven
A Highland Celebration

Egan knew he should leave. But he couldn't stop himself from opening her mouth and tasting her, sliding his hands beneath the dressing gown to cup her smooth shoulders.

She tasted like Highland sunshine, prized because it was rare. She was melting him like mountain snow at the first brush of summer.

Zarabeth made a small noise in her throat as she laced her arms around his waist and pulled him closer. He molded his palms to the small of her back, liking the swell of her buttocks beneath his hands. She smelled of lavender, tasted of the spiced wine they'd drunk to warm themselves downstairs after the search.

Sweet, sweet woman, I could kiss you all the night.

He knew she would let him into her bed if he asked. She was tired and afraid, and she trusted him. He could lay her down and peel the flimsy nightgown from her body, nuzzle between her breasts and drown in her scent.

He could kiss her all the way down her throat, suck her nipples into his mouth one by one, nibble his way to her navel, down to the soft place between her legs, to lick her and taste her and enjoy her. Then he'd kiss her mouth again as he eased himself into her.

He wanted it with every breath.

Ghosts from the past swam up to haunt him. Unbidden came the face of Zarabeth's father the night Egan had told him why he had to leave Nvengaria. Olaf had nodded solemnly and placed his hand on Egan's shoulder.

Thank you, my friend. I knew she'd fallen in love with you, and you were good to let her down so gently.

Best I leave, I think, Egan had replied. He'd still been tingling from Zarabeth's kiss, finding it hard to catch his breath.

Olaf agreed. *Only because it would hurt Zarabeth if she had to see you again. But be assured I'd trust her life with you. I know you'd never do anything to harm her.*

The vision faded, and Egan groaned. Why did Olaf have to reach out of the past to twinge him now?

Egan eased away from the kiss, feeling Zarabeth's fingers tighten on his arms. He took her hands and pushed her away. "Best ye go back to bed, lass."

She stared up at him, her lips damp with kissing. Outside the moon slid behind a cloud, the moon path on the loch faded, and the magic vanished.

"Egan."

He gently disentangled himself from her. "Best we don't, lass."

"I may not kiss you as a friend?"

"That was no friendly kiss, and ye know it."

She stepped back, anger in her face. "Thank you very much, Egan MacDonald."

"For what?"

"For telling me, ever so gently, that you still regard me as a child."

"I never said that."

She gave him a severe look. "I am three and twenty and have spent the last five years in a very bad marriage.

My father's innocent daughter is gone; she was trampled to death. And now the one man I thought a friend pats me on the head and calls me a ninny who understands nothing."

Egan stared at her in amazement, then pointed to his lips. "Did that come out of my mouth? Did ye hear it, or see these lips move?"

Her voice heated. "You think it, and you know you do. 'Sweet Zarabeth, still infatuated with her Highlander. I must be kind to the poor girl.'"

"Och, now ye're doing my thinking for me too. I'll tell my cousins t' take no more orders from me—they can just ask ye what I want."

"You are absurd, Egan MacDonald."

"As are ye, Zarabeth of Nvengaria."

She put her hands on her hips. "Perhaps you should shout louder, so Hamish and Jamie will come running to see what's the matter. Then my reputation will certainly be in ruins."

Egan took a step toward her, his blood singing with anger and exultation. "Mebbe you should have thought of that before ye started kissing me."

"I kissed *you*? Do not be ridiculous—you kissed *me*."

"I remember ye on your tiptoes, grabbing me around the waist."

"Absurd *and* conceited."

"'Twas not me lookin' my fill at a Highlander in his bath."

She gritted her teeth. "Will you be twitting me with that for the rest of my days?"

"Aye, I think so."

She was so beautiful when she was irritated, her whole body vibrant and alive. "You'll not use it as an excuse to kiss me again."

Egan wanted to laugh loud and long. "If I'm very

determined to kiss ye, I'll find a way. And what happens if ye want to kiss *me*?"

"I won't." She gave him a glare fit for an empress. "I will make sure of it."

"Good." He pointed at the door. "I'll be out there, trying to get some sleep."

She pointed to the bed. "And I will be over there, trying to shut out your snoring."

He stilled. "Oh, lass. Ye've done it now."

Apprehension entered her eyes. "Done what?"

"Insulted a Scotsman—a laird—in his home. The repercussions will no' be good."

"What repercussions?"

"I'll think of something. 'Tis my duty as laird to mete out justice."

Something flashed through her eyes, like deep fear, even panic. Then it was gone, even before he was sure he'd seen it.

She made a noise of exasperation. "You are teasing me again. You never leave off."

"No' much to do out here in the middle of nowhere."

Zarabeth pivoted on her heel and marched to the bed. "I'm going back to sleep. It seems to be the only way to avoid your condescension."

She scrambled up onto the sagging mattress and pulled the covers over her head. Egan chuckled at the lump under the blankets and walked away, shaking his head.

She didn't know how much he longed to tease her, even in bed. Their argument hadn't dampened his desire for her, and it had forced her spirit to blaze out. She had been her old self again for a few minutes, telling Egan exactly what she thought of him and his high-handed ways.

He left her room again, his humor restored but his

body aching. Yet if this was what it took to bring Zarabeth back to her former self, he'd pick an argument with her every day for the rest of her life.

It was too much to hope after Olympia's adventure that the girls would clamor to go back to Edinburgh, and Adam reported the next morning that this was not the case.

Egan was more a hero than ever for finding Olympia, Adam told him, and Faith had even gone so far as to try to run away so Egan would come after her. Her father had caught her and sent her to bed before supper.

"And anyway," Olympia had cried, "Adam Ross is hosting a supper ball at the end of the week, and it would be most unfair if we had to miss it."

In the end, both sets of parents relented.

"All they have to do is bat their eyelashes," Adam ended sourly, "and their dear papas will do anything for them."

"And this is what Mary wants me to have for a wife?" Egan growled.

Adam's smile was pained. "'Tis the curse of the MacDonalds at work. But count your blessings, man. It isn't your house they're stopping in."

Jamie moped at breakfast, sopping up his eggs with the heel of a loaf. He was sulking because Hamish and Angus had found the abductors' trail and had rushed off to follow it. Dougal and Adam had gone with them, but Egan had insisted Jamie stay behind and help look after those at the castle. The lad was too young to face paid kidnappers and assassins.

Zarabeth, awake early after her long sleep, sat next to Egan, saying little. She did not indicate any memory of their kiss or ensuing quarrel, but ate quietly, not looking at him.

Egan had tossed and turned on the cot in the gallery until dawn. Their exchange had awakened a fire within him, and the embers still had not gone out.

"Which of them will ye marry, Uncle?" Jamie asked suddenly.

"Eh?" Egan pulled himself away from thoughts of Zarabeth's soft lips. "Ye mean your debutantes? Neither one, lad."

"Ye have to marry, Uncle." Jamie cast Zarabeth a look of appeal. "Can ye no' persuade him?"

"Perhaps you should try another pair of ladies, Jamie," Zarabeth answered. "Your aunt said she had quite a list."

Egan snorted. "*More* debutantes? I want fewer of them about, not more."

Zarabeth's blue eyes sparkled like the loch in sunshine. "You'll need to meet others if you are to choose a bride."

"Exactly," Jamie said. "See reason, Uncle."

"Your father would have been laird after I was dead. The least I can do is see his son inherits what he should have."

"'Tisn't reasonable. Ye ought to have married and had twenty children by now. Da wouldn't have wanted the estate anyway. He told me back when I was a bairn."

Egan felt Zarabeth watching him. The mood had changed from light to deadly serious, and she'd sensed it.

"Ye'll say no more about it," Egan said firmly to Jamie.

Jamie looked rebellious. "He did tell me. He wanted to enjoy life and live in the city, not take care of this ruin."

"Go from the table, Jamie."

"But, Uncle—"

"I told ye t' say no more, and ye went on about it. Go from the table."

Jamie opened his mouth to argue, caught Egan's fury, and closed it again. He snatched up the last of his bread, made a decent bow to Zarabeth, then ran from the room, his kilt sagging on his lanky hips.

Zarabeth went back to eating. She took dainty bites of the porridge that Mrs. Williams made specially for her. Mrs. Williams had swirled it with butter and sugar and a dab of cinnamon, and preened when Zarabeth praised her.

The scent reminded Egan of his rough-and-tumble childhood, a childhood in which his younger brother had been the darling of the household. He'd had charm, had Charlie.

"Jamie's scheme will have to stop," he said. "It was amusing to play Mad Highlander for the young ladies, but it put them in danger, and 'tis no longer funny."

Zarabeth's eyes were serious over her porridge spoon. "Jamie wants your praise."

"He wants a thrashing."

"He is trying to please you. His father died when he was very young, did he not?"

"Jamie was four."

"And you are the next thing to a father to him."

Egan shook his head. "I wasn't much here when Jamie was growing up. My own father looked after him until he died, then Angus and Hamish."

"Not the same thing as a father, though."

She was digging too deep. He hadn't mastered her ability to hide behind masks, but he was good at growling until everyone left him alone. He tried this on Zarabeth. She simply leaned her elbow on the table and looked at him.

"Jamie means well," she said. "And he's right. You are head of the family and should carry on the line."

"As head of the family, I choose whom I want to carry on the line."

She raised her brows. She could always look at him so, making him argue with himself.

He leaned toward her. "I'll thank ye to stay out of it."

Zarabeth smiled, her lips too close to his, and echoed his words of the night before: "Not much to do out here in the middle of nowhere."

Egan smelled cinnamon on her breath. Her mouth would taste so sweet. All he had to do was lean closer.

He slammed himself back into his chair. "No more debutantes," he growled.

Zarabeth serenely lifted another spoonful of porridge. The Zarabeth he'd known might have fired the glob of it at him. This Zarabeth simply put the spoon in her mouth and smiled around it.

That evening Hamish returned with news. He and Egan's men had tracked the kidnappers to Inverness, where the abductors had been arrested. The leader and three other men had been up before the magistrate and now waited in jail for their trial. They'd confessed that they'd been paid by a foreigner to receive Zarabeth from the ship that went down and, if that didn't work, to seize her any way they could.

They did not know the name of the foreigner or where he could be found, and he'd paid them in English pounds sterling. A search of Inverness and surrounding areas had turned up no foreigners, except a few Frenchmen, elderly gentlemen who were friends of a local laird.

That seemed to be that.

Zarabeth knew it was not. The hired men might have been captured, but if Sebastian wanted Zarabeth dragged back to Nvengaria or killed in revenge, he would not stop. He'd simply hire someone else.

But for now she was determined to enjoy her stay.

Zarabeth's heart warmed as she descended from the carriage and entered Ross Hall the night of the ball. The house glowed against the autumn cold, the gardens hung with strings of paper lanterns. Music and laughter poured out of the open doorway, along with cozy yellow light. This was a gathering of families and old friends like the balls her father had hosted. Friendship and camaraderie prevailed here, and it touched her lonely heart.

Zarabeth smiled at Adam as he shook her hand and passed her to his brother, Piers, for a greeting. Mary flitted among the guests, acting as hostess, her face strained. Her thoughts came to Zarabeth clear and sharp—worry that the ball would not impress Zarabeth and that Egan would try something asinine again.

Warmth at Zarabeth's back told her Egan hadn't strayed far. He was keeping most insistently to his vow not to let her out of his sight. He looked particularly fine in his dress kilt and frock coat, a swath of plaid wrapped over one shoulder.

"You will have to dance every dance with me at this rate," Zarabeth told him over her shoulder.

"Aye. That was my plan."

"The other ladies will cry their eyes out."

He looked perplexed. "Why should they?"

Zarabeth flipped her fan open and waved it in front of her face, the room too hot with him so close. "A handsome laird, unmarried, who refuses to spread himself out among the single ladies?"

"That sounds a bit disturbing."

"Not for the ladies."

The idea of Egan lying spread-eagled on the floor in his kilt, smiling at anyone who'd take him, made her giddy. Zarabeth would be the first to fling herself upon him.

"I've made it plain I've no plan to marry," Egan said, oblivious of her lewd thoughts. "Jamie will inherit after me, if he'll push that through his thick head."

"He really does not wish to."

"And I really do no' wish to talk of it. I'm his guardian, and he'll do as I say."

Zarabeth raised her brows. "Forcing a person to be something he's not is the cruelest fate imaginable."

Egan narrowed his eyes at her. She quickly masked her expression, but it was too late. The man could worm truth out of her when she least expected it.

Egan took her elbow and marched her across the ballroom. Adam's friends hovered nearby, waiting for Egan to introduce them to her, but he sailed on by.

"You're being quite rude," Zarabeth said.

"Am I?"

"I should be meeting people and speaking to them. They'll think me haughty."

Egan shrugged. "Pretend ye cannot speak English. I find that works. The vacant smile and nod does wonders."

Zarabeth stopped and turned to him, and Egan nearly ran into her. He was too close, only an inch separating them, and she found she could not breathe.

The formal attire hid the true Egan. He looked more himself in the faded kilt and linen shirt he usually wore, though she decided the effect of him in ballroom clothes was not so bad. The coat hugged his broad chest and shoulders, emphasizing his narrow waist, and the swath of plaid over it made him look slightly wild and dangerous. He'd tamed his hair into a queue, forcing the curls to stay put by dampening them with water. This made his hair slightly darker and the gold flecks in his eyes warmer.

She'd seen his eyes so close the night he'd kissed her. The kiss had been unhurried, tender, not full of demanding passion. He'd kissed her because he'd wanted to.

"I don't wish to embarrass Adam," she said hurriedly. "Or Mary."

He looked impatient. "Ye didn't come to Scotland to win a string of admirers. Ye came for safekeeping. Remember?"

"You caught the men who took Olympia," she pointed out.

" 'Tis no' the end of it, and ye know it."

"I know," she said.

Candlelight burnished the whiskers that lined his jaw, the stubble almost auburn. She wanted to run her fingers along it, and then her tongue, enjoying the rough feel.

She wished he'd go away. It was torment enough to remember the kiss without him near her every moment to remind her of it.

Mary sailed toward them, full of distress. "Egan, you haven't even spoken to the Templetons."

"I'm here to protect Zarabeth, no' entertain your Edinburgh guests."

"You could at least *try*."

" 'Twas you who brought them, no' me. I'll no' risk asking one of the lasses to dance lest she think it a proposal of marriage."

Mary's face brightened suddenly. "I hadn't thought of that. . . ."

"Ye donnae dare go puttin' that into their heads," Egan said in alarm.

"It might save time."

"Ye'll no' do it. Ye'll no' embarrass yourself and the MacDonalds."

Mary stopped. "You sound like our father. I half expect you to threaten to lock me in the dungeon."

A grim look flashed in Egan's eyes. "I'd never do that, and ye know it."

Mary opened her mouth to continue the argument,

but something in his stiff stance made her stay silent. She shook her head and marched away to find something else to worry about.

Egan's jaw remained firm, brows furrowed as he watched his sister. Zarabeth squeezed his arm, solid under his coat. "I thought the MacDonalds never used the dungeon anymore."

"My father did from time to time," Egan said. "He thought it would teach us a lesson when we were disobedient, to stay a time with the ghosties beneath the castle."

"That's cruel."

"Aye, well, my father wasn't known for his kind heart."

"Is that why there are no portraits of you in the house?"

His gaze pierced her. "What?"

"I found a portrait of Mary and one of Charlie, but none of you. I looked on all the floors."

All humor and warmth left his eyes, leaving a bleakness that chilled her. "And you won't find one. My father destroyed it."

Zarabeth gasped. "Whatever for?"

"It was after I came home from the Peninsula and told him that I'd lost Charlie at Talavera. He fetched his dagger and slashed my portrait to ribbons."

Zarabeth danced with Adam Ross after supper, but her gaze followed Egan. He stood on the other side of the room, his hands behind his back, his head bowed as he listened with great attention to an elderly woman who sat against the wall.

Egan hadn't responded to her breathless question about why on earth his father would take a knife to Egan's portrait. He'd turned away instead, his countenance hard, and led her in to supper.

Supper ended at midnight, and as soon as the dancing began Adam had latched on to Zarabeth. Egan watched narrowly as Adam led her out to dance, but at least he didn't interfere.

This ball might have been any held in an English country house or a grand mansion in London. The food at supper had been refined and elegant, prepared by a French chef, and instead of Highland dancing, Adam led Zarabeth in a stately cotillion.

Zarabeth liked Adam. He embraced being a modern Scotsman without awkwardness, his Ross plaid trousers his one concession to his heritage. He wore his blond hair a bit long, in the romantic style, and his blue eyes showed he had a sense of humor.

During the cotillion he said the correct things to Zarabeth about the weather and asked if she liked the Scottish scenery. Usually Zarabeth was a master of inane conversation, but tonight she wanted to ask bald questions.

"Egan told me what happened to his portrait," she said when they walked in the dance down the long room. "Why?"

Adam's polite look faded, and he nearly missed a step. "Are you certain you do not wish to continue speaking of the weather?"

"Very certain. You're his closest friend—you must know."

"Aye, I do. It is not a happy tale, and Egan doesn't like it spoken of."

"Speak of it anyway. He isn't *your* laird. He's not even of your clan."

Adam shot her a wry smile. "True, but I remember stories of the days when the MacDonalds were my family's enemies. Egan's ancestors had vicious tempers and long memories and loved revenge."

"You can tell him I forced you to reveal the story, if it will make you feel better. He will believe you."

Adam gave a cultured laugh. "I doubt that. I'm surprised you don't know, though, since your father is Egan's friend."

Zarabeth glanced at Egan, still talking to the elderly woman, who seemed enchanted by his attention. "I imagine he did tell my father, but neither has bothered to tell me. Will it hurt him if I know?"

Adam considered. "I think it better you do know. Egan has been odd since he came home this time, even more melancholy than usual. He doesn't like to stay at Castle MacDonald for long stretches. Too many bad memories."

"But it's such a lovely place."

The castle was filled to the brim with Highlanders and their noise—Jamie and Dougal bellowing up and down the stairs, Hamish growling at them both, Gemma shouting to Angus to hurry and do something or other. The helpful, plainspoken Williams, his good-natured wife, the cheerful maids. She'd never felt a pall at Castle MacDonald, but perhaps the relief at having escaped her husband's prison of a house overlaid her impressions of it.

"Charlie MacDonald had a way with him—everyone liked him," Adam said as they turned in the dance. "Egan always felt awkward and gruff, while the family doted on Charlie. To be honest, Charlie was a bit spoiled, and in my opinion the lesser man. But never say I told you that.

"When Egan decided to join the Ninety-second Highlanders, Charlie didn't want to be left out. Egan's father gave up trying to persuade Charlie to stay home and admonished Egan to take care of him. Charlie and Egan ended up on the peninsula and were at Talavera."

"Where Charlie was killed," Zarabeth supplied. Egan

had told her that much when he'd lived with them in Nvengaria.

"I never heard the details of it, but yes, Charlie died, and Egan took leave to return to Scotland with the body. Old Gregor MacDonald broke down when he saw Charlie so battered and bloody that you couldn't tell it was him. He held Egan responsible. He destroyed Egan's portrait and rid the house of all Egan's belongings, while he set up a sort of shrine to Charlie. He pretended Egan no longer existed. Egan left Scotland and didn't return until after his father's death."

The dance came to an end. Adam bowed, and Zarabeth curtsied numbly and let Adam lead her from the floor.

"That's horrible," she said as he stopped with her near the French windows. "How could he blame Egan? A battle was hardly his fault."

Adam sighed. "The old man was insane with grief. He said Egan should have looked after Charlie better."

Zarabeth snapped open her fan. No wonder Egan never talked of his father or brother. She couldn't imagine her own gentle father being so cruel.

She said, "Egan mentioned that his father liked to lock him in the old dungeon to scare him. Did he do so to Charlie?"

"No. Egan yes, but never Charlie."

Zarabeth waved her fan faster as her face heated in anger. She wished Egan's father were still alive so she could tell the man what she thought of him and his cruelties.

"I've distressed you," Adam said.

"Not at all. I am simply . . . furious, if you must know. It rather overheats one to contemplate the ill treatment of one's friends."

Adam opened the door. "Come out and cool yourself. The night is not brisk, and I have a *real* terrace."

His attempt at humor didn't mollify her, but Zarabeth allowed Adam to lead her outside and close the door on the hot room.

Clouds obscured the moon, but the overcast sky kept the air from being too crisp. Below them Adam's lanterns lit the garden path like overlarge fireflies.

"It may not have the same place in your heart as the Ross castle," Zarabeth said, resting her fingers on the balustrade, "but you have a lovely home, Adam. Very tasteful."

She couldn't see Adam well in the darkness, but she sensed his pleasure at her words. "My father had a good eye, and I've tried to keep up what he began."

"It's impressive. So many wealthy people run to excess. The old imperial prince—my cousin Damien's father—loved opulence. He could have given Caligula pointers. Our nation heaved a collective sigh of relief when he finally died."

"Prince Damien is a better ruler?" Adam asked, but she sensed his thoughts flitting off, as if he were distracted.

"Gracious, yes. He was penniless at one time, had to work like a serf to survive, which gave him understanding of how many people have to live. Penelope, his wife, is English and quite sensible. She will keep any family tendency toward excess at bay."

"Excellent."

Adam was paying little attention to the conversation, but knew how to keep up the pretense. Zarabeth thought ruefully that both of them were expert at polite banality.

"I am pleased Egan has such a friend in you," she said, touching his arm. "His father might have been awful, but the rest of you have rallied around him. I am grateful for that."

Zarabeth felt a rush of warmth as Adam's attention

returned to her. She shielded herself as best she could, but intense thoughts could always penetrate.

You are winning her over, Adam was thinking. *Adam, you rogue.*

Oh, dear.

"Perhaps we should return to the ballroom," she said quickly.

"Not yet." Adam touched her cheek with a kid-gloved hand, and his voice went seductively soft. "Lady, will you do me the honor . . ."

He trailed off as he leaned down to kiss her. His lips touched hers briefly, and she stood her ground. A small kiss, nothing passionate, she could allow him that.

But as his lips slid along hers, she heard the smattering of his thoughts. *Touch her . . . taste her . . . have her tonight in my bed . . .*

His thoughts spun beyond words to a vision of her lying in a four-poster bed she'd never seen before, her breasts bare, Adam kneeling at the foot of the bed whispering, *Spread for me, sweet lady.*

Then darkness erased his features, his Scots plaid, his blond hair. She saw Sebastian instead, his mouth twisted in a grimace as his fingers gripped her ankles. *Spread your legs, Zarabeth; let me get this over with.*

Zarabeth tried to twist away, but he held her fast. The conflicting visions spun through her head and tore down her barriers.

She screamed.

Instantly Sebastian's features dissolved and became Adam Ross's again. He stood a foot away from her, eyes wide, mouth open in surprise.

The terrace door crashed open and Egan came barreling out. Growling like a madman, he seized Adam by the neck and hoisted him high.

Chapter Eight
The Cottages
at Strathranald

Egan, for heaven's sake," Zarabeth cried. Egan saw her start forward, reaching out to stop him.

Egan shook Adam once. "Ye dared put hands on her, is that what ye did?"

"I did nothing, man." Adam's brogue came back under stress.

"I see ye walk out here with her—alone—and then hear her scream. How can that be nothing?"

Zarabeth clutched his arm. "It was my fault, Egan. He did nothing—I saw something in the dark, and it frightened me."

Egan looked down at her. Her eyes were wide and anguished, but she couldn't quite meet his gaze. Another lie.

"Has anything ye told me since ye arrived been the truth?" he asked her.

She gasped at his abruptness. "Well, of course it has!"

"Egan, my friend," Adam broke in, tight-lipped. "You're upsetting my guests."

Egan felt the weight of stares behind him. As expected, Mary slipped out first, followed by the curious Faith and Olympia and their mothers. Piers Ross pushed past them, glaring at Egan.

Adam said, "If you plan to call me out, get on with it, but at least let me go. You're ruining my coat."

Egan opened his hand, and Adam thumped back to his feet.

"Ye touched her," Egan said in a deceptively soft voice. "Ye dared."

"Oh, for heaven's sake, Egan," Zarabeth exploded beside him. "He did nothing. I was frightened, but not of Adam. Stop being such an overprotective bully."

She pushed past him and stormed into the house. Adam straightened his cuffs, a grin flashing in the dark.

Egan turned after her. Piers still looked like a thundercloud, but Adam clapped his brother on the shoulder. "A misunderstanding is all. No need for clan warfare."

Now Mary got in his way. "Egan, leave her be. You ought to be attending to Miss Templeton and Miss Barton, in any case."

The two misses joined Mary, and their anxious mamas hovered behind them. More people in the way.

"She canno' be alone," Egan said. "Her life is in danger, if you haven't forgotten."

Mary gave him a maddening look. "Baron Valentin is looking after her."

Through the open door Egan saw the grim-faced baron slide Zarabeth's hand to the crook of his arm. Egan felt slightly better, knowing the half logosh could protect her very well.

"I will take her home," he told Mary. "Why I let ye talk me into bringin' her here in the first place is beyond my ken."

Adam barked a laugh. "You could always lock her in a cage and have done."

"If I thought it would help, I would."

Mary glared at Egan, then swung around and stomped back into the house. Mrs. Barton and Mrs. Templeton shooed their reluctant daughters inside, and Piers shut the door behind them.

"Egan," Piers rumbled dangerously, but Adam held up a placating hand.

"No harm done," he said. "I will admit to the pair of you that I did kiss her, but I swear on my father's bones I did nothing more than that, nor did I plan to ravish her out here with my own supper ball commencing inside. She must have seen a mouse or something."

Egan tried to unlock his clenched hands, tried to dredge up his sense of humor. He couldn't. The thought of Adam touching her, of brushing even a light kiss to Zarabeth's lips, churned fury through his gut.

"Do no' touch her again," he said, his jaw so tight he thought it would break.

For some reason, Adam's grin only widened. "That's how it is, is it? You might have told me."

"I have no idea what ye're talking about," Egan growled, then slammed his way past Piers and back inside.

Hamish and Angus met Egan halfway across the room, their eyes alight. "What is it, cousin?" Hamish asked eagerly. "Are we doin' battle?"

Egan ignored them and walked on. Across the room, Baron Valentin beckoned to a female servant and led Zarabeth into a small side room. The maid scuttled after them and closed the door.

Egan came to rest outside the anteroom, determined to plant himself there until Zarabeth came out. Unfortunately this made it easy for Templeton and Barton to find him. The two fathers stopped in front of him like a portly wall, stomachs in strained waistcoats arriving first.

"Mr. MacDonald," Templeton began. "You need to declare your intentions."

Egan fought to keep the berserker rage of generations at bay. While Egan's great-grandfather was dying a humiliating death at Culloden, these gentlemen's grandfathers had been hiding over the border in England, loudly declaring their loyalty to King George. He'd checked.

"My intentions," he said in a tight voice, "are t' take my friend Zarabeth home and not let her come out again."

Barton blinked, his mouth moving a little as he tried to work out what Egan meant. Templeton frowned. "No, sir, I mean your intentions toward our daughters. Which do you plan to marry?"

Barton leaned forward. "Our daughters are pestering us something terrible. If we knew which one, 'twould make life easier for us all."

Egan gave them a hard look. "I intend to marry no one. I thought I'd made that clear."

"No," Barton said, bewildered. "Mrs. Cameron said you were hanging out a shingle for a wife."

"My sister has it wrong. Take your daughters back to Edinburgh, where 'tis safer for them."

Templeton looked pained. "MacDonald, I don't think you quite appreciate the nature of the situation. My wife will have Olympia married, if not to you then to Adam Ross. If my wife knows where to aim, she will be much easier to live with."

As furious as Egan was with Adam, he wouldn't wish either of the young debs on him. "My neighbors will choose their own brides."

"That will not answer, sir," Templeton said. "If it is a question of finances, I assure you my daughter's dowry is formidable. I have connections."

"Would those be English connections?" Egan let some of his Mad Highlander persona slide into his voice. "Lordlings who evict their Scottish tenants so they can raise sheep in their place? Do no' try to win me over with Sassenach money."

Templeton drew himself up. "Then you have brought us here on false pretenses. There are laws against breach of promise, you know."

"I did not bring ye here at all. I canno' answer for everything my sister does."

"See here—" Barton began, but a commotion interrupted.

Faith and Olympia had stopped at the edge of the ballroom floor, facing each other with cherry-bright faces. As guests turned to stare, the room quieted until Egan could make out the girls' words.

"He will never dance with *you*, Faith Barton. Mr. MacDonald doesn't like colorless misses."

"Well, he doesn't like shameless hussies who get themselves kidnapped so he'll rescue them."

"I never did it on purpose!" Olympia shrieked.

"I'll wager you did!"

"I never! You walked outside with your bodice drooping, hoping you'd get kidnapped too."

Faith screamed. She seized Olympia's curls and yanked hard. Olympia's carefully coiled hair came straight off her head in one piece, and Olympia shrieked, trying to grab the false hair. Faith stared at the mass in her hand, then burst out laughing.

Olympia howled and flew at her, fingers curved, but Gemma suddenly appeared out of the crowd and jerked the girls apart.

"Shame," she shouted, shaking them. "Shame on ye both. Come away and stop this nonsense."

Gemma, half a head shorter than either girl, bore them away past the interested crowd and their mothers, who stood by with plump mouths open. As Gemma marched them out of the ballroom, Faith and Olympia finally subdued, the guests tittered a bit, then went back to their conversations.

Templeton and Barton looked Egan up and down again, and Templeton said, "Well, how about it, Mac-Donald? Which will you have? Faith or Olympia? Tell us quickly."

Zarabeth slept little that night, still disturbed from her overlapping vision of Sebastian and Adam. When dawn broke, she at last fell asleep, but she woke not many hours later to the sound of one of the redheaded maids laying a new fire.

Egan waited for her on the landing when she emerged washed and dressed, and he was deep in conversation with her Nvengarian footmen. They were blaming themselves yet again for failing Zarabeth, and Egan was trying to calm them down.

She was grateful that Egan could speak Nvengarian, making him the only Scotsman who could handle the two energetic lads. As Zarabeth descended the staircase toward them, Egan silenced them with a word, and the footmen made their bows and scooted down the stairs.

"What was that about?" she asked.

"They wanted to come with us today, but I told them they couldn't. We have an errand t' run."

"Do we?"

"Aye, and I don't want a great lot of Nvengarians tramping after us. My men grew up in these hills; they can follow us without blundering about and ruining things."

The window on the landing was streaked with rain, and the clouds obscured the mountaintops. The day wasn't much lighter than dawn. "More fishing?" she asked.

"No, something I need to do and something I need to show ye."

"And you'll not hint about either one?" she asked.

Egan flashed his grin, looking more like his old self. "No."

"And if I catch my death of cold?"

He looked her up and down, a hot spark in his eyes. "Ye look healthy enough. If ye can stand kissing Adam on a cold terrace in the middle of the night, ye can stand this."

"Adam kissed *me*," she said.

"And ye defended him strongly enough when I came t' see what was the matter. Did ye want to kiss him or no?"

"No. But he did not . . ." She stopped, exasperated. "Oh, never mind. Will you allow me to have breakfast before you drag me out to catch consumption?"

"Aye, of course." He took her arm, his fingers hard. "I wouldn't dream of keepin' ye from your morning porridge."

By the time Zarabeth had finished her delicious porridge and Egan led his horse to the courtyard, it was nearly noon. Williams clicked his teeth a little over the late night and late morning the family kept today, annoyed that his routine had been disturbed.

Keeping city hours, his sour thoughts touched her as he helped her with her wraps. *This is Castle MacDonald, no' a Parisian salon.*

Zarabeth hid her amusement and went out to meet Egan.

The rain was chilly, but not icy, the wind calm. The clouds were like a blanket holding warm air in the valley, while the rain fell steadily.

Egan insisted Zarabeth ride double with him again, as much as she protested that she did know how to ride a horse.

"I learned at an early age," she told him as he turned

the horse out of the courtyard. "As you know. I could beat you in a horse race anytime."

"Because ye told the horses t' give me trouble beforehand. I know ye for a witch, Zarabeth."

"A minor mage," she said quickly. "Talismans and potions only, and they don't always work."

"Mmph," was his only response.

He took a road that skirted Loch Argonne and rose toward the hills. Zarabeth put aside her worries to enjoy the beauty.

The loch lay in a cut of hills that rose steep and gray-green from the bowl of the valley. The water was dark gray today, rain churning its surface.

The road took them through a pass between the steep hills, then climbed through trees to the flat top of another hill. Heather bent under the rain, stretching across the rolling terrain, black rocks poking through its carpet. Behind them the land dropped, giving a spectacular view of the loch and purple hills beyond, all the way to the sea in the misty distance.

"You must love this place." She sighed.

Egan made a noncommittal noise. "Ye grow used to it."

"You do love it. I see your eyes when you look at it."

He turned the horse down a path that led toward a line of trees with mist in their branches. "We didn't come out here to talk about whether I love Scotland."

"What did we come out here to talk about?"

"I told ye. I have an errand."

"Always cryptic, is Egan MacDonald."

"Ye'll see soon enough."

She heaved a small sigh and stopped asking questions. Having his strong arm around her waist was distracting enough.

A hill dropped away on their right, and she saw white stone houses nestled in the fold of the valley. At first she thought them lovely against the green-gray heather, but then she noticed their air of desertion. The roof of one cottage had fallen in, and the windows in another house gaped empty and black.

"Does no one live there?" she asked.

Egan turned to look down, not slowing the horse. "No longer. There are clusters like that all over Scotland now because of the Clearances."

"Clearances? What does that mean exactly?"

Egan guided his horse under the darkness of the trees, shutting off the sight of the sad houses. "Large landholders in the Highlands are evicting their tenants. 'Tis easier to make a fortune raising sheep than to have tenant farmers pay ye from their crops. The farmers have nowhere to go. Most move to the cities to look for work."

"Did you evict yours? Is that why the houses are empty?"

"Nay, that's no' MacDonald or Ross land. Our neighbor Strathranald made friends with the English, bought a passel of sheep, and gave his farmers the boot—people whose families have lived on that land for hundreds of years."

"That's terrible."

"But what's the answer? Shall we all starve together?"

"The Rosses don't seem to starve. Did Adam turn out his tenants, too?"

"No." Egan looked somber. "When his great-grandfather was killed and the castle razed, the tenants' homes were burned and the folk either butchered or taken away. His family lost everything. Adam's father was smart enough to learn new ways and make money from them. Makes Adam insufferable, but he's good to his people."

Zarabeth fell silent, sad that there should be grimness in all this beauty.

The mists were thick under the trees, and they rode in solitude. Rain trickled through the branches to wet them, the horse's hoofbeats muffled in the mud. If Egan's men followed, they were keeping well out of sight.

The solid wall of Egan's body was comfortable to lean against and the woods peaceful with the quiet patter of rain on the leaves. She could ride with him here forever.

"Have you decided to tell me where we're going?" she asked after a time.

"Hush, lass," Egan said against her hair. "Not so much noise. I don't want to scare them."

Them?

"Who are we meeting?" she whispered. "The Fair Folk?"

She felt Egan start. "The wha'?"

"The Fair Folk. The Sidhe from the far realm."

Egan's snort was plenty loud. "Who's been telling ye tales? Jamie? Or Hamish?"

"Neither. I read about them." After meeting Egan long ago, she'd read as much about Scotland as she possibly could, fascinated by his native land and its tales.

"Ye read trash and nonsense. The creatures I'm tryin' to find are very much of this world." He shook his head, trailing off into a mutter. "Fair Folk."

"The logosh are true. Magic spells are true. Why not Fair Folk?"

"Aye, I grant ye that the Nvengarians and their Gypsy ancestry produced some strange creatures. But I've no' seen evidence of it in Scotland."

"I have that Gypsy ancestry," Zarabeth reminded him. "I do hope you are not calling me a strange creature."

"I know better than that. But I remember ye playin' with magic when ye were younger. Lookin' at grimoires and things."

She gave him an annoyed look. "Not playing. I have some minor powers. Not enough to threaten anyone on the Council of Mages. They rather sneer at women with magic."

"Shortsighted o' them." His grip tightened. "So ye truly can make a magic spell?"

"Small ones. In fact, I'll tell you a secret—I made one for you that night five years ago, when I asked you to kiss me. I thought it would make you fall in love with me."

She felt him start clearly that time, almost jerking the horse to a halt. "Did ye now?"

"It was on the silly necklace I wore. But there's no need to be angry with me—it didn't work. In fact, it appeared to have the opposite effect, as we discussed."

"Discussed? I thought we had a grand, loud argument about it."

"Whatever you'd like to call it. The point is the magic didn't work on you. Perhaps you are immune to spells."

"I don't think so. A few years ago, when Damien married Penelope, someone put a sleep spell on an entire household, and I succumbed."

Zarabeth clutched the horse's mane so he wouldn't see how her hand trembled. "Ah, well, perhaps it is only *my* magic that will not affect you."

" 'Twould be an interesting experiment."

She tried to stop her imagination, but she couldn't help picturing him lying on her bed, candlelight touching his bare skin while she chanted a spell over him.

His face was difficult to see in the gloom, but she felt the gleam of his gaze on her.

He ended the conversation by guiding the horse down a steep hill, and she had to concentrate on not slipping in the saddle. At the bottom he put his lips to her ear and whispered, "Be silent as a mouse. There they are."

She looked where he pointed and saw a tall, round-bodied horse that to her trained eye had good bloodlines. Excellent conformation, long racing legs, an intelligent face. It was not a wild creature but one used to a pampered, sheltered life. Escaped from the stables at Castle MacDonald?

She opened her mouth to ask when a shaking, weak-kneed foal inched around the other side of the mare. It caught their scent and sent up a shrill little whinny. The mare swung around, ears pricked, nostrils testing the wind.

Egan lowered Zarabeth from the saddle, then slid off beside her. He took some cloths from the saddlebag and started toward the mare and foal, his step silent but sure. The mare watched protectively, putting her body between him and her foal.

"Run off again, did ye, lass?" Egan's voice was soothing and quiet. "What have ye there?"

Zarabeth followed him as quietly as she could, holding her plaid skirts out of the muck. The gelding they'd ridden lowered its head and began to crop grass.

The foal peeked around its mother's hindquarters, curious. It was a bay, dark in the gloom, with a black mane and forelock. Large brown eyes peered at Egan, then Zarabeth, who halted a few feet away.

Egan moved with a gentleness his strength belied. He patted the mare, reassuring her, then held his hand out to the foal. The little horse took a step toward him, too newborn to be frightened.

"That's the way," Egan said, his voice softer than Zarabeth had ever heard it. "Come on, lad."

The mare nuzzled Egan, worried but recognizing him. The foal staggered forward, keeping one shoulder against his mother, and stretched his nose to Egan's hand. The foal lipped his fingers, then jumped when

Egan scratched his nose. Deciding he liked it, the foal stepped forward again.

"Good lad," Egan murmured.

Egan skimmed a cloth along the foal's side, and the foal did another small leap sideways into the mare. The mare swung her head around to watch, but less nervously than before. Egan's warmth and scent seemed to reassure her.

Egan stroked the foal with the cloth, wiping off rain and muck. The foal enjoyed it, half closing his eyes.

Egan was gentleness itself. He whispered to the foal and mare, rubbing the little horse dry while its mother hung her head over Egan's shoulder to watch. Zarabeth marveled how he could dampen his strength and his boisterousness so as not to frighten the animals. He'd be as good with children, she sensed. A pity he was so against marriage and having a family of his own.

A pang stole through her heart as she thought of how her ruined marriage had taken away her own chance to have a family. She could remarry, of course, but by the time her heart healed from what Sebastian had done she'd be too old for children. She had the feeling she'd be ninety before she was whole again.

Egan glanced over his shoulder at her. "Come see him, lass. He's not afraid."

The mare watched warily as Zarabeth walked quietly forward but seemed reassured when Zarabeth took Egan's hand. The foal was a handsome one, his conformation good, and the way he moved showed he was sound. He was also adorably cute.

He bumped his nose against Zarabeth's midriff, and Egan chuckled. "Only a morning old and already likes the attention."

"He was born today?"

"Early this morning. One of m' tenants sent word

the mare had dropped a foal in the woods, but none could approach her. She's always liked me, so I thought I'd have a go at getting them back." He patted the mare affectionately. "She ran off days ago, the hellion, but I knew she wouldn't go far. She never does."

"She has the habit of running away, does she?"

"She likes a bit of freedom. Wanders the lands and comes back when she's ready."

"Like you," Zarabeth said. "You wander the world but always come back here."

He slanted her a glance. "Not the same. I come back only because I have to."

"And if you make Jamie laird you won't have to?"

"Aye. I'll let him take over the place when he's of age, and I'll stay in Paris or somewhere."

"But you belong here."

His brows drew down. "Don't ye start. I was the oldest son by accident—Charlie was the darlin', loved by everyone. His blood should be here, not mine."

"That isn't what I mean." The foal nudged his way around Zarabeth and thrust his head under his mother. Zarabeth stroked the foal absently as he nursed, his tail flicking contentedly. "You belong to this place—you're part of it. Not because you were born first, but because it's inside you."

"Ye're dreamin', lass. I don't belong here, any more than there's Fair Folk lurking under the heather."

She beamed at him. "You're wrong about that."

"Ye know nothing of it."

"You're wrong about that, too." Her smile widened, to his consternation. "You belong to this place, and it belongs to you, and there's nothing you can do about it."

She looked so smug.

Zarabeth smiled as though she'd solved Egan's lifelong problems for him, as though he hadn't been burning for her ever since he'd pulled her out of the sea. Ever since he'd left her five years before, truth be told.

She was lucky he didn't want to frighten the horses, because he'd be making startling moves that would have her on the ground, her clothes covered in mud. She was safe for now, but later . . .

She was making his life a living hell.

He went back to his horse and quietly lifted a halter out of the saddlebag, hiding it with his body and closing his hands over the buckles so they wouldn't clink. The mare knew what a halter was, and a man had to sneak up on her with it.

"Pet her a moment, lass, if ye don't mind getting your hands dirty."

Zarabeth moved readily to the mare's head and began patting her neck and rubbing her nose. Zarabeth had always been fearless around horses, turning her father's hair gray by riding the most troublesome steeds in the stable. Once she'd shown the same fearlessness with Egan. Now she was as jumpy as the mare.

While Zarabeth distracted the horse, Egan managed to slip the halter over the mare's face. The mare gave him an annoyed look but didn't fight him. She was ready to get out of the wet and back to the warm stables under the castle.

"We'll have to go back slowly so the little one can keep up," he said.

Zarabeth was still petting the mare. "I'm in no hurry."

"Ye're a fool then. It's bloody wet."

She gave him an irritated look. "Would you prefer me to wail that my gown will be ruined, like your debutantes would?"

"They are not *my* debutantes, if ye please."

"I think you do want me to be spoiled and unmanageable. You are troubled that I'm bearing up so well."

He started to growl that of course he wasn't, but he stopped. Perhaps he did want Zarabeth to be nagging and petulant, because then he'd not have this consuming need for her. He could shut her in her room for her protection and ignore her.

Her eyes widened when he didn't answer. "Oh, you *do* wish I were horrible like your debutantes."

"They are not mine!"

The foal jumped and the mare bared her teeth. Zarabeth put a calming hand on the foal's shoulder. "Keep your voice down, Egan, or they'll be off."

Egan growled as he snaked the lead rope into a figure eight in one hand and hooked it to the halter with the other. He led the mare away without a word, but he saw Zarabeth's secret smile as she lingered to walk with the foal. The gelding turned and followed of his own accord.

The rain pelted harder, and by the time they emerged from the trees it was coming down in sheets. Zarabeth pulled her borrowed plaid over her head, but they were going to be soaked through.

"We can make it to the Strathranald cottages," Egan shouted over the rain. "One of them is bound to still have a roof. We'll wait there until the storm turns."

Zarabeth only nodded. The foal, too tiny for this weather, stuck to its mother, and Zarabeth tried to shield it on its other side. The mare was snorting and worried, shaking her head as rain ran into her eyes.

It wasn't far to the tumbledown houses, but too far in this weather. Egan tried to make Zarabeth ride the gelding, but she wouldn't have it. Bloody stubborn, as usual.

The sky was so dark it might be twilight, not high afternoon. Clouds lowered from the hills into the valley, blotting out everything in a haze of rain. Egan almost missed the buildings, but out of the corner of his eye he saw the white of one of them looming out of the gloom.

He followed the wall to the front of the house, Zarabeth close behind. The door of the cottage had been wedged shut, but Egan managed to shove it open and lead the horses and Zarabeth into a chill, musty room.

Chapter Nine
The Portrait of Charlie MacDonald

*E*gan thought it too much to hope that someone had left a handy pile of firewood, and he was right. These cottages had been picked over long ago.

He did find brittle pieces of broken furniture in the hole below the house that had served as a cellar. He brought them up while Zarabeth quieted the horses in the corner. Peering up the chimney showed him gray clouds above, not to mention getting rain in his face, so he laid the sticks and used flint and a slow match he carried in his sporran to strike a spark.

"Quite lucky you carry that about," Zarabeth remarked, still petting the mare.

"A habit from army days. Ye never know."

"I remember when you came back to visit us, the maids and I liked to speculate on what you carried in your sporran."

"Did ye now? And what did ye decide?"

She shrugged. "We thought there must not be anything important because you never opened it."

"No need, living in yer father's luxurious house."

"I declared I'd steal it and peek, but I never got the chance." She looked wistful. "You always carried it with you and locked your door at night. I once got the key and sneaked into your room, but you woke up and almost caught me. You thought one of the downstairs maids was trying to get into bed with you."

He stopped, a memory boiling to the surface. A dark night, the clean scent of female, a shadow in the gloom. He'd been avoiding the clutches of a particularly determined maid with a salty tongue and assumed she'd cornered him at last.

"God and his saints," he swore. "That was you?"

Egan remembered that his reply had been as salty and bawdy as the maid would expect. No wonder she'd started, then abruptly gone out.

"It was indeed, Egan MacDonald. Your Nvengarian was quite good by then—I hadn't realized you knew such words."

He stood up. "Ye shouldn't have known them either."

"I am Nvengarian. Ladies learn the arts of the bedroom when they are of an age to marry."

"Aye, but that's all flowers and poetic descriptions. This was bawdy backstreet talk, which you *still* should no' know."

Her smile was downright sinful. "Poetic descriptions? You do not know much about Nvengarian ladies. We learn the language of Eros—*érotique*, it is called."

"And ye should no' know *that* word either."

"I learned these words in exquisite detail." She hadn't moved from the horses, but Egan started to sweat. "I know many words that perhaps even you don't. I am not an innocent miss."

Was she trying to kill him? The thought of her sweet mouth forming naughty words sent his blood pounding.

"I am no' your husband."

"I know that." She started to laugh. "I am teasing you. Did you think I was trying to seduce you in a barren cottage in the wet and cold, with horse droppings?"

Her smile made her eyes sparkle, and he'd never seen her so beautiful. She was wearing MacDonald plaid, the same plaid that swathed his own body.

He crossed the tiny room, took her by the shoulders,

and kissed her. No calm tenderness this time. He pulled her head back and kissed her hard.

Her hair was black silk under his fingers, the loops and braids coming undone as he furrowed it. Her face was wet with rain, cool drops that tasted salty on her skin.

His groin tightened. Damn her for making him want her—when had she become so skilled?

Her body moved to his, fitting in the curve he made as he bent over her, her fingers latching onto his kilt. He couldn't stop kissing her. He swirled his tongue around her lips, tasting every inch of them, licking away moisture and the rain.

Her mouth locked firmly with his, tongue tasting him as much as he tasted her. He felt her hands part the laces at the top of his shirt, fingers finding the curled hairs that spread across his chest.

"Stop," he whispered. He pressed his face to hers, not wanting to let go. "Ye have to stop touching me."

"I can't."

Her breath feathered across his mouth, and her tongue followed in a sweet swipe across his lower lip.

She burrowed her hands beneath his shirt, fingers finding the tight points of his nipples, pebble-hard from the cold and her touch. She played with them while he kissed her, his honor going to hell.

When she pushed him away, he thought she had come to her senses. Before he could reel from the coldness of that, she yanked his shirt apart, leaned down, and sucked his nipple between her teeth.

He'd thought himself hard before. His head dropped back and he pulled her against him, the tingle from her teeth scraping white-hot needles through his groin.

"Damn," he whispered. "Damnation."

She started to suckle him, her hair soft and damp against his chest. He raked fingers through her hair as her teeth sank into him, sharp points of wanting. It would be so easy to scoop her up, to lay her on a bed of his plaids, to ruck up her skirts and enter her.

He wanted it. He wanted to feel her squeezing him and know he was inside her. He wanted to be complete with her; he wanted to ride her and not let her up until he was satisfied.

And then he'd use his hands and mouth to satisfy *her*. He wanted to see her face soften in longing, hear her moan as she came for him.

He made himself put his hands on her shoulders and force her away. "No, lass, ye're killing me."

She stared up at him, eyes wide, her hair a beautiful mess. "Don't push me away."

"I have to." He tightened his grip, giving her a shake. Her hair tumbled loose around her shoulders. "Do ye want me to have ye on this dirty floor, rutting with ye like an animal?"

Maybe on her hands and knees—it would be fitting in such a place.

Why did he have to think of things like that?

"Yes," she whispered. "I want that."

"No." He leaned into her, gritting his teeth. "No. I'll not do it."

Her eyes went still with shock. He'd never seen her like this—she was no longer the innocent maiden or the polished duchess. She was as wild as he in this place far from civilization, as wild as the heather and the rocks and cascading waterfalls. They could take each other in crazed abandon here, and it would mean nothing when they left.

Except it would mean something to him.

Egan peeled his fingers from her shoulders, swung

his plaid around his chest, and strode out into the chill rain.

By the time Egan returned, Zarabeth had mastered herself. She laid her plaid on the hearth and sat down, barely feeling the hard stone beneath it. The horses settled to munch on heather she'd brought in for them, the little one nursing.

She'd been able to braid her hair into a long, loose tail that hung down her back. What she couldn't stop were the tears leaking from her eyes. She wasn't sobbing, just sitting still while tears slid down her cheeks.

Egan banged back in, bringing with him the fresh smell of rain. He stopped in front of her, but she decided not to look up.

He had on over his muscular calves the dark, thick socks that Scots wore when informally dressed. His kilt swirled at his knees, tempting her to slide her hand under the hem and rest her fingers on his inner thigh. His skin would be warm there.

He brushed his knuckle across the tears on her cheek. "I never meant to hurt ye, lass."

"Go away, please," she said in a steady voice.

"I'll not let ye ruin yoursel' on me. I know what ye think ye want. . . ."

She glared up at him through her tears. His face was a careful blank, and as always she could not read what was behind his eyes. The horses were more open to her than he was. "I know precisely what I want. I'm not a child anymore, but it is clear that you do not want the same."

"I was no' exactly fleeing in disgust."

"No," she stopped him. "You might have wanted it because I threw myself at you. But you don't want me, not really."

"Because ye are still a married woman."

She shook her head. "As I traveled across Europe, I heard many tales about Egan MacDonald. In Vienna you were legendary, and you were not always interested in whether a woman was married."

Egan reddened. "That was a long time ago, and that was different."

"It was not so very long ago. Six months since you saw the Baroness von Traunberg. She remembered you fondly. In great detail."

Egan embarrassed was an amusing sight—or would have been if Zarabeth weren't so anguished.

"She should no' have said such things to ye."

"Why not?" Zarabeth lifted her shoulders in a shrug much like the languid baroness's. "I am a Nvengarian duchess, which meant I was sophisticated in her eyes. She knew I knew you and was happy to gossip. I'm not certain whether she wanted to make me jealous or give me pointers, but she enjoyed talking about you."

He groaned. "God help me."

"You are certainly famous throughout the bedrooms of Europe. Rather humiliating that I am the only one you push away."

"Because ye are the only one whose father I'd have to look in the eye. 'Beggin' yer pardon, Olaf, but I've seduced yer daughter. Do ye mind?' "

She dropped her gaze. "Stop. You've made it clear what you think."

"Ye have no idea what I think."

"I know that!" She jerked her head up again. She liked his eyes even when she was angry at him, deep brown and so warm and inviting. "I've never known what you thought."

"Listen then." He crouched next to her and grasped her chin. "Ye are a beautiful woman. But I'll no' take ye while you're wed, no matter what liberal rules ye have in Nvengaria."

"You have made that quite clear. We should cease speaking of it."

She had made a fool of herself over him again. Perhaps she would be doing this at regular intervals until they were both too elderly for it to matter.

Egan had wanted her—she'd felt it in the pounding of his heart and his hardness that pressed against her. His kiss had been that of a man craving a woman. If he'd let himself he would have, as he called it, rutted with her, and she'd not have stopped him. Her marriage was dead, her heart empty except for the places Egan touched.

But he wouldn't take her; he'd leave her to burn.

Egan rose to his feet. "The rain is slackening. We should get the mare and foal back to the stables." He turned away to the horses without another word, leaving Zarabeth to clench her hands in frustration.

Egan helped his groom safely stow the horses in the stables under the castle, hoping to work off his anger and frustrated need.

He wanted Zarabeth, and his desire was only getting worse. Damn the woman. When she'd jerked open his shirt to touch his nipples, he'd lost all sense of time and place. He'd felt nothing but her warm mouth on his skin and his own flaring need. He still didn't know how he'd gotten himself out of there without ravishing her. He had to stay away from her; that was all there was to that.

He grunted in frustration. Easier to make it stop raining in Scotland than keep away from Zarabeth. How he'd lived for five years without seeing her smile and her sparkling eyes or hearing her lilting voice, he had no idea. He had to have been out of his mind not to ride to Nvengaria, climb a rope to her balcony, and carry her off.

Ridiculous. Like living in an opera.

By the time he finished with the horses, he was sweating and somewhat in control of himself. Zarabeth had gone straight upstairs, thank God, to warm and dry herself from the rain. He wouldn't have to face her right away.

When he climbed out to the courtyard again, it was to see the MacDonald carriage squeezing through the gatehouse, followed closely by the Ross one.

"Bloody hell, not now," he muttered.

His fears were confirmed when girlish faces peered from his sister's coach and shrill voices sounded. "Is this it? Is this Castle MacDonald? Oh it is quite *bon temps*."

Egan stopped himself from rolling his eyes. The carriages halted and two debutantes nearly leaped out, followed by their equally silly mothers and fathers, then Adam Ross and Mary.

Olympia spotted him. "Mr. MacDonald, we have come to see your castle. Mrs. Cameron says it is quite grand."

Egan shot Mary an annoyed look, which she returned blandly. Of course, if the young ladies saw the wreck of the place perhaps they'd want to flee back to the comfort of Edinburgh. He pasted on a smile and invited them inside.

But the ladies seemed to like everything. They cooed over the entrance hall and the steep staircase. They demanded to see the great hall and exclaimed over the boars' heads and many-antlered deer on the walls.

Olympia and Faith tried to outdo each other in extravagant compliments, mostly in bad French, until even Mary blanched. Adam sat the fathers down out of the way in the great hall, and Williams brought them whiskey.

The ladies, however, clamored to see the portraits in the upper gallery. "All the MacDonalds," Faith purred.

Egan tried to escape around them up the stairs to wash and change, but the little group hemmed him in. Olympia and Faith strolled arm in arm, taking up the width of the gallery. The larger mamas were even slower and took up more space.

"Enchanting landscapes," Olympia crooned. "And here you are, Mrs. Cameron, and your charming son."

The painting had been done when Dougal had been five years old. Mary stood stiffly, her hand on the back of a chair, while Dougal held his puppy. Mary's gaze was prim and tranquil, at her most proper. Even the dog looked polite.

"And here is Egan MacDonald," Faith cried.

Egan stilled. Faith, in her ignorance, clasped her hands in front of the painting of Charlie.

He heard a door open behind him on the gallery. Zarabeth emerged, dressed in a clean plaid gown, her glossy hair once again in place.

"It is so like you," Faith bleated. "When you were *much* younger, of course."

Zarabeth sent Egan an understanding look. She might be angry at him—her pride hurt—but she still understood him like no one else could. She knew what he felt watching the young girls gaze adoringly at his brother's portrait. Charlie's death had cost him so much: his pride, his self-confidence, any chance at peace.

"No," Mary said in a strained voice. "That is our brother, Charlie. He died in the war."

"Oh, dear." Faith turned around, her eyes large, her lower lip trembling. "How awful. Poor Mr. MacDonald."

They both manufactured tears and told each other they could feel what a loss was in this house. Olympia sniffled. "I can sense him still here, poor Charlie Mac-Donald, his ghost weeping."

"If ye think that, it only proves ye know nothing about Charlie." Egan turned back the way he'd come and signaled to Zarabeth. "I need to speak to ye. Downstairs."

He abruptly descended the staircase, and Zarabeth, after a startled look, came after him.

He waited for her in the antechamber between the staircase hall and the great hall. She scuttled inside, and he firmly closed the door against the curious stares over the railing.

Egan had thought to invite Zarabeth to sit with him at the rather dainty table Mary had carted all the way up from London, but he was too restless. He paced, his hands behind his back, glancing out the window to where the rain had slackened.

"Are you all right?" Zarabeth asked.

"No, I'm bloody no' all right."

"I'm sorry. If I had been quicker I might have steered them away from the picture."

He stopped in surprise. "'Twas not your fault. Mary could have warned them."

"What happened to Charlie?" Elegant and serene, she glided into a gilt chair that matched the table. "Adam Ross and I were speaking of how he died at Talavera. I have been trying to decide how you are to blame for *that*."

Egan barked a laugh. "Did Adam tell ye I was to blame?"

"He said you blamed yourself. And that your father did as well."

"Well, that's true enough. My father thought I ought to have stopped the French from shooting at us long enough for me to get my brother to safety." His eyes stung, as though a bit of dust had gotten into them, and he put his hand over them.

When he looked up again, he found Zarabeth standing next to him, her blue eyes lovely and concerned.

Her tear-streaked face in the cottage had smitten him through the heart. He'd hurt her, and he'd never wanted to. But if she had let him take her on the floor, she'd have regretted it when she came to her senses. He knew Zarabeth—she'd be angry at herself, as much as he ground with self-anger over Charlie's death.

He suddenly wanted her to know the whole story. He gestured her to sit, and he scraped the other chair next to hers, sitting down and leaning his elbows on his knees.

" 'Tis a very simple tale. I was to lead a contingent of Highlanders and foot guards to charge the walls, since I was a captain and had experience already at Oporto. Charlie was new, having caught up to me after my first battle. Nothing for it but that he would join me at Talavera."

The memories of noise came at him, so much damned noise—shots firing, men shouting, artillery thumping, horses screaming. The smell, too, of mud and dung and blood was as fresh a memory today as then.

"I told Charlie to stay in the rear and not be a bloody fool. He barely knew what to do with his saber, though he could shoot a pistol well enough. He told me that the men needed good officers to spur them on, and he wasn't staying behind like a coward. I left him and joined my men, and got so caught up in the battle that I never noticed him there until too late.

"He fell in the first charge. The French were shooting from the walls, and Charlie walked right into a barrage of bullets. He died quickly."

Egan found his eyes closed again, and he pried them open. Zarabeth had her hand on his, her touch smooth and cool.

"I'm sorry," she said.

Egan knew she truly was sorry. Her eyes held so

much compassion he wanted to pull her to him and hold her for a long time.

"I could no' even get to him until after it was all over. Until we took the city and rode in, and then I had to go back out and look for him."

She watched him thoughtfully. "I am waiting to see how this is your fault."

Egan shook his head. "I should have persuaded him to stay behind. I was impatient, not paying attention. We had a row, and I stormed out—the last words I ever spoke to him were ones of anger. I go out to battle, and next thing I know he's trying to lead a charge. Bloody idiot."

"It was likely you could not have persuaded him, even had you tried harder. It sounds as though he was a bit of a hothead."

"Oh, he was, was our Charlie. Always got away with it, too. Bonny Prince Charlie, he was called, after another man who charmed other people into doing his dirty work for him."

Egan fell silent, staring at his big hands clasped between his knees. Charlie had sworn at him that afternoon and declared he didn't need a mother hen. And Egan had said, *Get yerself killed then; I care nothing for it.*

He'd had to return home and face his father, explaining that Charlie had died when Egan wasn't looking.

He shut the memory away. Enough for today.

"I did no' call ye in here to talk about Charlie," he said after a time.

"I thought not."

She looked at him over steepled fingers, calm as you please.

"I was thinkin' about the magic ye said ye could do." He leaned forward, lowering his voice. "Do ye think ye can conjure a magic charm to remove those bloody females from Castle MacDonald, the Highlands, and my life?"

Zarabeth's smile suddenly blossomed. "It would be my pleasure, Mr. MacDonald."

Chapter Ten
Spells and Rituals

The spell worked, but not, Zarabeth knew, in the way Egan had expected.

While Egan returned to his room to bathe and change, Zarabeth invaded the kitchen and, with Mrs. Williams's help, rounded up candles, twine, grease, and salt. She picked up a bit of stone from the ground beneath Castle MacDonald and borrowed a needle from Gemma. She spread these all on the table in the anteroom and invited the girls one at a time to have their fortunes told.

She could read from their thoughts that Olympia and Faith wanted to push each other away and go first. But they each smiled with sickening sweetness and told the other to go ahead.

Zarabeth settled it by choosing alphabetically— Faith, then Olympia.

Zarabeth lit the candles, rubbed the grease and salt on a stone, then asked for Faith's hand. Faith wrinkled her nose as Zarabeth set the stone in her palm, but she held still, not about to let Olympia see her squeamishness.

Zarabeth pricked Faith's finger until a tiny drop of blood dropped onto the stone. Zarabeth took the stone away, quickly wrapped it in twine, and dripped candle wax on it to seal it. She said a short chant in Nvengarian, and the spell was done.

"Wear this around your neck or keep it in your pocket," she told Faith, giving it back to her. "And the fortune I tell you will come true."

Fait looked excited. She wrapped the talisman in her handkerchief and plopped it into the bag she wore at her waist.

Zarabeth scanned the girl's mind and found what Faith most wanted—not long life and happiness, but the prettiest dress at the Season-opening ball. She gave Faith a vague reassurance that she'd find a most beautiful gown and sent her away satisfied. Zarabeth repeated the process for Olympia, but her fortune was different—Olympia would awe everyone next Season with her singing.

Egan entered the anteroom after the girls had run off to show their mamas the talismans.

"It won't hurt them, will it?" he asked worriedly.

Zarabeth's heart warmed. She knew Egan was sick to death of the determined young ladies, but even so he did not wish them harm. He was a gentle man for all his gruffness and strength.

"They'll take no harm from it," she assured him. "But I imagine they'll pester their parents to go home soon."

This prediction came true. Not an hour later, both girls looked at Castle MacDonald as though they never wanted to see it again. Jamie took them to the dungeon, hoping to thrill them with an old bit of chain still hanging near crates of whiskey, but their eyes glazed and they complained of the cold and their aching feet.

Mr. Templeton and Mr. Barton soon loaded them into Adam's carriage and rode away with them. In the courtyard, Egan waved cheerily, but the two ladies could barely be bothered to return the wave.

"How odd," Mary said beside him and Zarabeth.

"They were so eager to stay for supper and see Egan perform a sword dance."

"They are young," Zarabeth said, trying to sound wise for her twenty-three years. "Not long out of the schoolroom. Ladies tire easily of things at that age."

"I suppose," Mary said doubtfully. "Well, I shall be off back to Ross Hall to make sure everything is all right."

Egan handed Mary into her carriage, along with the mamas and Adam, and repeated the cheerful wave.

As the carriage squealed through the gatehouse, Egan put his hands behind his plaid-draped back and cocked a suspicious gaze at Zarabeth.

"What did ye do to them?"

The courtyard was empty, but Zarabeth looked around before answering in a low voice. "I gave them a dose of ennui. It was not difficult—they're already tired of being in the country, but neither wanted to admit it. They will badger their fathers to take them back to Edinburgh within the next day or so."

Egan started to grin; then his brow puckered. "They won't have ennui forever, will they? That would be a bit cruel."

"No, no. The spell will wear off in a few weeks, and Misses Faith and Olympia will find some new diversion to be excited about. But I'm afraid they'll always remember you as rather dull."

Egan's laugh rumbled through the courtyard. "Thank God for that. Ye're a devious woman, Zarabeth. Ye weren't lyin' when ye said your magic did no' work on me, were ye?"

"No, indeed. For some reason, you seem to be immune."

He gave her a long look, his eyes warm. "Immune to your magic mebbe," he said under his breath.

"What?"

Egan's plaid slid over his arm as he touched her face. "Nothing," he said. "Just passin' the time of day."

The debutants did go back to Edinburgh the next day. Adam sent a relieved message that his house had at last emptied of Mary's irritating guests.

Mary was all for returning to Edinburgh and convincing the next set of parents to bring their daughters to meet Egan, but Egan forbade it.

Zarabeth heard their argument as she was leaving her room the morning after the debutants departed. Egan and Mary lingered on the stairs, Mary breathing hard, Egan grim-faced.

"We are protecting Zarabeth, not hosting house parties. Ye'll stay home where ye belong."

"Yet *you* traipse about the world from Paris to Rome and back again. While I sit home and embroider."

"From the tales I hear in Edinburgh, ye do a damn sight more than embroider."

Mary reddened. "What I do in Edinburgh is none of your business."

"It is when I hear about ye taking a Sassenach lover."

Mary gasped, then leaned toward him in fury. "What was I to do when my husband died and left me nothing? I found cold comfort here."

Zarabeth tried not to listen with her mind, but Mary's distress worked its way through her barriers. She saw the loneliness in Mary, who was thinking that her affair hadn't comforted her as she'd hoped and that it was over. She'd mostly done it to defy Egan, and Egan hadn't noticed.

"This is your home," Egan said.

"Where I sit and sew. Such a life."

"Ye help me take care of Castle MacDonald and its inhabitants," Egan argued.

"You have Gemma for that now. She is much more efficient than I am. You don't need me."

"I do need ye, Mary. I need ye to stay here and look after Dougal."

"Who is grown-up enough to take care of himself. Don't placate me." Jaw set, Mary ran up the stairs and around the other side of the gallery, not seeing Zarabeth.

As her bedroom door slammed, Egan glanced up and met Zarabeth's gaze. They held each other's eyes for a few moments; then Egan shook his head and walked on down the stairs.

"She is lonely, that one."

Zarabeth gasped. Baron Valentin had come out of nowhere and now stood at her elbow, the part-logosh man able to move like a ghost.

"Yes," she said when she'd caught her breath. "She and Egan both are."

"It is sad," he agreed, his gaze lingering on Mary's closed door. His eyes were quiet, his strong hand resting on the gallery railing.

He didn't speak again, and after they'd stood in silence a few moments, he descended the stairs, his step heavy.

October wound into November, and November to December without much changing at Castle MacDonald except the weather. The temperature dropped week by week until snow fell in the first half of December, and Mrs. Williams began laying in supplies for New Year's or, as the Highlanders called it, Hogmanay.

No more attempts were made to kidnap or kill Zarabeth, which Zarabeth found disturbing rather than relieving. She was not naive enough to think her husband would stop trying to find her and punish her. He was that kind of man—he never let go of vengeance.

Egan's men continued to ride out with her whenever she left the castle, and Egan still stuck with her wherever she went, including bedding down for the night outside her room.

Though she didn't admit it to him, it was a comfort to know he was guarding her when she woke in the night.

The warmth and safety of Egan's castle made her realize that she'd lived a half life, brittle and polished on the outside, raging on the inside. Not until she'd arrived in the Highlands had she begun to come alive again. Egan's teasing, Jamie's antics, Angus and Gemma's good-natured shouting matches warmed her heart and filled her with hope that her life could begin again.

She threw herself into the Hogmanay preparations with enthusiasm, learning all she could about the customs of her adopted country.

"We should ask Baron Valentin to be the first-footer," Jamie said one cold morning while Zarabeth helped him and Dougal make garlands tied with tartan ribbons.

"First-footer?" Zarabeth asked.

Dougal answered her: "First man into the house after midnight on New Year's Eve. Supposed to be a stranger, but everyone around here's known each other forever. This year we'll have a real foreigner. And the baron is dark-haired, so it's better luck."

"Why is that?" Zarabeth tied a ribbon of MacDonald plaid around a green bough, liking as always to touch Egan's colors.

Jamie answered. "The worry about blond men goes back to when the Highlands were overrun with Norsemen. A dark man was all right—he was a Pict or a Celt, your neighbor. A blond man was a raiding Norseman, and ye didn't want him in your house because he'd steal your cattle and kill ye."

"A good worry," Zarabeth agreed with a smile. "But that must have been hundreds of years ago. I haven't seen many Norsemen traipsing about the heather."

"Aye, but Scots have long memories." Dougal grinned. "A dark-haired man is best. The baron will have to bring the right gifts, mind."

"I'll ask Valentin if he'll do it," Zarabeth offered. The taciturn, keep-to-himself Valentin would be non-plussed, but she'd do her best to persuade him. "It could not be me, could it? It sounds rather fun."

"Not a woman," Dougal said, sounding horrified. "That's the worst luck of all."

Zarabeth raised her brows. "Rather insulting."

" 'Tis tradition, is all," Jamie said. "No' meant to offend."

"Well, I would not want anyone to fall over in apoplexy if the first-footer is a woman. I withdraw my question."

"Good." Jamie grinned at her. "Somethin' else I've been meanin' t' ask ye."

"Oh?"

Zarabeth had grown fond of Jamie, who always seemed to be incurring his uncle's wrath. He kept getting into scrapes, mostly because of his own exuberance and youthful assumption that he was invulnerable. Zarabeth had wondered why he wasn't away at school, and Egan explained in exasperation that Jamie had been sent down from Eton for some disgrace. He was to attend Harrow when the Hilary term began.

Jamie took a length of paper from his sporran and spread it across the table. "Since Uncle Egan won't let us bring over any other ladies for him to get engaged to, I wondered if ye'd do it."

"Find eligible misses for Egan?" Zarabeth asked, pretending to be offhand. "I could write to some families I know, if you like."

"Nay, I didn't mean bring others here. I meant marry him yourself."

Zarabeth jumped in her chair. Dougal lost track of the bow he was tying and stared.

Zarabeth cleared her suddenly dry throat. "But I'm still married."

Jamie waved that away. "No' a bother. Uncle Egan says your divorce will be done soon, and in the eyes of your people ye won't be ruined. Not that Uncle Egan would mind it even if ye were."

Zarabeth flushed. "Your neighbors might mind."

"Nay. You're foreign," he said, as though that would excuse everything. "Ye'll be unmarried soon and of a good age to wed Uncle Egan."

"And I am not Scots. Don't your criteria say the lady must be a Scotswoman?"

Jamie shrugged. "We can get around that. But ye fit the rest. Good breeding—well, you were born a princess, weren't ye? You're young, pretty, of tolerable personality, and you're rich, Egan says. Very plump in pocket."

"Indeed." She felt herself sinking.

"And ye can do magic spells."

"A few." She frowned. "What about Misses Barton and Templeton? They weren't magical, surely?"

"Mr. Templeton and Mrs. Barton each claimed they had a witch in their family, way back when folk around here were hanging witches. We checked."

Zarabeth had no doubt he'd researched it with more care than he did his studies for school. "And this will not only save you from being laird but undo the curse," she said. "The one Egan wastes much breath insisting does not exist?"

Dougal chuckled. "He doesn't believe in ghosts either. He's too practical."

"Tell me how the curse started." Zarabeth gave a

quick glance out the open door, but Egan had gone down to the stables with Hamish and Angus. "Before Egan comes back and shouts that there's no such thing."

Dougal snorted, but Jamie shoved aside the garlands and eagerly began.

"'Tis a sad story about our great-great-great-great . . . I forgot how many greats . . . grandfather. His name was Ian MacDonald, and a beautiful but lowborn witch named Morag fell in love with him. She cast many spells for his safety and happiness, and he promised to marry her despite the scandal it would create. He was ensnared by her beauty."

"Course he was," Dougal said. "She enchanted him."

"But one day Ian went away to Inverness and stayed there for two years. When he returned to Castle Mac-Donald, he brought a lovely lady with him. He'd married her, and wasn't Morag crazy with rage?

"While Ian had been gone, Morag had borne him a son, but Ian now denied he was the boy's father, afraid his new wife would flee and tell her rich family of her displeasure." Jamie nodded at the sword hanging next to the fireplace. "Ian had left yon claymore with Morag to guard, and when he returned with the other lady, Morag cursed it and gave it back to him. He hung it up, none the wiser.

"And so the curse fell upon the castle." Jamie lowered his voice to dramatic tones. "Ill luck would fall on Ian MacDonald and his descendents down through the years. The curse canno' be lifted until a laird of Clan MacDonald isn't ashamed to marry a magical woman for love. Then the lady will help him break the sword and end the curse."

"And that's the story," Dougal said.

"'Tis no' the end," Jamie insisted. "Didn't Ian Mac-Donald drop down dead at Morag's feet? The son his

Inverness wife bore was sickly and died, too. Ian's brother had to become laird and was stalked by ghosts all his life."

"No," Dougal scoffed. "Ian MacDonald died in his bed of a fever five years later. His oldest son died of sickness, 'tis true, but the younger son lived to become laird. Look it up."

"All right, mebbe it was Ian's son who became laird, but he *was* haunted by ghosts, I know that much. Gibbering headless corpses on the top gallery."

"Have no other laird and lady tried to break the sword?" Zarabeth interrupted. She'd learned that Jamie could go on with enthusiasm about ghosts if not stopped. "You said it's been three hundred years since the curse began."

"Oh, aye," Jamie said. "My great-grandfather and great-grandmother tried it, but it didn't work. My grandfather was as skeptical about it as Uncle Egan, so my da told me."

A growl rumbled through the room, and Jamie jumped, looking guilty.

"Are ye fillin' Zarabeth's head with the curse nonsense?" Egan stood in the doorway, his arms folded across his broad chest, looking mouthwatering in plaids and a linen shirt. "'Tis no' but an old story, lad. Our luck has been good and bad, like anyone else's, and not because of a bloody curse."

Jamie stuck out his chin. "Zarabeth asked me to tell, because she knew ye never would."

Zarabeth rose to meet the fury that was Egan. "Leave him be, Egan. I did insist."

"Ye should no' have. He's usin' it to try to get me married off so he can gallivant around Scotland and England without a care. He's got t' learn responsibility."

"He is only fifteen," Zarabeth argued. "Plenty of time for him to grow up."

"He'll go to Oxford at seventeen. Not much time to finish at school, from which he keeps getting sent down."

"No' my fault," Jamie said, leaping up. "I only meant to set a *little* fire in the headmaster's room. He had so many papers around that it spread before I knew what was happening."

Dougal put his hands over his face.

"Ye need a thrashing," Egan rumbled.

"He needs someone to talk to," Zarabeth said.

"I grew up in a houseful of Highlanders, lass," Egan told her. "A thrashing is best."

"I see." Zarabeth gave him a frosty look. "Because it made you so kind and compassionate."

Dougal made a choking noise. Jamie only stared, openmouthed, as Zarabeth turned and walked past Egan out the door.

"Oh, no, ye don't, lass."

Egan was right behind her, his boots nearly scraping her heels. He caught her by the arm and spun her around before she could reach the stairs.

"Did ye mean t' come here and turn my house upside down?"

His hand on her arm was warm and strong, the look in his eyes not quite right for his words. He looked watchful, if anything, as though waiting to see what she'd say to him.

"I did not mean to come here at all," she said. " 'Twas the assassin creeping through the palace in Nvengaria that decided my fate. Damien sent me here."

"Why did ye agree to come? Ye might have asked to go elsewhere. I hear Virginia is quite civilized."

"I had little choice. Damien woke me in the middle of the night, put me on a horse, and bade me follow Baron Valentin as quickly as I could. I didn't even know where we were going."

"Aye, well."

She expected him to continue the argument and was gearing up to meet him, but he suddenly ceased.

"Is something the matter?" she asked.

He gave her a quiet look, his anger evaporating, if he'd truly been angry. She wished so much that she could read past the deliberately blank expression on his face.

"Shall we go for a walk, lass?"

"Isn't it rather cold?"

"Crisp and clear. We'll wrap up warm."

"Why on earth do you want to go for a walk now?" Aggravating man. He'd done his best to avoid her every day, while still seeming to know exactly where she was and what she was doing.

"I have something to show you."

He would not tell her what, of course. She peered at him a moment longer, then sighed. "Very well," she said, and went to get her wraps.

A quarter of an hour later, they tramped down the hill from the castle and followed what had become one of Zarabeth's favorite walks, winding down to the stream where they'd fished and along it to a glorious field of heather. The heather was buried under a thin layer of snow now, the stream running swiftly, black between the banks.

They walked in silence, Egan guiding her with a strong hand where the banks grew slippery. But instead of taking the path across the heather, he turned and climbed a steep hill in a direction she'd not gone before.

"I think you enjoy not telling me where we're going," she called up to him.

"Save your breath for th' climb. You'll understand later."

She bit back her reply and concentrated on the bend

and flex of his muscular legs, the sway of his kilt across his backside. She hadn't had another chance to peek at him in his bath again—he kept the door firmly closed now—but one night she'd risen to study him in his sleep.

She'd softly opened her bedroom door to find him on his cot outside it. He'd lain on his side, head pillowed on his arm, the blankets sliding down to reveal his hard torso. He'd slept in a linen shirt open to the waist, and she'd stood for a long time, mesmerized by the rise and fall of his chest.

She'd been sorely tempted to slide the blanket lower, to see what, if anything, he wore on his hips. But he'd shifted in his sleep, and she knew with certainty that he'd wake up if she even touched the blankets.

She'd gone back to bed, her dreams frustrating.

Egan crested the hill and waited for her to catch up. He stretched out his bare hand and boosted her up the last few rocks.

The top of the hill was flat and treeless. It sloped down slightly to a bowl-shaped valley, in the midst of which was a circle of tall, narrow stones.

Zarabeth gasped as the tingle of the stones touched her. They'd been erected at regular intervals, the monoliths standing high in their stately dance through the ages. The ground inside the circle and the stones themselves were untouched by snow.

"The Ring of Dunmarran," Egan said softly. "Come on."

He led the way down the hill, straight for the circle.

Chapter Eleven
The Ring of Dunmarran

Zarabeth caught up to him halfway down the hill and they walked the rest of the way side by side. The tingling she'd felt from the stones grew as they approached the circle, until Zarabeth's body vibrated with it.

"This is a magical place," she said.

"Dunmarran? I suppose. It's stood for a couple thousand years; at least, people think so. Even Roman records speak of it. No one knows what it was for, any more than they understand the other circles in Britain."

It was an ancient place, with the magic of aeons soaked into it. Zarabeth felt the weight of centuries past as she stepped inside the snowless circle. Whatever forgotten gods the stones had been erected to, the place was holy.

"That's why there is no snow here when there should be," she murmured.

"Mayhap," Egan said behind her. "I think there's a hot spring below it, deep underground, that melts the snow on the surface. That's likely why the stones are here, to mark the old spring."

The tingle she sensed came from something far stronger than boiling mineral springs. "Don't you believe in anything?"

"Aye, I do."

He spoke so quietly that she swung around. Egan stood behind her, a step away, his tall body blocking the wind.

"I have something t' tell ye, lass."

His expression was somber, his eyes dark. She felt a prick of dread. "What is it?"

The breeze tugged his kilt, and his brown hair escaped its queue as usual, wild and curling around his face. He might be an ancient Scot come to work magic in his stone circle.

"I had a message from Damien. Ye know he has a mage who has crafted a way to send messages by magic."

Zarabeth did know—Damien had explained that he'd be able to keep in touch with her through Egan.

"That's why I came to find ye." His voice was subdued. "I had a letter this afternoon that says your divorce is final. Ye are a free woman."

Free.

Zarabeth felt herself falling, but when she looked at the ground, she was still standing upright. She was supposed to be relieved and happy and exhilarated, but she felt as though she'd been cut adrift on a roiling river, her craft spinning out of control. She put her hand to her mouth and choked back a sob.

"Are ye all right?" Egan's hand was warm on her back. "Did ye love your husband so much?"

"Love him?" Zarabeth jerked away, her heart pounding until it sickened her. The band on her finger suddenly burned her, and she wrenched it off.

With a scream, she flung it away from her as hard as she could. The gold winked as it vanished into the tall grass.

"I hated him with every breath," she shouted. "So many times I wished him dead."

The words spilled out before she could stop them.

Zarabeth, who'd learned day by painful day to control her tongue, suddenly screamed what she'd truly felt.

"Why?" Egan asked in a hard voice. "What did he do t' ye?"

"Don't ask me. Don't ever ask me."

"But I am asking ye. Here and now. Tell me."

Zarabeth wanted to keep the shame quiet, at least, but the words jerked from her. "He punished me. If I did not do exactly as I say—speak, behave, dress, think—he punished me."

Egan's eyes went wild with fury. "He beat ye?"

"He didn't have to; he knew so many ways to be cruel. If I talked to someone he didn't approve of or went somewhere he didn't like, he locked me in my rooms for days and gave me no food or drink. My maid at first tried to smuggle me scraps from the kitchen, but I was afraid that if he caught her . . ."

Egan's rage grew. "What else?"

"If I did not dress the way he wanted, he took away my clothes and left me nothing but a shift. I could have defied him, but he did the same to my maids, and they were so miserable and humiliated."

"What else?"

"Why do you want to know all this? If I dared say anything he didn't approve of in public, he threatened to, he said, 'put me in my place.' What he meant by that I never knew—I didn't want to know."

Shaking tears rolled down her face. "I couldn't get away, because he guarded my every step. He watched me always, like a prisoner—no, more like a madwoman in an asylum."

She found herself against Egan's chest, buried in his scents of wool and male. Egan's arms came around her, shielding her like a blanket against the cold.

"Ye should have told me," he said into her hair. "Why didn't ye tell me?"

"I couldn't. He had his servants search my rooms and take away my paper and ink—I had to ask for them whenever I wanted to write a letter—and then his secretary took the letters to Sebastian for approval. I tried to devise ways to deceive him, but after a while it was easier to give in. If I gave in, he left me alone."

Under Egan's still chest his heart pounded rapidly. "Damnation."

She wiped her eyes. "You couldn't have known. Even my father didn't know, or Damien, so they couldn't have told you, either. No one knew. I became a master at hiding the truth. I don't even know why I'm telling you now."

"'Tis the Ring of Dunmarran," he rumbled. "Legend says that within its circle, ye can only tell the truth."

Zarabeth raised her head. "Really? How awful."

"Aye. That's why no one ever comes here."

His eyes were somber. She'd never seen him look so sad, not even when he spoke of his brother. Behind the sadness was the rage of the savage man he was deep down inside.

"Why did you make me tell you?" she asked.

"I thought ye could now that ye were out of his reach. I wanted to know what my Zarabeth was hiding." He put his finger under her chin and raised her face to his. "Ye are safe now. I'll never let ye be hurt again."

She shook her head. "I might be free of my marriage, but he won't let me go easily. Sebastian loves revenge. A man who voted against him in the council ended up violently ill. Sebastian would not have him killed outright because he might have needed the man again, but he let his displeasure be known."

"A monster."

"Oh, yes. But no one knows it, you see. He's more a master of hiding than I am."

"Well, ye don't have to hide anymore," Egan said.

"That's what I've been trying to tell ye, love. You're under my protection. As laird, I take care of all within my domain."

Standing against his hard body, protected from the cold, Zarabeth did feel safe. She let herself wrap her arms around his waist, which she hadn't done in weeks.

"Except now he'll try to kill you, too," she pointed out. "For hiding me."

Egan rumbled with laughter. "I'm a formidable enemy. I have every clan behind me if I need them, and besides, Prince Damien and Grand Duke Alexander count me as a friend."

Zarabeth rubbed her cheek on the plaid across his chest. "Sebastian is more insidious than that. He does not fight outright. He pays others to creep about and assassinate for him."

"I've cast a wide net. No fish will get in or out without my say-so."

She wanted to laugh at his metaphor but felt too brittle. "This isn't real freedom. I am confined here as much as I was in Nvengaria."

His voice softened. "Is it so bad? I know Castle Mac-Donald is no' elegant, and my family tumbles all over it. Enough to drive anyone mad."

"I like your family. They are wonderfully sane, and remind me of life in my father's house." She smiled. "Only a little louder."

"Aye, the battle at Culloden couldn't have been as loud as Angus and Hamish and Gemma when they get to shoutin' at each other."

"It is kind of you to let them all live here."

"Not so much lettin' them as I won't turn them away. Angus and Hamish's father—my uncle—didn't have a penny, and we all grew up here together. 'Tis their home. And now yours."

She sighed. "Sometimes I think I never want to leave

here. At others, I want so much to go home. Nvengaria has so much color and pageantry, and everyone lives so intensely. Sometimes it's wearying, sometimes exhilarating."

"Aye, it's an . . . interesting place."

She closed her eyes, suddenly able to reminisce without pain. Perhaps the Ring of Dunmarran's magic let her. "I remember the marvelous masked balls my mother used to give. I'd creep downstairs and watch all the guests, and when I came of age, I'd spend weeks planning my costume. Once I appeared as a frog princess. No one knew who was inside that giant frog's head. It was the very devil to walk around in."

Egan shook with laughter. "I am sorry I never saw that."

Sebastian would never have dreamed of letting her appear in green wool held in shape with wire with a little crown on top of her head. She had to wear magnificent and costly gowns and have her masks made to keep her identity obvious. Everyone should know that the best-dressed woman in the room was Zarabeth, wife of Duke Sebastian.

"Now I think I shall always attend balls in plaid," she said wistfully. "As a Scotswoman."

"It won't be so far-fetched. I'm t' make ye an honorary member of Clan MacDonald at Hogmanay." He made a noise of exasperation. "Damn the Ring of Dunmarran. 'Twas meant to be a surprise."

She took a step back. "Oh."

He frowned. "Ye don't look pleased. 'Twas Gemma's suggestion, since ye seem to like everything Scottish. And my clansmen will be loyal to ye as a lady of the clan."

"Oh," Zarabeth said again.

Then she nearly sagged to her knees as gratitude swamped her. She'd spent five years holding herself apart from the world so no one would be hurt because of her. Suddenly Egan's Highlanders were embracing her in a blanket of good-natured affection, welcoming her as one of their own.

"Not much of a gift," Egan was saying. "But I haven't had time t' visit our jewelers in Edinburgh and fetch a bauble for ye."

Happiness flooded her in spite of her worries. "I don't want a bauble."

"Are ye sure?" he asked, sounding surprised. "Ye'd turn down a diamond necklace for a pack of Highlanders?"

"Sebastian gave me boxes of diamonds. I hated them all. I'd rather have porridge and heather and tartan dresses."

"Ye'll be easy t' please, then." His half smile warmed her all over.

She knew right then that she'd better get herself out of the Ring of Dunmarran before she made a fool of herself again over Egan. She tried to push away from him, but his strong arms held her in place.

This was far too dangerous. She wanted to blurt that she loved him, that she always had loved him, even when she was angry at him.

"Egan, let me go."

"If I make ye an honorary MacDonald, ye have to pledge yourself to me. Ye do know that."

"Pledge myself?"

"Aye, t' have me as your laird. T' come to my aid when need be, to follow me when I ask it."

"Oh, is that all?" She wanted to laugh. Why, when Sebastian expected her unquestioned obedience had she been torn with rage and fear, but when Egan asked she felt only amusement?

Perhaps because Sebastian demanded submission without quarter, and Egan asked only for her word. One man bound her with chains; the other accepted her pledge as a gift.

"Is that no' enough?" he asked.

"I thought I'd have to polish your boots as well, o great laird."

His hold tightened. "Your pledge will be fine. At Hogmanay, in front of the clan."

"I will give it."

"Then I will swear t' protect ye with my sword and my strength."

Egan's eyes went dark, his body stilling. She could feel the foolish Zarabeth rushing up inside her, wanting to clasp her hands behind his neck, to draw his head down to hers for a long, tongue-tangling kiss.

She let her hands slide up his chest. "You never did tell me, you know," she said softly, "what a Highland laird wears under his kilt."

He started, as though that were the last thing he had expected her to say. Then he began to laugh, a slow chuckle that vibrated his body.

"I knew the first day I laid eyes on ye that ye'd be a vixen."

"I simply want to know, and if we're in the Ring of Dunmarran, you have to tell me the truth."

He pushed her away, still laughing. Then, before her startled eyes, he spun around and flipped the back of his kilt up over his shoulders. "There, now," he roared.

Zarabeth froze in place, unable to breathe. She'd seen Egan when he'd stood up in his bath, but that had been through a slit in the door. Now the winter sun touched his firm backside, everything bare for her to see.

Gods above, he was beautiful.

He dropped the kilt, but before he could turn around, Zarabeth went to him and slid her arms around his waist from behind. She leaned into his warm back, her body thrumming with need.

He didn't jerk away, not even when her hand found the arousal pressing the front of his kilt. She eased her fingers over its length through the fabric, her pulse fluttering as she felt every inch of him.

"No, lass." His voice was broken.

Zarabeth leaned her cheek on his back, enjoying touching him in a way she'd always wanted to. His staff was long and thick, and her cleft grew damp. She imagined him pressing his hardness into her and barely held back her groan.

"Gods, Zarabeth, stop."

"I don't want to," she whispered.

He made no move to push her away or still her hands. She loved the hard, full feel of him through the plaid. When she'd been eighteen, her innocence had run to kisses, but after she'd read about bedplay, her dreams of him had become specific and bawdy.

"*The Nvengarian Book of Seductions*," she said softly, "instructs a lady to measure her lover with a piece of ribbon and to keep it by her bedside as a reminder when he is absent."

"I've heard much about this *Book of Seductions*." He gasped. "Required reading, is it?"

"When a lady comes of age, she studies it most carefully."

"So she can drive a man mad?"

"I believe that is the intention."

His groan turned into a growl. He swung around and seized Zarabeth by the shoulders, backing her into the nearest standing stone. The magic from it seared her body, and she gasped at the heady sensation.

Even better was Egan leaning into her, his knee sliding between her legs. "Which seduction is this?"

Adolpho of Nvengaria's *Book of Seductions* was a practical manual, with elaborate seductions numbered one through three hundred and twenty. Each had specific accoutrements—dress, props, setting, and technique.

"I don't remember one for stone circles," she said.

"But ye remember others?"

"Oh, yes." She gave him an impish smile. "But do not worry. I am not one of your debutantes, chasing you through the halls of your castle to corner you."

"I keep telling ye, those young ladies were not mine."

"You didn't feel the least bit flattered by their determined pursuit?"

"No," he said flatly.

"You are a rare man, Egan MacDonald." She traced his cheek, fingers trembling.

"Are ye too cold, lass?"

"Not cold at all." Not with six feet and more of Highlander to warm her.

He pressed her shoulders into the stone and kissed her. No more slow, innocent exploring. He opened her mouth in hot, hungry strokes, lips and tongue demanding.

She melted back into the stone, feeling its magic surge through her body. Or perhaps it was her desires responding to Egan. She clutched his sleeves and closed her eyes, answering his kiss with a mouth as hungry as his.

Egan's hands left her shoulders. In a few swift moves, he pushed her cloak out of the way and unbuttoned the top of her bodice.

Her bosom swelled out into the cold, held in place by a small corset. The buds peeked over the top of the corset, the boning beneath her breasts holding her tight.

Still kissing her, Egan flicked one thumb over her nipple. She loved the feeling, the slow friction of his calloused skin. Her breasts were tight and hot, his touch a point of fire.

He would break away soon, as he always did. He'd

come to his senses and this sensation would be gone. And who knew when she could convince him to touch her again?

His tongue was strong in her mouth, pushing at her, probing. She had a heady vision of him pressing his tongue into her heat, and she shuddered hard.

She'd read the theory of such things, but never put it into practice. Her husband had taken her to bed only to produce a child—when he wanted, how he wanted. He'd needed a son to carry on his name and had been very angry that Zarabeth never conceived.

Egan would take her slowly, and it would be powerful.

I want this man, she thought desperately. She craved him with a hunger she hadn't imagined she could feel. She slid her arms around his waist and let her palms ease down to cup his buttocks through the kilt.

She couldn't read his mind, but she didn't need to this time. His restless fingers on her breasts and his hot kisses told her all she needed to know.

"Love," he whispered hoarsely. "Love, we have to stop."

"Not yet."

"They're watchin' us. My riders and your baron friend."

"They are too far away to see."

His breath scalded her. "Doesn't matter. I'll no' ravish ye out here with my men peering through the trees."

She pulled him against her, closing her hands on the tight roundness of his backside, loving the feel of his hardness against her abdomen. He wanted her, his desire made plain.

Very carefully, Egan eased himself away from her. She wanted so much to grab him and pull him back, but she made herself let him go. She had to agree—when he took her, she did not want his clansmen standing about laughing at them.

She knew exactly when and where she should seduce him, and she was both elated enough and upset enough by her newfound freedom to do it.

Zarabeth swallowed hard, hating her needy body. "You are right. We should go."

Egan let out his breath and quietly stepped away. They were both breathing hard, Egan's hair mussed and his face flushed as if he were drunk. With shaking fingers he pulled her placket over her bare breasts and buttoned the bodice.

"We go back now," he said.

"Yes."

He took her by the hand and led her out of the circle.

She remembered why he'd brought her here today: to tell her that she was no longer married to Sebastian. She was free. She could have Egan without breaking her vows; now she had only to find out whether he wanted her and how far his desire would go. Would she be like all the sighing ladies she'd met across Europe, fondly remembering their one night with him, and would she be able to bear that?

She was not certain she could.

As they stepped from the circle into the snow, Zarabeth thought she heard the stones murmur in satisfaction, but she couldn't be certain.

Christmas in Scotland was a quiet affair. Decrees in the time of Calvinistic reforms had declared Christmas just another day in an effort to distance it from the rather pagan rites of yuletide.

This did not keep the Highlanders from celebrating with a feast and the pipes and dancing until the small hours. In Nvengaria, yule was a full-blown affair, with mistletoe and a yule log and candles lit to Christian saints as well as to pagan gods. Nvengarians believed in honoring everyone, or at least any god that meant an extravagant celebration. Half of Zarabeth's married years had gone into planning the weeklong yule and Christmas feasts and balls, each one more magnificent than the last.

In Scotland, the Highlanders saved their exuberance for Hogmanay. Castle MacDonald burst with activity from Christmas to New Year's Eve, the servants and Highlanders both working to make Hogmanay a glorious celebration.

Angus and Hamish and Dougal brought in armloads of green boughs and let Gemma and Mary chivvy them to hang them here, there, and everywhere, and to change the hangings dozens of times.

Mrs. Williams baked and baked and baked. New Year's Eve supper would consist of venison and ham, shortbread, and a rich fruit tart called black bun. Zarabeth found herself helping Mary and Gemma and Mrs. Williams in the kitchen in the days before New Year's, cheerfully doing Mrs. Williams's bidding. Mary tried to prevent her, but Zarabeth insisted.

Zarabeth could make herself happy down in the kitchens, stirring batter and laughing with the female inhabitants of Castle MacDonald. She'd never had sisters, and her childhood girlfriends had faded into the woodwork after her marriage. She missed the girlish camaraderie, the jokes, the gossip, the laughter.

She was not afraid to go down into the cellars that Jamie called dungeons, and often ran down to fetch another bottle of wine or whiskey for Mrs. Williams while they cooked. Scottish cakes seemed to call for much whiskey. The kitchen maids were terrified of the dark cellar, but the former cells held no terror for Zarabeth. After living with Sebastian, she found a dank cellar full of bottles and old chains positively charming.

And Egan . . .

The man infuriated her. As much as he still insisted on keeping a close eye on her, he avoided being completely alone with her after their encounter at the Ring of Dunmarran.

He still bunked down outside her door in the drafty gallery, piling on blankets and fur rugs to keep warm. Whenever Zarabeth opened her door in the mornings, he'd be stretched out there like a great bear. A crotchety one, too, because he'd growl at her to go back inside until he could get himself up and out of the way.

Then he'd meet her at breakfast in the great hall, where he'd spring on her some outlandish thing he wanted her to do: fishing again, or horse racing in the snow, or visiting his tenant farmers and discussing the best points of pigs. Once she went with him to catch a few sheep that had strayed into the hills.

If she argued about going, he laughed at her and called her soft. In defiance she proved she had mettle enough to meet his every challenge.

In this way, Egan broke down the barriers her fear and self-preservation had erected. He let her remember what she'd been before she'd lived her life walking on eggshells. She recognized it and was grateful—if only he weren't so aggravating. Egan MacDonald never knew when to leave off.

New Year's Eve dawned crisp, clear, and bone-cold. Zarabeth spent most of the day in the warm kitchen, helping with the last-minute cooking. She'd learned to make bannocks and shortbread and even porridge, and she stirred the thick black bun that reeked of whiskey. When Mrs. Williams needed another measure of whiskey, Zarabeth readily trotted down the stairs to the cellars.

Despite the cold outside, the cellars were warm, insulated by the kitchen above and the thick earth and rock. It was dark as always, her candle a small circle of brightness.

Barrels of whiskey and dark bottles of wine and brandy marched in rows along the walls. The floor was swept clean, but the stones were uneven, making footing perilous.

A dark figure crouched in the corner, covered with fur. It gave a low growl as her candlelight touched it.

"Valentin?" she whispered. She held her candle higher, trying to see what kind of beast it was.

With a roar, the creature leaped at her. Zarabeth sidestepped just in time, and the shaggy body went tumbling end over end across the stones. The fur rugs fell away, and Jamie lay groaning in the middle of them.

Zarabeth leaned over him with her candle. "Are you all right?" she asked conversationally.

A great roaring laugh sounded behind her on the stairs. Egan came down and hauled Jamie to his feet. "I told you she wouldn't be frightened," he said, clapping his nephew on the shoulder.

Jamie winced. "All right, Uncle. Why did ye think I was Baron Valentin?" he asked Zarabeth.

Zarabeth hesitated, unsure how much she should reveal.

Egan answered, "He's a great one for jokes."

Jamie looked puzzled. "No, he isn't."

"Go on upstairs, lad. Ye had your fun."

Looking disgruntled, Jamie hauled the fur rugs into his arms and trundled up the stairs past him.

Zarabeth remained, clutching her candle, while Egan lounged against the door frame. This was the first time they'd been alone together since the stone circle.

"I've been meaning to ask ye . . ." Egan rumbled, his voice low.

Zarabeth's heart beat faster. "Yes?"

"Where is Valentin today? I haven't seen him."

Disappointment bit her. "I don't know. I've not seen him either."

"Well, if ye do, tell him I'm looking for him."

She swallowed. "I will."

He seemed to have forgotten all about pressing her against the stone and ravishing her mouth. She hadn't forgotten. She spent restless nights remembering the precise placement of his hands on her, and how he'd tasted.

"Come upstairs with me," he said. "This place is dank."

Her heart wished he'd meant go all the way upstairs with him, to his own room high in the castle, to make love with her. She knew he meant only that she should return to the kitchen, where the fire kept away the damp.

She snatched up the whiskey she'd come to fetch and started past him. He didn't move. When she was on the stair above him, she looked at him, nearly eye-to-eye.

His eyes were so dark in the shadows, gold flecks caught by the candlelight. She wished she knew whether he thought about their kisses or if they were a passing fancy for him.

Most people showed what they were thinking in their faces or eyes or the way they held their bodies. Really, it wasn't difficult to read people at all, even when she shielded herself from their direct thoughts.

Not Egan. His eyes could be blank, his face expressionless. He could show great mirth, anger, or frustration, but when Zarabeth wanted most to know what he thought, he could shut himself like an oyster.

His eyes betrayed nothing now. Stopping herself from heaving a sigh, she turned and walked up the stairs.

She felt his warm fingers on her elbow, guiding her up as he came behind her, but he released her at the top and turned to cajole Mrs. Williams into giving him a taste of the black bun. Mrs. Williams ran him off, and he whirled away, laughing. He never looked at Zarabeth.

The day was a whirlwind of activity. After all the cooking, they finally settled in the great hall to feast as darkness settled over the castle. The Rosses joined them, both blond men handsome in their most formal Ross kilts. Egan looked devastating as usual in his close-fitting frock coat and the MacDonald plaid around his shoulders.

Even Mary wore plaid tonight, a lovely dress in MacDonald tartan. Zarabeth wore plaid as well, loving being one of the MacDonalds. Egan, true to his word, had announced his intention of making her an honorary member of the clan. The others had enthusiastically cheered him.

Baron Valentin still had not appeared. When she had the chance, Zarabeth whispered her worry to Egan.

"He'll turn up," Egan said. "He's more comfortable on his own, I've noticed."

His words were nonchalant, but he looked troubled. Zarabeth wondered if Valentin were simply lying low to perform his role of first-footer.

The hard-faced baron had raised his brows when Zarabeth explained what a first-footer was, but he'd agreed to go along with the game. His blue eyes revealed little, but his thoughts showed amusement that he'd been chosen for the ritual.

She tried to cease worrying about him and enjoy the meal. Valentin was strong, fierce, and formidable, and could take care of himself.

They feasted long into the night, with Mrs. Williams and the red-haired maids bringing up platter after platter of food. The noise from the kitchens told Zarabeth that the castle servants were indulging themselves as much as the family was. She'd given Ivan and Constanz leave to join them.

Gemma made certain everyone knew which cakes Zarabeth had helped prepare, and everyone praised her or joked with her as the mood took them. Zarabeth glowed under their banter, for the first time in years truly feeling at home.

Near midnight, the household, including the servants, trooped to the front hall to ring in the New Year and welcome the first-footer.

Baron Valentin was supposed to, after the stroke of midnight, rap three times on the great door. Egan, as head of the house, would open the door to let him in. Valentin was to bring with him a stick of wood, a small measure of whiskey and one of salt, and the black bun Zarabeth had wrapped and put in his room. A stranger offering to share his fuel and supper with his hosts would be most welcome.

The great clock at the top of the stairs ponderously tolled the hour. Everyone turned expectantly to the door. The clock finished striking, the last chime dying away, and the chatter ceased.

Nothing happened.

Egan moved restlessly. She saw him exchange a look with Adam Ross, who shook his head.

Zarabeth swung toward the door again when she heard the latch lift. Valentin was supposed to have knocked, but Valentin often did things his own way.

The door swung open. Torches lit the foggy courtyard, and mists swirled around a figure in the ghostly light.

The man walked inside, pausing when he found the entire household assembled. He was tall, dark-haired, and Nvengarian, but he was not Baron Valentin.

Zarabeth shrieked.

Chapter Twelve
First-Footer

Father!"

The word echoed through the hall as Zarabeth launched herself past Egan to the man in the doorway. Olaf opened his arms for his daughter and swung Zarabeth off her feet.

Egan forced his heart back down from his throat, his pulse jumping. Bloody Nvengarians could give a man a heart attack.

Zarabeth was crying. She wiped tears of joy from her face and laughed shakily. "Welcome, Father. You're our first-footer."

Olaf looked perplexed, answering her in English. "Your what?"

Zarabeth tugged him around and presented her to the curious household. "This is my father, Olaf of Nvengaria. Father, these are . . . Egan's family."

Egan approached Olaf with mixed feelings. He was happy to see his old friend at the same time he couldn't forget what he'd done with Olaf's daughter. The passionate kiss—and beyond—with Zarabeth at the Ring of Dunmarran still floated in his mind.

Egan held out his hand and clasped the other man's strong one. "Well met. Or I should say, what the bloody hell are ye doin' here?"

Olaf smiled as he squeezed Egan's hand. "I wanted to see my daughter. And you, my old friend."

Zarabeth's eyes shone like sapphires. It struck Egan then that as much as she raved about Scotland and feared her former husband, Zarabeth was desperately homesick. She'd missed her father and her old life terribly. Now she clung to Olaf, love in her eyes.

Mary was thrilled to meet another Nvengarian aristocrat and instantly invited him into the great hall. The others followed, spirits rising in anticipation of more feasting and more whiskey.

As they filed in, Egan realized that in all the revelry, Baron Valentin still had not appeared. He waited for the last of his family to bustle into the great hall; then he slipped out of the castle.

In the quiet warmth of the stables, the mare greeted him with pricked ears and a whuff of hot breath. Her foal moved quickly to the front of the stall to see Egan. The swiftly growing foal was friendly and would follow Egan or Hamish or the grooms around like a dog.

Egan patted both mare and foal, but chose his steadier gelding to ride out into the night.

The fog had lowered, the air turning damp, and he knew there'd be more snow by morning. The night was not quiet, however. His tenants' cottages were alight with candles and torches, and a bonfire burned in the middle of the circle of houses.

Egan passed them by, although on any other New Year's he'd go down and join them. More firelight flickered in the distance, the next village with its bonfires. Everyone celebrated Hogmanay.

Egan turned from the homey fires to the cold of the open Highlands and rode off into the fog.

"Father, I have missed you so much." Several hours later, Zarabeth hugged her father on a window seat in a room Mary had hastily prepared for their visitor.

Her father's room was small, on the same floor as

Egan's. Angus had offered to let Olaf have the large chamber he shared with Gemma, but Olaf waved it off. There was only one of him, he said, he'd come unexpectedly, and he was happy just to have somewhere to lie.

The others still danced downstairs, and the strains of the fiddle and the drum wafted upward through the castle. The shrill of a bagpipe sounded somewhere out in the darkness.

Zarabeth hadn't seen her father since her wedding day. Firelight touched his face that would always be handsome to her, but emphasized lines that hadn't been there before and showed new gray threads in his black hair.

"Why have you come?" She'd been longing to ask that all night, but they'd been surrounded by Highlanders, without a moment to themselves.

"I did say," Olaf answered. They spoke Nvengarian, and Zarabeth felt a sweet relief that she could let her feelings flow in her native tongue. "I wanted to see you."

"But surely it was dangerous for you to make the journey."

Olaf's keen blue eyes missed nothing, and although Zarabeth knew he could not read minds like she could, he knew how to read people. She felt love emanating from him but also curiosity.

"Your old father is still up to facing a danger or two," he said. "Though our cousin Damien is not happy with me. It took much time to talk him into telling me where he'd sent you for protection, though I might have guessed. Egan always did have a soft spot for you."

A soft spot?

"He and his family have been very kind to me," Zarabeth said stiffly.

"They seem like kind people," Olaf agreed.

They fell silent, the notes of the joyful music below filling in the space.

"Egan seems different here," she said after a time. "He's still teases me something wretched, but he's very much in command. The others argue with him—loudly—but they obey him."

"He is laird. He explained it to me. It means he's a landholder, but it's more than that. He's their protector."

"He doesn't want to be." She explained the fiasco with Jamie and Mary trying to marry him off to one of the two anxious debutantes. Olaf began to laugh, a sound Zarabeth had sorely missed.

"Mary wants him wed because she thinks it high time he starts a family," she concluded. "But Egan wants to pass the lairdship to Jamie because of his brother. I've told him Charlie's death wasn't his fault—I don't know why he continues to blame himself—"

"I do," Olaf interrupted.

Zarabeth blinked. "You do?"

He nodded. "When Egan regained his health after we found him, he and I had many long talks. He was a very troubled young man."

"Can you tell me why? I am struggling to understand him."

Olaf barked a laugh. "I don't think anyone will truly understand Egan MacDonald."

That was very true. "He told me his father was angry at him for Charlie's death," Zarabeth said. "Adam Ross told me Egan's father even cut his portrait to ribbons. As though Egan should have tied up Charlie in his tent before the battle."

"That isn't everything," Olaf said in a gentle voice. "Egan had grown used to disappointing his father, more's the pity. What Egan can't forgive himself for is losing Charlie."

Zarabeth frowned. "But I've just said Egan couldn't have prevented Charlie from riding to battle."

"No, I mean *lost him* in the literal sense, child. After

the battle, Egan could not find Charlie's body. A blast during the battle had pulled down some of the walls on top of the bodies of Charlie and his men. What was underneath was a terrible jumble, with uniforms burned beyond recognition and limbs scattered, faces destroyed. Egan could never discover which of those poor broken men was Charlie."

"Dear God." Zarabeth imagined Egan, blood and grime on his face, sifting through the carnage. Knowing his brother was there and not finding him, searching frantically . . .

A tear trickled down her cheek. "Poor Egan."

"He brought a body back, so disfigured that no one could tell who it was, and helped his father bury him. Egan never knew if it was truly his brother. Perhaps some other family keeps Charlie's grave."

"And Egan never told anyone?"

Olaf shook his head. "He could stand his father blaming him for the death, but he'd never be able to explain that he'd had no idea which was Charlie's body. Egan quit Scotland and did some determined traveling on the Continent, which was how he ended up in Nvengaria for you to find."

"I'm glad I did find him," she whispered. "He would have died that night if I hadn't seen him, wouldn't he?"

"He's lucky you were such a watchful little girl."

Zarabeth remembered how she'd begged her father to stop the carriage on that brutal winter's night eleven years ago. She'd thought at first that she'd read Egan's mind, heard him silently calling for help, but later she'd learned she could not read him at all.

Then how had she known he was there? The darkness had been complete, snow falling, and she'd been snuggled warm in the coach with her mother and father. She should have passed on by and never noticed him.

Likewise, Egan had found her on the black rocks of

the Devil's Teeth, washed up by the sea, saying he'd heard her call out when she never had. Some magic was at work here that she didn't understand.

She peered out into the night, watching snow begin to fall. Egan had gone to look for Valentin; she knew that even though he'd not announced it. She wondered if she'd hear him again, calling out in the night.

Egan found Valentin huddled in his wolf form behind a standing stone in the Ring of Dunmarran.

Valentin snarled a warning, his blue eyes mad with rage and pain, as Egan slid from his horse. The gelding jerked the reins out of Egan's hand and bolted, the horse's dark rump disappearing into the fog and snow.

"Idiotic beastie," Egan called after him.

Valentin growled, his lips peeled back from knife-sharp teeth. The ground around him was dark with blood.

"Damn you too," Egan told him. "What happened to ye?" He crouched down, well out of the wolf's reach. "Can ye even understand me?"

Valentin's black fur glowed in the ghostly light of the fog, blue eyes piercing. Wolves had yellow eyes, Egan thought irrelevantly, but Valentin's kept their color when he changed.

"I can't leave ye here," Egan went on. "I'd have to face Zarabeth and tell her I didn't help ye. And ye know what she'd say."

The wolf watched him, his snarl quieting but fury remaining in his eyes.

"She'd say, 'Egan MacDonald, can't ye even look after one wolf? And ye call yerself a laird.' And she'd tell her father on me. He's here. Prince Olaf."

The wolf jerked upright, alert.

"Ah, that's interested ye. He arrived tonight—was our first-footer, what ye were supposed to be."

The wolf tried to rise, and Egan saw the wound, a bloody hole where his foreleg met his shoulder.

"What happened to ye?" Egan repeated softly.

Valentin buckled into a heap, staining the ground with more blood.

"Stay quiet, now." Egan began creeping forward. "I need to help ye, but it's best ye stay a wolf and stay warm."

Valentin subsided, watching warily as Egan made his way toward him.

"Someone shot ye, did they? A Highlander thinkin' ye were out to steal his sheep? Or someone else?"

The wolf's hot breath hissed between his teeth. As Egan leaned forward, Valentin's form shimmered and became demon.

Egan leaped back and rolled out of the way as the demon launched itself at him.

"Damnation," he muttered as Valentin's clawed hand came down. "This is why I hate logosh."

He got Valentin back to the house by at last persuading the man to shift back into his wolf form and let Egan carry him across his shoulders. Egan was bloodstained and exhausted by the time he reached the castle gate, much of it from fighting off Valentin's instinctive attacks. He'd finally got through the man's pain by admonishing him to protect Zarabeth. He must focus on that—helping Zarabeth.

Egan lowered Valentin to the stones of the courtyard. He could hear the fiddler playing away inside and the lively pounding of the drum.

"Ye'd better become a man," he told the limp pile of fur at his feet. "There'll be a fuss, but unless ye want to explain why you're a wolf . . ."

Valentin opened his eyes a slit. He made no noise, but

shimmered and became a man lying on the pavement, his skin caked with blood.

The door of the castle swung open, and Mary of all people ran out. "Egan, I thought I heard you out here." She stopped in horror at the sight of Valentin.

"He's hurt. Shot. Help me get him inside."

Mary stared at Valentin as though she'd never seen him before. He was stark naked, his clothes who knew where. When he was shifting, Egan had come to understand, a logosh's clothes didn't vanish—he had to remove them first or painfully tear them free.

"Mary," Egan said impatiently.

Mary shook herself, looking at Egan in a daze. "I'll get some blankets."

"Make no noise," he said. "I don't want the lot of them swarming out here."

Mary nodded and disappeared into the house, returning quickly with a pile of blankets. Egan wrapped them around Valentin's limp form, and Mary held the door open so Egan could carry him into the house. Egan lugged the unconscious man upstairs, Mary following anxiously.

The revelry in the great hall drifted up the staircase and into the bedchamber even after Mary closed the door. Valentin lay motionless on the bed, his face gray, his side covered in blood.

"He'll need a decent surgeon," Egan said, "t' find out whether the bullet's still inside."

"Who shot him?"

"I don't know, but I'll wager Zarabeth's husband is still after her, the bastard."

Mary, surprisingly, volunteered to stay with Valentin while Egan sent for a surgeon and broke the news to Zarabeth. Mary was calm, keeping the cloth pressed to Valentin's wound, no hysterics or distress. Egan patted her shoulder in thanks and left her to it.

Zarabeth and her father were not in the great hall. Egan took Hamish and Angus aside and spoke to them awhile; then his two cousins went out into the night. Adam came to see what was wrong, and Egan gave him the task of quietly ending the evening's revelry. Returning to Valentin's chamber, he found Zarabeth and Olaf already there.

Mary sat at Valentin's side, wiping his face with a damp cloth. The man was swathed in blankets but he shivered, his face too pale. Zarabeth stood on the other side of the bed, her hands clasped, blue eyes wide.

"Poor man," Zarabeth said when Egan came in. "If he dies . . ."

She did not need to finish. He saw the same rage reflected in her eyes that he felt in himself. Whoever did this would pay.

Olaf, on the other hand, showed no sympathy. He remained ramrod stiff and stared at Valentin with near hatred. Egan raised his brows at him, and Olaf turned, his expression furious. "Damien sent *him* to protect my daughter?"

"Yes," Zarabeth answered. "Why? He has been a most formidable protector so far, and there was nothing he could do on the ship—it happened so fast."

Olaf glared at Valentin's unmoving body. "Because he is a murderer, that is why. A trained assassin, an enemy of the state."

After her father's announcement, Egan shepherded Zarabeth and Olaf to Zarabeth's chamber. Mary remained with Valentin, the only one unmoved by Olaf's declaration. She turned her back on them and went on wiping Valentin's face, as though happy to have them out of the sickroom.

Once Egan closed the door in Zarabeth's chamber, her father told them a shocking tale—Valentin had tried to assassinate Damien and Grand Duke Alexander right after Damien had taken the throne, attempting to knife Damien while he ate supper with his wife.

Valentin had been thrown in prison and remained there for nearly a year, Olaf said. So why had Damien released him and told him to accompany Zarabeth on her journey to Scotland?

"Damien would not have sent him without reason," Zarabeth argued.

"Was the journey Damien's idea?" her father asked. "Or Valentin's?"

"Damien's." Zarabeth clenched her hands. "Damien guided me out of the palace himself. We met Valentin and the footmen in a tunnel that led out into the hills. Damien kissed me good-bye and told me that Baron Valentin would protect me."

"I'm inclined to agree with Zarabeth," Egan said. "Damien is a shrewd judge of character. He would no' have sent Valentin if he couldn't be trusted."

"There is something damn strange going on," Olaf growled.

Egan chuckled. "I agree with ye. That's what always happens when I deal with Nvengarians. But there's little we can do until Valentin wakes up and tells his side of the story."

"I suppose," Olaf said, scowling.

Egan cast a wary eye on him. Nvengarians were notorious for taking matters into their own hands, and Zarabeth saw Egan worry that Olaf would simply stick a knife into Valentin's chest—end of problem.

She'd have to explain that her father did not do things like that. Olaf was a fair man, although she had to admit her father looked grimly angry.

Egan declared that there was nothing left to do that night. He admonished Zarabeth to go to bed and Olaf to do the same. They parted for the evening, Egan giving Zarabeth a long look before he left her.

The surgeon arrived to work on Valentin soon after that. He removed the bullet and said that, providing the man took no infection, Valentin would be fine. His arm had been broken, but not irreparably.

Zarabeth went to bed after she heard this welcome news, but sleep eluded her for some time—her father's arrival, Valentin's injury, and her father's announcement about Valentin had left her excited and restless. She at last drifted off but was awakened by voices in the small hours of the morning.

Zarabeth sat up. The room was black save for the glowing fire, dawn breaking very late this far north not long after the winter solstice.

She strained to listen but heard nothing outside the door. The voices had been a faint whisper in her dreams and then they were gone.

Zarabeth rose and crept across the room. Egan made her lock herself in at night, so she softly turned the key in the lock and opened the door.

Egan lay across the doorway like a great bear, wrapped in blankets and fur rugs on a long cot. He slept, his snore evident.

Quick footsteps sounded on the stairs. Zarabeth peered into the gloom, starting when she saw a figure on the stairs.

She relaxed when she realized it was Constanz on one of his patrols. He opened his mouth, but she pressed her finger to her lips and shook her head. Constanz acknowledged her and went back down the stairs just as Egan emitted a particularly loud snore.

Strange that the voices had not wakened Egan, but Zarabeth might have dreamed them. Sometimes another's forceful dreams would whisper into hers, although that had not happened since she was a very little girl. Her mother, who could also read thoughts, had trained Zarabeth to block out thoughts, even in sleep, but with so many people in the castle and so many emotions spinning, someone's dreams could have gotten through.

One thing was for certain: she had a perfect opportunity to confound Egan MacDonald.

She began by pulling off the topmost cover, slowly dragging the fur into her room. Egan grunted a little in his sleep, but didn't wake.

Zarabeth pulled off the next blanket, and the next. The last was tricky because he had wrapped it firmly around himself and pinned it beneath his arms.

She tugged at the blanket, trying to ease it from under him. Egan's strength prevented that—she couldn't even budge him.

Finally she simply had to yank the blanket away. Egan came awake, clad only in a kilt pinned around his hips. He rolled off the cot into Zarabeth's chamber, his mouth open to roar.

Zarabeth slammed her finger to her lips and leaned around him to close the door. She surreptitiously turned the key in the lock.

"What are ye doin'?" Egan asked in a hoarse whisper. "What's the matter?"

Zarabeth dropped the last blanket and stepped back to stare at him. "You're sleeping in only a kilt now?"

He looked down at himself, naked from the waist up, his legs bare from the knees down. She watched the blush spread across his face. " 'Tis comfortable."

And delectable. His hair hung loose about his shoulders, dark curls mussed with sleep. His wide chest bore creases from the blankets, the wiry hair there as mussed as that on his head. His kilt dipped below his waist, giving her a tantalizing glimpse of his bare hips.

He stared her down, his eyes glittering in the darkness. "Has someone tried to hurt ye?"

She shook her head. She didn't want to stop looking at him.

Egan watched her a moment; then his muscles rippled in a shrug. "Well, if you're all right, I'll restore my bed."

He leaned down and gathered up his blankets, hips and thighs moving tantalizingly under his plaid. He reached for the door handle and found the door locked.

He swung around, puzzled. Zarabeth held up the key.

Egan scowled. "What game are ye playin'?"

He dropped the blankets and came for her, clearly intending to yank the key from Zarabeth's hand. She twirled out of the way as he lunged for her, and he came to rest with his backside against the bed.

"You're mad, lass. Give me the key."

Zarabeth smiled and flung the key to the other side of the room, where it clanked to the carpet. She put both hands on his chest and pushed him.

Egan's heels slid on the carpet and he fell back, half on the bed. Before he could recover, Zarabeth twisted off the ornate pin that held his kilt closed. The plaid slithered from his hips to the floor, leaving him bare as the day he was born.

Zarabeth's mouth went dry, but she held up the pin in triumph.

Chapter Thirteen
Hogmanay Night

Lass," Egan said in a stunned voice.

Zarabeth stood before him with the pin in her hand, her blue eyes sparkling.

His dreams of her had already made him hard, and he'd gone completely rigid when she'd shown him the key in her hand, a roguish little smile on her face.

The hollow of her throat was damp, and tendrils of her dark hair curled against her face. She smelled sweet, like sleep and herself, and her bed would be warm with the heat of her body.

She let her gaze rove downward to rest on his needy, rampant cock. He could never pretend he wanted to be only friends with her with it waving like a flag.

Zarabeth did not seem at all dismayed. She walked closer, her bare feet whispering on the floor, her gaze hot and blue. She placed her hand on his chest, fingers splayed right over his heart.

"My Highlander," she murmured, a sweet lilt in her voice.

Egan couldn't catch his breath. He should shove her aside, grab the key and his kilt, and get the hell out of that room. But he couldn't move. He who could have scooped her over his shoulder as easy as anything was pinned in place by her light, slender fingers.

"My Highlander," she repeated in a whisper.

He saw the hunger in her eyes. Women had been

hungry for him before, but they'd simply wanted a male in their beds, a skilled lover. Zarabeth wanted *him*, Egan, and he saw the difference.

The difference made his body roasting hot and rock-hard.

"Lass, you're killin' me."

Consternation flickered through her eyes, followed by another smile. She thought he was teasing.

Her fingers traveled his body, skimming over the ridges of his abdomen, across the flat of his pelvis, all the way down to his arousal. He groaned, heartfelt.

Zarabeth looked at him in surprise. But how could he not react? Her beautiful, questing fingers heated his skin, and he wanted her so much he throbbed with it.

Egan clenched his hands as she explored his cock, tracing the flange and the very tip. He was ready to grab her and fling her onto the bed, rip the night rail open to reveal her lovely body. Ready to part her legs and thrust himself inside her.

No preparing her, no tenderness, just lust that raced through him and made him insane.

She deserved better than that. Her husband had used her; she didn't need to be used by the man she called her friend.

She continued to touch his staff, her gaze riveted to it as though she were fascinated. He could tell she'd never touched a man like this before—her touch was too tentative, too light, and she hesitated a long time before she dipped her hand to trace his balls.

"Will you lie on the bed for me?" she asked shyly. "Please?"

I'm going to die right now, and it will be worth it.

Egan touched her cheek, loving the absolute softness of her skin. "Ye shouldn't be so beautiful when ye say that."

She blushed, but her eyes glinted with mischief. He

obliged her by lying back across the covers of her bed. This put him at exactly the right height for her to lean over him, rest her hands on either side of him, and fit her mouth over his cock.

Reason disappeared. All he felt was her hot breath on him, the wetness of her tongue, the swift scrape of her teeth. She was not schooled at this. She'd learned the theory, but not the practice, which meant he must be the first man she'd tasted thus. The thought absurdly pleased him. It also confirmed that her husband had been a complete fool.

Down comforters cradled Egan's back, a counterpoint to the warmth of her hands and the madness up and down his stem. He wound his hands through her hair, peeling apart her braid to let her thick curls fall onto his body.

He'd dreamed of this plenty of times, Zarabeth pleasuring him while he threaded his fingers through her silken hair, but the reality was so much better. His Zarabeth, learning the ways of pleasure on him.

He couldn't stand it. His muscles strained as he stopped himself from seizing her and taking her any way he wanted. Part of him urged, *Yes, have her!* Another place in his mind said, *No, don't hurt her; she is too fragile.*

His fragile lady nibbled his tip.

Egan roared, not caring who heard. He dragged her up to him, glorying in the friction of her nightdress across his bare body. He rolled her onto the feather bed and opened her mouth with his.

They sank into the down, Egan's lips slanting over hers, hungrily taking her. Zarabeth made a little noise in her throat, not of protest, but surrender.

He broke the kiss, and she clutched at him desperately. Her eyes were dark, lids heavy, her lips swollen and moist.

"Please," she whispered. "Please, Egan."

"Ye should leave me." Of course she wouldn't—this was *her* bedroom—but logic was not in the forefront of his brain.

"I don't want to. I need you."

Her soft admission broke him. He eased his weight off her long enough to hurriedly unbutton her night rail.

Her breasts came into view, soft mounds he'd bared in the Ring of Dunmarran. The same madness he'd felt in the stone circle permeated him as he tugged the night rail open to her waist.

Her lush body beckoned him, her waist curving to full hips, her naval a sweet oval. He leaned down and licked it, and she squirmed, laughing.

She stopped laughing when Egan smiled evilly and ripped the nightdress open all the way down.

Zarabeth gasped. Egan's smile vanished as their bodies pressed together, heat and sweat sealing them. His arousal lay heavy against her hip, and her breasts pressed against his pounding chest.

Everything slowed. He felt her warm breath on his face, smelled the scents of Zarabeth and the faint perfume she always wore. Not a heavy scent, just a light spice, a whiff of which could make him long for her.

Her hair had come all the way unbound, the black glory of it snaking around her. He wanted to bury himself in her hair, drag it across his throat, kiss it. Kiss *her*.

Her lashes swept down once, twice, his Zarabeth once more shy. Her eyes were midnight blue in the dark room, her gaze returning to his in hope.

She wanted him to take her. He saw in her eyes that she'd planned this, down to getting him into the room and tossing away the key. She'd seduced him.

"Lass," he said against her cheek. "You're a vixen."

For answer she kissed him on the corner of his mouth. Well, she'd pay for her seduction.

He slid his hand between her thighs, finding her wet and hot and ready. He nudged her legs open and pressed his tip to her opening.

They lay face-to-face, breath-to-breath, while he let her get used to him. She slid languid fingers through his hair, her eyes half-closed.

He shuddered. It was all he could do to stay calm, not to take her in a frenzy. She smiled at him, completely trusting. She thought she was still in control, that she could seduce him and have everything her way.

She was wrong.

Egan could do what he liked, and she couldn't stop him. Some ladies enjoyed that, thrilled at a frisson of fear as they surrendered control to him, wondering what he'd do.

Zarabeth only smiled, believing her Highlander would never hurt her.

She was right.

Egan very carefully took his weight on his hands and eased himself inside her. Her smile widened, and she skimmed her hands across his back.

He kissed her long and slow while she bent her knees, drawing her legs up and lifting her hips. He gently rocked in and out of her, gradually increasing his speed while he clenched his fists on the feather bed.

"Zarabeth." His voice was ragged.

He needed her, had needed this woman for the five years since he'd first kissed her. He'd roamed the world—seeking what, he did not know—moving restlessly from place to place, never wanting to come home.

Because Zarabeth hadn't been here. Castle MacDonald had been a *place* to him, not a home—it never had been a home. It was his father's house, and Charlie's, never Egan's in spirit.

Now that Zarabeth had come, he never wanted to leave.

But she'd leave him. She'd return to Nvengaria with her father once it was safe to live there, and Castle Mac-Donald would be cold and empty for him again.

He couldn't let that happen.

Egan let out a groan as his control snapped. Zarabeth gasped, then laughed out loud as he started to pump swiftly into her, the bed rocking and creaking.

She arched to him, lips parting in a soft sound of pleasure. Her faint moan, the passionate softness on her face, and the way she squeezed him finished it for him. He drove hard into her, spilling his seed into her welcome heat.

She writhed and laughed, enjoying every last second before he collapsed on top of her, breathing like a man running from what he feared most.

Zarabeth lay very still as Egan's weight covered her like the best blanket. His ragged breath heated her skin, and his sweat-soaked body was slick under her fingers.

She carefully said nothing. She couldn't bear it if he leaped away from her, snatching up his kilt to flee, leaving her bereft and cold.

He did none of these things. He kissed her face with swollen lips, mouth and tongue traveling over her cheeks, along her jaw, pausing to suckle her earlobe. He devoured her like he couldn't get enough.

Zarabeth put her arms around him and held on, scarcely daring to believe this was real. She'd made love with her Highlander, and he'd smiled at her and made her feel giddy and wanted. No wonder ladies across Europe had giggled madly when Zarabeth had admitted that, yes, she was great friends with Egan MacDonald of Scotland.

When she'd taken him into her mouth he'd tasted of salt and warmth, a heady spice. His staff had been smooth and tight, unlike what she'd thought it would feel like. She'd never tasted a man there before, never had the desire to.

Never until she had Egan stretched out before her, his hardness thick and ready for her. She hadn't been able to stop herself from licking him, tasting him, nibbling on him. How splendid that she could drive him mad with just the flick of her tongue.

Sleep began to come to her, and she didn't want it. Zarabeth knew that if she fell asleep, he'd be gone when she awoke.

Egan slid off her to land on his side against her, his leg twining with hers. He smoothed her hair from her face, and smiled, his eyes warm.

"Are ye sleepy, love?"

She nodded, still not trusting herself to speak.

"Before ye sleep, I want to do something for ye."

She couldn't imagine what. She nodded again.

Egan pulled the loose bedcovers around them, tucking them into a warm nest. Under the covers he smoothed her breast, circling the areola with his thumb until the nipple tightened into a hard peak.

A fiery tingle spread through her body, and then Egan's fingers were between her thighs, finding her sensitive places. He began massaging and rubbing, tickling and teasing, fingers moving swiftly and surely over her bud.

Zarabeth had never felt anything like it. She'd thought herself sleepy, but her eyes widened and her body came off the bed, eager for his touch. She screamed, and he laughed and caught her cries in his mouth.

She continued to writhe, her hips grinding against his palm. The intensity of it was incredible and flowed over her in huge waves.

Egan wound her to an unbearable point, and just when she thought she couldn't stand any more, he rolled onto her and entered her once more. The frenzy with which he rode her far eclipsed what they'd done the first time. She screamed like a wanton and begged him to take her harder, faster.

At last he groaned again, his hips stilling, and she came crashing down to the bed. She was awake, wide-awake, but at the same time utterly spent.

Egan kissed her for a long time, as greedily as before; then he rolled off her and tucked her with him into the blankets. As her body stopped moving, black sleep hit her. She reached for Egan, whispered, "Don't leave me," then fell into the abyss.

Baron Valentin's blue eyes snapped open, and Mary jerked back. The room was dark except for the firelight and a few candles, but his eyes seemed to glow.

He snaked one hand around her wrist, his fingers like steel pincers, and snarled words that sounded like nonsense.

"I don't understand," she said breathlessly. "Is that Nvengarian? I never learned it."

He growled in frustration, and then before Mary's startled eyes, his hand started to *change*. His fingers grew long and misshapen, his skin gray and mottled like a snake's. She tried to wrench herself away from him, biting back a scream when she couldn't escape his strength.

Suddenly, he released her and thumped back to the pillow. Heart racing, Mary ran for the door.

"Do not go." A hoarse whisper behind her pulled her up short. "Please."

Mary turned. Valentin lay exhausted on the bed, the white bandage on his shoulder stark against his chest. His skin was darker than a Highlander's, a line of jet-black hair feathering across his pectorals.

His hand had returned to normal, his face wan with fatigue. He regarded her with tired eyes, the glow gone.

Mary felt a twinge of remorse and returned quietly to the bedside. Her arm ached where he'd seized her, but she would not abandon him when he was so ill.

She sat down, reaching for the cool cloth to wipe his brow.

"What happened to me?" he whispered.

"You don't remember? Someone shot you. Egan found you out by the Ring of Dunmarran—without your clothes."

"Who shot me?" He grasped her arm again, but this time kept his touch light. "It is important."

"You don't know?"

"I don't remember it at all."

"Egan didn't see anyone. He found only you."

"Is Zarabeth hurt?"

"No," she assured him. "She is safe in her room, and Egan is guarding her."

"Thank God."

He subsided but kept his hand on her forearm, blunt fingers brushing her skin as though to make up for hurting her. She chose not to ask how his hand had seemed to change into that of a monster. Egan had told her that Nvengaria was full of magic and magical people, and Mary believed him. She had been raised a Scotswoman—her childhood filled with tales of selkies and brownies and Fair Folk and the mischievous Red Cap, until she half believed them.

"The shot was clean, the surgeon said," Mary told him briskly. "If you rest and we keep the wound clean, you should take no harm from it."

He touched her face. She stopped, mesmerized, letting the cloth drip water on her skirt.

"You are lonely," he said softly.

"No." Her voice sounded raw and wrong. "I have Dougal, and Egan, and my cousins and friends."

His fingers slid down to rest between her breasts. "Your heart is lonely. I can feel it."

She could feel it too. Her husband, Neil, had been popular in Edinburgh, but he hadn't been much interested in the wife he'd married to give him an heir. Mary had enjoyed being a hostess, had thrilled with pride when Dougal was born—and then discovered that her husband was an inveterate gambler who'd run through his fortune and hers.

Neil had taken sick and died when he'd learned of his complete ruin, leaving Mary and Dougal penniless. Egan had paid the debts and brought Mary home to recover.

It had taken years before she'd gotten over the shame, and she'd lost her trust in dashing, handsome men. She'd had a brief, discreet affair with an Englishman this year, but she'd been unable to engage her heart and had parted from him.

"I choose to be lonely," she said.

Valentin did not answer. He traced her cheek, sliding his fingers to the line of her hair. Before Mary could stop herself she leaned over him, closing her eyes as their lips met.

He made a noise in his throat, and then he was kissing her brutally, lips opening hers and tongue probing her mouth. He tasted wild, like midnight air—dark and exciting.

Mary had never had a kiss this fierce. She found herself responding, her lips as bruising as his, her heart hammering. His unhurt hand slid through her hair, loosening her curls.

For an injured man he was very strong, and she knew he could do to her what he wanted. The thought should have frightened her, but exhilaration tingled through her body, and she knew she'd not even try to stop him.

"Mary," he murmured against her skin. "Your name, it is beautiful."

She felt herself blush. " 'Tis plain and dull."

"No. Simple and lovely."

He kissed her again, slowly this time, as though memorizing her taste.

All at once he thumped back to the pillow, his strength spent. Mary sat up in alarm, realizing the wet cloth had soaked through her skirt. Valentin's face was gray again, his breathing shallow, but his hand locked around hers as his eyes slid closed.

"Stay with me, Mary. Do not let them . . ."

His words trailed away to silence. Sick with fear, Mary put her hand over his heart but found it beating hard and strong.

"Do not let them what?" She bit her lip as he lay silently, but she closed her hand over his and held it tight. "Don't worry," she said, though she knew he couldn't hear. "I won't leave you alone. I promise."

Chapter Fourteen
The Ancient Tunnels
of Castle MacDonald

When Zarabeth swam awake again, the window was gray with dawn. She tried to sit up but found the bulk of Egan pressed against her side.

She sank down with relief. He hadn't left her.

Egan was awake. He smiled at her, the gold flecks in his eyes alive with warmth.

"Good morning, love. Ye slept well?"

"You know I did." She pushed hair out of her eyes, realizing she must look horrible. Whenever she'd dreamed of having Egan in her bed, she'd forgotten that she'd look like she always did in the morning, her face lined with sleep and her hair everywhere. "What happened exactly?"

"Ye mean ye don't remember?" He grinned. "'Tis a bit unflattering."

"Of course I remember. I mean . . ." She blushed, suddenly tongue-tied. "I mean, when you touched me . . . when you were in me it felt wonderful, but when you touched me it was more than I could stand."

His brows shot up. "Ye never?"

"I never felt anything like it. What was that?"

A teasing light entered his eyes. "But ye told me ye studied treatises and books all about the art of lovemaking. Ye've never heard of orgasm?"

"How do you say that in Nvengarian?"

He started to laugh. "I have no bloody idea. I only

know the naughty Nvengarian, no' the refined words for it." He rubbed his finger along her cheek. "But it sounds t' me like ye had your first one."

"It seems that theory and practice are two different things."

His laughter shook the bed. "Aye. It also says that your husband didn't take proper care of ye."

"I don't wish to talk about my husband."

"I know." He cuddled her close, but his eyes shuttered to her. "I know ye don't, love."

"I like it here. With you."

"I know."

She bit her lip. "But I'll have to leave. Nvengaria is where I belong. That is likely why my father came, to take me back when it's time."

"Mayhap."

Zarabeth wanted to stay in this castle with this strong man the rest of her life—going would tear away an irreplaceable part of her. Egan smiled at her as though he weren't contemplating much more than what Mrs. Williams was cooking for breakfast.

"You'll let me stay, then?" she ventured.

He stroked her hair. "We'll talk about what happens to ye when the time comes. Your father says Nvengaria is still not safe, so you'll stay for now. We'll worry about later, later."

"Very philosophical."

Egan shrugged, muscles rippling in splendid strength. "Scots are philosophical."

And handsome and strong and wonderful lovers. She brushed her fingers across his chest and rested them on his armband. It was silver, its pattern an intricate interlaced design she'd seen on some of the weapons in the great hall.

"Why do you wear this? I don't remember you with it before."

He touched it. "Something m' mother left me, from her side of the family. She was a MacLean, a distant cousin of Gemma's. I'd had it up in my chamber since her death." He shrugged. "When I came home this time I decided to wear it."

"It looks old."

"Aye, supposedly handed down through the centuries."

Perhaps he'd taken to wearing it because he'd decided he'd have no son to pass it to. The thought made her sad. "You don't speak much of your mother."

"She was long-suffering, married to my father. She died when I was at university."

"I'm sorry."

"She was a kind woman, but got pushed aside by my father. And she wasn't like Gemma, strong enough to take matters into her own hands. I was surprised she made sure I had this." He touched the band again. "But the day after she died, I found it in the drawer in my bedside table. She wore it as a necklet or around her head like a diadem, but 'tis too delicate for my thick neck." He smiled a little.

"I like it where it is. Something for you to remember her by."

"Aye, I suppose it is."

It was; he was trying not to admit to doing something sentimental. "She was lucky to have such a son," Zarabeth said.

"Was she?"

"Of course. And I am lucky to have you as a friend. What would I do without my Highlander?"

"Likely get more sleep." To her disappointment, he threw aside the covers and rolled out of bed.

He was a splendid sight. His tall body was well proportioned and moved with grace. Zarabeth's gaze riveted to his well-muscled thighs as he bent to retrieve his kilt from the floor beside the bed.

"Don't go yet," she said.

He slung the kilt around his hips. "I want to, before anyone sees me coming out of your room."

She reached for him, closing her fingers on the wool plaid. She knew she was being shameless, but she couldn't bear to lose him.

"Please, Egan."

He looked down at her, not pulling away, but she couldn't see what was in his eyes.

"May we . . ." The words stuck in her throat, and she tried again. "May we be lovers?"

A faint smile flickered on his mouth. "I thought we just were."

"No, I mean for longer than one night."

"An affair, ye mean?"

"Yes, I think so."

He was quiet for a long time, the folds of his plaid hanging still. "Is that really what ye want?"

She released him, her face heating. "If it's not what you want, then never mind."

Egan sat on the bed again, quiet. "It's not something to do lightly, lass. It makes ye a certain sort of woman in the eyes of the world. Is that what ye want?"

Zarabeth dragged the covers to her chin, hiding her body. "What I don't want is for you to patronize me. I am a woman of the world. . . ."

"No, ye are not." His hand came down on her arm with weight. "Ye have no idea what the world can do to ye. You are innocent, despite all your talk about learning things the Nvengarian way. I said I wouldn't ruin ye, and I won't."

"We must always play by your rules," she said bitingly.

"I am the laird." He stood up. "And we aren't play-ing. This is no game."

"And I am no schoolroom miss. I was five years married and hosted gatherings for the very top of

Nvengarian society. You don't have a dozen dukes and duchesses staying in your house without learning a thing or two about the world."

"Aye, now you're about to remind me how sophisticated is Nvengaria and how backward is Scotland."

"I don't know enough about Scotland to make a judgment."

"Lass." Egan's voice gentled, and she saw him try not to smile. "Ye are not a worldly woman, ye are still the daughter of a close friend, and I don't plan to be the man who ruins ye."

Her anger mounted. "Well, you have made it plain how you feel. Go and have your breakfast."

He rose, smoothing a lock from her forehead, then wrapped the kilt around him, hiding his delightful nakedness. "Ye rest now. I'll see how Valentin is faring."

She fumed. Was he admonishing her for not rushing to see if her bodyguard was all right?

"Oh, do go away," she snapped.

To her surprise, he grinned at her, like the sun coming out from behind a cloud. "That I can do."

He walked unerringly to the key she'd flung away, picked it up, and went to the door.

She put aside her anger long enough to admire his backside as he bent for the key, but the knowing look he gave her as he exited made her rage flare again.

No matter how long she lived, Egan would not see her as she wanted him to. He could make love to her like an angel, but he'd never equate her with the countesses and duchesses he'd wooed across the continent.

He hadn't wanted to come to her bed at all—she'd had to trick him into it. And he couldn't see that of all the lovely ladies across Europe who sighed over Egan MacDonald, Zarabeth needed him the most. She needed her old friend who fished with her and raced horses with her to take her in his arms and make everything better.

She lay down again, burying her face in his warmth and scent that lingered in the sheets.

Hamish grinned at Egan as he made his way to the great hall for breakfast. The place was still a mess from Hogmanay revelry, with Zarabeth's footmen sleepily tidying up.

Egan tried to tell the lads not to bother—Hogmanay would continue for several more days, and the house would be a wreck in the end. They'd all sleep it off, then dive into putting the castle to rights again. The footmen stubbornly continued to work.

"So, cousin," Hamish rumbled as Egan piled sausages, potatoes, bannocks, and toasted bread on his plate. "Worked up an appetite, did ye?"

Egan gave him a sharp look. "Your meaning?"

Hamish leaned to him and lowered his voice, though there was no one else in the great hall but the footmen, who spoke little English. "My chamber's right next to Zarabeth's. I didn't think that headboard would stop bangin' into the wall all night. And then I poke me head out of the door in the wee hours and see ye traipsing out, naked as a weasel."

"Ye keep that to yourself." Egan scowled. "And I was wearing a plaid."

"Barely. So will ye make an honest woman of her?"

Egan thought about Zarabeth sleeping in the nest they'd made together, her sweet body curled among the pillows. It had been difficult to leave her, difficult to walk away and not make love to her all day long. What better way to celebrate the coldest days of the year than lying in bed with Zarabeth?

"'Tisn't what she wants," he said. "I think she's had enough of marriage. 'Twas no' a happy one, as you might imagine."

"I didn't ask what she wanted," Hamish said amiably. "I asked if ye'd make her honest."

"That's my intent." Egan studied his charred bread, wondering what Olaf would say when he learned what Egan had done. Olaf had not wanted Egan for Zarabeth before—had things changed?

Hamish burst out laughing. "First poor Angus, then Egan. I'll be the only MacDonald bachelor left."

"I'll send ye to Nvengaria," Egan threatened. "The ladies there are beautiful, and they'd be happy to have a go at such a strapping man as yourself."

An apprehensive light entered Hamish's eye. Egan continued eating his toast, perfectly serious.

While Hamish continued to torment him, Egan finished his breakfast, then went upstairs to check on Baron Valentin.

To his surprise, he found his sister curled up in a chair next to the bed. "Have ye been here all night?" he asked her.

Mary remained where she was, head resting on her arm. "Yes. I worried for him."

Valentin still lay unmoving under the covers, but his skin was no longer waxen, and he breathed easier. Egan checked the wound, happy to see it wasn't hot or swollen.

"He'll feel like hell when he wakes up," Egan said softly.

"He did wake."

Egan stared at Mary. "Ye didn't call me."

"He didn't stay awake long. I thought it best to let him sleep."

She sounded subdued—shaken, even. Egan wondered what had happened in here, what Valentin had said to her, if anything. The way Mary pressed her lips together told him she wasn't about to reveal it.

should sleep," Egan told her.

think I should stay, in case he wakes again."

an frowned, but Mary returned his look inscrutably. He shrugged. "Just be careful, and call out if ye need anything."

"Yes."

He waited, but she said no more than that one word. Very strange. Usually his sister didn't hesitate to voice an opinion on anything.

He gave up and left her there. He wanted to talk with Olaf, but Angus had taken him out, "to show him a bit of the land," Gemma said.

Angus's wife was elbow-deep in dough, helping Mrs. Williams prepare the next round of Hogmanay feasting. Egan got away with stealing only one sugar-coated dried apple before Gemma and Mrs. Williams ran him out. He had many things to do this morning, so he headed out of the castle.

As he passed the staircase, Zarabeth's door above him opened a crack. He sensed her behind it, watching him closely, but she made no attempt to call out. She hid while he continued through the hall; then he heard the door close behind him with a soft *snick*.

Hogmanay wound on. The MacDonalds ate a modest meal just after midday, then prepared to visit their tenants, crofters, and neighbors. The night would culminate in bonfires and a huge gathering at Ross Hall. Adam Ross had set up fireworks in his gardens, and the inhabitants of every village for miles around would be there.

Egan told Zarabeth not to go.

"And why not?" Zarabeth demanded as they stood outside the great hall after luncheon. She hadn't seen Egan all morning, not since she'd observed him hurrying downstairs and out of the castle earlier. "I think I will be safer in a crowd of Highlanders than left behind with my footmen and Valentin in his sickbed."

"Ivan and Constanz will go," Egan said, sounding offhand. "They've worked hard and deserve a treat."

"So I should stay here, completely unguarded?"

He had no business looking so cool and calm, his hair brushed and tamed instead of in its usual wild abandon. His eyes were carefully blank. "Of course not. I'll be here, and your father. And Mary, who's looking after Valentin."

She stared at him, her anger rising. "Of course. I'm certain two women, my father, and an injured logosh can withstand an army of assassins."

"We can, and I don't think we'll have an army. I need to show ye something."

"Another adventure?"

Egan nodded. "Dress warm and prepare to leave after the others depart for their revelry."

He walked away from her, perfectly confident she'd do what he wanted. She ground her teeth. *Insufferably arrogant Highlander.*

Even so, she dressed in the warmest of her plaid gowns and fur wraps borrowed from Mary, thick gloves, and stout boots, and met Egan downstairs after the others had gone to Adam Ross's. She was still angry with him but also curious as to what he wanted to show her.

The Williamses and the other servants had been given the night off as well—that morning Egan and Mary had bestowed gifts on them and bidden them a happy New Year. The staff would attend the merry-making below stairs at Ross Hall, just as the Ross servants had enjoyed themselves at Castle MacDonald the night before.

When Zarabeth descended to the cavernous kitchen with Egan, she found the room deserted and the fire banked for the night.

"Is this what you wished to show me?" she asked Egan. "You raiding the larder?"

"Hush now," Egan said absently. "Ah, here he is."

He was Zarabeth's father. Olaf waited in the shadows of the stairs that led to the cellars, a shuttered lantern in his hand. He looked alive with anticipation, his blue eyes sparkling over the scarf he'd wound about his throat.

"Are we going to look at the bits of manacles?" Zarabeth asked Egan. "There isn't much to them."

"Trust me, lass," Egan said.

"Don't I always?"

Egan opened his mouth to answer, then closed it and shook his head, ignoring Olaf's amused expression. "Follow me."

Olaf motioned for Zarabeth to walk ahead of him, while he brought up the rear. Both Egan and Olaf had lanterns, the candlelight reflecting eerily on the walls around them.

Egan walked past the barrels of whiskey and the rusting manacles left over from the clan's more ferocious days. At the end of the cellar, farther than Zarabeth had yet explored, was a door about four feet high and wide. Egan took a thick key from his sporran, inserted it in the lock, and creaked the door open.

"Will we have to crawl?" Zarabeth did not have a horror of closed-in spaces, but that did not mean she wanted to get herself dirty crawling on a floor.

"Nay, the door is small, but the passage was dug so a man can walk upright." Egan shone his lantern inside a rough tunnel shored up with hand-cut stone. The cellar, though several hundred years old, looked modern compared to the tunnel, which must have been ancient.

Egan ducked through the doorway, shining his lantern around. Zarabeth came next, and then Olaf. The passage was wide enough for only one at a time—or rather, one Highlander like Egan at a time. Zarabeth and Mary would be slim enough to walk side by side, although they'd have to squeeze next to each other.

The stones had been unevenly cut but fit together almost perfectly, and were smooth with age. The tunnel floor sloped upward, until Zarabeth's legs ached with the constant climb.

"What were the tunnels for?" she asked.

Egan shrugged. "In ancient times, I don't know. When MacDonalds first lived in the castle they used the tunnels t' get behind their enemies or t' flee to safety. I canno' find out whether the tunnels were here first and the castle built on top, or they were made after the MacDonalds chose this place to live."

"What do you use them for now? Entertaining foreigners?"

Egan barked a laugh. "Ye have a fine sense of humor, my lass. Ye raised a termagant, Olaf."

"She does have a forthright manner," her father answered, amusement in his voice.

"Thank you, gentlemen, you may cease now."

Zarabeth kept her tone crisp, but tears in her eyes threw the light of Egan's lantern into spangles. It had been so long since she'd heard her father's gentle banter, so long since he and Egan had bantered together. Her father was here, Egan was here, and maybe . . . just maybe everything would be all right.

Egan stopped walking and looked up. Zarabeth and Olaf followed his gaze and saw a black iron grille set into the ceiling. The grille was fairly new, likely fashioned by the village blacksmith to keep animals and people from falling or wandering into the tunnels.

Egan unlocked the grille with another stout key and pushed it open. He caught the low opening, hauled himself up to sit on the ledge, and reached back down.

"Send Zarabeth up," he told Olaf. "And don't let her look up me kilt."

Snorting with laughter, her father lifted Zarabeth around the waist up to Egan. Egan caught her under the arms and pulled her through the hole to deposit her gently on snowy ground.

Zarabeth gave him a lofty glance and looked around. It was dark, the stars and moon glittering on the thin snow cover. The lights of Castle MacDonald shone far away, and bonfires dotted the hills above the village.

Egan helped Olaf climb out of the hole; then he replaced the grille, locking it.

"Where are we?" Zarabeth asked.

"On the hill behind the Ring of Dunmarran." Egan signaled them to follow and trudged down the low rise.

The standing stones were ghostly in the moonlight, like giants marching in a stately circle. The middle was clear of snow, as before, the ground covered with brown-green grass.

"A magical place," Olaf breathed. "I once saw a stone circle in Nvengaria, high in the mountains of the north. No one knows what the stones were for—they are far older than Nvengaria itself."

"This one makes you tell the truth when you're inside it," Zarabeth said. "Or so Egan tells me."

"That's the legend. But that's no' why I brought ye here. Tread carefully."

They followed him to the first stone. The ground on the outside was snowy, but here the snow had been trampled, and something dark stained it. Egan flashed his lantern over the spot.

"This is where I found Valentin."

Zarabeth gasped.

"That's no' all." Egan held his lantern high. "I came out here this morning and had a look at the place. No else one has been here, because I didn't let on where I found Valentin. I discovered a trail leading back to the tunnel entrance. Whoever shot Valentin was waiting for him—inside the tunnel. When they saw him, likely in his wolf form, they charged out. Valentin was shot as he attacked, by someone ready for him."

Zarabeth listened in shock. "You unlocked the grate from the inside. Was it locked when you came here this morning?"

Egan nodded. "But I'm no' the only one with a key. Adam Ross has one, which hangs on a peg in the back stairs of his house, where anyone might take it. Another hangs in the kitchen of Castle MacDonald. There was a horde of people at the castle for Hogmanay, so anyone might have found a key or stolen one."

"Still," Olaf said slowly, "that indicates someone who knows your family's habits."

"Yes." Egan gave him a pointed look. "Someone who for some reason wants Valentin dead."

Olaf held up his hands. "Not I, my friend. I arrived at Castle MacDonald when you first saw me in the middle of the night. I did not know Valentin was here, or who he really was until I saw him unconscious in your guest chamber."

Egan turned his questioning gaze to Zarabeth. She returned an amazed look. "Why should I try to shoot Valentin? I barely know him, despite traveling with him. He's . . ." She stopped, wanting to say, *He's nearly as unreadable as you*, but she changed her words: "He's enigmatic."

"I don't think either of ye did," Egan said. "But I wanted to show ye. To warn ye that this is close to home."

"I see that," Zarabeth said. "Do you have any idea who?"

He shook his head. "I'm sorry t' say no. But I have something else to tell ye."

Egan came close to Zarabeth. In spite of their quarrel this morning and Egan's avoiding her the rest of the day, her heart beat faster as he slid his arm around her shoulders and pulled her close. "I had another letter from Damien today."

Likely on their magical paper. "What did he say?"

Egan's eyes were quiet. "I'm sorry, love. Damien wrote that your husband was killed. There was fighting when Sebastian and his crowd tried to storm the palace, and Sebastian was shot. He died almost instantly."

Chapter Fifteen
The Stone Kirk

Zarabeth stared at him in shock. She didn't move for an entire minute while she watched him with wide blue eyes; then she wrenched herself from him and whirled to pound her fists on a standing stone.

"How could he?" she cried. "How could he?"

Egan had no idea whether she meant Sebastian storming the city or Damien letting his men shoot him. He started to go to her but Olaf held him back. "Let her rage. She deserves to."

Zarabeth continued to pound the stone; then her fists stopped and she leaned into them, her body shaking.

Egan couldn't keep himself away. He went to her and gently drew her into his arms. "Hush, now," he said, stroking her hair. "Hush, love."

He half expected her to burst out in anger, to say she was glad Sebastian was dead. He realized he wanted her to say that, to tell him that Sebastian meant nothing to her. But as horrible as her husband had been, she'd lived with him nearly five years of her life, shared his house, shared his bed. . . .

He glanced at Olaf and found his emotions mirrored in the older man's eyes—anger, love, guilt, relief.

"Olaf, my old friend," he said softly, "I'd like to marry your daughter."

Olaf's eyes widened. Egan waited for the man to deny him, to tell him again that he wanted much more for Zarabeth. Egan was a laird, but he was merely a landholder, not a clan chief or a titled man. Egan's father had once been offered an earldom but had turned it down with scorn—no MacDonald of his line would accept a handout from a bloody English king. Egan wasn't even Nvengarian—if Zarabeth married him, her home would be far, far away from her father's.

Olaf hesitated a long moment, then nodded. "I should have given you my blessing five years ago, when I realized she loved you. I thought it a passing fancy of hers—I never knew how much unhappiness I would cause her."

"I haven't changed much since then," Egan said.

"You have, you know." Olaf looked sad. "I was cursed with stubborn pride, and had such ambitions for my only daughter. But my ambition should have been for her happiness, not her position in society—or mine. I should never have sent you away."

"Aye, well, at the time I was a drunken fool and probably would no' have done well by her." He gave Olaf a nod. "We'll go to the kirk in the village and have it done in the morning. I know 'tis not the Nvengarian way."

"No matter. A marriage in another country is still legal in Nvengaria, and when we return we can have a proper ceremony at my house, with all our old friends. As it should have been."

Zarabeth suddenly flung herself out of Egan's arms. Tears streamed down her face, shining in the cold moonlight.

"Was either of you going to bother to ask me?" she demanded, glaring at her father. "'One husband is dead—here, Zarabeth, take another'?"

Egan said quickly, "Of course I intended t' ask ye, love. But ye're grieving."

"Planning it out while I stood here, like I couldn't

hear you? My wedding." She jabbed her finger to her chest. "*My* life."

Egan raised his brows. "Are all Nvengarian girls so defiant, Olaf? A Scottish lass does her father's bidding wi'out question."

"Ha!" Zarabeth shouted, but as he'd intended the tears stopped. "I will tell Gemma and your sister that you think so. I am sure they will want to have a talk with you. Mrs. Williams, too."

Egan imagined the three ladies backing him against a wall, three pairs of Scottish eyes glaring as they told him what they thought of him. He blanched. "No, thank ye."

Olaf remained somber. "Being the widow of Sebastian will be dangerous. His faction will want their vengeance. Allying yourself with another family will help, and Egan's family is well respected and strong."

Egan nodded. "Aye, I thought of that. I intended to make ye part of Clan MacDonald, but as laird's wife, ye'd have even more protection. And ye need a husband who can look after you."

Zarabeth clenched her fists. "Don't you dare marry me because you feel sorry for me, Egan MacDonald. Poor Zarabeth, all alone in the world. I am acquainted with plenty of widows who muddle along just fine, thank you, and in fact lead fuller lives now that they're not married. I do not need a husband."

"But those ladies have money," Olaf pointed out. "Sebastian's lands, wealth, and title were stripped from him when he turned traitor. Damien took everything back to the Crown."

Zarabeth made a noise of exasperation. "Damien will not leave me destitute. He's not a despot—he's family. And then there's my mother's legacy, which Sebastian couldn't touch, not to mention I'm my father's heir. I thought you'd ask me to keep house for you now, Father, seeing *you* are alone."

Olaf looked embarrassed. "Of course you're welcome to come home when it's safe to. But I have only half the wealth Sebastian had, and you're used to moving at the top of society."

"I care nothing for that. I am more than ready to let the cream of society do without me."

"And then there's Lady Beatrice," Olaf said, looking sideways at her. He pronounced it the Italian way, *Bee-ah-tree-che.*

Zarabeth blinked. "Who is Lady Beatrice?"

"A widow I happen to know." Olaf reddened. "She has taken to staying with me."

"Oh." Zarabeth stared as though seeing her father for the first time. "Oh. I see."

"That is not to say I would not welcome you home, daughter," Olaf said hastily. "I have told Lady Beatrice everything about you, and she so hopes to meet you."

Zarabeth clenched and unclenched her hands, not looking at her father. Egan's heart ached for her as she realized that the world had moved on, that her father perhaps didn't need her as much anymore.

"It seems my choices have been narrowed for me," she said.

Egan gentled his voice. "I told ye a long time ago, I'm no' but a whiskey-soaked Scotsman in a wreck of a castle. It wasn't good enough for ye then, and it isn't now, but as ye say, your choices aren't much."

"Thank you, Egan," Zarabeth said coolly, her sad look vanishing. "A proposal every young lady dreams of."

" 'Tis the middle of the night and bloody freezing. 'Tis the best I can do."

Zarabeth seized his hand. "Come with me."

Her fingers were warm in his as she dragged him within the boundary of the Ring of Dunmarran. They stumbled out of the snow onto damp grass, which did feel warmer. Perhaps his theory about a hot spring was not so far-fetched.

Zarabeth put her hands on his shoulders and studied him. He'd seen that look before, when she took the measure of a person—her eyes steady and clear and not a little unnerving.

"Why do you want to marry me?" she asked.

He cupped her shoulders, knowing that here she'd believe he spoke true. "To keep ye safe, love."

"What about Jamie? What about him inheriting and becoming laird?"

"He still can. I dislike t' ask ye this, because I don't want to hurt ye. But can ye have children?"

If the legend of the Ring were right, she wouldn't be able to lie to him. He wondered—she'd been married to Sebastian for five years, and Egan knew from last night that she was not a virgin. Unless Sebastian was daft or impotent he'd have bedded her often. No man in his right mind could have stayed away from her.

Zarabeth answered in a low voice, "I never conceived."

Her expression broke his heart. She was trying to be brave about it, hiding her longing for children, her deep hurt that she'd not been gifted with any.

"I don't mind," Egan said. "Children come or don't. I have a ready-made heir in Jamie, much as it pains him."

"It seems the perfect solution," she said hollowly.

"No' perfect. But the best I can do."

"I never wanted to marry again," she answered almost savagely. "Not even you. Especially not you."

The words stung, but he only nodded. "I'll no' let ye regret it. I promise."

She looked as though she regretted it already. Egan gathered her against him, vowing to make it all right for her. He was laird; he could keep her safe at Castle Mac-Donald, as he'd always longed to.

Zarabeth didn't struggle to get away from him, but neither did she respond when he brushed a kiss to her lips. He kissed her again, harder this time, never mind her father standing by, but she barely moved her mouth beneath his.

His heart sank as he saw the road ahead of him and the challenge that would be more difficult than any other. But he'd win and make Zarabeth happy, whether she liked it or not. As long as it took.

Zarabeth wore plaid for her wedding the next morning—she insisted, to Gemma's and Mary's distress. They tried to persuade her to wear one of the numerous silks that had been made for her since her arrival, but she stood firm.

"I will be a laird's wife," she told them. "I should look the part."

For their sake, she softened her tone. Both ladies had been ecstatic when Egan made the announcement at breakfast, and both had whisked Zarabeth upstairs to get her ready with much hugging and tears. Jamie had whooped, his cry shaking the high windows.

When Zarabeth entered the small stone kirk where Gemma and Angus had been wed, Egan was the first thing she saw. He waited patiently by the altar in formal kilt and subdued coat, a sword at his side—Ian Mac-Donald's sword from the great hall.

Egan's family surged in, followed by the Rosses, the kirk filling with plaid and laughter. Jamie capered about, unable to keep still.

The villagers had followed them down the hill and now swarmed through the kirk with sprigs of holly and ribbons in cold fingers. What better way to end Hogmanay than with the wedding of their laird?

Olaf had tears in his eyes as he led her to Egan's side. "All those years ago, I should have understood and encouraged him to marry you. I made many mistakes, but now I'm putting it right."

He looked so pleased and so relieved that Zarabeth didn't have the heart to do anything but press a quick kiss to his cheek.

The ceremony was a blur to Zarabeth, and she wasn't quite certain what she felt: anger at Egan and her father for their pity, grief over her marriage and five years lost, fierce joy that she'd be with Egan at last.

Her body remembered Egan's lovemaking, his hot hands on her, his kisses, the way he felt inside her. Egan was her lover. She wondered if that would change when she became his wife, or if he'd ensure that Jamie inherited the lairdship by avoiding sleeping with Zarabeth.

Egan's eyes gleamed in triumph when he slid a ring on her finger, a huge sapphire that he produced from his coat pocket. The band didn't quite fit, and the gold looked old.

As soon as the vicar pronounced them man and wife, the Highlanders sent up a huge cheer. Egan turned and lifted his hand twined in Zarabeth's to them. He was their lord and master, and he'd just become Zarabeth's lord and master, too.

Back at Castle MacDonald, a piper met them in the courtyard and piped the laird and his lady inside to more cheers. In the great hall, Williams and his helpers served up another enormous feast. The fiddler and drummer played as they ate, and Egan's family and friends continuously congratulated them.

Adam Ross leaned down and lightly kissed Zarabeth under Egan's scrutiny. "Egan was quick enough to land you after you became a widow, the scoundrel. If I'd had more warning, you might be a Ross today."

"Not likely," Egan growled.

"You're very kind." Zarabeth gave Adam a warm smile, which only increased Egan's frown.

"You're a true Highlander now," Gemma told her, throwing her arms around her. "And a cousin. Welcome to th' family."

"I always wanted a large family," Zarabeth told her, kissing her cheek. "Thank you for everything."

"Well." Gemma's cheeks went pink. "Seeing as now we're family, I wondered if ye could help me with a wee problem. Not now," she said hastily, glancing at Egan. "Tomorrow. When you've done with your weddin' night."

Zarabeth blushed. She wondered at her own shyness— she'd already shared a bed with Egan, but the thought of going upstairs with him tonight filled her with trepidation. "Very well, we'll talk tomorrow."

Gemma nodded happily and left her alone.

Jamie came bounding over with the sword of Ian MacDonald in his hands, likely the happiest Highlander in the room. "Ye have to do it now, Uncle. It's time to see if ye can break the curse."

Egan growled. "Will ye leave off the curse, at least until tomorrow? I carried the sword at the wedding for ye. Isn't that enough for now?"

"But everything's right. Ye married a magical lass without shame. Ye need to openly declare the marriage and then break the sword."

"What about the rhyme?" Zarabeth asked, looking with interest at the sword. "You said we have to chant a rhyme or a spell."

Jamie looked momentarily downcast. "If it exists, I can't find it. I thought mebbe it had been etched on the sword, but no."

He showed her the blade, polished for the occasion. It was clean and plain, a workmanlike sword.

"It's likely to have been in Scots," Egan said. "And probably destroyed long ago, either by the English or by the laird trying to avoid arrest or fines. The Gaelic language was banned after the 'Forty-five."

"Ye can try it anyway," Jamie said. "Ye met the requirements."

"What about the brave deed?" Zarabeth broke in.

"Aye, lad, it's been a while since I performed any kind of bravery."

"Ye rescued Zarabeth from the ocean," Jamie insisted. "And carried Baron Valentin home."

"And faced down the debutantes," Zarabeth pointed out.

Egan looked pained. "All right, lad. Give me the sword, and let's get it over with. If it breaks, will ye leave be the curse nonsense?"

Jamie grinned. "Gladly." He jumped up on the table and yelled for silence.

"My friends," Jamie proclaimed, "at last we have a laird who has taken a witch to wife, who has a chance at ending the curse of the MacDonalds. Give your attention now to Egan MacDonald, laird of his clan."

The Highlanders roared enthusiastically, banging on tables with fists and cups. The drummer and piper and fiddler kept up the din until Jamie waved for silence again.

Egan leaped to the tabletop and lifted Zarabeth up beside him. He was so strong she landed lightly next to him without losing her balance. Jamie, smiling hugely, handed him the sword.

"T' please Charlie MacDonald's beloved son . . ." Egan began.

He paused encouragingly, and every glass shot high. "Charlie MacDonald!"

Egan waited until they had drunk. "T' please my nephew, I'll have a go at breaking the curse of the Mac-Donalds."

"The curse of the MacDonalds!" they roared.

"I thought *Jamie* was the curse." Dougal snickered.

"Hush, lad. I have married today a lovely lady of Nvengaria, a magic woman of her country. She is now the Lady MacDonald."

"Lady MacDonald!"

Egan thrust the sword high. "This is the sword of Ian MacDonald, who thwarted a witch three hundred years ago. Legend says that when a laird of Ian's line and his lady have broken it, the curse itself must break."

More roaring. Egan brought the sword down and positioned it to break the blade over his knee. "Take hold of the hilt, love," he said to Zarabeth under all the noise. "But be careful. I'll try not to hurt ye."

Zarabeth laid her fingers on the hilt. She felt it then, a light tingle of magic, but it was not benevolent magic. A trickle of darkness touched her, anger old and honed. Jamie wasn't wrong. The witch had cursed this sword, locking a piece of her anger inside it.

She gripped tighter, wanting to rid the castle and Egan's family of that anger.

"One," Egan said, looking at her. "Two. *Three.*"

He brought the blade down across his rock-hard knee. A hollow clang sounded through the hall, but the sword stayed whole.

"Ouch," Egan shouted. "Damnation."

"Are you all right?" Zarabeth gasped.

"Bloody swords. Bloody curses."

Someone below them laughed. "Now then, Mac-Donald, mebbe ye got soft in the army."

"Stubble it," Egan snarled. "I'm trying not to hurt me wife."

"More like preserving yer fishing tackle. It'd be a short weddin' night."

Zarabeth blushed, but Egan ignored the laughter. "Now then, let's try again."

She put her fingers on the hilt again, flinching as she felt the tiny tingle of malevolent magic. Egan brought the sword up, then swiftly down again.

The blade banged off his knee, flew into the air, and clattered on the table as the guests jumped back. Egan cursed and wrung his stinging hand. "Ye all right, love?"

"Fine." Zarabeth bit her lip in trepidation. If there truly was a curse and they couldn't break it, things could become very bad.

The jesters in the crowd were enjoying themselves. "Did ye hear him scream? He really did cut it off, hard luck to his missus!"

"He'll have to find a new one, mebbe buckle it on."

The shouting grew more lewd. Apart from Mary the ladies didn't seem to mind, and in fact joined in. "Well, he can't borrow yours, Geordie Ross," a woman shouted. "Ye must have lost it because I've not seen it these five years."

Amid the ensuing laughter, Hamish yelled, "Och, Geordie, where've ye been keepin' it?"

"Ye're one to speak, Hamish MacDonald. I saw ye eyeing that sheep like a man with something on his mind."

"Aye, mutton chops and potatoes."

As the laughter burst out again Egan gripped Zarabeth's hand and pulled her down from the table. Jamie looked glum, but the rest of the party got caught up in the bawdiness.

"Now then, Hamish," Angus roared. "Gracie MacLean doesn't look much like a mutton chop, does she?"

Hamish turned beet red, and while all attention was fixed on him, Egan and Zarabeth slipped away.

The gaiety faded behind them as they climbed the stairs through the middle of the castle. Before they reached the second floor, Egan stopped and lifted

Zarabeth to the step above him. He was still taller than she even then, but she could look into his eyes without having to tilt her head much.

Egan studied her in silence. They hadn't had a moment alone since the day began, and now Zarabeth felt the awkwardness between them. The loose sapphire band hung heavy on her finger.

"I'm sorry you couldn't break the sword," she said.

"I'm no' bothered. Jamie needs to learn no' everything in life can be so easily solved."

"But there really is dark magic in the sword. I felt it. He's not wrong about that."

Egan stilled her words with his finger on her lips. "Tonight I'm not interested in dark magic or the curse."

"We shouldn't pretend it away. . . ."

"Not tonight." His eyes went stern. "There's something else I want to do tonight."

She was his wife now, *his*. She belonged to him. Gemma and Angus seemed to be partners and friends, Angus good-naturedly giving in to Gemma's bustling bossiness. What Egan expected of this marriage she couldn't guess.

Right now he expected to kiss her. He bent his head to slant his mouth across hers.

"Egan."

"What is it, lass?"

"I should look in on Valentin."

"Aye, we will. But I'm sure he won't mind if I kiss my wife first."

Zarabeth wanted to respond, but the will went out of her as his mouth connected with hers. He skimmed his hand down her back, scooping her against him.

She felt him hard through the folds of his kilt, smelled his warmth and the tangle of his hair. He pushed his tongue into her mouth, mastering her, tasting every inch of her.

When he released her, she would have fallen but for his arm around her. He must feel her shaking, must sense her need and her worry.

He gave her a little smile, his eyes sparkling. "Let's go visit your baron."

Still shaking, she took his hand and let him lead her up the stairs, and they entered Valentin's room.

Valentin had been left in the care of Mrs. Williams's mother, an elderly woman called Rose who had sharp eyes and a no-nonsense attitude. The baron was awake, but his face was flushed with fever.

"You married him," Valentin said to Zarabeth when she and Egan entered the room. "That was wise."

"The best solution," Egan agreed.

Zarabeth kept her temper and held her tongue. She took the damp cloth from Rose and dabbed it across Valentin's hot forehead. "Can you tell us what happened to you now?"

"I remember very little." Valentin's voice was weak, and he stuck to Nvengarian, as though it cost him too much effort to speak English. "I was patrolling the grounds—I don't remember why I went to the standing stones. Perhaps I heard something there. Whoever shot me came out of nowhere."

"The tunnels," Zarabeth said. "Egan thinks they came from the tunnels that run under the castle."

"That could be. I never saw him. I smelled fear, a swamping wave of it. I sprang at it, and then he must have shot me. I went down, and he disappeared. That is all I remember."

Egan folded his arms and regarded Valentin thoughtfully. "Did you glimpse anything—clothing, hair color, the man's build?"

"If I did, then pain has wiped away the vision. I could scent him again, I think. But not like this."

He motioned to his inert body. From what Valentin

had once explained to Zarabeth, because he was only part logosh his predominant form was human, and he had difficulty changing from one form to another when he was hurt. Full logosh would revert to demon form when hurt and remain that way until they healed, but Valentin had too much human blood in him. He'd have a hard time shifting until he was better.

"We will get ye well, my friend," Egan promised. "Then ye can go out and nose around—so to speak."

"I will do so." Valentin gazed at Zarabeth, his hard face softening the slightest bit. "Be happy."

This was the closest thing to sentiment she'd ever heard from him. He surprised her again with his next question. "Mary—Mrs. Cameron. She is well?"

Egan's brows climbed. "Aye, she's downstairs trying to keep the guests under control, and failing miserably. But that's a Highland fling for ye."

Valentin looked as though he wanted to say more, but subsided against the pillows.

"You rest now," Zarabeth said, patting his shoulder. "I'll look in on you in the morning."

Valentin's eyelids eyes drooped and he merely nodded. Mrs. Williams's mother shooed them out then, and Zarabeth and Egan went back to the cold staircase.

Chapter Sixteen
Revelations

Instead of heading for Zarabeth's bedroom, Egan led her up two more flights to the floor where his own chamber lay. Zarabeth paused at the top of the stairs to catch her breath.

"Why up here?"

"Less noise. And the lads will be too drunk to climb this high and cheer me on."

Zarabeth's face heated as she slid inside Egan's chill room. The chamber was small, dominated by the fireplace on one side and a huge walnut bedstead on the other. When he'd had his bath in here, the tub had taken up most of the extra room. He didn't have much in the way of other furniture, pictures, or decoration. A plain room for a man who traveled most of the time.

"Now I know what Gemma meant," Zarabeth remarked.

"Meant?"

"After she married Angus. She said that when you marry a Highlander, you marry the pack of them. I suppose I should get used to it."

Egan grinned. "I never have." He went to the fireplace and bent down to add logs to the fire and stir it to life. His kilt stretched enticingly over his backside, and Zarabeth couldn't look away.

"We don't have to stay in Scotland, ye know," Egan

said as he worked. "We can go to London or Paris if ye like, and as soon as Damien declares it safe, I'll take ye back to Nvengaria."

"I like it here."

Egan looked at her over his shoulder. He saw the direction her gaze had taken and roared with laughter.

"Ye have a strange fascination for my fundament, love. I'd be flattered if I didn't think ye liked it better than my face."

Heat fluttered through her body. "Nonsense, you are a very handsome man, Egan."

"You're kind t' say so, but Charlie had the looks."

"I didn't marry Charlie MacDonald."

He straightened up, going still. "Don't tease me, love."

"I'm not teasing. I decided years and years ago I wanted to marry you—the minute you woke up and looked at me in my mother's best guest room. And now I have. I'm no better than Gemma, chasing Angus all her life until she got him to the altar."

"She didn't have to chase him hard. Angus had always been in love with Gemma, only he didn't know how to show it."

"It seems she taught him."

His expression became thoughtful. "Ye liked me all that time, did ye?"

"I was twelve, and you were so handsome. I knew you'd make the perfect husband—all I had to do was grow up." She sighed. "Life is simple when you're twelve."

"Some things are easier, and some things get better with age."

She folded her arms, suddenly nervous. "Such as what?"

"Don't be afraid of me, lass."

Egan came toward her, backlit by the fire, moving as

slowly and quietly as he had when he'd rescued the mare and foal.

"I'm never afraid of you, Egan MacDonald."

He stopped in front of her. "I like ye in plaid. Did I ever tell ye that?"

She fingered the cloth, a lump in her throat. "The tartan wears well. A very practical material."

"We're a very practical people." He cupped the curve of her waist. "For instance, we don't have long books and years of study about lovemaking. We just do it."

"And what exactly do you do?"

She thought of the bawdy talk downstairs in the great hall, earthy people laughing with one another about lust.

His smile was feral. "We're not skilled seducers, not like a certain Nvengarian lady who seduced me in her bedchamber two nights past."

"No?"

"No. We just say what we want without flowery language. Sometimes we don't say anything at all."

"I see. What would you say to me now?"

Egan bent closer, his breath hot as he whispered, "I'd say, 'Get out of that pretty dress before it's in tatters.'"

She gulped. "You wouldn't really tear my gown."

"I would. I'm the Mad Highlander, remember?"

"That's an act to make people laugh."

His eyes sparkled dangerously. "Is it? Or is it what's truly underneath honorable Egan, everyone's friend?"

Zarabeth gave a breathless laugh. "Are all Scotsmen this insistent?"

"Well, I wouldn't know. I don't know all Scotsmen."

"Perhaps we could ask them."

Grinning savagely, Egan put his hand to the top of her bodice and, with one twist of his wrist, tore it open.

Buttons popped and zinged around the room, one heading straight into the fireplace with a loud *crack*.

"Egan." She gasped.

He placed his huge hand inside her bodice. "I remember ye yankin' the pin out of my kilt and lettin' the plaid slide right off. Why shouldn't I do the same t' ye?"

"I didn't tear anything."

"Ye have seamstresses at your beck and call t' sew it back together. Mary saw to that."

"But what on earth would I tell them?"

"That your husband was impatient. They'd know what ye meant."

She thought of the joking in the hall beneath her. The seamstresses probably *would* give her knowing looks and laugh.

Egan jerked the bodice open to her waist, revealing her short stays over her chemise. He expertly unlaced them both and pushed the garments down, baring her breasts. He studied her, his eyes dark.

"You're lovely, lass."

He cupped her breasts and leaned to kiss her. His body dwarfed hers, his hands could easily crush her, and yet he could be so gentle. The tenderness with which he'd made love to her two nights before made her throat tighten.

He was rougher tonight, more playful, but still he held himself back. Speculating what he'd be like if he chose not to hold himself back made her shiver with delight.

"Are ye cold?" he asked.

"No. I'm fine."

"We'll get into the bed. The middle of winter in Scotland's not the best place to be undressed."

He turned away from her, and now she did shudder with cold. With him against her, she'd always be warm.

Egan raked the covers back from the bed, the pillows

flopping across the mattress. Without waiting for her to approach, he swept her into his arms and tossed her on the bed.

She landed with a bounce on the feather bed. He yanked her gown all the way off and tossed it to the floor, then proceeded to strip himself.

First his coat fell, and his lawn shirt followed it, becoming a wrinkled mess. He kicked off his shoes, polished leather tumbling end over end. Socks next, a bright plaid pattern crumpled on his shirt. Last his kilt, unpinned and unwound from his hips.

Zarabeth couldn't take her eyes from the beauty of him. He might think himself world-worn, but he'd always be handsome Egan to her.

Need welled inside her to feel his weight on her, his sweat against her skin. He snatched the covers from her hands and climbed in with her, pulling the quilts over their heads. In the dark nest inside, he cradled her firmly against him.

"I don't know if I can go slowly," he said. "I'll try, but I don't know."

Zarabeth had no desire for slowness. She wrapped her hand around Egan's staff and squeezed hard.

"Oh, lass, don't do that."

She let go. "Did I hurt you?"

The bed shook with his laughter. "Nay, but ye might turn me into a wild man."

"I see." Smiling to herself, she reached out and squeezed him again.

He let out a moan. "I'll have to make ye pay for that."

"Pay? But you said it didn't hurt."

"Always teasin', aren't ye, Zarabeth? Fooling everyone with that sweet little smile, but not me."

"I never tried to fool anyone," she said, pretending innocence.

"Ye were always a hellion. No matter how pretty ye looked, no matter how ye smiled, I knew."

She gave in. "Thank you for never telling on me."

"I never did, did I? Just let ye run wild and told your father it was my fault ye came home covered head to foot in mud. I wonder what I deserve for being so good to ye?"

Zarabeth's heart pounded. She loved when he was playful, loved the spark in his eye that said maybe the Mad Highlander really did lurk there.

She ran her finger down the bridge of his nose. "In return I always made sure your favorite Nvengarian cakes were on the table."

"That ye did." He captured her finger and nibbled on it. "Ye taste better."

"There are more cakes downstairs."

"Where they should stay. But I don't think cakes are enough. Ye owe me more than that, love."

"Really, Egan," she said with pretended hauteur. "I can't imagine what you mean."

"My Zarabeth," he said in tones so low they made her shiver. "I so want to make ye understand what pleasure can be. But I don't want to scare ye."

"I am quite brave." Her racing heart belied her words. "I traveled all the way here with two footmen and a logosh."

"Aye, Ivan and Constanz are terrifying." He smiled briefly, then sobered. "I want ye to know I'll never hurt you. No matter what I do or ask ye to do, I'll never hurt ye. Do ye believe me?"

She nodded.

"All right then." Egan lowered his head and licked from the hollow of her throat to her lips. "I'm going to show ye what pleasure is, Zarabeth. Never mind your books."

She nodded again, her mouth too dry for speech.

Egan shoved the quilts off them. Cool air touched her skin, but the fire had started warming the little room, and against Egan she would never be cold.

He slid his arm all the way around her and rolled her onto her stomach.

"Are you going to admire *my* backside?" she asked. "Since I admire yours so much?"

"Only partly. Get on your knees, love."

Zarabeth started to get onto her hands and knees. Egan's strong hand eased her down until she hugged a pillow, while her backside stuck up behind her.

"Egan?" she asked in trepidation.

"I promise, lass." His voice had gone dark and sultry. "I promise ye only pleasure."

His big hands moved her thighs apart, and then she felt the heat of his tongue. She gasped and tried to squirm away, but she learned then and there how strong he truly was.

He held her and made her take every lick, every stroke, every suckle. His practiced tongue knew exactly where to touch her and how fast and for exactly how long.

At first she tried to control her cries, but she soon gave up and squealed and writhed against his hot, wet, very gifted tongue. She'd never felt anything like it, not even when he'd played with her with his hands.

She moaned his name over and over, begging him, but she wasn't sure what she begged for. She couldn't take any more; he had to stop.

She cried out in pure disappointment when he did stop. But he rose over her, a great bear of a man, and nudged her knees even farther apart. His chest closed on her back, and he whispered soothing words into her ear as his blunt hardness prodded her opening.

"No," she whimpered. "I can't."

He nipped her ear. "Yes, ye can. I've got ye wet enough and open enough. Ye can take me."

He smoothed his hand over her hair and across her shoulder, and started to press inside. He was huge.

"Shh," he whispered. "Ye're beautiful, Zarabeth. Hot and wet for me."

"I don't know what to do," she moaned.

"Ye don't have to do anything. I'll do it all."

His hardness throbbed inside her. He stayed still a moment, his arms taking his weight on either side of her, his body draped over hers, so wonderfully warm.

She'd never known it was possible to feel this way. She realized she'd never truly coupled before Egan, not like this, with a man who did it for the joy of it.

Egan nipped her cheek as he slid even farther inside.

"No," she groaned. She couldn't do this; there was no way she could take him.

Her body had other ideas. Without realizing it she thrust her hips back to his, rocking on his hardness. She was behaving like a wanton, like the mistress she'd offered to be.

"Zarabeth." The whisper dragged out of him. "You're so beautiful, my Zarabeth. God help me."

He started to move his hips, scraping his length in and out of her in slow movements. She clung to the pillows, tears streaming from her eyes, but she wasn't crying. "Egan, *please*."

He didn't answer in words. He moved faster in and out of her, the heat where they joined beautiful. His sweat mingled with hers as he sexed her, and she balled her hands and let it happen.

He covered her fists with his hands, the two of them sinking deeper into the feather mattress as the bed strained with the onslaught. Just when Zarabeth thought it would break or she would, Egan shouted his climax.

He went on and on, pumping into her until she screamed herself, everything hot and slick and tight where they joined. Zarabeth fell to the bed, half-numb, Egan on top of her, his breathing harsh.

They lay that way for a time, tangled in each other, while everything stilled.

Egan touched her wet face. "Are ye all right?"

"I'm . . . just . . . fine," she panted.

Egan cuddled her close, and they lay together touching and kissing in silence. Zarabeth for once felt no need to talk. Just basking in his warmth made her sleepy and happy.

She traced the lines of his face, liking how his mouth naturally curved down. He had tiny lines in the corners of his eyes, white patches from squinting at the sun.

She wished with all her heart that the wasted years between them hadn't happened. If she hadn't been so foolish, if she'd not frightened him away, they might have remained friends, and she wouldn't have married so rashly.

Her father had encouraged the match with Sebastian and had been happy when she acquiesced, but Zarabeth knew in her heart that she'd jumped at the chance to marry Sebastian because she'd been angry with Egan.

How dare he? she'd thought. How dared Egan call her a child when a sophisticated duke wanted her? She would show him to what lofty heights she could rise. When Egan returned and begged to be her lover, she might condescend to think about it.

Five years of misery for one hasty, pride-filled decision. She realized she'd blamed Egan at first for Sebastian's abuse, because he hadn't come back to rescue her. He'd left her alone to pay for her own mistake.

"I wish . . ." she whispered.

Egan trickled her hair through his fingers. "You wish what, lass?"

"I wish I didn't love you so much."

He stilled, and she wanted to bite off her tongue. His eyes shuttered to her, as they had last night after she'd accepted his proposal.

"Is that a bad thing?" he asked.

She'd wanted to say, *I wish I hadn't been so angry at you. I wish I could have sent for you. I wish I could have had you in my life.*

"Many things would be easier," she said.

"What things, love?"

"I don't know. Never mind. I meant nothing."

He continued to stroke her hair. "Ye flatter me, saying ye love this wreck of a man. Do ye know how old I am?"

She shook her head, pretending, but of course she knew—she knew everything about him. He was thirty-six, exactly thirteen years older than she was.

"Nearly forty."

She gave him a mock amazed look. "As much as that? Dear me, you ought to have told me before I agreed to marry you."

He didn't laugh. "Lass, ye want a young man to be young with. I was used up and spent when ye first met me."

"I thought you quite dashing."

"Nay, I'd already dashed. I'm finished w' dashing."

"Don't be silly, you run about quite well."

Egan nuzzled her cheek. "Ye make an old man feel better."

She wished she knew what he was truly thinking. Regret for marrying her or what he thought was the necessity of it? Regret that he'd bedded the daughter of his friend when he'd vowed not to?

When Zarabeth read people, she had only to open her mind to their thoughts, to slide between the layers of chaos in their minds. It was easier when she looked into their eyes, as she had to with people like Valentin, who knew how to keep their thoughts controlled.

She rose up on her elbow and gazed into Egan's eyes, the gold flecks in the deep brown mesmerizing.

Nothing. As usual.

She didn't understand why his mind was closed to her, the clamor that surrounded most people utterly silent.

He cupped her cheek in his palm. "What is it, love?"

"Nothing."

His brows lowered the slightest bit. "Why do ye look at me like that? You used t' do it when ye were a girl, and then ye'd look away like you were disappointed."

"Disappointed?" she asked in surprise.

"Finding me lacking. I see ye give that penetrating stare to others and then look satisfied, like ye understand something."

"I do?"

Oh, dear. She'd always prided herself on having learned to control her gift so the barrage of thoughts didn't crush her. All the while she'd never thought that other people might be reading her—perhaps not her thoughts, but her face.

"Ye do." Egan stretched himself out next to her, sharing her pillow, his broad hand splayed on her waist. "I wonder sometimes. Ye can make potions and charms, simple magic, ye say. But what else can ye do? Can ye see what people are thinking?"

She sat up, startled. He shouldn't know that. He couldn't.

"I'm right, aren't I?" he asked. "I've been watching ye all these years and thinking it through. You're Nvengarian; why shouldn't ye have such magic?"

She felt queasy. Never in her life had she admitted to another person except her mother what she could do, and then only because her mother had the same gift.

"My mother could read thoughts," she said slowly. "As a child I could always hear her in my mind, and she could hear me. I thought everyone could do such things, but she taught me that what we had was unusual, and she taught me how to control it."

"Ye never told me." His tone was flat.

She looked at him, stricken. "How could I? I didn't want you to look at me the way you're looking at me now, and besides, I didn't think you'd believe me."

"Does your father know?"

"I think so. Because of my mother. We never talked of it, but he must know or have guessed."

Egan laced hands behind his head and lay back, taking up most of the bed. "I've always wondered how ye found me in the dark the night ye rescued me. It was pitch-black, and I was well off the road, and yet ye knew to stop for me. Ye must have heard my worries that I'd never get out of there alive."

She shook her head. "No, I don't think I did."

He gave her a skeptical look. "Ye might have warned me ye know everything I'm thinking. Did ye not think to save your old friend embarrassment?"

"But I can't read you. I don't know why. I can sense everyone's thoughts, even Valentin's, although he's very difficult. But not you. I didn't find you by reading your mind that night in Nvengaria—I have no idea how I found you."

His eyes were cool and still. He didn't believe her.

"Please, Egan. It's true."

"Then why did ye not tell me, if I had nothing to fear?"

She put her hands to her face. "Because it is difficult to speak of, and I knew you'd never believe me. One of the reasons I like being with you is because I *don't* hear your thoughts; I don't have to shut them out or guard against them."

"I see."

No, he didn't. This was too new to him, too strange. Charms and potions he could handle—what she did was mostly harmless. He could even accept logosh, because he'd gotten to know several of them.

"My mother taught me never to tell anyone. She said it was dangerous, and she was right. I learned that as I grew older."

"But your father knew."

"She must have told him, but I don't know—we never discussed it. I didn't tell you because I knew I couldn't make you understand, and I didn't want you to avoid me."

He let out a long sigh and scrubbed his hands over his face. "Just when I think I fathom ye, when I think I can hold ye in my hand like a tame bird, ye prove what a wild creature ye really are."

"I would have told you someday; I swear to you. I planned to work up to it. But you guessed."

"Aye, that I did. Serves me right for speculating."

She caught his hand. "Please don't pull away from me."

He closed his fingers around hers, but she saw that it was already too late. He needed time to think about this and decide what to feel. She was pushing him away as surely as had her foolish attempt to seduce him when she'd been eighteen.

She kissed his palm. "I said I wished I didn't love you so much because it hurts so."

His expression at last softened. "Hush, now, lass."

He pulled her down onto him, and she pillowed her head on his chest, her dry eyes burning.

She thought he would lie quietly with her until she went to sleep, but after a moment he rolled over onto her and slid himself inside her again. He made love to her, face-to-face, gaze-to-gaze, but without the previous frenzy. Just long, slow loving that lasted until she was boneless and exhausted.

When he climaxed, he turned his head and squeezed his eyes closed, moaning low in his throat. She was excited and desperate, climaxing so new to her that she didn't want it to end.

He quieted her cries with his kisses, then slid out of her and held her until she succumbed to sleep. When she awoke, the sun was high and Egan had gone.

Chapter Seventeen
Lessons from Friends

Egan rode out early in the morning to check on his tenants and see what repairs needed to be done now that Hogmanay was over, but his mind was not on his work.

When Zarabeth had said, *I wish I didn't love you so much*, he'd stopped breathing. That revelation and the next, that she could hear what people thought, had sent waves of conflicting emotions through him.

He'd been angry that she hadn't trusted him enough to confide in him. He hadn't believed her at first when she said she couldn't read him—that he was the only person she couldn't read—but sincerity had rung in her declaration, and he'd changed his mind.

He also believed her because his thoughts about her since her arrival had been incredibly carnal. If she'd heard *those* thoughts she'd have been shocked senseless and fled Castle MacDonald long ago, never mind her husband's minions lurking in wait for her.

He also felt annoyance and jealousy that he should be the only one she couldn't read. The only one she couldn't touch. *Why not me?*

Damnation.

As he spoke to the villagers, who were cleaning up from Hogmanay revelry as well as the marriage celebration, he tried to shut out his feelings and inquire about any sightings of strangers in the last few days. None had seen anyone out of the ordinary except Olaf. There'd been no witnesses to the shooting of Valentin—no one had even noticed a wolf prowling.

Either Valentin had been very careful, or Egan's tenants had been very drunk. Both probably.

Egan headed back to the castle, not liking to leave Zarabeth alone for long. Hamish and Angus and even Williams would defend her, but with Valentin injured he wanted to stay as close as possible to her.

Her sweet voice came to him again, her sigh of anguish. *I wish I didn't love you so much.*

Beautiful Zarabeth, filling the hollow spaces of his heart.

When he reached the castle, it was still early, but Olaf was pacing the courtyard.

"I needed to walk," he said when he saw Egan. "But I didn't want to go far."

"Walk down to the bottom of the road with me," Egan replied, handing his horse to a groom. "I want to talk with ye."

Olaf nodded and fell into step with him. Once they'd left the courtyard and were trudging down the steep hill, Egan said conversationally, "Tell me about your wife."

Olaf glanced sideways at him. The man walked with his hands behind his back, still upright, like the soldier he'd been many years ago. Gray barely touched his hair, though the lines on his face were deep.

"Mariah. You knew her."

"Sadly, not for long. Zarabeth was how old when she died? It was after I left again for the Peninsular War."

"Zarabeth was fifteen. Mariah died of a fever—swift and sudden. Poor lamb." His eyes shone with tears.

"I'm sorry," Egan said sincerely. Mariah had been a kind woman, and Egan had never guessed her secret.

"Zarabeth told me a little about her. That she could read thoughts."

Olaf glanced quickly at him, then nodded. "I knew that she could, though not when I first met her. Zarabeth . . . I never asked her, but I am certain she can as well."

Uncertainty twisted in Egan's gut. He'd believed Zarabeth, but to hear it confirmed in the light of day by her father made it starkly real.

"How did ye . . . ?" Egan groped for words. "How did ye manage?"

Olaf smiled. "I loved Mariah. She gave me her vow that she would never pry into my head." He tapped his forehead. "She said she'd respect my privacy. We never talked openly about Zarabeth, but my wife taught her well. I know she did."

"And ye trusted her?"

"Mariah? Implicitly." He gave a rueful laugh. "After I got used to it, that is. Besides, I'm certain she did not want to know everything I thought. I think she was more afraid of what she'd find in my head than of me knowing she knew."

"Did it make ye more . . . guarded with her?"

"I admit it did at first. What a thing to be told, eh? That the woman you love will know everything you think about her—and everything else? I was angry with her, and I tested her, thought odd or bizarre things to see if she would react or know things I didn't speak of. She never did. I realized then that she'd been true, and I was ashamed of myself for not trusting her. I told her what I'd done." He smiled. "It would have served me right if Mariah had given me the boot, but she forgave me. That's a rare quality, the ability to forgive from the heart. Zarabeth has it too, despite what her husband did to her."

Egan wondered how much Olaf knew of what her husband had done. "I'm not sure she'll forgive her husband. I'm not sure I want her to."

"Maybe not, but she won't let what he did harden her or bury her in bitterness. She's free of him to get on with her life, and she knows that."

"But does she want to get on with her life with me?"

Olaf stopped walking and faced him, his smile sunny on this cold winter's day. "You know Zarabeth, Egan. Do you think if she truly didn't want to marry you that anything we said would have persuaded her? You'd still be trying everything in your power to make her accept you. She is her own woman. I feared Sebastian had broken her, but when I saw her on New Year's Eve with you and your family, I knew she'd be all right. The same exuberant Zarabeth. And for that I thank you." Tears filled his eyes and spilled down his cheeks.

"I canno' take credit for her strength," Egan said gently.

"I believe you can. Damien told me how numb she'd been when she first came to him. And now she's dancing and laughing without constraint. Whatever else has happened at Castle MacDonald, you've brought my Zarabeth back to me."

Tears still streaming, Olaf clapped Egan on the arm. Egan returned the clasp, hoping he could live up to what Olaf thought of him.

"Why didn't it work?" Jamie MacDonald sat at the table in the great hall, staring morosely at the sword that lay lengthwise in front of him.

Zarabeth ate her porridge hungrily, her appetite huge after the previous night's activities. Gemma sat at the table with them, her red hair neatly in place, her round face pink with health.

"Ye didn't have the rhyme, did ye?" Gemma asked.

"The legend goes that the laird and lady have t' chant the rhyme together, and *then* break the sword."

"Where are we going to find th' rhyme?" Jamie scowled. "I've been over every box of old papers in this castle, and none even mention it."

Zarabeth looked up. "Maybe Ian MacDonald was like Egan, not believing in curses. Maybe he felt no need to keep any kind of record of it."

"That's a thought," Jamie agreed glumly. "Uncle Egan can be bloody stubborn about it."

"But perhaps Morag's family kept the record," Zarabeth went on. "You said she bore a son, Ian's child. What happened to him?"

Jamie perked up, but Gemma shook her head. "Folk like Morag were peasants, tenant farmers. Most could no' read nor write."

Jamie thumped the table in sudden excitement. "But someone might have written it down, maybe their parish priest. Parish priests were always sticking their noses in where witches were concerned. I'll go talk to the vicar, see if anything survived."

"It'd be unlikely," Gemma warned.

Jamie leaped up, a bright grin on his face. "I'll find it. See if I don't." He raced out like a shot, boots clattering.

Gemma moved down the table to sit opposite Zarabeth, then waited while Williams and a maid cleared the breakfast things.

"Poor Jamie," she said. "I hope he's not too disappointed, but it gives him something to do."

"You don't believe in the curse?" Zarabeth asked.

Gemma grinned. "Well, of course I do. I live with it every day, and I don't believe that a few words from long ago can break it. Morag probably never thought a laird would openly marry a witch, not in those suspicious times. Why would she leave a convenient spell to end it?"

"Perhaps to plague him with false hope?"

"From what I hear tell, Ian MacDonald didn't much believe in anything, least of all hope. A right bastard he was."

Zarabeth blinked in surprise. "But the MacDonalds are so goodhearted."

"Aye." Gemma smiled fondly. "But that's after they started marrying good peasant stock. The 'Forty-five took many a fine lad to their deaths, and lasses of the families had to marry where they could. Things are a bit mixed-up nowadays, for the better, I'd say. Egan's father, now, he was another right bastard, and Charlie was just like him."

"Truly? But Egan and Adam told me everyone loved Charlie."

"Oh, aye." Gemma nodded wisely. "I should no' be telling tales, but everyone knows. Charlie could wrap people around his finger, he could, but Egan's ten times the man he was. Charlie was his father all over, but used his charm t' get his own way, didn't matter what. Well, he's gone, and no' much we can do now."

Zarabeth felt a pang of anger for the departed Charlie and his father. They'd been horrible to Egan, as horrible in their own way as Sebastian had been to Zarabeth.

"What did you need to talk to me about yesterday?" Zarabeth asked.

Gemma leaned forward furtively. "Breedin'. Me and Angus, specifically. Ye made a charm to send those two silly girls back home, but can ye do something a bit more complicated? Like making sure I get with child next time me and Angus go to bed?"

She looked worried, and Zarabeth's heart squeezed in sympathy. She well remembered her dashed hopes each time she began her menses during her marriage, the disappointment that she still hadn't conceived. Her initial, girlish interest in Sebastian had faded quickly enough once she learned his true character, but she'd still wanted a child, someone to love unconditionally. She'd grieved when she finally accepted that a baby was not going to come.

"You and Angus only married in October," Zarabeth pointed out. "These things can take time, you know."

"Nay. Angus and me have been tumbling for a year now, ever since he bent his knee and asked me t' be his wife. We thought if a baby started, we'd just up the date a bit. But nothing." She sighed.

"There are charms I can give you," Zarabeth said. "Though I can't guarantee they'll work." They hadn't worked on herself, but she'd helped other ladies in the past.

"I'll try anything, I don't care. The quack in the village gave me some potions, but they're useless. Quacks usually are."

"They are fond of their books and mathematics," Zarabeth agreed. "In Nvengaria, wise women with herbal lore are far more respected than doctors and their bloodletting."

Gemma grinned. "I think I'd like Nvengaria, what Egan's told me about it. Is it true that wives there rule their husbands?"

"Not exactly. But they can own property and run businesses and do as they like."

Gemma shrugged philosophically. "Aye, well, I likely wouldn't know what t' do wi' myself in Nvengaria— I've never been twenty miles from Castle MacDonald in all my life. I'll stay here and run Angus's life for him."

Zarabeth hid a smile. From what she could see, Angus loved being bullied by his gentle wife.

Gemma said suddenly, "Ye aren't going to run off back to Nvengaria and leave Egan here alone, are ye?"

"No." Zarabeth stopped. Things had been such a whirlwind in the past few days that she'd ceased worrying about what she'd do when the time came to go home.

"Good. Because he needs ye here. After Charlie died, ye couldn't even talk to Egan. He just shut into himself. He didn't shout at his father for blaming him for Charlie's death or for cutting up Egan's picture. Egan walked away and never came back until Gregor MacDonald was dead and buried. Even now, Egan's been distant, like he's not really here even when he is."

Zarabeth pushed aside her now empty porridge bowl. "He was not like that in Nvengaria. Or . . . maybe when he first came to us, but I was only twelve and didn't really understand his grief. He talked to my father at length about it, says my father gave him back his will to live. Egan seemed almost happy at my father's house."

"Ye did him good, then. I'm glad. Poor Angus had to look after the castle and the farms and do his best while Egan was gone. He's a good and competent man, is Angus, but he's not the laird, and the people know it." She laced her fingers together. "So I don't want Egan runnin' off and leaving Angus to it again. Not if I have to chain him to the castle gates."

Zarabeth smiled at the idea, because she knew the fiery Gemma would do it.

"You don't want me to take him away," Zarabeth said.

"We need him, Zarabeth. Ye've given him back a bit of life, and that can only be good for Castle MacDonald. Do ye know Egan is one of the few landholders around here who hasn't given all his tenants the push so he can load the land with sheep? He's got a few flocks, but he hires local men to look after them, and the rest continue to farm. The people stay loyal to him because he's loyal to them."

Zarabeth remembered what Adam had said about Egan making sure his tenants and crofters were snug and dry even if Castle MacDonald leaked. "I have some money," she said. "My mother left me a substantial legacy. The tenants never need worry, because the income from my legacy can repair all the roofs in the county. Including this one."

She looked up at the torn plaster where the ceiling beam had come down. It still hadn't been mended, and with all the bouncing she and Egan had done on the upper floors . . .

Gemma gave her a grateful look. "I think you're the answer to our prayers, lass. We've been prayin' an awful lot that Egan will stay home and be laird, as he should. And from the noise comin' from your bedrooms, I'd say we'll have a little lairdling soon?"

Zarabeth lost her smile, her heart squeezing again. "I don't know if I can. I've never had a child."

"This Nvengarian husband of yours, he came to your bed, didn't he?"

Fortunately Sebastian's visits to her had been few and far between. He'd been too busy to demand her compliance in that area very often, and he'd made it clear he was bedding Zarabeth only to get an heir.

"He did. Every few months—when it was clear I hadn't conceived."

Gemma's mouth dimpled. "Well, ye need t' try harder than that. With Angus and me, it's been near every night for a year. That's why I'm askin' for help. But ye and Egan—ye keep at it every day, and ye'll get there. My ma had a hard time conceiving, so I'm not surprised I do, too. There was only ever one of me at home."

"There's only one of me, as well. Perhaps my mother had difficulty, too."

"Do ye know for certain?"

"No," Zarabeth said with regret. "She died before we talked about starting families."

"Well, I know I need a bit of a boost, which is why I'm willing to try your charm—as well as frolic with Angus every chance I can get. But ye find out before ye give up. And take Egan t' bed as often as ye can. The MacDonald men have stamina."

Zarabeth's face heated as she recalled just how much stamina Egan had. She'd been half-dead with sleep by the time he'd stopped the second time, and then he'd sprung up and ridden off over his lands, while she'd blearily scrubbed herself and stumbled downstairs for porridge fortification.

Gemma laughed out loud. "There, now ye know why the ladies love a MacDonald." Zarabeth's blush deepened, and Gemma laughed harder.

"Tellin' funny stories, are ye?"

Egan's voice rumbled from the doorway, and Zarabeth jumped a foot, her face scalding. He could move quietly for such a large man, drat him.

"Nothin' that would interest ye," Gemma said innocently.

Egan gave her a suspicious look. "Where's Jamie?"

"Gone t' the village," Gemma answered.

"Doing research on the curse," Zarabeth put in. She hoped her face had returned to its normal color.

"Och, Jamie and his curse."

Gemma rose from the table, her face merry. "Thank ye, Zarabeth. Ye tell me what I need t' do, and I'll follow your instructions to the letter." With a smirk at Egan, she left the room.

"What was that about?" Egan asked in suspicion.

"She wants a baby. She and Angus."

"Aye, well, she's always loved bairns. She'd have the castle running over with children if she could."

"It should be." Zarabeth looked over the vast great

hall, with its heads of slain animals and weapons of war. Egan, Mary, and Charlie had played here as children. Mary's and Charlie's sons had grown up here, and Egan's should as well.

"There's Jamie and Dougal," Egan pointed out.

"They're almost grown now, too. In a few years they'll be having children of their own."

"Dear God, do no' remind me."

"I look forward to it."

Egan came to her, his presence filling the hall and making her feel very small. She stood up to meet him, her body growing hot with longing, as usual. All he had to do was slant that lazy smile at her and she melted into a pool of lust.

"Look forward to it?" he repeated. "But you'll return to Nvengaria soon."

"Will I?"

"Aye, with your husband killed, Damien and Grand Duke Alexander will put down the uprising quick enough. It will be safe for ye to go with your father in a few weeks, I'll wager."

"And you?"

"I'll journey wi' ye, if I may."

"No."

Egan had opened his mouth to continue the conversation but stopped in surprise. "No? Are ye tired of this marriage already?" He spoke lightly, but she saw watchfulness in his eyes.

"I should stay in Scotland and be the lady of Egan MacDonald."

Egan raised his brows. He looked at the ruined ceiling and the cold walls, then back to her again. "In this tumbledown place? I can never match what ye had in your father's house, lass, nor the riches your husband gave ye. Here ye'll be hostin' fairs with farm women, not entertaining royalty."

She tried a laugh. "Goodness, I don't care about that. You belong *here*. This is your land, your clan, your castle."

"Ah, Gemma's been talking at ye." He gave her a wise nod. "Keep the family together, tend to my duties as laird, that sort of thing."

"But she's right. The castle needs to be filled with family. That's what will drive away the curse, not breaking the sword or saying the right words."

Egan glanced at Ian MacDonald's sword, lying where Jamie had left it on the table. "Five Highlanders live in the castle already. Seven, if ye count the Rosses, who are here too often. Isn't that enough?"

"You have a fine family, Egan. It shouldn't die out."

"There's small danger of it dyin' out. Angus and Gemma will have children, and Jamie and Dougal. And Hamish has yet t' wed. The place will be knee-deep in bairns before long."

"With you to look after them all."

Egan's good humor vanished. "Ye can never understand what this place means t' me—or doesn't mean t' me, Zarabeth. I was never happy here, not like ye were as a girl in your father's house. My memories are haunted, and I do no' think that can ever change. Curse or no curse."

Zarabeth went to him, liking how he towered over her. It wasn't just that he was so tall, over six feet to her five feet. There was so much of Egan, a force to be reckoned with.

"Perhaps we should fill it with happy memories, then," she said in a low voice.

His eyes darkened. "Are ye trying to seduce me again, love? Last night didn't sate ye?"

"Are all Scotsmen so certain of their prowess?"

A flush stained his cheekbones. "Well, I *am* a Mac-Donald."

"Gemma mentioned that you are all full of yourselves."

He cupped her shoulders with warm hands. "And ye are the lass so keen to get a MacDonald into bed."

"Must it always be in a bed?"

She felt his heartbeat quicken. "Little vixen."

"I've read so many books, you see. And lovers do not always stay in bed."

"No, but the great hall is no' very private."

"Perhaps not." She smiled and ran her hands down his chest to his kilt.

He pulled away, breathing hard. "What were you and Gemma truly talking about?"

"I told you." She thought about Gemma's advice to keep trying for bairns—children—every chance she had. If nothing else, the deep pleasure Egan made her feel would be worth the effort.

She smiled at him, the flirtatious, winsome smile she'd practiced, turned her back, and sauntered out of the great hall. The little anteroom that lay just across the landing was far more private. It also had a dainty key to fit the gilded eighteenth-century lock.

Before she was halfway across the landing, Egan overtook her, growling like a bear. He snatched her up in his arms and barreled into the anteroom, slamming the door and locking it tight.

Chapter Eighteen
The Lineage of Morag the Witch

*E*gan's blood boiled hot, and Zarabeth's sly little smile didn't help at all. He'd never understand her—never, ever—and it didn't matter whether she could read his mind or not.

Trust her, Olaf had been trying to tell him. *Believe in her.*

Of course, Olaf didn't know what a mad seductress his daughter was. She stood on the other side of the gold-leafed table, watching him while her teeth worked her full lower lip.

"Are ye enjoying yourself?" he asked her.

"I don't know."

"Ye must be. You're driving me mad."

"Am I?"

Oh, God, that innocent look. "Come here."

He sat down on one of the absurd gilded chairs his sister liked and nearly dragged her to him. He rucked Zarabeth's plaid skirt to her thighs and pulled her down to straddle him.

She sat face-to-face with him, her arms around his neck, and watched him with an expectant smile.

"Now then," he rumbled. "What exactly are ye trying to do to me? You've been driving me mad since ye first set foot in Scotland."

She looked surprised. "How can that be?"

"Don't play the innocent, lass. Ye snuggled your bum up t' me in the inn by Ullapool and then again on our way home. Ye lured me into kissing ye, first in your chamber and then in the Ring of Dunmarran. Ye wanted so badly t' know what was under my kilt that ye spied on me when I got out of the bath, and *then* ye tricked me into your room and pulled off my kilt. Ye like the sight of my bare arse so much, I might have a painting done of it and hung in your room."

Her eyes were round with fascination. "Don't be absurd."

"I haven't even mentioned how beautiful and wicked ye were last night."

To his satisfaction she blushed. "I can't help rubbing my backside against you whenever we are on horseback. You make me sit in front of you. And at the inn, you were the one who got into bed with me."

The mirth left him. "I was so afraid for ye, Zarabeth. So afraid ye'd die of cold before I could stop it."

"I knew I'd be fine, once I saw you were there to take care of me."

"Now, don't come over the sweet maiden on me. I know ye better."

"I am not joking." She traced his lips, her soft fingers doing insane things to his private places. "I knew you'd come for me, somehow. Like a knight in shining armor."

"That's only in fairy stories."

"You live in a castle in a faraway land."

She tilted her head as she studied him. Her lashes were long and black, sweeping down over her sparkling eyes.

He found it difficult to breathe. "I live right here in Scotland."

She brushed back a lock of his unruly hair and kissed him softly on the lips. He swallowed a groan as she explored his mouth and dipped her fingers inside his half-unlaced shirt. She was not even touching his intimate places, and still he was ramrod hard.

"I love your hair," she murmured.

He laughed. "A rat's nest, m' sister always calls it."

Zarabeth wound one of his long curls around her finger. "It's thick and soft. I liked it on my face last night."

He started to throb. This was why he was happy he hadn't married a virginal miss, one who had no idea how to set a man's heart pounding. Zarabeth likely wasn't doing it on purpose, but she wasn't afraid of saying what she liked.

He wove his fingers through her coiled braids, pulling them loose. "I like yours, too. Like gossamer."

She smiled as her dark hair tumbled about her face. He feathered kisses across her lips, loving the little flicks of her tongue as she tried to catch him.

"Do ye know what else I like?" he asked between kisses. "Your hair all sweet and damp for me between your legs."

He heard her intake of breath, and the heat inside him nearly exploded. He thought of how he'd tasted her. She tasted of salt and spice and smelled better than the best Parisian perfume.

My Zarabeth. My wife.

He slid his hands up her thighs and dipped his thumbs into that beautiful tuft of hair, all wet and warm for him. She gasped when he fingered her opening, rocking on his lap as he began to pleasure her.

"Do ye still love me, Zarabeth?"

"Yes." It was a moan.

"Good."

"You don't want me to, but I do."

"I'd never stop ye from doing what ye truly want," he whispered.

She had no idea what she was saying. Her eyes were half-closed, her lips parted in pleasure.

"Ye make me want you," he told her. "Ye make me want you *now*."

"*Yes*."

Her languid moans turned to a frenzy of cries. It was easy to lift her skirt all the way, to shove his kilt aside and impale her right there on the chair. He caught her cries with his kisses, snaked his arms around her, and held her tight.

"Well, now, lass," he said, his voice strained. "Is this better than a bed?"

"Egan," she breathed.

"I agree with ye."

She felt so good squeezing him, her thighs smooth against his, her body arched so he could kiss her throat and face without moving.

He made sweet love to her on that chair, while the gilt ormolu clock ticked crisply in the corner, and the laughter and shouts of his cousins came through the partially opened window.

He did not agree with Zarabeth that he belonged at Castle MacDonald—too many bitter memories—but right now, at this moment, he belonged here with her on his lap. He'd never much liked this room, but now it would hold this memory of him making love to Zarabeth while ordinary castle business went on around them.

When she gasped her climax, he was not far behind with his. He held her hard, burying his face in the curve of her neck, as she writhed in a frenzy on top of him.

If only life could be as simple as a fairy tale. The valiant knight married the beautiful princess, and they lived forever in a palace in which all rooms looked like this one—overly ornate English frippery. He much preferred whitewashed stone and echoing halls and a plain table laden with bannocks and Mrs. Williams's porridge.

He hoped for his sake that Zarabeth did too.

When they at last emerged from the anteroom, Egan saw Jamie seated on the lower stairs, his kilt dangling between his spread legs, fingers twitching impatiently. When he saw Zarabeth he sprang up like a young hunting dog scenting a grouse.

"Ye were right, Zarabeth," he shouted. "Ye were right about Morag."

Jamie's brown eyes glowed with excitement. He didn't seem to notice, or care, that Zarabeth's hair hung in long, mussed waves, or that her skirt was wrinkled and askew.

Egan stepped protectively in front of her. "What are ye on about, lad?"

Jamie loped past him and seized Zarabeth's hands. "I went t' see the vicar. He said parish records didn't go back very far, but Morag was so famous that people wrote down stories about her, and he had some locked away. We read them all." He bounced up and down on his toes, squeezing Zarabeth's hands until she winced. "Morag's son lived, but he had no sons of his own—only a daughter."

The curse again. Egan tried to keep impatience from his voice. "Her line might be hard t' trace if her descendants were peasants, lad."

Jamie turned to Egan with a wide grin. "That's what I'm trying t' tell you, Uncle. They were no' peasants. Morag's granddaughter, she married a *Ross.*"

He pulled Zarabeth out into the hall and started dancing a jig around her.

Zarabeth laughed. Her hair swung around, dark as midnight, her blue eyes flashing as she let Jamie spin her around. Jamie tripped over his own large feet, and Egan caught Zarabeth before Jamie could barrel her to the floor.

"Stop before ye hurt yourself," Egan admonished.

Zarabeth, still laughing, leaned back against Egan, pulling his arms around her. "Well, if she became a Ross, hadn't you better go ask Adam if you can look through his papers?"

Jamie's grin dimmed. "But Ross Castle was destroyed after Culloden. The bloody English might have burned all the papers."

"I wager some got out," Egan said, interested in spite of himself. "A Scotsman's greatest treasure is his family, and tracing that family is most important. A few family trees will have survived somehow."

Jamie leaped to his feet. "I hadn't thought o' that!" He spun and dashed away madly, kilt swinging.

"I'd better send Angus after him," Egan said, releasing Zarabeth with reluctance. "Lord knows what he'll be telling Adam Ross, tearing up the man's house without leave. You know 'tis a long shot, Jamie finding anything about this granddaughter of Morag's."

"I know," she said. "But he's happy. Let him believe what he can while he's young. Time enough for him to grow up and lose what's important."

Egan dropped a kiss to her hair. "That's a bit cynical, love."

"Perhaps I learned too many lessons too quickly. I had to grow up before I was ready, when I was still waiting for my knight in shining armor. Let Jamie believe in the end of the fairy tale for a while."

Egan swept her up for a hard hug and a kiss. "All right, I'll let him. But he still needs t' not pester the Rosses too much. Let me explain things t' Angus. Then I'll come back and we'll talk."

"Talk about what?"

"Many things, love." They had so much to decide.

He didn't like the slight worry that entered her eyes, but she'd understand. "Ye go on up and tidy yourself— even though I like ye mussed. I'll run Angus t' earth and find ye."

She seized him before he could turn away, pulling him to her for another kiss. He made himself disentangle from her after a time and sent her upstairs with a pat on her backside. She glared at him over the railings, and he walked away, whistling, to scour the castle for Angus MacDonald.

Zarabeth ducked into her bedroom, bathed her face in cool water, and brushed and repinned her hair. What a wanton she looked! She'd let Egan take her three times in three days, once on a gilded chair in the anteroom. She blushed hotly.

Yet she longed for him already. She wanted to spend the rest of the afternoon and on into the evening exploring him, learning what he liked. Lovemaking for pleasure was a new sensation to her. She'd read about it, but it had seemed distant and unreal, like reading travel literature about exotic lands where she would likely never go.

From Egan's expression, he was eager to continue their journey into their newfound world. She knew he hadn't accepted what she'd told him about her ability to read thoughts, but he was willing to put it aside while they made love. There would come a time when they had to sort things out, but for now, she would enjoy his body and his touch.

She smoothed her gown and left her room to look in on Valentin while she waited. She wanted to ask him a few things while she had the opportunity.

Ivan and Constanz, stationed outside her door, snapped to attention when she came out, and followed her to Valentin's chamber, where they took up sentry stance again. Zarabeth thanked them, rapped softly on the door, and let herself in.

Valentin was better. Mrs. Williams, who was just leaving with a tray, reported that he was eating well and demanding more. Valentin did look stronger propped against the pillow, the bandage on his shoulder a white slash on his dark skin. His face was still pale, but his blue eyes glittered with impatience.

Zarabeth closed the door behind Mrs. Williams and came to sit by Valentin's side.

"Will you tell her, please, to bring something besides broth?" Valentin growled.

Zarabeth smiled at him. "There is always porridge."

He looked horrified. "No."

"I was only teasing. I will talk to Williams and see what I can do. No one knows there's a wild animal inside you, you see."

Valentin moved restlessly. Zarabeth recognized the symptoms of a man who felt better but had to lie quietly or risk growing worse. She'd seen it in her father, who often fell off horses while riding hell-for-leather, and in Egan after they'd rescued him in Nvengaria.

"Where is Mrs. Cameron this morning?" Valentin asked abruptly. "She said she would read to me."

Zarabeth's interest perked. He'd asked about Mary before, seeming embarrassed about it. "She went shopping with Dougal, Gemma told me at breakfast. She did sit with you when you were first hurt. You might not have realized."

"I realized." Valentin clamped his mouth shut as though fearing to elaborate.

To change the subject she told him of Jamie's research into the curse and what he had discovered. Valentin did not look terribly interested.

"I can read to you, if you like," she offered.

"No." He softened his irritated grunt. "Forgive me."

"Not at all. I hate being laid up myself." She leaned her elbows on her knees and studied him, a square-faced man who would be handsome if it weren't for the hard, rather forbidding cast to his features. He was younger than Egan—she guessed about thirty years old.

"My father recognized you," she said quietly.

Valentin's gaze instantly locked on hers. The atmosphere in the room changed from sickroom boredom to the tension of a general's battle tent.

Zarabeth went on. "I told him that Damien would not have sent you with me if he couldn't trust you."

Valentin watched her for a long time, his too-blue eyes harsh. "You are right. He would not have."

"I do wonder why you agreed to come with me at all. I would have thought that once you got out of prison you'd want to go home."

"Atonement." Valentin sank back to the pillow but remained alert. "For my sins."

"For trying to kill Damien?"

"Among other things. I reasoned that if I volunteered to protect something precious to Damien, he would believe in my contrition."

"I see."

His expression turned fierce. "You do not see. I failed on the ship; I failed by letting myself get shot. If not for Egan MacDonald and his family, you would be dead."

Zarabeth held up a placating hand. "I know that. I also know that protecting me by yourself would have been impossible. If not *for* you, I'd be dead, too. We could not have anticipated the ship breaking up off-shore, and likely you frightened away whoever was lurking in the tunnels the night you were shot. No one has attacked me."

"But I lie here, ineffectual and weak."

"You look plenty strong to me. Anyone else would have succumbed to fever, or at least slept for a fortnight."

"Do not try to appease me," he snapped.

"Very well. You have not been the perfect bodyguard, but who could be? You found Olympia Templeton before she froze to death, and your patrolling has likely helped keep assassins from creeping close to the castle. It has been a great comfort knowing I had a logosh to look after me. Because of you, I made it to Scotland, where Egan could keep me safe. I have written Damien to tell him so."

"Yes, but—"

"Wallow in misery if you like, but Damien would not have chosen you if he did not think you could protect me, atonement or no."

"I volunteered."

"Even so." She raised her brows at him. "You know Damien. He is not persuaded to do anything against his better judgment. He's the most cautious man in the world."

Valentin relaxed a little. "You are kind to comfort me."

"I want something in return. Two things, actually."

He tensed again. "What are they?"

"I want you to pledge yourself to me as a lady of Clan MacDonald. Your loyalty to me—not to Damien or Egan, but to me."

He looked surprised. "Why?"

"Because I want you protecting *me*, not simply pleasing Prince Damien. Are you willing?"

He hesitated a long moment, searching her gaze. As he did so, Zarabeth lowered her shields a little bit, letting herself touch his thoughts.

As usual, she could not see much. Valentin was a man who knew how to keep his true self tucked into a secret place—perhaps it was a trait of the logosh. But what she found in him was truth. He'd pledged himself to Damien, and he sincerely regretted any mistakes he'd made while protecting her.

"What are you doing?" he asked.

She quickly broke the contact. "Nothing."

Valentin's blue eyes narrowed. "I am a magical creature, so I can tell when magic is directed at me. But if you would like to pretend, I will say nothing."

Zarabeth stared at him, and he stared back, meeting her gaze without blinking. "You are a frightening man, Valentin," she said at last.

"And a dangerous one. But very well, I will pledge my loyalty to you." He paused. "What is the second thing?"

Zarabeth regained her composure and sat back, pleased. "I want to know your story. *All* of it."

Chapter Nineteen
Baron Valentin's Story

*Y*ou do know it." Valentin shifted on his pillow, wincing when he moved his injured arm. "I tried to kill Prince Damien. He caught me and imprisoned me. I changed my mind, and he let me out."

"No, no. The real story. You've pledged your loyalty to me; now I command you to tell me."

Valentin shot her another look that she recognized: that of a man annoyed that a woman had gotten around him. He couldn't simply protect her in silence—she insisted he open himself to her.

He gave a resigned nod. "I worked in Grand Duke Alexander's household before Damien became imperial prince. I believed in Alexander and what he tried to do—undermine and overthrow the prince of Nvengaria and instill a rule by the Council of Dukes, with the grand duke at its head. The imperial prince was a monster and ruining the country. His son Damien was a frivolous playboy who never came home."

Zarabeth felt chilled. Sebastian had also wanted to overthrow the imperial prince in the dark days when Grand Duke Alexander had virtually ruled the country as its dictator.

But with a slight difference, she realized as Valentin went on. Valentin had been fanatically devoted to Grand Duke Alexander, while Sebastian had been fanatically devoted to grabbing power for himself. Valentin truly wanted what was best for Nvengaria; Sebastian had wanted what was best for Sebastian.

Then Grand Duke Alexander did the unthinkable. He was unable to stop Prince Damien from returning to Nvengaria to take up the throne, and then Alexander turned around and actually supported him. Not only that, Alexander had fallen under the influence of Princess Penelope, the English girl who'd married Damien. Alexander had pledged himself to Damien and Penelope and appeared to be content working for them both.

To make matters worse, the logosh from the mountains—the pureblood shape-changers—had become Princess Penelope's sworn protectors. It seemed that Damien had undermined everyone in the country.

Valentin decided to act on his own. He'd crept into the palace and tried to kill Damien as he dined with his wife, as Zarabeth's father had described. Damien's bodyguards had been alert enough to stop him. Damien, cool as you please, had called for a new coat to replace the one Valentin's knife had ruined, apologized to the concerned Penelope, and resumed his dinner as Valentin was dragged away.

Valentin had been given a trial, found guilty of attempted assassination, and put into the dungeons under the palace.

"I was surprised I wasn't executed the next morning," Valentin continued. "But Damien was interested in me. He visited me several times and kept putting off the execution. At first I thought he was trying to break me, but I came to realize that he wanted me to get to know him. He got me to talk to him about being part logosh, and seemed to understand how difficult it had made my life.

"One day he brought Princess Penelope with him." He smiled, an unusual expression for Valentin. "I think

I became a little smitten with her. There she was, a golden-haired young lady with a strange accent, wanting to know all about me and why I'd tried to kill her husband. After meeting her, I grew certain that Prince Damien wasn't the monster his father had been. A woman like that wouldn't have married a monster and remained so . . . happy. She radiated happiness, and not because she was too foolish to know any better. She'd seen the world and its darkness and had found a home."

Zarabeth nodded. "She struck me the same way."

Sebastian had viewed Penelope as a harpy who'd snared Prince Damien in her claws. Zarabeth had known that couldn't be true, because her cousin Damien would never fall for such a woman. She'd been pleased to become friends with Penelope when they'd at last met.

"I became devoted to her, as have all the logosh," Valentin said. "Damien released me from prison and gave me a job. When Damien made plans to get you here, he let me in on the secret. I asked to be the one who guided you to Scotland and guarded you. Damien decided it was a good idea."

"And you didn't fail," Zarabeth said as Valentin's expression clouded again. "I am here, am I not?"

Valentin subsided. He'd probably learned not to argue with determined women.

"Now that your husband is dead, his cause will subside," Valentin said after a moment. "When Prince Damien declares the danger past, I will return to Nvengaria, where I belong. What will you do?"

Zarabeth went silent. She was almost glad Damien would still have mopping up to do so that she could put off making the decision. Egan was restless and wanted to leave. Gemma thought Zarabeth should make him stay at Castle MacDonald. Jamie wanted Egan to settle down and start a family so Jamie wouldn't have to inherit. Angus wanted Egan here so he'd not have to be head of the house. Olaf wanted to return to his Lady Beatrice—he'd said he wanted Zarabeth home with him, but she was not certain how Lady Beatrice would feel about that.

If she returned to Nvengaria and Egan came with her, would he be happy so far from home? If she stayed at Castle MacDonald, as she'd declared to Egan she wanted to, would Egan, restless and impatient, travel the world without her? She thought of the baroness in Vienna, the one who'd described her love affair with Egan in lavish detail, and lapsed into boiling fury.

A thought came to her from outside the door, one sharp and clear enough to penetrate her barriers. She could not tell what language it was in, because it was more an urge than a word.

Now.

Zarabeth jerked around to face the door. Nothing happened.

Valentin raised himself on his elbow, trying to adjust his bandaged arm. "What is it?" he whispered.

"I don't . . ."

Her mouth went dry. She felt determination from outside, guilt, and fear.

Valentin eased the drawer of the bedside table open and withdrew a pistol. One-handed, he primed and cocked it, then told Zarabeth, "Open the door."

The door was not locked—any intruder could have burst in. Zarabeth quietly glided to the door, shielding herself behind it as she pulled it open.

Valentin pointed his pistol at empty air. No one was there.

Zarabeth tentatively peered around the door. Ivan and Constanz stood in their places, blinking at her in surprise.

"Ivan, was anyone out here?" she asked.

"The cook came out and went downstairs," he answered readily.

"I mean besides Mrs. Williams. Did anyone else come up to see Valentin?"

"No." His surprised, innocent stare told her he wasn't lying.

Valentin lowered the pistol. Zarabeth turned back to the room, and as she did, she caught another thought—strong relief.

She whirled and stared at Constanz, who looked back at her with guilt large in his eyes.

"Oh, no," she said, her voice sad. "Oh, Constanz."

Ivan grabbed her arms in a hard grip and shoved her back into the room, the cold blade of a knife at her throat. Constanz followed and shut the door.

"Please put the pistol away," Ivan said clearly. "I will try not to kill her, but you must not shoot and make noise, or I will cut her."

Valentin, glaring his fury, uncocked the pistol. Constanz hurried over and took it from his grip.

Zarabeth, for some reason, felt no fear, only profound sorrow. "You could have taken me or killed me at any time during our journey, Ivan. Why have you waited until now?"

Constanz stared as though she'd said something puzzling. "Because we wanted to protect you. We need you. We did not lie when we said we'd die for you. We several times almost did."

"Then why do I now have a knife at my throat?"

Ivan answered: "We did not mean for this to happen. But we cannot let Baron Valentin kill us. He is not on our side, and we still need you. You will come with us, and we will explain."

Valentin snarled and kicked back the covers. He was naked under them, making it all the easier for him to

surge into his demon form. He became something in-
human, large-eyed, sharp-toothed, and growling. He
was still injured, making the change hard for him, but
his limbs were bursting with muscle, his hands curving
into razorlike claws.

Constanz fired the gun.

The ball hit Valentin as he leaped, sending him crashing back into the bed. Zarabeth screamed.

Ivan swore. "Now they will all come running to the
noise. Help me!"

Constanz dropped the gun. Zarabeth struggled against
Ivan's brutal grip, crying out as the knife blade bit into
her neck. Constanz yanked a thick wad of cloth out of
his pocket and pressed it over Zarabeth's mouth.

She gagged and tried to turn away from the strange,
sweet odor, but the two footmen were strong. Her head
spun, blackness whirling before her eyes.

She heard running feet as she drooped, nearly senseless, against Ivan. Then Williams's voice, and Hamish's.
Where was Egan?

"Ze baron," Constanz shouted in his broken English.
"He attack our lady. I shoot."

No. Zarabeth struggled to speak, to tell them Constanz lied, but her tongue was heavy and she couldn't
make a sound.

"Good lad," Hamish said. "Bloody bastard."

Again Zarabeth tried to correct him, and again her
lips would not form words. She was vaguely aware that
the knife and the cloth were no longer there, but she
could not make her body respond.

The last thing she knew, Ivan had swept her into his
strong arms and was carrying her away, past Hamish
and Williams, who let her go without question.

Egan returned to Castle MacDonald after having to
search too bloody long for Angus. He'd found his

cousin halfway along the road to the village, talking with Olaf, who'd just returned from a walk there. Egan had sent a resigned Angus after Jamie, and climbed back up to the castle with Olaf.

As soon as Egan entered the castle he knew something was wrong. The servants were bustling up and down the main staircase, Gemma shouting above, Hamish cursing.

Silence fell the moment Egan set foot into the hall. Hamish looked over the gallery, then hurried down, his face gray. "Egan."

No.

Egan felt something fierce and hard well up inside him. Every vestige of the cheerful Mad Highlander, the friendly Egan, shattered like brittle glass.

"Where is she?" he asked, his voice deathly quiet.

"I don't know. She's gone, her two footmen are gone, and the baron . . . he's gone, too."

Olaf made a noise of rage. "I knew he could not be trusted."

As Egan raced up the stairs, shouting for Williams, Hamish choked out the story. He'd found Valentin naked and spilling blood on the sheets in his bedroom, Constanz the footman claiming Valentin had attacked Zarabeth.

The two footmen had taken Zarabeth, who'd fainted, out. Hamish swore they'd taken her to her room, but once they had Valentin subdued, Zarabeth and the footmen had vanished. By the time Hamish organized a search for *them*, Baron Valentin himself had somehow slipped away.

"Egan," Hamish said in a near whisper, "I'm so sorry."

"Don't be sorry," Egan snapped. "Find her."

Olaf stepped forward, his face grim. "What about Baron Valentin?" He had murder in his eyes.

Egan preferred that Valentin remain alive so he could

answer questions. "Search for him, too," Egan told Hamish. "Injured, he canno' have gone far. If ye find him you'll likely find Zarabeth." He started to turn away, then decided to trust Hamish with the truth. "If ye see any wolves, don't shoot. That will be Valentin."

Hamish started. "Wha'?"

"Valentin can turn into a wolf. He's part logosh—a shape-changer. Keep it t' yourself; I'll explain later."

Hamish's mouth hung open in astonishment. But he nodded and turned away, bellowing at the servants to search the castle top to bottom one more time.

The tunnels under the castle were the most likely places for an abductor to get Zarabeth out, but they'd have to have gone through the kitchens to do it. If everyone in the castle had been running in seven different directions, likely the kitchen and cellar would have been unguarded just long enough.

Egan couldn't think clearly. In the depths of his panicked brain, one thought pounded.

Get her back.

No more noble ideas of letting her go home with her father, sending her back to Nvengaria, where she belonged. The ancient Scotsmen whose blood ran in his veins, the ancestors who'd fought and died at Culloden, wound him into berserker rage.

Get her back.

He needed a weapon. Somewhere in the house were pistols, but he didn't know where. Aggravating not to know his own house well enough to put his hands on a pistol. Valentin had used one, but when Egan grabbed Williams to question him about it, Williams said they couldn't find it. Valentin must have taken it with him.

The gillie had hunting guns, but his cottage was half a mile from the castle. Egan rushed into the great hall, eyeing the ancient—and rusted—weapons hanging on the walls. The now-polished claymore of Ian MacDonald still lay on the table where Jamie had left it, and Egan snatched it up.

It was a well-balanced sword with a good hilt, made by a fine craftsman. Egan had carried it at the wedding, liking the weight of it by his side, and the scabbard and belt still lay across the chair where he'd dropped it. He buckled it around his hips and slid the sword home.

If Jamie wanted this sword to perform a brave deed, Egan would give him a brave deed. He'd find Zarabeth and slice up anyone who had dared touch her.

He headed for the tunnels, growling at Hamish to gather the men and follow.

Zarabeth awoke in the dark. She tried to move and found her hands painfully bound behind her and ropes around her ankles. She lay on something hard and unforgiving, but lifting her head to look around gave her a pounding headache. Wherever room she lay in was dank, warm, and smelled of earth.

Ivan and Constanz. It made no sense. They'd been loyal to her, very worried about her well-being, and adamant about keeping her safe. They'd had plenty of opportunities to abduct her or kill her on their journey and at Castle MacDonald, and they hadn't. After Egan had rescued her from the Devil's Teeth, they'd wailed in self-castigation, offering to kill themselves to atone.

What had happened to change them? And had it been one of *them* who'd followed Valentin to the Ring of Dunmarran to shoot him?

They hadn't gagged her, and for that she was thankful. She moved her tongue, which felt foul and sticky, cleaving to her parched mouth.

A blinding light flashed in her eyes. "She needs water," came Ivan's baritone.

After a moment, a dripping cup touched her lips, but Zarabeth closed her mouth and turned her head.

" 'Tis not poisoned, I promise," Constanz told her. In the glare of the lantern light, he sipped from the cup himself, then offered it to her again.

A very good assassin learned to take an antidote to a poison before sharing it with his victim, but she knew that neither Ivan nor Constanz was a trained assassin. She had an advantage—she could read her captors' thoughts.

From both Constanz and Ivan she felt only concern to keep her alive but confined, worry that she would be angry, hope that she would understand, and no intention of letting her go.

Zarabeth gulped the water. It tasted muddy, but it wet her throat and let her draw a clean breath. She looked up at Constanz as he gently dabbed her lips with a handkerchief.

"Why?" she croaked.

Ivan and Constanz exchanged a glance. They were wondering exactly how much to tell her, and each worried that the other would tell her too much.

Tell her what? She silently urged them to think, but Ivan and Constanz were simple lads, not much given to deep contemplation. She sensed something in the back of their minds, something important, something big, but their immediate worries were keeping it silent.

"I know you mean me no harm," she prodded. That was, no harm but brutally tying her wrists and ankles and dragging her out of Castle MacDonald. "My husband did not order you to kill me."

They exchanged another glance, and Ivan spoke: "No. We keep you safe."

"Why?" she asked again.

Their thoughts came to her at the same time as Ivan's words. "For the cause."

She was pulled into a vision of their triumph. She saw glorious battle, Prince Damien covered in blood, and herself stepping over Damien's dead body with the crown of Nvengaria on her head.

She choked, sickened. "You cannot."

Constanz started, spilling the water. "Cannot what?"

"You cannot put me on the throne of Nvengaria. Have you run mad?"

Ivan swung to his brother. "Constanz, you told her."

"I did not." Constanz was wide-eyed. "I told her nothing, I swear it."

"Constanz did not tell me anything." Zarabeth firmed her voice, as she often did when she admonished them for mistakes in their duties. "I am a powerful witch, as you must know. That is why Egan married me, because he can break his curse only if he weds a witch."

Constanz took a step back, but Ivan remained in place. "Your being a witch will be even better. You will be a great imperial princess, a finer ruler than your husband would have been. The cause is not dead."

She blinked. "But Sebastian did not want to rule, not as prince. He wanted the Council of Dukes to rule, with him as Grand Duke."

Ivan shook his head. "He did at first. But after you were kidnapped by Prince Damien and held hostage, he decided it was better if he took over entirely. He vowed revenge on the prince for taking you."

Zarabeth went silent in shock. Had Sebastian truly thought Damien abducted her, or had he told his followers that lie so he'd not have to admit that his own wife had betrayed him? She could never know now. Looking into Ivan's and Constanz's minds showed her that they believed Damien's perfidy wholeheartedly.

She wondered what to do. If she pretended to go along with their scheme, perhaps they'd untie her and she'd stand a better chance of getting away. But their thoughts told her that while they were not the most intellectually gifted young men, they were cunning.

They needed her, but they did not trust her. She'd have to win them over gradually.

"May I have more water, please?" she asked.

Ivan nodded at Constanz. Constanz lumbered into the darkness, clinked the cup against something, and returned with it brimming with water. She drank gratefully, trying to ease her position to relieve her cramped body.

"My hands hurt," she said as she licked droplets from her lips. "I cannot run away if you loosen the ropes— I'm much too sore and tired."

"We do not mean to hurt you," Ivan said, believing it. "We brought you here to protect you from Valentin and the Scotsmen, who wish to keep you here forever."

"They are trying to protect me, too."

Constanz shook his head. "I hear them talk. They think we understand so little English, but we understand more than they know. They want you to stay and be the lady to Egan MacDonald. To live in this wilderness as nothing, when you could lead your people in Nvengaria."

Zarabeth stifled a groan. Ivan and Constanz were fanatics, certain their way of thinking was the only way, and simplistic enough not to easily be turned aside.

"Can I start leading you by having you untie my hands?" she asked. "My arms ache so."

Constanz looked to Ivan for guidance, and when Ivan nodded, he leaned down and quickly cut away the bonds.

Zarabeth hadn't lied when she said she was too sore and tired to run away. She eased her arms out from behind her back and rubbed her hands together, trying to work the blood back into them. She didn't ask him to unbind her feet—she'd have to work up to them trusting her that much.

She began her questions again. "Are there others in

Nvengaria who are interested in my becoming imperial princess?"

"Oh, yes," Ivan answered, and she eagerly touched his thoughts, looking for information. "Plenty of men were devoted to Duke Sebastian and his cause, and are happy to have you as the symbol for the new Nvengaria. Prince Damien must die."

"He is powerful," she pointed out. "And so is Grand Duke Alexander. They have the army with them."

"Not all. There are those who have had enough of Damien and his family. You are connected to the royal blood, but distant enough not to be tainted by the cruelty of them. We have watched you and your father for a long time, and know you to be good people."

Oh, dear. "My father . . . does he know of this?"

"No," Ivan answered. "He likes Prince Damien too much, but when you are put in Damien's place, he will follow you."

This was worse than she'd expected. Zarabeth delicately rubbed her hands, wincing at the pins-and-needles feeling of blood flowing through them again.

Ivan and Constanz and Sebastian's followers wanted a puppet queen, a woman who was popular and young and pureblood Nvengarian. The average Nvengarian might balk at rule by the Council of Dukes, whom they didn't much trust anyway, but might accept a pretty young woman connected to the royal family.

The two footmen hadn't mentioned Princess Penelope and her tiny son. Zarabeth found the vague thought in Ivan's mind that Princess Penelope would be sent back to England, but he was comfortably avoiding the question of what would happen to the baby, Damien's son and heir. Ivan might naively believe that wife and son could be exiled, but Zarabeth knew Nvengarians. Assassination was much more likely.

Bloody hell.

The epithet Egan liked to use was strangely satisfying. Zarabeth came from a long line of people who'd lived close to the bone, who'd fought vicious battles in the mountains of Nvengaria for survival. She had that survival instinct in her; Sebastian had not been able to suppress it.

She would survive this—she had to in order to warn Damien and Penelope and stop this stupid plot before people died for it. She had to tell Egan, who could send messages to Nvengaria in the blink of an eye.

She touched Ivan's mind, wondering what they intended for Egan, and found bright, vicious anticipation. Egan would be a pleasure to kill, Ivan was thinking. Egan had tried to take their beloved princess away and mire her in this nowhere place called Scotland. He had to die.

Zarabeth knew they'd find Egan harder to kill than they imagined, but still, enough blades turned at him would do the job. She flinched away from a vision of Egan's kilt stained red with his blood, and blocked Ivan's thoughts from her head.

Egan searched every inch of the tunnels under Castle MacDonald and out into the Ring of Dunmarran, but found nothing. She could not have been taken far, the reasonable part of his mind said. No horses had gone missing, and there were no signs that other horses or carts or even people on foot had come to the Ring to meet them.

He sent his men to check the abandoned cottages at Strathranald and the homes of his own tenants. He believed his tenants loyal, but times were hard in the Highlands, and if someone had offered thousands of pounds to kidnap or hide Zarabeth, it might have been difficult for a poor crofter to resist.

Adam Ross came over to help, with Jamie in tow.

Egan tried to keep his emotions under control as he divided his men and family into teams, gave everyone maps, and carefully blocked out a grid to search.

Inside he raged and fumed. If Valentin had hurt Zarabeth despite Zarabeth's insistence that he was trustworthy, he'd break every bone in the man's body, logosh or no logosh. He also wondered what had become of Ivan and Constanz, and whether he'd come across the lads' bodies strewn along the way.

Over all this, he ached for Zarabeth. He needed to touch her, to assure himself that she was all right, and whole, and alive. He was to have protected her, and he'd failed her. He'd thought leaving her snug in the castle while he walked a hundred yards down the road outside it would be adequate, and he'd paid the price.

He'd search every inch of the Highlands and beyond, if it took him the rest of his life to find his Zarabeth. No one would part him from her ever again.

The winter day grew short, and darkness began to fall soon after four. Egan and his men and cousins and Adam and his men continued to search for hours, and still found not a trace of Zarabeth, her footmen, or Baron Valentin.

Chapter Twenty
True Colors

Mary Cameron learned about Zarabeth's abduction while still in the village with Dougal—one of Egan's retainers rushed into the shop where Mary was hesitating over a skein of ribbon and blurted the news. Dougal joined Egan's retainer, and Mary hurried home on her own.

Egan would be beside himself, she knew. Her brother loved Zarabeth; she could see that clearly in his eyes.

She heard the details of the abduction when she arrived home, how the two Nvengarian footmen were missing as well, how it looked as though Valentin had orchestrated the kidnapping. She didn't understand how he could have, and, to be honest, she didn't want to believe it.

She should have been sitting with Valentin herself, but she hadn't been able to bring herself to enter his room today. His kiss on Hogmanay night had taken her breath away and stolen her sanity, and she no longer trusted herself near him.

She could swear that Valentin was too injured to have abducted Zarabeth, but perhaps he had tricked them all, and seduced her to make her believe in him. The thought both humiliated her and made her angry.

She went to the kitchens and helped Mrs. Williams prepare cold meals for the searchers; then she took a lantern and went down to the tunnels to search herself.

She was not afraid of the darkness, and if she could find something that could help she wouldn't shirk.

She found nothing. Tired and downcast, she returned to her own chamber. It was well after dark, and lanterns bobbed along the hills and roads in the distance.

"Mary." The low voice came from the darkness behind her. She swung around and pressed her hands to her mouth to stifle her scream.

Valentin stood a few steps from her, his bandages stained with new blood. He'd pulled on a pair of breeches, which were stained and torn as though he'd run through bracken, but the rest of his body was bare.

"Do not be frightened," he said in his dark voice. "I promise not to hurt you."

Mary gaped, feeling the edge of hysterics. "What happened to you? They think you've taken Zarabeth— were you shot?"

"Shh." His scent and warmth spilled over her, the smell of the outdoors and blood and wildness. "I must find her. Damien charged me with protecting her, and protect her I must. Help me, Mary."

"How can I possibly?"

"I can scent Zarabeth, but I need to get outside."

"*Scent her?* I don't understand."

He hesitated a long moment, his blue gaze shuttered to her. "You will see."

"They think you kidnapped Zarabeth, or at least helped."

Valentin cupped her shoulder, his calloused hand hot. He put his face close to hers, and she saw that his irises had widened strangely, the pupils nearly swallowing the blue.

"I must ask you to trust me." He leaned closer, his breath scalding her face. "Trust me, Mary."

All her life Mary had avoided making difficult choices. As the only daughter in the family, she had been petted and spoiled, never experiencing the rivalry Charlie and Egan had lived through. She'd been able to keep her father's bullying distant by pretending Egan's and Charlie's troubles had nothing to do with her.

She'd been a coward, and she knew it. After Charlie's death and Egan's departure, she'd buried herself in her married life in Edinburgh, taking care of her husband and Dougal. By the time her husband had died, her father had passed away also, and she'd returned to Castle Mac-Donald, pretending that all was well.

Valentin was forcing her to look things in the eye. She'd never been comfortable looking things in the eye, but he gave her no choice.

Trusting him went against every grain of common sense. The woman inside her who liked to run away from problems wanted to flee from this one. Valentin frightened her as much as he intrigued her. She remembered their kiss, and how hot her blood had pounded. She pressed her hand to his unbandaged shoulder, even now thrilling to the hard muscle beneath silk-smooth skin.

"Mary," he said. "I need you."

She wished he meant he needed her body, but she knew he only needed her help.

Mutely she nodded. "Tell me what to do."

Valentin traced her cheek, his eyes so close, so dark. "Get me out of the house with no one seeing." His lips pressed her skin, and then he turned away, leaving her cold and bereft.

Egan searched for hours. He rode along the shore of the loch, trying not to think of Zarabeth's body floating lifelessly on its black surface. The edges of the loch were thick with ice, but the middle still flowed deep and cold.

I'll find you, lass. I won't stop till I find you.

It was well dark, the stars out in a white mass, when Egan finally rode back to the castle. His mount was tired and cold, and while Egan could have ridden all night, he knew his horse could not continue.

He remembered his desperate search for Charlie's body, and his despair when he could not find his brother anywhere. Zarabeth could be dead as well, her body lying in the heather, her black hair trailing across the snow. Or she could have been carried off, perhaps to a ship waiting at Ullapool to bear her away.

A sudden rage washed over him as he crested the hill to the castle. Zarabeth had been right: Egan could never have stopped Charlie from joining the battle at Talavera. Charlie had never listened to Egan in his life, blithely doing whatever he pleased, and laughing when his older brother advised caution.

Egan's father had expected Egan to have full control of Charlie in a way Gregor MacDonald never had. He'd sliced Egan's portrait to ribbons, had told Egan to his face, *I wish to God ye were a bastard so I could have pinched out your life when ye were a bairn.* Charlie, with his laughter and his charm, had deliberately set his father against Egan so subtly that no one, not even Egan, had understood what he'd done until it was too late.

If Charlie hadn't died, Egan was certain that his father would have come up with schemes to keep Egan far from home while he and Charlie ran the place. Egan might be the rightful heir, but if he were not there, Charlie could do as he pleased.

Egan's chest tightened with emotion he'd never let out, anger and rage he'd bottled up all these years. He'd accused Zarabeth of being a shell of a woman, when all this time he had denied his bitter anger at his father.

Egan reached the courtyard and slid from his horse just as a figure loomed out of the dark. "Anything?" Olaf asked him.

"No." It took all of Egan's energy to say the one word.

Olaf's face was lined with grief. "I can't lose my Zarabeth. I lost her when she married, and I didn't know it. I drove her away because I did not understand what would make her happy. Seeing her with you now . . . I can't forgive myself. . . ." His voice broke.

Egan growled at him. "We'll find her. I'll no' stop looking for her. Ever."

He threw his reins to the groom and strode into the castle. Gemma met him inside the door with a new problem: Mary had vanished, and Gemma had found blood in her room.

Egan swore in every language he knew, then bellowed for a fresh horse.

Olaf followed him, eyes wet and red. "What are you going to do?"

"Go after them. I think I know where my sister is and what she's up to."

"I want to come with you. I'm an old man, but I swear I won't slow you down."

Egan gave him a grim nod. "I want you with me. Mary's a fool, but this time I think she's done the right thing. And I'll need you there to help calm down that bloody logosh."

"May I have more water?"

Constanz looked at Zarabeth in concern, and she sensed his worry for her. He and his brother could hardly expect to put a figurehead princess on the throne of Nvengaria if the figurehead princess died along the way. Ivan, not as concerned, nodded at him, and Constanz refilled the cup.

As the footman brought it to her, she wondered where they were getting the freshwater. It tasted as muddy as before, but also wonderfully cool and bright.

Were they near a well or a stream? She thought about the land she'd ridden over with Egan, of the loch, the streams where they fished, the pools filled with roiling water that cascaded from the hills. Of Castle MacDonald poking up in ancient majesty from the rocks around them, in stark contrast with Adam Ross's elegantly modern house. Egan wild, Adam cultured.

The Ross family hadn't always been cultured. They'd lived in a stout castle like the MacDonalds had until the day it had been razed by the English. *Until not one stone was left standing on top of another,* Adam had said.

Zarabeth wondered suddenly what lay under the ruins of Castle Ross.

"Where are we?" she asked, trying to sound merely curious.

"In a safe place," Ivan assured her. "No one will hurt you here."

"Are we near the coast? How will we get away?"

"We'll go soon," Constanz said before Ivan could answer. "Everything will be all right, and you'll be back in Nvengaria, where you belong."

Zarabeth nodded, pretending hauteur. "They *are* a bit barbaric here. Not much in the way of society, not even a spa or casino next to the lake. And my clothes . . ."

She plucked at the plaid of her gown, and then her heart nearly broke. MacDonald tartan, the same as she'd worn to her wedding. *Egan, please find me. I love you.*

"You'll have all the clothes you want, and jewels," Constanz assured her. "You'll be the most beautiful princess that ever lived, and we will be your slaves."

Zarabeth stifled a sigh. Constanz read far too many fairy tales, which all ended with the beautiful princess loved by everyone in the kingdom. This princess never had much to do, Zarabeth mused, except look lovely in a tiara and wave at her adoring subjects.

But Constanz had forgotten that every fairy tale had

its prince—the handsome man who usually eked out life as a farmer before he decided to ride off to rescue the captive princess. In this case her handsome prince, or knight in shining armor, was a Highlander in a rough kilt.

Egan had found her on the Devil's Teeth when she thought herself beyond help; perhaps he would find her now. Of course, at the moment, even Zarabeth didn't know where she was.

The flickering light of Ivan's lantern showed little—hard-packed earth on the floor, walls too far away to see. It was cool but not cold, as though they were far from the winter chill. She strained her senses to hear or feel thoughts outside the room and found nothing.

"Is there anything to eat?" she asked. "I've had nothing since breakfast, which I assume was a long time ago." Her stomach recoiled at the thought of food, but her question would tell her how well they'd planned.

"Give her the bread," Ivan said.

Constanz faded into the darkness. "I need the light; I can't see."

Ivan uttered a profane word and caught up the lantern to assist his brother.

Zarabeth sat in darkness, watching Ivan and Constanz, who were lit like actors in a play. Ivan's lantern showed her board shelves against ancient stone walls—man-made stone, not natural rock. She'd seen similar stones in the cellars and tunnels under Castle MacDonald.

She knew she could not be under Castle MacDonald, because Egan and his cousins and nephews would have found her by now. They knew every inch of those tunnels, and they could use Valentin to sniff her out.

Zarabeth remembered Valentin falling with the shot, and her heart squeezed with worry. He was a good and noble man and did not deserve to die.

Constanz brought her half a loaf of bread, which looked suspiciously liked the kind Mrs. Williams baked every morning. Zarabeth took it gratefully and chewed the nutty crust.

She blinked back tears—the taste reminded her of every meal she'd eaten in Castle MacDonald. The mornings when Jamie goaded Egan, and Egan snarled at him. The family suppers with Hamish poking fun at Angus and Gemma, Angus blushing and Gemma smiling. Mary trying to keep them all civilized while Jamie and Dougal argued, and Williams joining in debates while he served the roast or venison with his wife's bread.

I've finally discovered what true happiness is, Zarabeth thought. *I can't lose it now.*

"I hate to mention this," she said when she swallowed the last bite, "but I will have to use the necessary, you know."

"There isn't one," Constanz said at once.

"Oh dear. Well, I suppose a far corner will have to do, as long as you don't wave the lantern about. I'm shy."

Ivan shook his head. "We can't let you wander about alone. You might get hurt. This place is strewn with rocks and debris."

"You ought to have thought of that before you brought me down here. If you'd brought a maid to help me, she could tend to my needs and make sure I didn't trip in the dark."

"We did not know who we could trust," Ivan told her. "The maids are all Scottish and could force you back to Egan MacDonald."

"That is true, but I will need a maid eventually. All kinds of servants—ones who are loyal—to tend to me."

"We know. That will be taken care of, he assured me."

"Who did?"

"Your benefactor."

What benefactor? One of Sebastian's friends, or a leader of a new faction? She smothered a sigh. Never a dull moment in Nvengarian politics.

"Be that as it may," Zarabeth said primly, "there is still the question of the necessary. Perhaps you or Constanz can lead me across the room with the lantern, and then return for me when I am finished?"

Ivan thought that through. "Very well. I'll take you."

He pulled out a knife and cut the knots that bound her feet. When he hauled her up she had to cling to him, gritting her teeth as the blood flowed back through her limbs. She realized she'd never be able to run until her legs uncramped and her feet lost their numbness.

Ivan simply stood, patiently waiting until she felt better. He was a well-trained servant, raised to wait on his master's or mistress's every need.

When Zarabeth thought she could walk, she nodded to Ivan. He carried the lantern in one hand and supported her firmly while she hobbled with him across the vast room. Ivan stopped in a corner and discreetly backed away until she was alone in the darkness.

Zarabeth knew better than to run. She was weak and tired, and Ivan would pounce on her and drag her back to the middle of the room if she tried, where he would likely tie her even more securely. She needed to take her time, win their trust.

She did not have to relieve herself, but she scuffled against the wall as though hiding embarrassing noises. She felt her way along the stone, wincing as she found moss and slime from who knew how many centuries. This was a dead place.

When she guessed she'd been long enough, she called to Ivan, who immediately started for her. He steered her back to the middle of the room and silently handed her a handkerchief when she said she'd touched the wall and gotten ooze on her hand.

She sat down, but when Ivan bent to tie her feet again, she let out a true moan of protest. "Please don't. It hurts so."

Ivan did not quite trust her yet, but Constanz looked distressed. She heard Ivan's thought that when Zarabeth became princess over Nvengaria she perhaps might remember how kindly Ivan and his brother had treated her. He nodded and didn't bind her, then brought her more bread and water.

Zarabeth asked a few more curious questions, probing gently at their thoughts as she did. She could discover only that a highborn Nvengarian man had given them orders to hold her under their protection, but she could not discern his name or face. He'd communicated with them by means of the magic paper that Damien's old tutor had invented, the same way in which Damien communicated with Egan. A message had come during Hogmanay instructing Ivan and Constanz to get rid of Valentin as soon as possible. Ivan had followed Valentin out and shot at him, then fled.

Ivan and Constanz now were waiting for the search to die down so they could get her to a ship. They'd found this place while they explored the hills searching for those who wanted to kill Zarabeth, and decided to hide her here.

Ivan let Zarabeth lie down on his coat, and she dozed, trying to conserve her strength. She watched with half-closed eyes while Constanz, bored, explored the room. His lantern revealed a door on one side and the black opening to a passage on the other. The door had a new lock with no key in it; probably one of the footmen had pocketed it.

"Are we under the old Ross castle?" she asked, sitting up again.

Ivan glared at Constanz. "You told her?"

"He never said a word," Zarabeth assured him, as

Constanz reddened. "I concluded it. Do you know about the ghosts?"

Both brothers glanced around uneasily. "We have not seen or heard any ghosts," Constanz said. "Don't be afraid."

Zarabeth recalled Adam's story and embellished it a little. "Adam said that many Highlanders were killed here after Culloden. They tried to stop the English from destroying the castle, and the English killed them and buried them down here. 'Tis said their ghosts walk on midwinter nights under the moon. But I am not worried. 'Tis likely it's only an old legend."

"Likely," Ivan said, but he shot a nervous glance around the room. Constanz silently lit a second lamp, and Ivan did not admonish him.

The black maw of the open passage gaped, and she could imagine the ghosts of angry Highlanders pouring out of it, screaming for revenge. She wished one live Highlander would dash in, ready to wreak havoc on anyone who dared touch her.

Egan. Please find me!

She cast her thoughts wide, trying to reach up through the stones for anyone hunting for her, and again found only silence. Either the walls were too thick, or no one had thought to look for her here. She could not project thoughts herself, so she could not guide them to her.

Still, she could do more than search for thoughts. While Ivan and Constanz worried about ghosts, she put the remainder of her plan in motion.

Chapter Twenty-one
The Secret of Castle Ross

$\mathcal{M}$ary did not find it difficult to slip from Castle MacDonald with Valentin, because every inhabitant had rushed out to search the night. Valentin consented to sling one of Egan's plaids around his torso, but he discarded it almost as soon as they left the path to cut across the heather. When Mary started to ask what he was doing, he swung to her.

"Thank you. You should go back now."

She stuck out her chin. "Not a bit of it. I want to help find Zarabeth, not wring my hands in my bedchamber."

"I admire your courage."

She thought he'd add a caveat, such as, *But a woman should stay out of this kind of business,* but he did not. He leaned toward her as he had in the bedchamber, nuzzling her hairline as though taking in her scent.

"This will frighten you," he said. "I did not want to tell you, but you will have to know. You might hate me for it."

"Hate you? I could never—"

"Mary." He gave a heartfelt groan, pain in his eyes. In the moonlight, his body was sleek and muscled and taut, like a statue come to life. "You are so beautiful."

He lowered his head and kissed her. Heat flared as he parted her lips and tasted her as wildly as he had the first time. She touched his chest, loving the hardness of his body.

"I wish this could be easier," he said.

She loved his accent, so rich and full. He gave her a look filled with darkness and sorrow, then unbuttoned his breeches and pulled them off.

Before she could do more than gape—his body was perfect—his limbs began to change.

It happened very quickly, but it also seemed to take forever. His face elongated, his ears rising, hands curving into massive claws. She gasped and jumped away as black fur sprouted on his body, and he landed on all fours, the largest wolf she'd ever seen. He looked at her with wolf's eyes that were blue rather than tawny.

Mary pressed her hands to her face. "What are you?"

He couldn't answer her, of course. He gave her a look of sorrow, then brushed past her and loped away into the darkness.

When Zarabeth calculated that a few more hours had passed, she announced that she needed to relieve herself again. Ivan looked pained but again led her away from the center of the room. She asked to go to a different corner, and he took her there without question.

Once he backed away, leaving her in darkness, Zarabeth quickly and silently felt her way along the wall to the open passage. Walking carefully through, she found a staircase that went down into deeper darkness. She had not truly thought it would lead up and out, because Ivan and Constanz would have blocked it in some way if it had.

Keeping her hand on the wall, Zarabeth picked her way down, testing each stair before putting her weight on it. She wanted to hurry, but tripping and falling or tearing her way through rotten floorboards would not help her.

She counted the steps as she went down, and reached twenty before she heard Ivan calling to her. Still, she made herself go carefully, holding her skirts out of the way, fighting the urge to move faster.

She heard Ivan curse when he realized she'd fled. He called to Constanz and told his brother to follow him, then bellowed in anger when Constanz refused. Constanz was afraid of the ghosts.

A dozen Highlander ghosts with murder on their minds didn't sound at all bad to Zarabeth just now. Perhaps she could persuade them that a horde of English were trying to capture her, and they'd fight on her side. She half laughed, then bit back a sob.

Her body jarred as her foot came down on level stone, the stairs ending. She groped until she found another wall, then felt her way along it as fast as she could, reasoning that the floor would be sounder against the walls than in the middle of the passage.

She felt coldness brush past her, and she froze. A ghost? Or fresh air?

She hurried toward the sensation, holding in the shivering that suddenly racked her body. Worse, she heard Ivan and Constanz bravely start down the stairs.

The tunnels beneath Castle MacDonald led to the outside air, and she reasoned that Castle Ross might have had similar tunnels for similar reasons. She had no way of knowing where the tunnels would lead or whether they had been blocked, perhaps for centuries. She could only limp along, biting back tears, and hope.

Far back in the passage, she saw the warm glow of the lamp, heard the angry thoughts of Ivan and Constanz. They moved faster than she did, and not as cautiously. Zarabeth kept groping her way along the wall, praying she'd find her way to the surface so she could run fast back to Castle MacDonald. She wanted to scream loud and long, to have someone find her, help her, carry her to safety.

One someone in particular.

She thought of Egan's wild hair sweeping across his shoulders, his brown eyes that sparkled gold when he smiled. His firm mouth that could open in roaring laughter, turn down in fearsome frowns, or kiss like fire. She thought of his hands cupping her face as he leaned in to kiss her, of his hard body on hers in the night, of the rightness of him firmly nestled inside her.

I love you, Egan MacDonald.

Her previous infatuation for him had dissolved and gone. That had been a selfish love, a girl wanting a man to pay attention to her. She loved what he was now, her Highlander who made fierce love to her, who growled at his family but loved them, who teased and cajoled Zarabeth until she'd put aside the horrors of the last five years and laughed out loud.

Egan had made her live again, and she loved him for it.

A whisper brushed past her, a wisp of words she couldn't quiet hear. Ghosts again?

Ivan and Constanz behind her seemingly hadn't heard; nor did they feel the breeze that touched her skin. They were afraid, but not panicked, nothing on their minds but retrieving Zarabeth so they would not fail their cause.

Abandoning care, Zarabeth ran forward, praying not to trip on a loose stone or fall into a hole. Not many steps later, her hands banged painfully into a wall ahead of her, stone scraping her skin.

Choking back sobs, she felt her way along it until she found the boards of a door. She pushed at it, but it was locked.

No. Giving up on trying to be silent, she pounded on the door, hoping the wood around the lock would be old and rotten. She heard Ivan shout and the brothers run forward.

She hurled her body into the door and was rewarded

as the boards in the middle splintered. She felt stinging cuts on her face, but kicked her way through, hoping against hope to find a way out. Once in the snowy fields, she could run, calling out to those who must be roaming the hills looking for her. Neither Egan nor her father would give up searching for her—she knew that.

Zarabeth fell through the door, hearing Ivan and Constanz sprinting to find her. She climbed to her feet, slivers stabbing painfully into her hands, and found herself in a stuffy, warm place that smelled of steam.

She groped and couldn't find walls to guide her. Ivan and Constanz kicked in what remained of the door.

Ghosts of brave Rosses, please help me.

Whether it was the ghosts responding or simply a ruined house falling further into ruin, the door beam and the wall it held up collapsed behind her. The room filled with crumbling earth, choking her, cutting off Ivan and Constanz and the light of their lantern.

The rumbling of the fallen wall faded, and perfect blackness seemed to smother her. Zarabeth struggled to stay on her feet, tears trickling down her filthy cheeks.

Egan! she cried again, but only silence answered.

She thought the warmer air came from her right. Carefully stepping on the uneven stones, she put her hands out in front of her and began to explore.

Egan pulled up his horse so abruptly the gelding skidded on the snow. The night was quiet, punctuated only by the faint calls of searchers far away. Olaf reined in his horse next to him. "What is it?"

Egan held up his hand for silence. He'd heard it: a faint cry, his name. Or at least, he thought he had.

"Zarabeth?" he shouted into the night.

His voice echoed from hills and down into the loch, the land empty and cold.

Nothing.

"What did you hear?" Olaf asked after a few moments.

"I thought she called me." Egan shook his head, his heart like lead. "A trick of the night."

"They must have taken her away by now." Olaf's eyes were dark with despair.

"I know this land. There're places to hide her everywhere, hidden holes and deep woods, plenty of choices for a man who knows his way around here."

"And who does know his way around here? Not a Nvengarian."

"No, but several Nvengarians have been all over since Zarabeth came and could have discovered many things."

Olaf's lips tightened. "Valentin."

"Mebbe not. I believe in Valentin now."

"Then why has he disappeared as well?"

Egan swept his gaze across the snowy hills, coming to rest on the stark black stones of the Ring of Dunmarran. "Either he's hunting for Zarabeth, or he's been taken as well." He turned his horse. "I want to look down there."

"We have been there," Olaf reminded him.

"Even so."

The land was silent, the moon and stars glittering in silver profusion. Zarabeth would love it; she loved beauty of all kinds.

He reached the first stone and dismounted. The horse wandered into the ring, which was free of snow, as usual, and bent his head to crop grass.

Egan thought of how Zarabeth had wrapped her arms around him when he'd playfully flipped up his kilt for her in the middle of the circle, intending to give her a glimpse and no more. She'd leaned her lush, warm body right into his back, making his cock rise hard and tight. He'd wanted her with intense longing he'd barely been able to hold back. If he hadn't known other riders circled the stones that day, keeping watch, he would have taken her on the warm, damp ground.

The image of her under him came to him powerfully, her eyes heavy with desire as she lay under his body, her hair spread across the pillow like black flame.

I love ye so much, Zarabeth. . . .

Egan!

He snapped his head around, hearing her voice loud and clear. He started to call out, but then words died on his lips.

He remembered what she'd told him the night after their wedding, how she must have heard his thoughts when he'd lain half-dead in snowy Nvengaria. She'd never heard them since, but she could not explain how else she'd known to stop and go to him.

Egan closed his eyes, imagining her beautiful face, the wicked blue of her gaze, her red-lipped smile.

Zarabeth.

Zarabeth sobbed with relief when she heard the voice in her head, the full, rumbling baritone of Egan Mac-Donald.

Egan, I am here. Help me, please!

Zarabeth.

The word was full of longing, of hunger, and of love. She clung to it, praying she was not imagining it in her desperation.

Egan, help me.

Where are ye, lass?

She stopped, hugging herself, tears of joy replacing those of fear. *I don't know. I was under Castle Ross, and then I found a tunnel. I ran—Ivan and Constanz were chasing me, and I fell through a doorway. It collapsed. . . .*

She broke off as Egan's anguish reached her. *Are ye all right?*

I think so. But it's so dark.

His voice moved to its commanding tones, Egan the soldier trying to plan. *Do ye know which direction ye went? Where ye are in Castle Ross?*

I have no idea. I didn't wake up until I was inside. I went downstairs in a corner.

I'll send for Adam. I wager he knows every corner of that castle, even if he lives in luxury now.

And then he went silent. The voice vanished from her head—perhaps he was shouting orders to find Adam and drag him there—but it left her bereft.

Egan, don't leave me.

I'm here, lass. I'll never leave ye.

I love you.

I love ye too, lass. Before she could cling to the happiness of that simple statement, he was moving on. *Can ye tell me anything else about where ye are? A hole, a room, a cave, a tunnel?*

I don't know. I can't see anything. But it's warm and a little smelly, like the baths at Baden.

Baths?

The word cut like a whiplash, and Zarabeth felt his surging, joyous triumph. He shouted so loud in her head she thought it would vibrate the room. *I knew there was a bloody hot spring under the Ring of Dunmarran. I've found ye, lass!*

Oh, good. She laughed shakily. *Hurry. And please don't leave me again.*

No, lass, came his voice and the heady feeling of his love. *I never will.*

The first thing Zarabeth saw when moonlight sliced through the roof of her prison was paws—enormous clawed feet that raked dirt out of the way faster than the sharpest spade.

"Valentin," she called.

A moment later the face of a huge wolf hung in the

hole, eyes shining. It vanished, to be replaced by the human face of Egan MacDonald. "Hello, lass," he said.

Zarabeth's throat squeezed shut, and she couldn't speak. *I knew you'd come.*

To her joy, she could still hear his answering thought. *Did ye? Ye seemed scared, for a lass who believed I'd rescue her.*

That does not mean I wasn't terrified. Get me out of here.
We're coming, love.

He disappeared, but the link to him still held. Zarabeth did not need to think in words; she simply let herself wrap around the feel of his presence.

It seemed so natural now to reach out and touch him with thought alone. She'd been able to do that with her father when she'd been a child, although he had never known it. Egan responded by caressing her thoughts as gently as he caressed her skin. He did it in wonder, a new thing for him.

She wondered what had become of Ivan and Constanz, but she could tell that Egan didn't know. She stood well away from the opening while the men with Egan dug a shaft to her. She sensed her father, too, his gladness and relief, plus worry that the tunnel would collapse around her. She no longer felt Valentin's presence— likely he'd slipped away into darkness again. She hoped he was all right.

But the old walls held, and the moonlight pouring in showed her a ceiling shored up with thick beams, carved arches that looked ancient. The arches led down the tunnel to another huge, dark opening that swallowed light.

A lantern came down on a rope, its warm twinkle welcome. This was followed by Egan, who lowered himself into the hole, holding on at arm's length before dropping to the floor. His kilt swirled around him, a long sword strapped to his side.

Zarabeth flung herself at him, and Egan caught her tight, squeezing the breath out of her. He cupped her face in his hands and kissed her, never minding how filthy she must be. He kissed her lips, her face, her hair, holding her hard.

Men were calling out above, including Zarabeth's father. She dragged her hair from her wet face and shouted up that she was fine. She heard her father break down in relief, and then the other men started talking about the logistics of putting down a ladder or ropes or both.

Egan skimmed his hands through Zarabeth's hair and kissed her again, smiling the smile she loved. "I thought I'd lost ye, lass."

She hugged him without words, shivering now when she thought about what could have happened to her.

"Ivan and Constanz . . ." she began.

"We didn't find them. They must have run away somewhere, but never fear, love. We'll have them."

"They were coerced by someone else. I don't think they deserve to be hurt."

"That doesn't make them less dangerous, love. They could have gotten ye killed, bringing ye down here, and were ready to turn ye over to a fanatic, whoever he may be. Ye couldn't discover who?"

"No," she said. "They might not have known themselves—it was vague in their heads."

"Aye, well, when we find them, I'll pry it out of 'em."

With his grim look and his sword, he looked more fearsome than the ghosts she'd been imagining. He snatched up the lantern, but instead of waiting for the ladders and ropes, he took her hand and led her on into the tunnel.

The light shone on stone pillars that were fantastically carved with interlaced flowers and leaves and the occasional animal—badger, deer, hawk—and wild-looking men and women. The tunnel led downward in a short slope until it opened into a natural cavern in which a sheet of water steamed.

"This is why there's no snow in the Ring of Dunmarran," Egan said. "A hot spring. Marked by our ancient forefathers by a ring of stone."

"Or perhaps they marked it because it was a sacred place," Zarabeth suggested, "and the spring was part of the sacredness."

"Either way, they cared enough about it to decorate it well."

Egan rubbed his hand across an intricate carving and strolled to the spring, leaning down to poke his bare finger into it. "That feels fine. Want to test it?"

Zarabeth glanced back up the tunnel. "Father and your Highlanders are trying to rescue me."

"They'll be at it a while. Come on."

He unstrapped his belt and sword, peeled off his coat and shirt, and unpinned the kilt to let it fall. Naked except for his armband, he sat on the stone edge and dangled his feet in the water. He looked like one of the old gods, Thor perhaps, god of thunder, deciding to rest his huge body in a hot spring under the earth.

Winking at her, Egan slid into the water. "'Tis not deep," he said, up to his neck. "And nice on the muscles. Join me, love."

Zarabeth was cold and bone-tired and aching, and the steam, despite its odor, beckoned her. With a glance up the tunnel, she unbuttoned her gown with stiff fingers, tossed it and her underclothes onto the ground, and sat down beside the spring.

Egan slid his hands around her waist and pulled her into the spring with him. The hot water bit her skin, stinging the cuts and abrasions from her frantic escape.

The heat was heavenly, Egan's arms protective, the water letting her float in warmth and peace.

"This *is* a sacred space," she murmured. "Can't you feel it?"

"I feel you," Egan said, his grin as wicked as ever.

He cupped her bottom with his hands and coaxed her legs around him. His hardness nudged her, and dark warmth twisted through her belly. She nuzzled him, hands sliding on his slippery body.

Egan cupped water to her face, cleaning the dirt and tears and blood from her skin. The tingling water felt good, and she found her fear dissolving. She was here with Egan, the thought connection between them still strong.

She kissed him again, and he slanted his mouth across hers, scooping up the taste of her. His hair wound to wiry kinks in the steam, curling around her fingers. He was delectable.

I love you, Egan.

She wanted to say it over and over, directly into his mind, coupling the words with her thoughts. Anyone could repeat the phrase, but this way he'd know she was sincere.

He smiled as she filled his mind, and kissed the tip of her nose. "Ye know I love ye back, Zarabeth."

The words made her toastier than the hottest spring ever could.

Shouting in the tunnel broke their next kiss, and the room suddenly filled with the enormous shadow of a Highlander, kilted and booted, with a gun in his hand. The shadow shrank down to meet Hamish as he charged into the tunnel; then he stopped short when he saw them in the pool.

It was dark and the water was murky, but Zarabeth shrank shyly into Egan's side. Hamish straightened up and pushed his hair from his sweating face.

"Disturbin' ye, are we?" he said. "I beg yer pardon, we didn't mean t' rescue ye so loud."

Angus MacDonald piled in behind Hamish, followed by Adam and Piers Ross, then her father and Dougal. Last came Baron Valentin, dressed in tattered breeches and a coat over his bare body. Bandages smeared with dirt showed in the shadow of his coat, but he stood upright, his face calm.

"Och," Angus said, leaning on his brother Hamish. "Look at him, if ye please. We're breakin' our backs diggin' him out, and his lairdship is having a swim."

"Really, Uncle," Dougal chimed in.

Olaf simply smiled, his face wet with tears that Zarabeth was all right. Adam peered about the room, taking in the carvings and the pool with a proprietary gleam in his eye.

"A natural hot spring underneath Castle Ross. Look at it, Piers, and think of the possibilities."

"I am," Piers answered, the lantern light catching on his blond hair. "Paying guests, the aristocracy of Europe come to relax at Castle Ross and its healing spa. A hotel, perhaps, with a chef from Paris to cater to well-bred tastes."

"You're forgetting," Egan said from the water. "This spring is under the Ring of Dunmarran, which belongs t' the MacDonalds."

Adam pursed his lips. "There has always been some dispute whether the Ring stood on Ross land or MacDonald."

"Aye, well, I have the maps at home t' prove it."

Zarabeth glanced up from where her head rested on Egan's shoulder. "Perhaps we can talk of this later?"

Adam had the grace to avert his eyes. "Of course, Zarabeth, forgive me."

"Uncle!" The shout came from the outer tunnel, followed in a hurry by Jamie. "Did ye find . . ." He stopped short when he saw the pool with Egan and Zarabeth, the rest of the Highlanders standing by with hands on hips. His mouth dropped open. "A hot spring, by all that's holy."

His words rang to the corners of the cavern as he quickly stripped off his clothes and dived in, his body a lithe white streak. The rest of the Highlanders looked at one another, and suddenly kilts tumbled to the ground in a tangle of Ross and MacDonald plaid, and the water splashed to the ceiling as five more Highlanders leaped in.

Even Zarabeth's father stripped off and joined them, modestly staying at the far side of the pool. Valentin, on the other hand, shook his head and faded back into the tunnel, a thread of amusement touching Zarabeth's senses.

She smiled at Egan while the Highlanders splashed and shouted and dunked one another in the middle of the pool, her thoughts and his still entwined.

Och, she thought, imitating the broadest Highland Scots she could. *'Tis true. When ye marry a Highlander, ye get the pack of 'em.*

Chapter Twenty-two
The Inn at Ullapool

*W*hen Egan awoke the next morning, curled around Zarabeth, he realized that the thought bond between them had gone.

He'd brought her here to the castle after the Highlanders had had their fun in the pool and gone. He and Zarabeth had helped each other dress in the cavern, kissing and laughing as they tried to pull clothes over wet bodies. His cousins had rigged a hoist that hauled Zarabeth, unhurt, to the surface.

Bundled against the January cold, Egan had ridden Zarabeth back to Castle MacDonald, determined to keep her warm and safe while his cousins hunted for the elusive Ivan and Constanz.

He'd made love to Zarabeth in a frenzy, still terrified at nearly losing her, and worried that he would again. Being inside her while their love twined through each other's minds had been the most erotic thing he'd ever experienced. He loved her, he needed her, and he knew without doubt that she felt the same.

They'd fallen asleep, Egan still inside her. Sometime in the night, he must have rolled away, because when he woke, he was spooned against her as he had been in the inn near Ullapool, when he'd rescued her the first time.

She opened her blue eyes and smiled at him. "Good morning, love."

And then he knew the thought bond had truly gone.

He couldn't feel what she was thinking or sense her love or her thoughts. He started up in panic. She stared at him, surprised; then he saw her also realize the silence between them.

Her eyes filled with tears. "What happened?"

"Ye canno' tell what I'm thinking at all?"

She held him with her gaze for a moment, then bit her lip and shook her head.

Egan's heart nearly broke. The closeness he'd had with her last night had been unlike anything in his life, and he'd wanted to hold her with it forever. At last someone who saw his true self—Egan MacDonald—not the Mad Highlander or Charlie's brother or the laird of his lands or his father's hated son. Just Egan, the man who loved Zarabeth.

"Oh, lass," he said. He gathered her close while her tears fell on his skin.

"What do we do?"

Egan stroked the midnight silk of her hair. "What we always did, lass. Quarrel, make up, quarrel some more. That's what most of us do, talk and argue and try to figure out what the devil is goin' on in the other's head."

"It has only ever been a problem with you." She traced her thumb over his cheek. "The only person I could never read."

Egan forced a grin. "Maybe 'twas meant that way, love. Maybe if we're meant to be together, we have to poke and pry to see what each other's feeling. So we'll keep poking and trying to understand for years to come."

"You mean if we could read each other's thoughts, it would be too easy?"

"Aye. We'll have to muddle through like any other couple in love."

"But it was so . . ."

Egan chuckled. "I know, lass." He thought about the

wildness he'd felt when he'd pumped into her last night. They'd been together like never before, bodies and thoughts entangled. It had been insane and wonderful.

"I suppose," Egan said in a soft voice, "we'll just have to keep trying until we find something that resembles what we had last night."

He saw a wicked smile sparkle behind her tears. "Perhaps we can spend much time on this."

"I was thinkin' that."

Zarabeth twined her arms around him, nails lightly scratching his back, and moved her foot firmly against his thigh. Egan was hard, in love, and ready. He kissed her, tentatively probing for the thought bond they'd had, but he did not find it.

What he did find was Zarabeth, the spice of her, the softness of her breasts against his chest, and the slick moisture between her legs that said she was just as ready as he was. He groaned as he entered her, and was rewarded with a soft look on her face, her lips brushing his, and love in her eyes.

Ivan and Constanz were found that morning on the road to Ullapool. When they tried to run away, Egan put the sword of Ian MacDonald to Ivan's throat, and Constanz immediately gave up.

Egan and Adam Ross with the help of Egan's Highlanders dragged them back to Castle MacDonald. Constanz was terrified, though Ivan tried to brave it out.

"You have no right to keep our princess from us," Ivan said, standing in the great hall in front of the collected Highlanders.

"And ye had no right to abduct Zarabeth like brigands," Egan said severely. "I want to know who put you up to this, how much he paid you, and where I can find your mysterious benefactor."

Ivan lifted his chin. "I will tell you nothing. We do this for the good of Nvengaria."

Egan, who still gripped his ancestor's sword, again put its point to Ivan's throat. Amazing how effective a fine blade was. "For the good of your hide you'll tell me."

Constanz broke in. "We never meant to harm the princess. If she'd done what we said she would not have been hurt. She belongs in Nvengaria."

Olaf, standing next to Egan with a grim look on his face, said, "She'll not go there against her will. She's chosen Scotland, and that is good enough for me."

"But she is Nvengarian," Ivan argued. "She does not belong in this barbaric, cold place with backward Highlanders."

Hamish said mildly, "Careful, lad—you'll have a ton of backward Highlanders on you if you don't watch yourself."

Egan held up his hand. What he really wanted to do was thrash Ivan and Constanz until they couldn't see, and send their broken bodies back to Nvengaria. He'd have Damien lay them at the feet of whoever had hired them as a warning to all who threatened the lady of Egan MacDonald.

He stopped himself, knowing that he needed to use the two young men to catch the bigger fish. Zarabeth's continued safety was more important than his immediate need for vengeance.

He modulated his voice to the tones of Captain Egan MacDonald of the Ninety-second Highland Regiment. "If ye want to continue living, ye will lead me to the man you intended to take Zarabeth to. No arguing, no running, no quarter."

Ivan might be a Nvengarian and a fanatic, but he understood when he was up against a more formidable man than himself, not to mention a sword point. Add to that Egan's family and friends, all large men with weapons, surrounding him and his brother.

Egan stared Ivan down. Constanz was in tears.

"We only meant to help the princess," Constanz repeated. "I knew it was wrong."

Ivan glared at his brother. "You are weak."

"No, I am loyal to the princess."

Ivan realized his brother was against him as well. He did not have a strong enough personality to stand against Egan, and finally bowed his head. "I will do as you say. Spare my brother—he did what I told him. You may take my life afterward, and know that I gave it for the good of Nvengaria."

Egan silently exhaled, his gaze connecting with Zarabeth's. The last thing he needed was Nvengarian dramatics, so he said quickly, "Never mind that. Just tell me who the bloody man is and where I'll find him."

He sensed Zarabeth tensing, felt her rage. She was strong and brave, and though he wanted to protect her more than anything, she was no wilting flower. They had a few things to talk about, but right now Egan needed to put an end to this opera.

He leaned toward Ivan, making his voice menacing and low. "Tell me, lad. I'm running out of patience."

Ivan swallowed. "His name is Baron Neville."

Zarabeth gasped, and Egan jerked his attention to her. She'd gone deathly pale, her blue eyes glittering like sapphires.

"Who the devil is Neville?" Egan demanded. "I feel stupid even saying that."

"My husband's secretary." Zarabeth's lips were white. "He was his most trusted aide and adviser."

Egan felt the ancient MacDonald rage once more welling up inside him. "And this Neville is dangerous?"

"Extremely." Color began to surge back into Zarabeth's face. "Shall we find him and inform him just how dangerous Highlanders can be?"

Hamish bellowed with laughter. "Aye, lass, we'll give him the thrashing of his life. Are ye with me, lads?"

"Aye!" the Highlanders roared, holding up fists.

In the ensuing noise, Egan lowered the sword and had his men surround Ivan and Constanz.

He determined then and there that he never wanted to see Zarabeth looking that terrified again, not if he had to lock her in Castle MacDonald and never let her out.

Zarabeth insisted on accompanying them to Ullapool. "I want to," she said, when Egan, predictably, wanted to argue. "Baron Neville used to steal all my correspondence and helped Sebastian devise punishments for me. I want to look him in the eye and let him know that Sebastian didn't break me."

Egan eventually gave in, mostly, she knew, because he still did not want Zarabeth out of his sight. Valentin rode with them, and so did Adam Ross and his brother. Jamie insisted that Egan take the sword of Ian MacDonald again.

"Ye must have it, Uncle," Jamie retorted when Egan growled at him. "Ye must carry it until Zarabeth is completely safe."

To her surprise, Egan didn't argue with him, but strapped the sword to his saddle. He either had begun believing in the curse or was softening toward Jamie.

Ivan and Constanz had been instructed to meet Baron Neville at Ullapool in the very tavern in which Egan had waited for Zarabeth's arrival months ago. Ivan and Constanz were to enter first, Zarabeth and Egan and Valentin right behind them. Hamish and Adam Ross and other fighters would surround the tavern.

Valentin was angry. His logosh body had healed, more or less, his flesh mending more quickly than that of a man. Zarabeth wondered if he would be able to control the beast inside him when he saw the villain.

When they reached Ullapool, the Highlanders surged apart, riding to cover the waterfront before they could be seen from the tavern. The whitewashed building opened right into the street, and Egan sent Ivan and Constanz in while he and Valentin waited on either side of the door.

Zarabeth entered behind the two footmen, her heart beating swiftly, but she tried to stay cool and collected. In his thick English Ivan asked the landlord if a foreign gentleman waited for them.

The landlord peered at him. "Oh, aye. He's in th' parlor, and a strange-looking man he is. All in blue and covered with medals. Never seen anything like him."

Zarabeth's pulse sped up . Ivan took a deep breath, marched toward the door the landlord indicated, and opened it. He went inside, followed by Constance, Zarabeth on his heels, and Egan hulking right behind her. Egan had the sword of Ian MacDonald in his hand, ready to fight.

The Nvengarian rose. He was tall, with a hard face, a hawklike nose, and ice-cold blue eyes. He wore black boots muddy from the damp outside but beautifully made, the best money could buy. Medals hung all over his chest, as though he'd brought them out to terrify anyone he encountered, and a gold-and-blue sash slashed from shoulder to opposite hip. His gaze raked Zarabeth and then Egan, and, without changing expression, he looked at Ivan.

Ivan screamed. Constanz gasped and turned green, then fell, half fainting onto the nearest chair.

Ivan turned to run but was stopped by Egan and his

sword. When the Nvengarian's large hand landed on Ivan's shoulder he stopped moving like a dog who had been bested by his master.

Zarabeth stared at the man in shock. "Alexander, what are you doing here?"

The Grand Duke Alexander, the second in command of Nvengaria, known in England as the Mad, Bad Duke, gazed down at her from his height. He was a cold man, ruthless and terrifying, although Zarabeth could see a sparkle in the back of his eyes that might be amusement.

Egan answered her. "Damien thought the problem complex, so he sent Alexander to beat your enemies into submission." He grinned. "Of course, all he has to do is give them that look, and they run away with knees knocking."

Zarabeth stared at Egan, mouth dry. "You knew he was here."

"Damien told me he was coming. I had no idea he'd actually arrived."

"Then what happened to Baron Neville?" Zarabeth demanded, as Alexander's gaze flicked behind her.

Valentin had come in and stopped short at the sight of Alexander. "Your Grace."

Alexander gave him a cool nod. "You have done well," he said.

Zarabeth balled her hands and approached Alexander. Her cousin Damien was far more charming, but she'd gotten to know Alexander in the brief time she'd stayed at the palace and learned that his cold demeanor hid a man of deep feeling. His wife, Meagan, a fun-loving young woman, had become Zarabeth's friend.

"Alexander, where is Baron Neville? I want to tell him what I think of him."

Alexander's blue gaze pierced her. "I already took care of him."

Ivan and Constanz cringed. Grand Duke Alexander had a bad reputation as a man who "took care of things," which usually meant quiet, swift, and violent justice. Damien wooed and charmed his subjects, but Alexander simply let his enemies know what would happen to them if they disobeyed him. Alexander was a hard man.

Zarabeth decided to ask no more questions. Alexander could have killed the man or tied him up and put him on a ship ready to be sent back to Nvengaria and Damien.

The door opened on the other side of the room. "May I come out now?" A red-haired woman peered around the door frame at them. "It is quite dull in here, Alexander, and I did want to see Egan before you sent him away."

Zarabeth was already across the room, pulling Alexander's wife into her embrace. Alexander's grim look softened as he turned to the woman he loved.

"My dear, I intended to begin the visit when our work was done."

Meagan came into the room, her arm around Zarabeth. "Your work *is* done—you men simply enjoy posturing. Now that you've terrorized these lads, can we all have tea and enjoy ourselves? I haven't had scones, *real* scones, in a very long time." She waved at the man behind Egan. "Hello, Valentin, how are you?"

Alexander said dryly, "My wife believes in keeping to essentials."

Egan laughed, his rumbling baritone filling the room. "I think we're going to be henpecked husbands, Grand Duke. But I can't imagine anything better than my wife pecking me."

Alexander raised his brows, not as comfortable bantering about his married state as Egan was bantering about, well, anything.

Zarabeth said to Meagan, "And they believe *we* believe they'll listen to us."

"Oh, they do listen," Meagan said, "when it is beneficial for them, and especially when it is time for bed."

This time it was Egan who blushed. Meagan had wholeheartedly embraced the Nvengarian enjoyment of lovemaking, and Egan was still uncomfortable with women who talked unashamedly about it.

Zarabeth winked at him. She would have to get Egan used to Nvengarian wives and their willingness to seduce their husbands as often as necessary. As she caught his sparkling gaze, she decided that it would be quite satisfactory to teach him.

Chapter Twenty-three
The Sword of Ian
MacDonald

Upon returning to Castle MacDonald, Meagan whisked Zarabeth away, leaving Egan and Alexander to resolve things between them.

Alexander was bloody closemouthed as usual as Egan took him to the great hall, but Egan did notice a change in him. The last time Egan had interacted with the man had been in London, after Alexander had married Meagan, when he'd still been a cold bastard. Now Alexander's eyes had softened, and his gaze followed Meagan whenever she was within his sight. Also he seemed more at ease and comfortable with himself, and Egan guessed he'd come to terms with his logosh nature.

Like Valentin, Alexander was part logosh and had grown up human, learning of his shape-shifting abilities as an adult. Both men still bore a slightly distracted look, as though they were on edge, keeping control of the beasts inside them.

Egan knew that Alexander had gained some mastery of himself, because Meagan was utterly unafraid of him. Their two children, Alexander's son by his first marriage and the tiny daughter he'd had with Meagan, had come with them, and they tumbled around their father without the least worry.

"Your castle," Alexander began, looking around at the plaster dangling from the ceiling and the old weapons in the great hall.

Egan braced himself for Alexander to decry his home. Alexander had been raised in utmost luxury and still wallowed in it.

"It is a fine place," Alexander pronounced. "I envy you."

Egan raised his brows. "The great grand duke envies a simple Scottish laird like me?"

"Yes, because this is a home. Generations have lived and died here. I can feel the connections between them all the way to the bones of the castle. You have a family, the support of those who love you. I was always alone, until Meagan came into my life."

"And it looks like she's staying."

His white teeth flashed in a brief smile. "I wouldn't have it any other way."

"And I want Zarabeth in my life." Egan paused as Olaf joined them, nodding a greeting to Alexander. "I assume you're prepared to escort her back to Nvengaria," he continued.

"If she wishes to go," Alexander said.

Olaf shook his head. "I believe Zarabeth wishes to stay. I've been watching her, and she has never been so happy as she is here. Keep her safe for me, Egan, and bring her to visit when you can."

Egan's throat tightened. "That will have to be up to her. She misses Nvengaria more than she lets on. I've not much more to offer her than I did five years ago, though I suppose Adam is right and that hot spring can generate some income."

Olaf gave him an amused look. "What you can offer her is a home and a family. She and I and her mother were very close, but her marriage destroyed her childhood illusions. She needs a real life, a real family, not to bury herself at my estate remembering and regretting the past. You will let her go forward."

"Still." Egan swallowed, remembering how heartbreaking losing the thought bond had been. Had Zarabeth withdrawn from him, and did it mean she wished to return to her father now that the immediate danger was over?

"The danger is over, isn't it?" Egan asked Alexander. He looked the man in the eye, knowing Alexander would tell the truth, no matter how painful.

Alexander gave him a wintry smile. "For now. Nvengarians are always plagued with assassins and plots—it is in our blood. But for now, the faction that followed Sebastian and the splinter group that wanted to use Zarabeth as a figurehead have been mopped up. You and your Highlanders will have to remain vigilant as long as she is with you, but meanwhile . . ." His smile warmed, and he waved his hand like a prince granting his subjects a boon. "Enjoy the peace."

"Peace." Egan grunted. " 'Tis unlikely with a pack of Highlanders in my castle."

As if confirming his words, Jamie bounded into the room. "Uncle, ye haven't broken the curse yet. All this chaos—assassins, kidnappers, wild wolves—will go away once ye break the curse."

Egan caught Jamie by the scruff of the neck before he could dance into Alexander. "We tried, lad. The sword wouldn't break, and ye and Adam never found the rhyme we have t' say."

Jamie looked glum. "True. Adam and I turned his house upside down. Adam said he'd keep looking."

"Nay, lad, Adam is now looking for proof he owns that hot spring or part of it. I wager he's no longer interested in the curse."

Jamie stopped, indignant. "Ye aren't going to let him have it, are ye?"

"Of course not. But it might be good business if I

share it with him. His family knows how to turn a penny into a pound."

"That's as may be," Jamie said. "But nothing will come of it if ye don't break the curse."

Egan gave up. "All right, lad. Let me fetch Zarabeth and the sword, and we'll break your curse."

Alexander's brows quirked. "This sounds interesting."

"Not really, but I know what to do now."

Jamie stared. "Ye do? But what about the rhyme?"

"I have the feeling I know where it is. Gather the family, lad, and we'll do this."

Shut in Baron Valentin's chamber, Mary wordlessly watched Valentin tuck his few belongings into a bag. He was leaving.

"Why do you have to go?" She pressed fingers to her lips, wondering why her heartbeat skipped and jumped.

"Zarabeth will be protected now. My task is done, and I need to return to Nvengaria."

"Forever?"

His dark hair slid over his shoulder as he turned to look at her. "I belong there."

"But you could visit. Zarabeth will want to see you again—she is grateful for what you've done for her."

"Perhaps."

"Others might want to see you, too. Egan and Jamie—Jamie finds you fascinating. Egan needs to rein him in before he destroys himself with his exuberance, and I know you could teach him a thing or two. He grew up without a father, and even with Hamish and Angus, it's not quite the same. . . ."

Valentin was suddenly in front of her, stopping her babbling words with his fingers. It unnerved her how he could move like that, from dead still to lightning speed in a heartbeat.

"Mary." He kissed her once, his lips hard and hot. "Come with me."

Her eyes widened. Her safe, dull life, which had run like a longboat in a narrow canal, suddenly halted.

"To Nvengaria?"

"Yes, to my home. Let me show it to you, the beauty of the mountains, the harsh blue of the lakes, the meadows with colors you've never seen the like of."

She swallowed, throat tight. "But I have duties here, a son. . . ."

"Bring him along. You are no longer the lady of Castle MacDonald. Egan has married, and Zarabeth will fill your place."

Mary felt a brief, illogical hurt that she could so easily be replaced. She'd done much for Egan and Castle MacDonald over the years . . . but Valentin was right. Angus had brought Gemma here, and Zarabeth would be lady of the manor now, and likely Hamish and even Dougal would marry soon and bring their wives to live here.

Mary would always have a place, a room of her own, but she'd be a hanger-on, a mother living to push her son into a good marriage. Valentin was offering her a way to take life by the hand, to live it on her own terms.

"I could not leave right away. There are things to be done. . . ."

He kissed her again, this man of wild strength and mysterious power. "You will come when you are ready. I will be there, waiting."

Her heart leaped in hope. "I would scandalize everyone." She laughed as she said it.

"You do what you must."

One last kiss; then he took up his bag. He was tall, powerful, strong, frightening. She thought she could follow him anywhere.

"I will be there," she whispered.

Valentin turned back, his blue eyes dark. "I know."

Then he slipped out the door and was gone.

Egan came to Zarabeth's chamber, where she and Meagan were poring over the seamstress's sketches for more plaid gowns. He was smiling over some secret amusement as he pulled her into the gallery and would not tell her what he had in mind, as usual.

The rest of the Highlanders gathered, including Adam and Piers Ross, who looked as mystified as Zarabeth. Mary joined them, her eyes red, but Valentin did not appear.

They crowded into the gallery, the seven Highlanders and their ladies, with Olaf and Alexander watching from behind. Egan, his hand firmly gripping Zarabeth's, raised the sword of Ian MacDonald.

"With this blade, I rescued my lady, Zarabeth, from the clutches of her enemies. Zarabeth is a magical woman from a land far away, who has come to help break the curse of the MacDonalds."

"But the rhyme," Jamie bleated. "What about th' rhyme?"

Egan pointed dramatically at a faded painting at the end of the hall. "Behold the portrait of Ian MacDonald."

Zarabeth craned to look with the others. Ian's portrait was dark with age, painted in the style of Holbein. Ian had red-brown hair, the characteristic MacDonald face, and an aquiline nose. He wore a plaid kilt and a bonnet stuck full of feathers, and carried a sword that looked like the one Egan held.

"I noticed this when the two debutantes ye brought to plague me were staring at portraits of our ancestors." Egan brought a rag out of his pocket, walked to the picture, and began to scrub at the painted sword.

Zarabeth watched, eyes widening. "There are words on it."

"Aye." Egan continued rubbing. "When Jamie said he thought the words might be on the sword itself, I wondered."

"Did ye?" Jamie turned an anguished glare to him. "But I crawled through the attics at Ross Hall for hours. They have boxes and boxes of old junk up there."

Egan grinned, and Zarabeth saw a triumphant twinkle in his eyes. "Kept ye out of trouble, didn't it? I wasn't certain, though, so ye didn't look for nothing." He straightened up and tucked the dirty handkerchief back in his coat pocket.

The sword bore markings, tiny letters that had obviously been added after the portrait was finished. The letters were clear now, but she couldn't make out the words.

" 'Tis in Scots." Angus snorted. "Can anyone read it these days? Bloody English made our fathers stop teaching us the old language."

"I can," Egan said calmly. "As Jamie said once, Nanny Graham was a wise old woman and knew the laird would need to know Gaelic. 'Tis not that difficult, only two lines." He read them out, the musical lilt of them pleasing.

"What are you saying?" Zarabeth asked him.

Egan translated; then the two of them held Ian Mac-Donald's sword and said it together:

> *When the sword is broken,*
> *Love will prove its worth.*

Egan looked at Zarabeth, his brown eyes as warm as his grin. "Shall we?"

Zarabeth closed her hand over his on the hilt, and as before, Egan brought the sword up over his bent knee. "One . . . two . . . *three!*"

The blade broke over his powerful thigh, and a ringing note echoed all the way to the top of the castle.

Zarabeth sensed the sigh of something released, a thin darkness that flowed through an open window and dispersed.

She also sensed her bond with Egan. She quickly looked at him and saw that his eyes had gone dark, his thoughts reaching for hers. But as she reached for him, the bond dissolved once more, leaving her bereft.

Egan blinked as though waking, then handed the pieces of sword to a triumphant Jamie. "There ye are, lad. One curse, broken."

Jamie grinned at the sword, then thrust the pieces into the air. "God save the laird and his lady."

"The laird and his lady!" the Highlanders shouted with him.

Egan waved for silence. "Now if you lot will clear off, the laird and his lady have something to discuss. Alone."

Hamish whooped, and the younger MacDonalds followed suit. Angus thumped Egan on the back. "Aye, I know what that means."

He winked at Gemma, who blushed and said, "Ye have work t' do, ye great lummox. We'll have our . . . talk . . . later."

More whoops from the others; then Adam rounded them up and shooed them away. As he passed Egan, he said, sotto voce, "Don't make too much noise. I haven't the head today to suffer through the lady and laird drinking game."

He moved on down the stairs with the others, Meagan on Alexander's arm, Mary slowly following.

"The lady and laird drinking game?" Zarabeth asked when they were gone.

Egan steered her into her bedroom and closed the door. "The lads bring out the best malt and throw back a glass of it every time the laird and lady make a noise of passion. Ye know what I mean."

"Oh, dear."

"Adam and your father will keep them under control," Egan said.

"I hope so. How unnerving."

More unnerving was the way she melted inside when he cupped her face in his hands. "Ye felt it."

She did not even need to ask what he meant. "When the sword broke? Yes."

"But now there's nothing. We canno' see each other's minds anymore."

"I know."

Egan's hand drifted down to splay warmth at the base of her spine. " 'Twas cruel to give us that taste of it. Mebbe Morag hasn't forgiven the MacDonald line yet."

"Or perhaps it was part of breaking the curse. Us coming together to drive her magic out."

"Mebbe. But to lose that is like losin' part of myself."

"I know."

Egan skimmed his hands to her shoulders and held her at arm's length. "To be with ye like that, especially when I was in ye . . ." He shook his head.

Zarabeth's throat ached. He looked sad and worried, as though he feared they'd never share anything so special again.

"As you said," she ventured, "we'll have to muddle through like any couple in love."

A few lines on his face relaxed. "I don't want to disappoint ye, lass."

She started to laugh. "As though you ever could. Egan, I have been trying to get you into my bed for five years. I'm not letting go of you now."

"Aye, ye've been a bit of a seductress."

"I've had to be. You would never look at me."

His eyes widened, and suddenly he crushed her to him. "Never look at ye? Damn ye, woman, I could never keep my eyes off ye. You swaying and sashaying all over the place, and me trying to keep my kilt from tenting up in front of me. I was afraid I'd ravish ye, I wanted ye so bad. It hurt me, watching ye and not having ye."

She tried to catch her breath. "You must have known I wanted you."

"I knew it. But ye teased me with it, like ye knew I was dying inside whenever I couldn't touch you."

She shook her head. "I never meant . . ."

"Didn't ye, vixen? Did ye no' like having that power over me, knowing I'd do anything for ye?"

She flushed, knowing she did enjoy seducing him, liked watching his longing flare. "So you plague the life out of me in return?"

His eyes sparkled with a vicious light. "Of course I do. 'Tis the only way to stop myself taking ye whenever I have the chance."

She touched his face. "You wanted me that much?"

"Love, I want ye all the time. I burn for ye every minute. If my large and inconvenient family would disappear for more than five seconds at a time, I'd have ye constantly."

"Then it doesn't really matter whether we can read each other, does it?" she asked softly.

Egan groaned. "Nay. I want ye always. I love ye, my lady."

Her pulse sped, heat spreading from her heart to every limb. "Perhaps the link will come when we most need it. You needed me to find you in the dark ditch in Nvengaria. I never called out to you at the Devil's Teeth, not out loud, and you found me. You heard my thoughts. Perhaps it works when one of us is in danger—calling out to the other. Do you not think?"

Egan mulled this over. "Ye might be right, lass. Ye have an uncanny way of knowing what's what."

"When the curse broke, perhaps we connected again

to protect each other from the dark magic trapped in the sword."

" 'Tis a theory worth considering, I grant."

She went on excitedly. "So when we most need it, I'm certain it will return. When we're both safe and sound, we'll be silent to each other, but the bond will be there underneath."

Egan kissed her hairline. "Aye, lass. 'Tis called love, I believe."

She found herself suddenly swept up in his arms, then flying through the air to land on her back on the bed. Before she could squeal, he was on her, tearing away her gown.

"This is how much I love ye. And this."

He lowered his head and took her nipple into his mouth. He traced it with his wet tongue, suckling her, and she arched into the incredible feeling.

"Want me t' show ye more how much I love ye?"

She could barely speak. "Please do, my Highlander."

He laughed at her, low and wicked, and did. She opened her arms and welcomed him in.

Two Months Later

March blasted in and lingered, windy and cold, but Zarabeth found it as rosy as the brightest days of summer.

In the great hall, workmen high on a ladder repaired the ceiling beam, with Jamie angling to get up a ladder as soon as Egan's back was turned. Mrs. Williams had joined the watchers, hands on hips, wondering loudly where she was to serve supper.

So much had happened since Hogmanay. Alexander departed with Meagan and the two footmen, and soon after that, Olaf set off. Zarabeth wept when she said good-bye to him, but they made many plans for Zarabeth and Egan to travel to Nvengaria in the summer.

Lady Beatrice, Olaf assured her, was a kind lady and truly did want to meet her.

Valentin had gone the day Zarabeth and Egan had broken the sword. Mary told her of his departure and of Valentin's invitation for Mary to come to him. Zarabeth promised Mary that when she and Egan traveled to Nvengaria, she was welcome to come with them.

Mary accepted the offer calmly, but Zarabeth wondered if she wouldn't depart for Nvengaria before then. Dougal returned to school in mid-January, taking a reluctant Jamie with him. Jamie had managed not to disgrace himself and returned at the end of the term in March, chatting about the friends he'd made. Mary had talked about traveling south with them when they started the next term in April, and Zarabeth wondered if she didn't plan on going farther.

For Zarabeth's part, she wanted to wait until late summer to travel anywhere. There was plenty to do at Castle MacDonald, and besides . . .

Gemma, a broad grin on her face, sought out Zarabeth where she stood with Egan to watch the repairs.

"Well," she said brightly, "I thank ye, Zarabeth. It worked."

"Worked?"

Gemma dipped into her pocket and drew out a stone with wire wrapped around it. Tiny marks had been etched into the crystal. "Whether it was your magic or me and Angus pumpin' every night, I've done it. I'll be havin' a bairn come autumn."

Zarabeth gasped in delight. She threw her arms around Gemma and hugged her hard.

Egan watched them with a blank look on his face.

"Ye gave Gemma magic?" he asked Zarabeth as Gemma rushed to spread her good news to the others.

"Of course. A little magic always helps."

Egan's brows rose. He was dressed in his great kilt, the plaid looped around his shoulder over his linen shirt. He'd tried to tame his hair into a queue, but as usual, curled locks had already escaped to brush either side of his face.

They had not shared their thought bond since Zarabeth's rescue and the subsequent sword breaking, but she'd come to realize it didn't matter. They had a strong connection no matter what, sharing their thoughts in words without secrecy. And every night when she lay in the warm nest of their bed, she felt it stretching between them, the shimmering, silken bond of love.

"Helps?" he asked.

"With conception," Zarabeth answered cheerfully. "But do not worry, I have not brought any charms to our bed. My magic never works on you, remember? Instead, I simply followed Gemma's excellent advice."

Egan glanced at Gemma, who was being hugged by Mrs. Williams. "And this advice was wha', exactly?"

"To take you to bed as often as I could." She slid her hand into Egan's strong one, feeling hugely satisfied. "She is very wise. Our bairn will come along about August."

Egan stared at her in shock. "Our bairn? Did you say *our* bairn?"

"I believe I did, yes."

Zarabeth waited in some trepidation for his reaction. Egan had so wanted Jamie to inherit the lairdship of the castle, although lately he seemed to have made his peace with Charlie MacDonald and his offspring.

Egan suddenly whooped. The workers jumped and cursed, catching the beam before it fell. Hamish and Jamie whirled around, looking for the problem.

Egan swept Zarabeth into his arms and twirled her

off her feet. "Did ye hear?" he bellowed. "Fetch up the best malt, Hamish. I'm t' be a father!"

Hamish gaped. Jamie went round-eyed, then launched into the air, screaming madly.

Then Hamish was pounding Egan on the back, Mrs. Williams wiping her eyes, Gemma shouting for the rest of the family to come hear the news. Egan held Zarabeth safely away from the mob, but she was so happy, she didn't mind being mussed by their bear hugs, and a tearful, gentler one from Mary.

"I'll be an aunt." Mary sniffled, then laughed. "Again." She whispered in Zarabeth's ear, "Thank you for making my brother so happy. You worked a miracle."

Jamie did cartwheels all along the perimeter of the room and finished in front of them. He pointed at Zarabeth's abdomen. "All hail the new laird of Castle Mac-Donald!"

The whiskey had arrived by then, and the glasses shot high. "The new laird of Castle MacDonald!"

"It might be a girl," Zarabeth pointed out.

"Doesn't matter." Jamie clutched a brimming glass of whiskey, not minding Egan's frown. "I expect ye'll have many, many children, the way your bed creaks every night. One of the lot will be a boy, and I'll never have to be laird—thanks be to God and Zarabeth of Nvengaria."

"Zarabeth of Nvengaria!" the others chorused, and drank to it.

Egan pulled Zarabeth aside from his dancing, whiskey-quaffing Highlanders and gathered her into his arms. "You're the brightest light that ever entered this castle," he breathed. "Thank ye for keeping the light here with me."

Her heart filled, but she answered lightly. "Well, now that the curse of the MacDonalds is broken, there should be much more light and laughter."

Egan groaned in mock despair. "Och, will I never hear the last about that bloody curse?"

"Probably not. It makes an excellent story."

"With a happy ending," Egan said in a dark voice. He kissed her, his lips warm, and she felt the passion behind the caress. "Do ye like happy endings, Zarabeth?"

"They are the best kind, my Highlander."

His next kiss stirred fires. "Perhaps we can slip away from this lot and celebrate the end of the curse by ourselves?"

"I'd like nothing better."

Egan gave her a wicked smile, his brown eyes twinkling. He slid her hand under his arm and proceeded to lead her out past his cousins and nephews and even his sister, who busily toasted one thing after another.

Behind them, high on the wall in its place of honor, the broken sword of Ian MacDonald glinted in satisfaction.

LaVergne, TN USA
26 December 2010

210020LV00001BA/2/P